Where the Waratahs Bloom

An Australian Saga

Ingrid M. Smith

Book Design by Linellen Press
265 Boomerang Road
Oldbury Western Australia
www.linellenpress.com.au

Dedication

For Peter

Disclaimer

Apart from the general locations of Sydney, Bondi, Lithgow, the Blue Mountains and Jindabyne, all names of persons and places are purely fictional.

Cover Acknowledgments

Watercolour editing of front cover pony photograph: Emily M. Smith

Windmill photograph on back cover: Noel McShane

Waratah image on back cover: Free Vintage Art:
http://www.freevintageart.com/waratah-flower

Mine shaft image on back cover:

https://pixabay.com/en/mine-shaft-machine-mining-shaft-2269513/

Contents

Acknowledgments

The poem in Chapter Nineteen was written by Jeremy Martin and is reproduced with his kind permission.

The poem *Little Eohippus* by Elwyn Hartley Edwards was reproduced with the kind permission of @Elwyn Hartley Edwards/Riding Magazine/IPC+ Syndication. Thanks to Lucy Cox at IPC Media for all her assistance.

Warmest thanks to Frances Richardson for the charming waratah drawing on the title page.

Prologue

September 1991

The man had been driving for a long time when he finally saw the old poppet-head silhouetted against the night sky. The wooden framework above the abandoned mineshaft stood tall and menacing. The gold mine at Sentinel Hill had not been worked officially since 1891, one hundred years ago. One day the poppet-head would collapse, timber by timber and yet another legacy to New South Wales' past would vanish, but for now it stood proudly, even arrogantly, dominating the landscape and towering above the nearby rusted iron stamper battery.

A wry smile crossed the man's face as the battered old sign appeared in his vehicle's headlights. It was skewed at a crazy angle, the words, **Danger — Do Not Enter**, having long peeled away from the dry board. The sign stood in front of the remnants of what was meant to be a perimeter fence encircling the mine: three rusty strands of barbed wire trailing on the ground. It had been like that for as long as the man could remember.

He stopped his vehicle just past the old sign. The track which led up to the poppet-head and stamper battery began here. It was a cool night for late September and the man was glad of his thick, warm jacket and heavy work boots. Faded blue jeans, a khaki work shirt, long woollen socks — hand-knitted — and broad-brimmed felt hat completed his clothing. Day or night, he felt naked without the hat clamped to his head. However strong the wind, the hat never shifted so much as an inch yet it was held in place by no stampede string. The man scorned such frivolous non-essentials.

A light mist drifted silently through the night, partially obscuring the landscape. The man removed his large torch from the front passenger seat of the ute and headed for the sign. He carefully stepped over a twisted tangle of barbed wire, the strong beam of the torch guiding him.

A five minute walk took him along the overgrown track and up to the poppet-head. The uneven ground bore testimony to those men who had gone before: pieces of once-loved mining machinery, a heavy old black kettle with a long, curved spout, corrugated iron, massive bolts, heavy timber mine supports, a stamper stem. The man's eye was caught by a sudden gleam as the beam of his torch touched a patch of rough grass. A pair of eyes stared at him for a long second then vanished: probably a member of the possum family.

The man walked a few paces beyond the relative safety of the track. The leather boot of his right foot knocked against a small object. The torch revealed a glass bottle, seemingly whole. He bent to retrieve it, his strong fingers handling the bottle with surprising gentleness and delicacy. Carefully he played the light of his torch over the bottle, whistling silently between strong white teeth. His eyebrows shot up in disbelief as he read the base mark: Bishop & Co, Makers, Adelaide.

He allowed himself a moment to appreciate this possible treasure. The aqua-coloured bottle had a round blob top and was cylindrical in shape with semi spherical ends. Round enders some people called them. He knew that C. Bishop stood for Cornelius Bishop, an early manager of the South Australian Bottle Factory. The bottle, oddly shaped to the modern eye, was about ten inches long and two inches in diameter, and had once held roughly ten fluid ounces. It probably dated back to the late nineteenth century, perhaps 1886, when the Sentinel Hill mine was in full operation. One corner of his mind slid back to that time: he pictured a miner, thin yet well-muscled from ceaseless labour, a young man, old before his time thanks to his endless toil at the mine. Perhaps the miner had paused for a moment, leaning on his long-handled shovel, to drink from this very same glass bottle. Mentally chiding himself for creating this impossibly romantic vision, the man slipped his find into an inside coat pocket.

Returning to the track, the man glanced up at the looming poppet-head, dwarfing the neighbouring stamper battery. He was almost there. The huge winding wheel, long fallen from the poppet-head housing, lay to the left of the track. He could now see the main shaft, an inky black well of darkness beneath the poppet-head. It was a treacherous area; as well as the deep main shaft which was at least marked by the poppet-head, other open mine shafts, some partially overgrown with rough grass and spindly trees, dotted the surrounding land.

The man stood perfectly still, his eyes taking in the deep main shaft. He then turned and looked back down the track towards the rusty perimeter fence. His ute was hidden from view by the contours of the land and a group of straggling gum trees. He nodded once: nothing appeared to have changed here since his previous visit. A quick glance at his wrist-watch told him it was past midnight; it was time to get on with the job. As it was, he wouldn't be back home much before three.

The man returned to the ute and carefully placed the round ender bottle on the passenger seat before opening the rear door. His toolbox sat next to the wheelchair. Both items were deftly lifted out. He had not had time to collapse the wheelchair earlier so he did it now. Grasping the well-used toolbox in one hand and the collapsed wheelchair in the other, he walked steadily back up the track, guided by the poppet-head hovering possessively over the main shaft.

The toolbox was opened and the necessary tools selected with care. With a calm deliberation that would have both frightened and puzzled an onlooker, the man began to break down the wheelchair, piece by piece. The two armrests, the backrest, the two large rear wheels, the two push rings, the pair of castor wheels, the castor forks, two footplates, the calf strap, the anti-tip bar and the cushioned seat; the wheelchair was stripped right down to the frame.

One at a time, each piece was then thrown down the hungry, gaping mouth of the main shaft, fodder for the poppet-head. The man worked steadily, not hurrying. He barely saw each condemned piece as it made the final journey; his mind was filled with the vision of a female face. He saw her eyes as he had last seen them, eyes full of bitterness, despair, desperation, eyes that were stunned in disbelief that this could be happening to her. Life just didn't work like that, the bad things always lashed their cruel whip at other people. It had been when he had seen her eyes flicker in the direction of the polished stock of his prized rifle that the man realised he had to act that night.

He stood there, the final piece of the dismembered wheelchair in his hands. It was the backrest. He looked closely at it, seeing it properly for the first time. It struck him how incredibly ugly a wheelchair was, lacking any form of visual appeal. Couldn't the so-called experts who designed the damned things come up with something better? Did they ever spare a thought for the poor people whose lives were controlled by these abominations? Even the upholstery was a dull black, the tone which represented death, darkness, night, negativity, the unknown, fear, evil, mystery, mourning and grief. Hell, black wasn't even a colour. With a muttered oath the backrest was flung away. The throw had been poor and the backrest hit the edge of the mineshaft, throwing up a small rock before dropping into the bowels of the earth.

The sharp edge of the rock cut the man's right cheek, drawing blood. The wheelchair had made a single but lasting statement, refusing to quietly submit, branding him in a defiant gesture. The man wondered how deep the shaft was: two hundred metres, four hundred metres, perhaps even more? He had no idea, it was deep enough which was all that mattered. He ignored the blood running down the right side of his face.

The light mist had moved away and the moon was attempting to break free of the clouds. The scene, with the poppet-head in the leading role and the stamper battery as a supporting player, held a dramatic quality, a stark and haunting beauty that even a film producer would not dare to imitate. The man stood quietly, staring up at the poppet-head. He heard the screech of an owl in the distance. It probably had a roost in one of the dilapidated mine buildings.

It would be many months before it would occur to the man that perhaps the wheelchair might have found a different fate. Tonight, all he could see were those female eyes turning towards his rifle.

It was getting colder now, beginning to edge remorselessly towards the chill hours and the man thrust his hands deep in his jacket pockets. His job was done and it was time to return home. The rifle now lay safely in the back of the ute, wrapped in an old blanket. It would not be used to end a human life tonight.

Chapter One: One Day in April

April 1990

Max Richards sat the dapple grey mare with ease, his hand light on the reins, a faintly rueful expression on his tanned face. Like many competitors, he detested the Grand Parade. He knew, however, that for many who came to watch and enjoy, it was the highlight of the show, perhaps the only chance they ever got to see such beautiful animals.

The huge spiral of animals, handlers and riders was barely moving. Spectators crammed the ringside rails, ten deep, eager to get close to the action. A small boy wearing a striped shirt and brown shorts was suddenly lifted onto a man's shoulders. Laughing with delight, the child pointed at Max. Max touched his broad-brimmed felt hat and turned Misty's head in the direction of the boy. Just for a few strides before he was obliged to return to his place in the never-ending spiral, Max and Misty belonged to the child. This was what shows were all about, or should be. Max saw the boy urgently whisper to his father. The father looked uncertain, unsure of what to do.

'Sir, what is your horse's name?'

Max caught the words because he was half expecting them. The man looked embarrassed and apologetic.

'Misty,' Max called back, wishing he could stop beside the pair. But he had already done enough to exasperate the stewards and well he knew it. Trying to organise many hundreds animals and people in some semblance of order was no joke and he had no right to make things harder for the stewards.

Overhead movement caused Max to look up. A vivid scarlet cable car was passing above him. He grinned up at the bright bubble slowly moving along its planned trajectory. How many years had it been since he had last ridden the cable cars? Stella had been a toddler and Toby in his early teens.

He felt a thrill of pride as his eyes fastened on Stella. Her usual riotous chestnut curls were sternly curbed by the net she wore beneath her navy velvet riding helmet. The sturdy tanned limbs, so vigorous and strong, were hidden beneath the beautifully cut jodhpurs, long sleeved white shirt, navy blue jacket and string-backed gloves. She had her hands full with the young mare she was riding.

As the two horses came abreast, albeit from opposite directions, Misty pricked her ears in recognition. Desert Star, whose name admirably suited her unusual rose grey dappling, whinnied, pranced and gave little half rears. Max noted with approval that Stella kept her hands low and light on the reins.

'Family reunion,' Max spoke incisively.

'Dad.' A pair of laughing grey eyes met his for a quick moment and the two riders passed on, Desert Star disapproving of the parting. His mind dwelt on his daughter. She was a natural horsewoman, born with the gift that could never be taught. He had not yet told her she had been selected to represent her state later in the year, requiring travel to Victoria for the national event. Plenty of time for that later, they were all busy enough with the current show.

A man mounted on a daintily stepping thoroughbred came alongside Max, keeping in step with Misty.

'I've just been 'stewarded' to pair with you for the Grand Parade,' he spoke politely.

Max nodded and the two men exchanged a few words, their mounts eyeing each other with disdain. Max's sharp blue eyes were scanning the Parade Ring for the rest of his family.

He finally spotted Toby and Jester in a line of led horses and handlers. The two-year-old colt pranced along, glossy bay neck arched, ears alert and pricked. Like most two-year-olds, Jester was still lacking in muscle development and definition but the promise was there. His breeding showed in every step he took and in another two years, he would be outstanding. Max patted Misty, Jester's dam, in appreciation; she was the best damned mare he'd ever seen and what a broodmare she was! Thank God he'd had the sense to send her to a top stallion, even if it had been half way across the state. The result was there, in Jester. Now, where the heck was Kirsty?

As so often before, it had been a wet show this year. Misty fastidiously picked her way around the puddles; she had always detested stepping in water. The thoroughbred beside her appeared to share her feelings, also sidestepping the muddy pools with elegant precision. At least the worst of the rain had stopped for the Grand Parade.

An excited murmuring heralded the appearance of Kirsty Richards on Serenade. Dressed in the black broadcloth habit that had belonged to Max's grandmother, Kirsty rode the bay Anglo-Arabian gelding sidesaddle. Max felt his heart turn over as he gazed at the woman who was his wife. She sat with grace and elegance and the top hat and veil were a perfect foil to the clear pallor of her oval-shaped face. The dark curls had been firmly restrained in a tight chignon which she wore netted at the base of her hat. A steward stopped her, spoke a few words and pointed, explaining her role in the Grand Parade.

For Kirsty's sake, Max was relieved the day was cool and wet, but not windy. The clothes she had to wear for this sidesaddle get-up were ludicrous. Beneath the elegant habit she was clad in breeches, long sleeved shirt and vest. At her throat she wore a cream-coloured stock. The ensemble was finished with long black boots, the left one spurred, and cream-coloured gloves. She carried the sidesaddle whip which had belonged to his grandmother.

A traditionalist at heart, Max bore a deep rooted love for his land and family. To him, it seemed right that the very saddle and habit his grandmother had brought with her all the way from Hertfordshire in England should now be used by his wife. So many of the old ways were too fast disappearing; these days, shows like this were the only place people could see ladies riding sidesaddle, and harness horses. Just look at that fine team of Percherons over there — what a role the breed had played during the first world war in France and Belgium — what deep chests and heavily muscled quarters, yet those small, neat and alert ears wouldn't have been out of place on a Welsh Mountain pony. A lot of hours had been spent braiding those manes and tails with scarlet and gold ribbons. It was grand to see such a spectacle. His gaze flickered back to his wife, her right leg neatly hooked over the pommel, her left leg in the single stirrup iron. What a woman and what a helpmeet she was! Looking at the calm, serious face, intent on the task in hand, it was hard to believe in those four sturdy pine trees flourishing at Cheshunt. Each tree represented a child she had borne, dead in infancy.

A sudden shower of rain, cool and sharp, broke across the train of his thoughts. The thoroughbred next to him shook her head and flattened her ears, protesting at the intrusion of rain drops. He could see Desert Star taking exception to a line of alpacas, staring at the strange and fluffy creatures as if she could hardly believe her eyes. She dug her hooves into the turf, refusing to move. His lips twitched as he waited for the little drama to reach its climax.

'That little lady's got her hands full,' the thoroughbred's rider, his parade partner, suddenly spoke.

'She'll manage just fine.'

The man looked surprised. 'You know her, then?'

'My daughter,' was the laconic reply.

The man felt discouraged by his 'partner's' disinclination to talk. He would have enjoyed a discussion about the show. Somewhat to his surprise, his mare had performed well above expectations and wore the two broad sashes to prove it. He soothed his slight pique by brushing away a bush fly which had had the temerity to alight on one of the sashes.

The alpaca line was almost past Desert Star. The final animal in the line turned his long neck and stared at her. It was too much for the young mare and she shied violently, an enormous bound away from the terrible beast. Stella, who hadn't shifted an inch in the saddle, patted her mount reassuringly, collected her and returned to their place in the parade spiral. It was all part of the learning experience for young animals. Stella wouldn't be here if she weren't capable of doing what was required.

'Are you local?' the thoroughbred rider tried again.

'Depends what you call local. We have a place north-west of the Blue Mountains.'

'I'm from Mildura.'

'That must be a bit of a hike,' Max was mildly interested.

'Twelve plus hours when we're towing the float,' the man smiled. 'What about you?'

'Nothing like as bad — around five hours in the old truck.'

'In Australia, that probably counts as local,' said the man with a wry smile. He spoke with a slight accent which Max couldn't place.

The conversation was suddenly interrupted by a mettlesome Shetland taking momentary charge of his young rider. Ducking away from his place in the Grand Parade, the chestnut pony gave a series of lighthearted bucks, ignoring the small hands frantically tugging at the reins. The rider, who could have been no more than seven, lost her stirrups but managed to keep her seat. The Shetland then plunged between Misty and the thoroughbred and abruptly halted, the rider clinging to the pony's neck, her crash helmet precariously balanced on her nose.

Red faced and furious, the child wriggled down her pony's short neck and settled herself back in her saddle. An impatient hand pushed her helmet back to where it should be, more or less. One chubby hand took a firm grip of the reins, the other grasped a small whip. Two piercing, dark blue eyes gazed up at Max, partly defiant, partly beseeching. He was instantly reminded of Stella at that age.

'He looks quite a handful,' he spoke seriously, reassuring Misty who was eyeing this minute member of the equine race with disgust.

'I can manage him most of the time.' The small, stubborn chin tilted upwards. 'He didn't like those funny sheep with the long necks.'

'Funny sheep with the long necks?'

'Yes, there was a long line of them. Jack didn't like them.' She patted the pony fondly.

'I think she means the alpacas,' the man from Mildura spoke up, eyes twinkling.

'Can I stay and ride with you for the rest of the parade? I don't like my partner — she was mean about Jack — she said he looked like a bushy mop and needed clipping!'

Beneath the brave front, small lips were trying hard not to quiver.

'I think he's a beautiful pony,' Max spoke gravely. 'He looks exactly like what a Shetland pony is meant to look like.'

The young face lit up. 'That's what the judge said. His show name is Blue Waterfall Creek Jackson, but we call him Jack. Can I ride with you in the parade? My partner won't care — she was mad at being put with me — please?'

The two men exchanged glances over the top of the small pair.

'What say you ride just ahead of us?' suggested Max. 'I don't think the stewards are very keen on three riding abreast — they seem to like pairs the most — but some very special people are allowed to ride by themselves — like that lady riding sidesaddle over there — and the man on that nice palomino just in front of her.'

The expressive face, which had fallen at the first of Max's words, beamed a huge smile as he finished speaking.

'I think the sidesaddle lady looks beautiful,' she told the two men.

'So do I,' said Max seriously.

The child competently turned Jack and, using her heels and whip, trotted on ahead.

'A typical upset between two youngsters,' the man from Mildura raised his eyebrows at Max, 'or something else?'

'Something else, I rather think,' was the short reply. Max's eyes followed the compact, stocky little body, the short, powerful legs, the dense bushiness of the chestnut mane and tail; this little fellow was all of nine hands tall. The kid managed him well enough. Shetlands could be real a handful if not fed and handled properly. Too many people had a tendency to regard them as sweet pets. He gave a wry grimace. Pets indeed! All horses were real live animals, God's creatures and should be treated as such. What was that quotation he'd always liked? *First, God made Man, then He made Woman as a companion to Man. Then He made the Horse, with the strength of Man and the beauty and grace of Woman.* He knew he hadn't got the words quite right but the sense of them was there.

Beneath his imperturbable facade, Max longed for this parade to finish. He needed to get back to Cheshunt. A stately Clydesdale pulling a bright yellow buggy trotted by, his well-groomed bay coat a perfect foil for his white feathered legs. Even the mud and dirty water thrown up by trotting hooves couldn't really spoil the smartness of the turnout. A shaft of sunlight broke through the sullen clouds, causing the well-polished brasses on the Clydesdale's harness to gleam brightly; it turned the vivid scarlet sash with its gold fringe — the spoils of victory — into a splash of medieval motley. Horse and driver had their proud moment in the sun.

'When do you hope to leave for home?' the man from Mildura tried again.

'Tonight. My daughter's got another class shortly after all this.' Max nodded at the controlled melee all around them. 'She's riding a young novice but with a bit of luck we'll be away by seven.' His thoughts flew to the young mare in the stables. She was that rarity, a genuine black, the only bit of white being the four-pointed star almost perfectly centred on her forehead. From that pure white star came her name, Star of Bethlehem.

Part of the spiral that was the Grand Parade swung close to the rails, granting eager spectators a closer view. Hands pointed, voices cried out, cameras clicked. A green balloon, the string held by a small child, slipped away from the sticky fingers and floated away. The child scarcely seemed to notice the silent flitting, so entranced was she by the colourful living spectacle taking place before her widened eyes.

Suddenly, it was all over. The stewards gave their directions and the beginning of the seemingly endless spiral turned towards the exit. Some animals left the ring with orderly dignity, others pranced and curvetted, requiring the experience of their handlers to curtail too high spirits. The loudspeakers coughed, struggled to life and died. The expectant pause was broken by another cough and followed by the first notes of *Mammas, Don't Let Your Babies Grow Up to be Cowboys*. Max grinned to himself: he had always liked this song and it was good way to end the Grand Parade.

Blue Waterfall Creek Jackson trotted in front of the two men, his youthful rider's two plaits bobbing on her shoulders. She had to keep the Shetland trotting to remain well clear of the two bigger horses following in her wake. Every so often the child would turn her head and beam a huge smile at her protectors. Both men were faintly worried about this child yet neither knew why.

Riding near the end of the spiral, Max was the last of his family to leave the orderly confusion of the Parade Ring. He had been relieved to see that Stella, after a few words with a steward, departed quickly, heading for the stables and Star of Bethlehem. A prettily marked goat broke away from her handler, enjoying a few dainty steps of freedom before being recaptured — *attractive with those brown and white patches* — he wondered what breed she was; he knew nothing about goats. *What a magnificent animal that Red Angus over there is* — he'd bet she'd produce some grand calves in her time — *beautifully presented, too.*

'You naughty girl! Why didn't you stay with Tiffany? How dare you go off with a pair of strange men?'

The shouted words jolted Max back to the scene immediately in front of him. His small group was passing through the exit gates and the Shetland's bridle had been seized by a woman. Scarlet faced, furiously angry, she glared at Max and the man from Mildura.

Of medium height and build, she wore a powder blue pantsuit, long dangling earrings which matched it and black, high-heeled shoes. Artificially blonde curls hung messily around her shoulders.

Behind his usual inscrutable facade, Max inwardly shuddered. She represented the four things he found anathema in a woman: creating a scene in public, shouting — how he hated women who yelled and screamed — wearing that repulsive pantsuit, and hard eyes. Beneath the too thick mascara and plucked brows, the blue eyes were acquisitive and ice cold. *That poor little kid and her Shetland!*

'I think we're blocking the exit from the ring,' the man from Mildura spoke quietly and politely.

'Yes, the stewards will be after us soon,' Max hastily supported him.

Grudgingly, but without relinquishing the bridle, the woman moved aside. Behind her hovered a tall thin man dressed in an extremely expensive business suit, a white shirt and striped tie. The child on the Shetland brightened a little. Casting a partly defiant, partly terrified glance at the woman, she piped up:

'Hello Daddy.'

'Hello, Adeline. Jack looks very smart.' He moved closer to the child and pony.

'You had no right to leave Tiffany,' stormed the woman. 'I arranged specially for the two of you to parade together so she could keep an eye on you. She's such a nice child —'

'I hate her! I hate her! She was mean about Jack! He got upset and these nice men helped me. I hate you, too!'

This speech, which was followed by a storm of tears, caused a momentary stunned silence. Before Adeline's mother could retaliate, Max swiftly stepped in. Bending from his saddle to face the father, his words were nevertheless meant for the woman.

'Sir, I am sure you will agree that this is no place for an upset or argument. Jack was worried by the alpacas, as was the pony my own daughter was riding.' Aware of the woman's slight change of expression at the mention of Stella, he continued, 'Jack got away from Adeline for a moment and they stopped next to my friend and I. It also appears that Adeline's partner had been somewhat unpleasant to the child — instead of displaying the kindly responsibility an elder child should have shown — and Adeline was naturally rather upset by both incidents. Your daughter, who is an excellent young horsewoman by the way, felt happier riding in front of two rather older people.' Max paused before making his final thrust. 'I am afraid I will have to leave you now as my wife is waiting for me, but if you have any doubts as to my respectability, or that of my friend, I am sure numerous people here today will vouch for us.'

'I support my friend in every word he has said,' chimed in the man from Mildura.

The effect of these words was remarkable. The woman, whose complexion could have reddened no further, dropped Jack's bridle and stared at Max. The man, gazing at Max as if he were a saviour, nodded, helped his sobbing daughter from her saddle and wrung the saviour's hand.

Adeline, now realising that her mother was a back player — for the time being, at least — stopped crying, and clinging to her father's arm, called up her thanks to her two mounted heroes. It was then that the woman's jaw dropped and she stood, mouth openly gaping, blue eyes widened.

A slight whicker from Misty had already alerted Max that a fellow stablemate was close by. He knew it was Kirsty before he turned his head. You could always rely on her to sense when trouble was brewing and, if at all possible, come to your assistance.

'It's the beautiful sidesaddle lady,' cried Adeline in delight.

Max watched as Kirsty smiled down at the little girl. She nodded gravely to the small group clustered just outside the exit laneway before turning to her husband.

'Stella would like a hand with Star of Bethlehem. I was sent to try and find you.'

'Tell her I'm on my way,' Max exchanged a meaningful look with his wife.

Kirsty spoke directly to Adeline. 'I saw you in the ring yesterday with your Shetland. You did a beautiful workout. He's a wonderful pony.'

Stars shone in the child's eyes as she gazed up at this supreme being. Not only was she almost magical, riding sidesaddle, but she was kind as well. And she had noticed Jack, and liked him! The supreme being nodded to her husband and rode slowly away.

Adeline's father, taking swift advantage of his wife's state of shock, thrust a glossy business card at Max.

'If I can ever be of any service —' he mumbled. Still holding his daughter's hand, he led her and Jack away, quickly vanishing into the crowd. The woman slowly followed after, still seemingly mesmerised by the appearance of Kirsty.

'Nicely handled,' observed the man from Mildura as the two of them rode in the direction of the stables. 'That could have got quite nasty. You have a very clever, as well as an exceptionally talented and beautiful wife.'

'Kirsty's the best there is!'

'The lady most certainly took note of our numbers and will be checking the show catalogue within ten minutes,' observed the man from Mildura.

'Hardly a lady!' growled Max.

'Look, *friend*, what the heck *is* your name? Do I have to wait to read my catalogue as well?'

Max stared at him for a long moment before throwing back his head with a roar of laughter. He thrust his right hand at the man riding close beside him.

'Max Richards.'

'Rene Guisard.'

The two hands clasped briefly but warmly.

An hour later Max and Kirsty sat together, high up in the grandstand, waiting to watch Stella and Star of Bethlehem. Kirsty, now clad in worn jeans and a cotton shirt, with a warm waterproof jacket around her shoulders, leaned against her husband. He slipped an arm around her.

'Tired, my girl?'

'A bit.' She closed her beautiful warm brown eyes momentarily.

'We'll be on the way home soon.' He lightly touched an errant dark curl which had escaped from the hairnet she still wore. 'Are you sure you're warm enough? Your blouse is very thin.'

'I'm fine. I'm glad they've brought the working hunter classes back. They've always been one of the best classes — you can't beat that combination of flatwork, jumping and conformation. It's usually about seven or eight jumps, isn't it?'

'Yes, rustic or natural jumps. Looks as though today's course is a figure of eight.'

'They've made a nice job with that artificial stone wall.' She craned her neck to get a better view.

'If that hay rack didn't have such a clear ground line it would cause a few problems.' Max quirked an eyebrow. 'Even with that ground line I think there will be some stops. I hope they jump first.'

'They usually do, don't they?'

'Depends on the judges. Makes more sense to do the jumping first because it's worth the most marks — and jumping faults makes the judging easier.'

'Here they come.' Kirsty gazed down at the riders entering the ring, some in pairs and some singly.

Stella and Star of Bethlehem rode in at the end of the somewhat straggly line. Their number, 112, was printed large and black on a white cardboard rectangle and displayed on the mare's chest, held in place by a number holder. There were fourteen competitors in what was one of the final classes of the multi-day show.

The first to jump was a sturdy flea-bitten grey who refused the hay rack at his initial attempt. At his second try, he cleared the obstacle with an enormous leap and only the rider's skill kept the two together. They completed the course without further difficulties. The judges wrote on their clipboards.

Next to go was a prettily marked pinto, well-balanced with beautiful paces. He jumped at a strong canter, clearing each fence neatly and received a round of applause from the half-full gallery.

There were two judges: an elderly man, his immaculate dress topped by a grey fedora with dark-coloured band, and a stout woman clad in a smart black and white ensemble: well-cut pants, white silk shirt, black and white silk scarf, black cartwheel hat and yellow rose buttonhole. They were assisted by a steward. The day was drawing to a close and the vast ring was now shared by just three classes, the competitors almost looking lost in the huge space. The judges encouraged their riders to make good use of the larger area now available to them.

'All this wet weather's made the ground pretty slippery,' observed Kirsty.

'Working hunters have to be able to cope with it,' pointed out her husband. 'Imagine living where horses have to cope with very thick ice underfoot. Now that would be a headache and a half — but I take your point. Any horse not being held together could take a fall.'

Waiting quietly on Star of Bethlehem, Stella watched the competitor before her present to the judges. If all went well for this rider, and it probably would, Stella only had a minute or two left. Unobtrusively she touched the place where the tiny gold cross always hung from its slender gold chain around her neck — it was buried under her jacket, shirt and tie, but no matter, she knew it was there, which was all that counted. She lifted her head high, searching for her parents up in the grandstand — she knew roughly where they would be sitting, just as she knew they would be there, and finding them, gave a small salute. Then closing her legs against Star of Bethlehem's glossy black sides, Stella began the walk to the judges. She knew that judges hated having to look around for a missing competitor; some refused to do it. The previous rider cleared the final obstacle, completing a faultless round. Applause rippled from the gallery.

Up in the grandstand Kirsty gripped Max's arm tightly as Stella rode forward. More than thirty-five years of showing still had not dulled the excitement, the anticipation or the tension Kirsty felt. It was all part of the game, and she wouldn't have it any other way. The day one felt blasé or apathetic about showing horses was the day you stopped, according to Max, and she agreed with him completely.

Max looked down at Star of Bethlehem with approval. Carefully bred with stunning bloodlines, sturdy with a touch of refinement, she held her head proudly, ears pricked and alert. The mare had been what Max termed an unforeseen purchase. She had been bought from her breeder as a promising two-year-old; the buyer, a local acquaintance of the Richards family, had gifted the filly to his seventeen-year-old daughter, a talented rider. Unfortunately the buyer had been two years too late. His daughter, a keen and enthusiastic horsewoman since the age of four, had discovered other interests.

It had been Kirsty who had first come across the filly, attracted by her beauty, grace and elevation of movement as she cantered about her paddock. One winter's day, Kirsty, driving past the paddock, had stopped as usual to admire the youngster. Unchecked by her owner for several days, the two rugs the filly usually wore were dragging behind her, the twisted leg straps chaffing in a tightened tangle above her hocks. Horrified, Kirsty quickly climbed through the fence and caught the frightened animal, whose head-collar was partly off. Unable to untangle the rug straps, Kirsty resorted to the small pen knife she always carried and cut the filly free.

She had righted the head-collar, adjusting it to fit correctly and was just wondering what to do with the pile of torn and useless rugs when a utility truck drove up. The man who had bought the horse for his daughter jumped out. He listened to Kirsty's explanation, carefully checked the filly over and thanked Kirsty for all her help. His last words had rather grimly indicated that his daughter would shortly be arriving with new rugs. Three days later he had rung Cheshunt and spoken to Max, offering him Star of Bethlehem at a price far below what she was worth, and, far below what he himself had paid for her. She was rising four and had received little training or handling in the past two years. The man would like her to go to a good home, feeling she had been given rather a raw deal so far. Max thanked the man and refused the offer. Cheshunt was home to far too many horses already. He had, however, reckoned without Kirsty.

She had taken one of her passionate likings to Star of Bethlehem, deciding the youngster was the ideal mount for Stella; the two could grow and develop their talents together. She had managed to somehow find out that the current selling price to the Richards family was a quarter of what had originally been paid for her. Max, on arriving home at Cheshunt after a two-day absence looking at possible stock purchases, found Star of Bethlehem happily settled in the smaller of the two home paddocks, already passionately attached to Nugget, her orphan sheep paddock mate. She had come complete with two bridles, grooming brushes, a handsome black sheepskin numnah and a set of travelling bandages, all included in the quoted selling price. Max, on observing all of this, was grimly amused. If his wife had been anyone other than his Kirsty, he would have been inclined to wonder what services she had offered the seller to obtain such a bargain!

The quarrel had been short but stormy.

'We don't need another horse, Kirsty, you know that!'

'She's so perfect, Max. Surely you can see it: a year of careful training and she will make a working hunter; they could do a bit of pony dressage – she's just a pony – she could be the ideal all-rounder for Stella.'

'Kirsty, we do NOT need another horse!'

'Look at her properly and tell me if she wasn't worth it!'

'What's wrong with all the horses we have?'

'Please, Max, please — do look at her closely. She is that one in a million. She's got that something special — she's ideal for Stella. They will learn and grow together.'

'How was she paid for?'

'Out of my private account — my money, Max — get that clear! Look at the bargain we got: the horse plus all that gear, most of it unused.'

'The gear was included for the quoted price?'

'Yes!'

'You're telling me you paid a total sum of four hundred dollars for horse plus equipment?'

'Yes.'

'The man must be mad!'

'Not really.' Kirsty, seeing she was winning the battle, put a tentative hand on her husband's arm and led him towards the smaller of the two home paddocks. Star of Bethlehem was being lunged by Stella in the far corner, well out of earshot. Seeing Max's eyes follow the trotting pony, his wife continued, 'I think he feels very bad about his daughter pretty well ignoring the youngster for the past two years. I also think he wishes to be rid of the pony as quickly as possible, but only to a good home — and I think he would like her to stay within the district, to see how she gets on, if you see what I mean.'

'Pity he didn't pay a lot more attention over the past two years,' growled Max.

'It's easy to say, Max, but the pony was under the daughter's care — he assumed she was looking after her properly — she's nearly twenty, after all. You shouldn't need to chase someone of that age to make sure she is managing her responsibilities.'

'The daughter should have a damned good hiding!'

'She's a bit old for that, dear!'

'Anything happening on his land is his ultimate responsibility,' but Max was speaking absently by now, his attention taken by the grace and beauty of the circling black pony. After some minutes he turned to his wife, a reluctant grin on his face. 'All right, my girl, you win. Let's see what Stella can make of her. It's a damned shame about those two wasted years though. Later on she'll be competing against animals up to two years younger who have more experience, but we'll see.'

He was rewarded by Kirsty throwing her arms around his neck and kissing him. Pleased, yet determined not to make his capitulation too easy, he couldn't resist enquiring, 'I suppose you're going to pay for all the shoeing and feeding bills as well?'

'Now that,' replied his wife, linking hands with him, 'is just being plain nasty.'

They stood, fingers entwined, watching girl and pony.

That had been eighteen months ago.

In the grandstand, Kirsty and Max watched as Stella and Star of Bethlehem presented to the judges, cantered a small circle and headed for the first jump, the usual inviting brush fence, this time a sloping one. The mare's stride was smooth, confident and steady as she neatly popped over it. The second obstacle, the log pile, was angled in such a way that Stella had to curve around to the left to approach it correctly. Larger than the first jump, the log pile was appealing. Stella closed her legs firmly against the mare's sides and Star of Bethlehem soared over as if winged. The course then followed a tight turn to the right but again, the jump was angled so that the rider had to swing out to the left to approach it, thus involving two changes of legs. Serenely and with confidence, the pair flew over the hay rack. Sensing the slight apprehension of her pony as they neared the narrow wall, Stella spoke soothingly, inspiring confidence by strong use of her legs, seat and body. Keeping her hands light, she increased her speed a little — better to lose a few point for inconsistency of pace than risk a refusal — and responding to her training and the voice she knew so well, Star of Bethlehem jumped cleanly, if a trifle big. They turned left for the fifth jump, a tempting hedge, neatly trimmed along the top. The mare popped over easily and a few strides later, soared over the hay bales. The seventh jump was the first, taken from the other direction, the sloping brush fence. Less inviting this way, Stella had always been aware that this was her most likely nemesis. Perhaps the many hours working over the hills and valleys of Cheshunt had helped Star of Bethlehem, for it was there that she was asked to jump anything her young mistress considered jumpable, however strange it may seem. She had learned to trust her rider's judgement. When she was told, by voice, by leg, by hand on rein, that the strange sloping fence was fine, she accepted it, jumping strongly with plenty of impulsion. The final jump was the log pile again, the number two jump taken from the other direction. As if aware she was almost home, the mare headed for the obstacle with enthusiasm, her neat little ears pointing forward. Amused, the decreasing crowd in the gallery laughed, some beginning to applaud. They were over and clear.

Stella patted the hot, damp neck and quietly brought her gallant pony to a halt next to the judges. She saluted and waited for the return acknowledgement before retiring to a discrete distance.

'Not too dusty,' thus spoke Max, although the smile on his face spoke volumes.

Kirsty's heart was too full for words. She leaned her head on her husband's shoulder, blinking back the tears. There was so much pride and satisfaction in seeing the results of all those months of hard work, patience and perseverance — there was nothing in the whole world quite like bringing on a green, untrained young horse, and when the animal had been through a rough time the pleasure was all the deeper.

The first rider was commencing his workout on the flat. This was the last of the working hunter classes, the others having taken place earlier in the day. The chill of the autumn evening was slowly creeping into the muscles and bones of those who were stationary. Kirsty shivered and slipped her arms into the sleeves of her warm waterproof jacket. The thick fleecy collar fit snugly around her neck, comforting and cosy.

'Hungry?' asked her mate.

'Yes!'

'Stella will be the last to work out so there's plenty of time to grab a bite to eat. You stay here — you've had a rough day and look tired. I won't be long — there's plenty of eat places handy. Any preferences?'

'So long as it's hot and filling and there's lots of it,' she returned.

She watched him descend between the tiered seats, tall, broad shouldered, slim hipped, his black hair, barely streaked with grey. Once or twice he paused to exchange a few words with an acquaintance. Kirsty was growing very weary. These multi-day shows really took it out of you. As much as she had enjoyed it, she was pleased that this show was drawing to a close. Home was starting to call very strongly. She settled back in her seat and concentrated on the workouts taking place below.

The gallop was obviously the bête noire of many of the ponies, as was so often the case. The first two competitors performed well, both the flea-bitten grey and the prettily marked pinto finishing their workout with a beautifully controlled gallop. The third rider lost control of her somewhat nervous mount; the pony, ignoring the frantic tugs on the reins, took hold of the bit and hurtled around the trotting track which edged the enormous ring. He ploughed through another class before finally running out of steam and drawing to a gradual stop, sides heaving, nostrils flared.

'Poor kid, that must be very frightening,' murmured a man sitting in front of Kirsty. Earlier she had noticed him turning the pages of his show catalogue in obvious bewilderment.

The runaway obviously upset the other horses; the next three to work out were unsettled and uneasy although they stayed under control. None of them gave a full gallop, settling instead for the hand gallop.

'Do you happen to know what they're placing to?' the man with the catalogue suddenly asked Kirsty.

'I think to seventh but it often depends on the judges,' she replied, her eyes following the sturdy bay which was just commencing its workout. His number was 273 and Kirsty liked his looks: quiet but with plenty of impulsion; on the stocky side yet with that touch of quality which always spelled good breeding. His rider, a boy, had the bay nicely on the bit. Too many horses were ridden over-bent, people wrongly believing the head practically on the horse's chest meant being on the bit.

'My son is competing in that class,' the man with the catalogue told her, needing to confide in someone.

Kirsty smiled at him. 'The suspense is hard, isn't it?'

'You have someone competing?' he asked eagerly.

'A daughter.'

The bay pony, number 273, was completing his workout with a spanking gallop. The pony flew around the track, rider lightly poised in the saddle, leaning forward with shortened reins, his weight in his stirrups and off the pony's back.

'That,' said Max, suddenly at her side, 'is one very nice pony ridden by a very talented youngster. How did he jump, I wonder? Here, Kirsty, take some of these before I drop something — more of a crush at the food stands than I expected.' Two hot dogs, a huge cardboard bucket of hot chips, two cups of tea in cardboard mugs with folding handles and their own little cardboard tray and two massive rock buns, sultana-studded, were thrust at Kirsty. 'How far through the class are they?'

'About halfway.' She neatly arranged the food on the empty seat beside her, relishing the heat and savoury smells.

They ate together contentedly, keeping a steady eye on the ring below.

'Ground's a mess,' commented Max. 'Glad this is the end of the show.'

Down in the ring awaiting her turn, Stella was aware of the damp chill of the fast approaching evening. She kept Star of Bethlehem walking steadily around: it was not good for young horses to be kept standing in line for ages. She was not nervous or worried but there was always tension before a class. She had learned many years ago if you didn't feel that tension, you wouldn't give your best. Her lips twitched into a faint smile as she recalled the day that particular lesson had been well and truly drummed home. It had been made abundantly clear to her that the only thing that mattered was giving of your best in every class; much better to come last after having given your all, than winning by a lazy ride or judge preferment. No, Mum and Dad had not been impressed with that second place ride at all.

No thoughts went to the recently completed jumping round. What was done was done and could not now be changed. What mattered lay ahead and all her efforts must go there. Back-tracking over past events was useless; Stella had learned that very early in life.

Stella would not have admitted it to a living soul but one corner of her mind was very set on being in the top three. Before her jumping round she would have thought that to be an impossibility — only too well she knew that a clear round would be almost essential to score a top three finish — but she thought she might now be in with a chance, albeit a long one. She knew, again from much experience, that the gallop was nearly always the sorter-outer as she called it to herself, in these classes. This puzzled Stella, who galloped on horseback pretty well every day of her life.

With only two ponies left to work ahead of her, Stella began paying attention to the workouts. It was rather unusual, she noted, much less circle work than the hack classes — also much less trotting — plenty of cantering with that glorious gallop at the end. She patted the black neck encouragingly. It was almost time.

Her heart rate increased as she went through her private ritual of touching her little gold cross followed by the discreet salute to her parents. She felt shaky inside as she rode across to the judges. She saw the steward glance at her, write something on his clipboard. Her number, probably, and her heart beat even faster. Inside her gloves her palms felt wet with apprehensive sweat. Suddenly, she was terrified. She couldn't do this. She would make a fool of herself and a wonderful pony.

'Hello again,' smiled the stout woman judge. She looked closely at Star of Bethlehem. 'That's a beautiful pony you have there. How old is she?'

'Five,' Stella answered.

'Do you know her breeding?' asked the woman.

'Welsh Section B sire, Connemara dam.'

'Ah, she gets her height from her mother then,' the judge nodded.

'Do you know the workout, my dear?' the other judge spoke up.

As she had been taught, Stella asked for the workout instructions before repeating them back to the judges. You never did your workout based on previous performances by others because they may have made mistakes.

'When you're ready.' It was the man judge nodding at her.

'Full gallop if you can manage it; hand gallop if you're worried about control.' It was the woman now. 'Take your time — there's no need to rush things. Use as much space as you like, you've got all the room in the world.'

Stella tried to smile, collected herself and closed her legs against the mare's warm sides. She took clear note of the marker cones placed for guidance, then she was ready. All fear vanished within the first few strides. She was doing what she loved best, working with a horse she had helped train from nothing.

Star of Bethlehem trotted out strongly as they headed for the first orange cone. It was very different from the usual figure-of-eight of so many classes; it was harder, she thought. Cantering a horse in a straight line was not the easiest thing in the world to do. She had decided to treat the workout rather like a dressage test; it would be easier to manage that way, and each sharp turn at the canter could be treated as riding a corner. It was rather like a trigonometry lesson: three large triangles followed by a square and ending in a huge circle.

Watching intently from the grandstand, Kirsty's acute hearing picked up comments from the people around her.

'Nice pony — can't quite pick her breeding — got some Welsh in her, though.'

'Doesn't canter as straight as she might.'

'That kid handles that little mare rather well — pretty pony — wonder what they'd take for her?'

'That pony jumped very well — should be in with a chance if she doesn't screw up this workout — not too bad so far.'

'Pretty green still but plenty of hope for the future. Not often you see a real black horse.'

'Let's see what she'll make of the gallop.'

'Some Coed Coch blood there, I'll bet you a tenner.'

She wished she could nudge Max and share her enjoyment of all the remarks but he was very hard of hearing, especially in a public area. She would tell him later. In the ring Stella was finishing the last of the cantering and preparing to gallop.

Star of Bethlehem was pleased to stretch her legs. She had been getting tired of all that cantering. She stretched out her neck, gave a little toss of her head, and with one neat black ear pinned back, the other pointing ahead, literally flew around the ring. Stella, leaning forward with her weight in the stirrups, let the little mare show her speed yet always remained easily in control. At the end, she reduced speed, coming quietly back down through the paces to the walk and finally, the halt. To finish up, she reined back four neat steps, walked forward again, halted and saluted the judges.

There was quite a long wait while the judges, assisted by their steward, added up the points, double-checking their mathematics. The two judges deliberated together, talking earnestly. A brisk nod from the cartwheel-hatted woman and she stepped forward, clipboard in hand. Walking down the line of riders, she spoke a few words to each. Some left the ring while the chosen stayed in line.

'Does that mean they're placing to eighth?' the man with the catalogue turned again to Kirsty.

'Not necessarily,' she told him with a smile. 'They might have ended up with say, two fifth places or maybe two seventh places — it all depends on the mathematics.'

'My son wrote asking me to come,' the man confided. 'My wife and I are divorced and Piers lives with his mother and stepfather most of the time. He's only gotten into this riding business since his mother married again. I don't know anything about horses but Piers seems to love them.'

'Is this your first show?' asked Max.

'Yes,' the man grinned ruefully. 'It's fascinating but rather hard to understand.'

Down in the ring the judges were conferring together again. Then a sheet of paper was handed to their steward who, stepping forward, called out:

'Please come forward and line up in this order: 273 — 112 — 303 — 515 — 104 — 57 — 528 — 65.'

He spoke slowly and clearly, leaving a long pause between each number called.

'That's to avoid any possible mishearing and misunderstandings,' explained Kirsty to Piers' father. She wondered which number Piers was, presuming he was still in the ring. There were three boys in the line.

Piers' father wondered which girl belonged to the nice couple behind him and tried not to think of what it would be like to be here as a proper family. He still missed Clare shockingly yet couldn't bring himself to start looking around for a possible new mate.

The bay pony, number 273, which Max had admired, was sashed with the blue first place ribbon. Kirsty and Max watched with pride as Star of Bethlehem was awarded the red ribbon for second place. The prettily marked pinto, number 303 was third and arched his neck proudly once clad in the broad white sash with the gold lettering. The gleaming chestnut coat of a young mare was the perfect foil for her fourth place yellow ribbon.

'See, the judges are giving two fifth places,' Kirsty pointed out as the attractive, tobacco-brown ribbons were tied around the necks of numbers 104 and 57.

'That's Piers on number 57,' his father confided.

'He's done very well,' said Kirsty warmly, 'and what a beautiful pony.'

'Ah — what colour would you call it?'

'That's a liver chestnut,' she explained.

They watched as the last two ponies were sashed in emerald green and a pretty pale pink.

'Which is your daughter?' the man suddenly asked.

'112,' answered Max.

'But that's wonderful,' he exclaimed, 'you must be delighted.'

'Oh, she's done all right,' was Max's laconic reply, so characteristic of him. The prouder he was of Stella, the less he showed it, especially to strangers. He rose to his feet, stretching cramped muscles. 'Thank God that's finished and we can go home! Kirsty, come on girl, up you get. Time to move!'

Piers' father was longing to go and congratulate his son but, unsure of his welcome by Clare and her new husband, felt it best to stay away. He abhorred shouting, scenes and conflict and Clare was virtuoso at all three. He could always write to Piers. His attention was caught by a small cluster of ponies entering the ring.

'Championship contenders,' explained Kirsty, who was in the process of being hauled to her feet by her husband.

Piers' father looked bewildered and Kirsty laughed understandingly. 'It's not quite as complicated as you might think. We've had four of these working hunter classes for ponies today, right?'

'With you so far,' agreed Piers' father.

'Well, the judges are now looking for an overall champion and a reserve champion, which almost always come from the winners. With working hunter classes, things are a bit different because usually the judges base the championship on the scores. Do you understand?'

'No.'

'The champion will go to the rider and pony who have gained the highest overall score. But the standard can vary quite a lot between classes you see, so the second placed pony in one class might have a higher score than the winner of another class. It doesn't happen very often and usually only with second place getters, but it does happen when it all comes down to the numbers. Makes for some interesting results too.'

'I think I'm with you now,' Piers' father nodded. 'So it's just a matter of the judges comparing all the numerical totals of the four classes?'

Kirsty grinned. 'It should be, but I've never yet seen a judge give a champion award to a pony he doesn't think deserves it.'

Piers' father groaned. 'Just as it was starting to make sense —'

'I wish Stella would get that pony back to the stables,' Max glared in the direction of his distant daughter. 'It's getting cold and the mare needs rugging after all that work.'

The judges were in deep consultation with their steward, clipboards being passed between hands for checking and double-checking. The small cluster of champion hopefuls hovered at a short distance. Finally, the steward stepped forward and beckoned to the winner of Stella's class, the boy on the sturdy bay.

'Glad to see that some boys still have manners,' murmured Max, watching in approval as the bay's rider removed his hat when approached by the lady judge. The brave little bay was sashed with the vast three-coloured ribbon which proclaimed champion.

The steward stepped forward again, checking the numbers of different ponies. 'Number 112 please. Number 112!'

Stella, hurrying to the exit, stopped Star of Bethlehem dead. 'Did you mean me?'

The steward grinned at her. 'I certainly did, young lady. You're going in the wrong direction!'

Barely comprehending what was happening, Stella turned the little mare, and, as if in a dream, followed the steward back to the judges.

'In a hurry to go home?' asked the elderly male judge, a twinkle in his eye.

Stella blushed crimson and managed to say, 'No, sir.'

'Congratulations on a very nice performance.' The beautifully clad, stout lady judge tied the thickly fringed, green and white satin sash around Star of Bethlehem's black neck.

'We see it came as a bit of a surprise,' commented the male judge.

'It was a very close call,' said the lady judge. 'You were just two points ahead of the winner of another class.'

'Doesn't often turn out that way. You certainly kept us busy with the mathematics today,' said the male judge, handing Stella a large trophy, a thick white envelope and a neatly wrapped box the size and shape of a shoe carton.

'Can you manage all that?' asked the lady judge rather doubtfully.

Stella clutched the box and envelope to her chest with her right arm then balanced the trophy on top. She too appeared somewhat doubtful. Then her face lit up. 'There's Mum at the exit gate. I can give it to her.'

The professional photographers had been busy and two weeks

later the proofs would arrive at Cheshunt. Kirsty's favourite would show a beautiful black mare ridden by a happy, healthy, laughing girl, lightly poised in the saddle.

Chapter Two: Morgan Luck

August 1990

Stella leant on the massive five-barred, heavy wooden gate of the smaller of the two home paddocks. The early morning was cold and frosty, the grass the wonderful colour of Allen's Spearmint Leaves. Stella grinned to herself as she recalled the bags of sugar-frosted, leaf-shaped, mint jellies, a much loved childhood treat. At just sixteen years old she still loved the sharp yet sweet taste of the Spearmint Leaves.

Desert Star galloped past the gate, nostrils flared, mane and tail flying. One ear was pinned back, the other pricked forward. She was followed by another set of thundering hooves: Star of Bethlehem had no intention of being left behind. Suddenly the two young mares stopped. Their elegant necks reached out, they touched noses and squealed. A snort, a high pitched neigh and legs kicked out in pretended rage, and they were off again. Their warm breath steamed from their nostrils in the just above freezing air.

Nugget, the coal-black Corriedale ewe, flew along behind the ponies in her own unique style — what Kirsty always called *sheep leaps* or *jumbuck jumps*. It was as if she were a giant spring; all four hooves would leave the ground in a magnificent bound. She would sail through the air, touch down for a second and leap through the air again. Nugget would hurtle around the paddock in this fashion, connecting with Mother Earth for the least possible time. It was always vastly entertaining to watch.

From the neighbouring larger home paddock, Serenade and Misty regarded the antics of their juniors with superior benevolence.

"

The pair stood quietly together, their rumps turned to catch the first approaching rays of the late winter sun. They were warmly clad in snugly fitting New Zealand rugs. Stella had already broken the thin layer of ice on their water tub.

Misty was the elder states-mare of Cheshunt and the pride of Max Richards' heart. She had been at Cheshunt longer than Stella had. Her story made people shake their heads in wonder, commenting that fact was so often stranger than any imaginative storyteller's fiction.

In 1969, Kendrick Tenny left his Vermont farm in the more than capable hands of his son-in-law and paid a visit to Australia. His aims were threefold. He desired to observe some of the nation's working horses in action; his sights were especially focused on the Australian Stock Horse, the almost forgotten Waler, and the Australian brumby. He was also hoping to purchase a few broodmares, if he found what he hoped to find. Thirdly, he needed a break from his wife for a while, and three months in Australia was just what the doctor ordered. Unfortunately, Eunice was one of those women whom increasing affluence did not suit.

Eunice's initial wish to accompany him was speedily put to rest by crafty references of roughing it with the boys, sleeping under the stars in a swag, eating beans by the campfire whilst a friendly crocodile winked from nearby, and the merciless Australian sun. Kendrick Tenny rarely argued with anyone but somehow, he almost always managed to get his own way. Eunice decided she would visit her second daughter instead: Carol lived in a smart apartment block in New York City with nary a crocodile, friendly or otherwise, in sight.

Humming, *'Australians, all let us rejoice, for we are young and free,'* which was not yet the Australian National Anthem, Kendrick left for Australia. Was the word 'free' sung with a trifle more zest than usual? Perhaps it was, yet he did not travel alone. He was accompanied by his magnificent dapple grey Morgan stallion, Son of Saratoga.

He explained his reasons to Max Richards, whom he met by pure chance at the Thoroughbred Sales in Sydney. 'Well, son, if I take a fancy to a couple of fine broodmares, the owner might not be too happy to see them depart for such far distance shores as Vermont. He might just bump up the price somewhat to help ease his pain at losing such lovely ladies. Now with old Sonny Boy along for the ride and him having plenty of juice in the tank, if you'll kindly excuse any crudeness, I kinda figure he might sort of help ease along the business arrangements. I just point out that this grand country of yours isn't exactly overrun with Morgan horses. I produce old Sonny Boy's papers and some photos of his progeny winning at big shows. Heck, they've even had wins at the Saratoga Classic and Madison Square Gardens. Now that sort of stuff doesn't overly excite me but brother, it surely does impress some people. It impresses them enough to make them forget all about the fancy prices they were going to put on their horses; all the money they were going to squeeze out of this fool of a rich American.'

Max enquired if this business arrangement had proven fruitful.

Kendrick admitted that while the business side of the plan had prospered even more mightily than he hoped — Australian owners were practically lining their broodmares up in rows, hoping to exchange them for a share of that precious Morgan blood — the transportation issues were proving a tad bothersome.

'How did you manage with the quarantine laws?' Max couldn't help asking.

Kendrick waved the quarantine laws away with an airy hand. 'One can always find a way to navigate these little obstacles, my boy.'

His only concern at present was the Morgan stallion he fondly called 'old Sonny Boy'. Kendrick would like to give the hard working stallion a bit of a vacation somewhere whilst he took a quick look at the Northern Territory and North Queensland. Could Max recommend a suitable establishment worthy enough to be granted the honour of looking after Son of Saratoga for three weeks? He then suggested that he and Max finish their conversation in the bar over a late lunch and 'something long and cool'.

Max thanked the kindly American but declined, explaining he had been accompanied to the Thoroughbred Sales by his wife and small son. They were having a general look at everything and he was due to meet up with them for lunch, in fact, he would have get moving right away. Max would never know what induced him to add the final few words, so uncharacteristic of him:

'My wife's had a bit of a rough time recently, so we are spending a week in Town.'

The piercing blue eyes of the American swept across Max's face, seeing far more than Max could have ever imagined or wanted. Kendrick Tenny, incisive, intelligent and shrewd, made one of his snap decisions.

'Bring her and that boy of yours to dinner in Town tonight. That fancy new place in George Street, The Summit, I think it's called. We'll make it nice and early — I hate late dining — and it'll probably suit your good lady and son better. Six-thirty do you?'

'But sir, I can't possibly —'

'Stop dithering, boy, and go meet up with your family! See you tonight and don't be late. I'm off to visit my old Sonny Boy: he's staying down the road at some swanky horse joint — charging me an arm and a leg for it too!'

Max waited until his family were back at their hotel before telling Kirsty of the invitation. Toby, tired out by the morning's activities and the newness of the city surroundings, was fast asleep. Clutched in one small hand was a model of a thoroughbred horse.

Max looked down at his wife. She was curled up against a bank of cushions on their bed. Kirsty got very tired very easily since the twins.

The twins had been born early, at thirty-four weeks. They had also died shortly before birth. Max would never forget the expression on Kirsty's face as she cradled the tiny, perfectly formed baby girls in her arms.

Noël Flora and Naomi Laura had been cremated, their ashes carefully dug in around the two tiny pine trees planted at Cheshunt. Kirsty had wanted it that way.

It was three months now since the death of the twins and Max was seriously worried about Kirsty. It was as if something within his beautiful, spirited wife had frozen over. Her dark brown eyes, now appearing larger than ever, wore a permanently haunted look.

Once she had physically recovered from the actual birth process, she quietly and steadily went about her usual daily tasks. Max sometimes wondered if she hoped to physically exhaust herself each day in a desperate and useless attempt to suppress both thought and memory. Always, Kirsty saw those two little babies, felt their tiny bodies in her arms, felt the ache in breasts that were not needed…

Max seriously wished she would let go and throw the contents of the kitchen drawers at the walls, maybe break a window or two. What the heck, such breakages could always be mended or replaced.

Peter, the brother closest to Kirsty both in age and affection, had suggested the week in Town to Max. He and his young wife, Louisa, would come and manage Cheshunt, giving Max the opportunity to take his small family away for a break. By this time, Max, who normally detested being absent from Cheshunt, was desperate enough about Kirsty to gratefully accept his brother-in-law's kindly offer.

Curled up against her pillows, Kirsty listened while Max told her about his meeting with Kendrick Tenny. The story of the American and Son of Saratoga brought a faint flicker of interest to his beloved Kirsty's face. Observing this, he mentioned the invitation.

'He invited all of us to The Summit?' Kirsty sounded bewildered.

'Sure did. Six-thirty sharp.'

'Well, I don't know,' she sounded dubious.

He knelt beside the bed. 'Please, Kirsty, for my sake, please come.'

Perhaps she sensed the underlying tinge of desperation in her husband's voice and dimly realised he might be suffering in his own way. Reaching out to touch a gentle hand to his cheek, Kirsty agreed to accept the invitation.

Kendrick Tenny was no fool. Waiting in the lobby by the lifts on the forty-seventh floor of Australia Square, his keen eyes observed the trio as they exited the lift. The woman was tall, long limbed and moved rather awkwardly — it was almost as if she was unsure of where to place her next step — he noted that her husband guided her discreetly with a gentle hand on her left arm. The clear pallor of her oval-shaped face was dominated by enormous dark brown eyes. Dark hair was drawn back from her face and twisted into a neat roll on the back of her head. She was very quietly dressed in a navy blue frock ending just below the knees. It had a big white collar and six large white buttons. With it she wore low-heeled black pumps, or what he knew the Australians called court shoes, and nylon stockings. Most unusual for a woman, she carried no handbag and if she wore makeup, it was so discreetly applied as to be invisible.

Small pearl earrings adorned her neat, well-shaped ears, the only jewellery she wore except for the two rings on her wedding finger.

Kendrick thought of his wife, Eunice, whose dress code could be best described by the word flamboyant. He rather liked bright colours himself but she did take things a bit too far. Loud checked pants with gaily coloured striped shirts were okay — yes, he could live with that — even that red and white plaid blouse and those huge orange and blue flowers on the skirt she wore with it. Well, it could be worse, he supposed. He mentally winced as he recalled the day she had appeared in something from what she called 'the latest designer collection'. To Kendrick, it seemed as if someone had emptied a tin of oil over a piece of black material. He had very nearly got it right.

'It's called Iridescent Oil Spill,' she had announced proudly, modelling the creation for him.

He stared in amazement at the pantsuit his wife was wearing.

'It's from Henri's special designer collection for the mature woman,' she told him, parading around the large dressing room.

'Mature woman?' spluttered Kendrick.

'Henri says the mature woman mustn't hide her light under a bushel. She must show her potential and not be shy.'

'Be hard to find any bush big enough or dense enough to hide that creation behind,' Kendrick most unwisely replied.

Rather fortunately Eunice missed most of the sentence, being far to enraptured by her reflection in the huge triple mirrors of her dressing room.

'Bushel, dear, not bush,' she called absently.

Kendrick deliberated on how to tactfully tell her that the spilled oil getup, or whatever in creation the wretched thing was called, was hardly suitable for a woman of over sixty with a queenly figure. To be honest, he couldn't see it looking good on *any* woman, regardless of age or figure. How in the name of Jeremiah did these dress designing queens get away with it?

'It is the Pick of the Season at Henri's Salon,' Eunice spoke proudly.

'If that bloody fairy has ever spent one day of his life in France, then my name's George Washington,' snapped Kendrick.

No, he certainly couldn't imagine this wife of Max's ever wearing something resembling an oil spill in his garage.

He was much struck by the gravity of the small boy holding his mother's right hand. Clad in spotless moleskin strides, well-polished, elastic sided ankle boots and a beautifully ironed checked cotton shirt, the child had the same dark hair and expressive brown eyes of his mother. He held his mother's hand protectively.

Introductions were made. Kendrick Tenny learned that the woman's name was Kirsty; that the boy was called Tobias, Toby for short and that he was in his seventh year. Kendrick was worried; this woman had been hurt and hurt badly by something. This was no instance of a woman hiding behind her partly imagined health issues. One part of his mind dwelt resentfully on Eunice and her bloody headaches, every time he wanted a bit of a cuddle in bed. What the hell was the point of being able to buy one of those new-fangled large beds if you couldn't make proper use of it?

Behind the polite conversation, his mind worked like lightning. It would be just his luck to make some innocent seeming remark which flicked this woman directly on the rawness of her wound. He had to find out what the problem was before the whole evening turned into a right mess. All he needed was a minute alone with young Max. Spotting a flower wagon being pushed carefully out of a lift, he had a brainwave. He turned to young Toby, hoping the child was old enough to understand.

'Son, see that lady over there with that flower wagon?'

'Yes, sir.' A pair of dark eyes steadily gazed back.

'Can you take your mother over and buy her the biggest bunch of flowers you can find?'

'Yes, sir.' The small face lit up.

Kendrick caught the flower seller's eye and she nodded understandingly. He tucked a banknote into the boy's shirt pocket.

'Come on, Mum.' The boy eagerly yet gently tugged at her hand.

Max, seeing signs of protest on Kirsty's face, squeezed her left arm warningly. 'Lucky girl, Kirsty, I can see some lovely roses on the wagon.'

She allowed herself to be drawn towards the flower-laden cart, attracted as always by the colour and scent of flowers. Max waited till the flower seller had engaged her in conversation before turning to Kendrick.

'Nicely done,' he spoke softly, 'now please tell me what that little charade was in aid of?'

'Look Richards, it is as clear as water to me that your beautiful wife is not —'

Max cut him off abruptly, 'Twin girls, dead at birth.'

Kendrick's jaw dropped. 'Both?'

'Yes.'

'Oh my God, son, I had no idea!'

'How could you? So, no mention of babies, pregnancies, increasing the family — that sort of thing — you get the picture? Stick to horses and you can't go wrong. Kirsty loves them as much as I do. I suppose I should have told you but —' He shrugged his shoulders.

'I shouldn't have pressed you into coming tonight!'

Max shook his head. 'No, I wanted her to come. You've probably done us a favour.'

Both men looked up to see mother and son coming towards them, Kirsty holding a beautiful bouquet and Toby proudly clutching a single, partially opened yellow rosebud.

'The lady gave me this,' Toby told them. 'She said it was because I was accomp-compan-ing Mum so I had to have the same flower. She said it's called a button-hole.'

'That's right, son,' Kendrick agreed. 'The gentleman who accompanies the beautiful lady must always have a flower to match her bouquet.'

'It's always worn on the gentleman's left side,' Kirsty carefully handed her bouquet to Max, produced a safety pin from beneath her large white collar and deftly attached the yellow rosebud to her son's shirt. Then she turned to Kendrick. 'That was very kind of you, Mr Tenny. Thank you so much for such lovely flowers.'

'Thank you, sir,' added Toby, smiling up at the big man.

'That's enough of that, and what's all this 'Mr Tenny' nonsense? It's Kendrick to you, Mrs Max, and how about Uncle Kendrick for the youngster? Any objections?'

Smiling, Kirsty shook her head.

'Well, that's grand. Now we've settled all that, let's go find our table. Hey, waiter, you there, where's the maître d'? I had a table booked in the name of Tenny. Take this lady's flowers and make sure they are properly arranged on our table. Thanks, son.' A banknote discreetly changed hands.

During the first part of the evening, all three members of the Richards family listened entranced whilst Kendrick Tenny told how Son of Saratoga had travelled to Australia.

'He came over in a Boeing 707,' explained Kendrick, 'along with eight beautiful broodmares for company. Normally, on a plane, there is one groom for every three horses but this time was different. Five grooms came with the nine horses, instead of the usual three.'

'Why?' asked Kirsty, who had been listening intently.

'You see, the insurance people got a bit worried about my old Sonny Boy and insisted he had his own groom. They seemed to think he was getting along a bit in years. Absolute rubbish! Then some dude who only deals with paperwork, saw the words 'stallion and broodmares', and promptly had kittens. Seemed to think the trip would turn out to be an experiment in international, mid-air, free-for-all breeding, if you get my drift. Stupid clot! Well, the powers-that-be decided that five grooms would be essential for the safety of all concerned.'

'Was there any trouble?' asked Max.

'Trouble? All the horses dozed pretty much all the way and so did the grooms,' snorted Kendrick. Suddenly his wide smile broke out. 'Still, better safe than sorry, I guess.'

From the breast pocket of his dazzlingly white shirt, Kendrick produced a packet of photographs. To the amazement of Max and Kirsty, they were in colour. When spread out across the white damask cloth they revealed a horse who took Kirsty's breath away. This was the first time she had ever seen a Morgan horse.

Son of Saratoga resembled an illustration from a child's book of magical creatures. He was a glorious dappled grey with a flowing waterfall of a thick, silky silver mane. His high set tail almost swept the ground. The beautifully defined head was poised upon an upright, strongly arched neck, giving him a stylish, proud carriage. He had small neat ears and large, dark, expressive, intelligent eyes. The compact body was short-backed with well-muscled hindquarters and chest; the overall impression was one of powerful elegance and refinement. He stood proudly on strong, clean legs, and looked about fifteen hands tall.

'Wow,' wide-eyed Toby stared in wonder at the dozen photographs.

'Wow, indeed,' agreed his father. 'That's some horse you've got there, Kendrick. I'm not surprised the Australian owners find him irresistible.'

'His progeny seem to favour him: they call it prepotency,' the American pushed three photos across the table. 'Two colts and two young mares, taken at the Saratoga Classic and Madison Square Gardens a couple of years ago.'

'What are their names?' asked Kirsty.

'New England Lass, Massachusetts Marianne, Burlington Bertie and Lancaster Lord,' was the reply.

Whilst the Richards trio poured over the pictures of the beautiful Morgans, Kendrick continued talking:

'I'm leaving for the Territory on Saturday and I'll be gone three weeks. Not too happy with that smug place where Sonny Boy is boarding at present — it's all fancy matching blankets and bandages, and even fancier charges. I'm not saying they are actually mean to the horses but the whole place lacks the homely touch. Trouble is, I've only got three days to find somewhere better, and get it all arranged. Say, Mrs Max, you ever heard of a place called Stormy Ridge or Thunder Ridge, a place with a weathery sort of name?'

'For boarding horses?' asked Kirsty.

'No, no, for opals. Up near the Queensland border, I think.'

Max's lips twitched involuntarily. 'You mean Lightning Ridge?'

'That's it, my boy. I figure that I might as well return to Sydney via that Lightning Ridge place. I need to get a peace offering for Eunice, my wife, and some fine opals should just be the ticket.'

'They are very beautiful stones,' Kirsty offered shyly.

Kendrick beamed at her. 'Eunice likes lot of bright colours so opals should be the very ticket.' Turning to Max, he asked, 'Now where's this farm of yours? Far from here?'

'About five hours drive. We're north-west of the Blue Mountains,' explained Max.

'What do you have on your place? Cattle, horses, crops?'

'Bit of a mixed bag.' Max was always reticent when speaking of Cheshunt to people he barely knew, however friendly they might be.

'We've got lots of horses,' Toby spoke eagerly. 'I've got my own pony, he's called Casper.'

Most untypically, the American did not immediately respond. Max had already observed he was exceptionally punctilious when talking with Toby, treating the boy with serious attention and respect. The silence grew and Toby bit his lip, his face flushing slightly. Anxiously he looked up at his mother who smiled reassuringly at him, drawing his attention again to the photographs. Mother and son, so alike, bent their heads over the wonderful Morgans, a breed practically unknown to Australia in the 1960s.

'Lots of horses, have you?' Kendrick spoke absently, breaking the silence, a calloused hand thoughtfully rubbing his jaw.

Kirsty sensed what was coming and a tiny bubble of amusement, the first she had felt for three long months, stirred within. She kept her eyes fixed on her husband's face.

'Jumping Jeremiah! I have it! Sonny Boy can go to you good people for three weeks!' Delighted with his decision, Kendrick crashed his huge fist down on the dinner table.

In the silence which followed this far from quietly spoken declaration, the sound of delicately breaking glass was heard; Kendrick had knocked two finely engraved wine glasses to the floor. A hovering waiter hastened to the rescue. Covert looks came from diners at the surrounding tables: really, such behaviour! At The Summit too, of all places. Disdainful noses tilted as whispers were exchanged.

Max Richards appeared to be struck dumb. He shot a quick glance at the beaming American, hardly believing what the man had said. Was Kendrick Tenny seriously proposing to entrust a highly valuable stallion to people he had only met that very day? He seemed far from satisfied with the obviously luxurious accommodation provided by the current equine boarding establishment. What the blazes was he going to think of Cheshunt? A beautiful property, certainly, and one with enormous potential, but Cheshunt had deteriorated sadly under the last years of Max's father's ownership. Max, backed by Kirsty and his small team of employees, was working steadily to repair, replace, improve and update, yet Rome couldn't be built in a day. His eyes met those of his wife and to his astonishment, he saw something approaching a twinkle in them. He cleared his throat and swallowed twice.

'You know, our place isn't anything fancy, Kendrick.'

'Is that so? White painted fences and fountains in the front yard doesn't mean good horse care in my experience.'

'I still don't think we're quite what you're looking for,' Max persisted.

Kirsty had rarely seen her husband so unsure of himself. She reached out a hand and gently touched his arm.

'What do you say, Mrs Max?' Eagerly, the big American turned to her.

Toby, aware that some momentous decision was hovering in the air, fixed his dark, expressive eyes on each adult face in turn. He wasn't quite sure what was happening but it seemed to have something to do with horses. Anything to do with horses interested Toby, so he kept quiet and still, carefully observing the grown-ups.

Max looked up from the tablecloth and met Kirsty's eyes. She gave a nod so small that only he noticed it. There was a pause and again he cleared his throat and swallowed hard.

'Well, Kendrick, I guess we've got one fine Morgan stallion coming to pay us a visit!'

It was much later on that same night and Max Richards was sitting alone in the hotel bar. Upstairs, both Toby and Kirsty were fast asleep. Max had agreed to meet up with Kendrick the following morning to make the arrangements for transporting Son of Saratoga to Cheshunt. In his right hand Max cradled one of his extremely rare drinks: Southern Comfort and dry. What in the blazes had he gotten himself into?

Visions of accidents, of massive insurance claims, of fights between this excessively valuable stallion and his own two, far less valuable stallions, all this and more danced before his eyes. Theft, my God, what about theft? He would be the target of every damned horse thief in the country! Perhaps arrangement should be made for armed guards? Furious with himself, Max downed the contents of his glass and left the bar.

Upstairs in their bedroom, he stood quietly and looked down on his sleeping wife. Through a partly open door, Toby slept peacefully in the adjoining bedroom. The huge bunch of golden-yellow roses stood on the glass-backed dressing table. They had been carefully arranged in the ornate glass vase supplied by the obliging housekeeper. The anger, the strange and unfamiliar lack of confidence in himself, both began to slowly drain away. The room was full of peace and its gentle fingers reached out to touch him. He bent low and kissed the bare white shoulder from which Kirsty's pale pink nightgown had slipped.

So Son of Saratoga came to Cheshunt, one of the first purebred Morgan's to visit Australia. None of Max's fears materialised: the beautiful Morgan was a model visitor.

Max had iron-clad rules for keeping stallions, having too often seen them restricted to tiny yards. Each Cheshunt stallion had its own paddock, double-fenced, with a laneway between the fences. This meant that whilst the horse had complete freedom to gallop about, graze and see everything that was going on, it had no physical contact with any other horse across paddock fences. The result was happy, contented, well-behaved stallions. Max saw no reason to change what had always worked so well, so Son of Saratoga was given his own doubled-fenced paddock, nicely sheltered by radiata pines.

Kirsty spent hours grooming the beautiful horse, paying special attention to the mane and tail. One day Max found her riding the horse around his paddock. She was bareback and instead of a bridle, Son of Saratoga wore his usual head-collar, to which Kirsty had attached both ends of a lead rein. Toby, seated on the rail fence, was clapping his hands in delight.

Max was horrified but daren't bellow at her: this might frighten the horse. Instead, he joined his son and grimly observed his wife. She and the Morgan made an enchanting picture; the horse with his proudly arched neck, alert ears and flowing mane and tail was the perfect foil for the woman who sat him so easily and lightly. Seeing her husband, she trotted over to the fence.

'Kirsty, may I ask what you think you're doing?'

'It's all right, Daddy. Uncle Kendrick said she could,' piped Toby.

'Kirsty?'

'Kendrick rang up last night — remember, I told you? He's finishing up in the Territory and moving on to North Queensland. He's bought some mares to take back to America but I'm not sure what breed. The phone line was bad and kept dropping out — he sounded very pleased, anyway. Just before he hung up he told me I could ride our boy —' She patted the strong neck lovingly, '— and that he was as quiet as a lamb. He is too.'

'I don't remember you telling me that bit about riding him.' Max frowned. 'And what's all this *our boy* business? Don't you go getting too fond of him now.'

'Show Daddy how he can canter.' Toby looked proudly at his mother.

'Kirsty!'

Father and son looked on as Kirsty touched her heels gently to the dapple grey flanks. Horse and rider flew across the grass, the Morgan moving as smoothly as a rocking horse, the rider part of the powerful stallion.

'Aren't they lovely, Daddy.' Toby looked up at his father.

Max gave in to the inevitable, relaxed and laughed. He ruffled his son's hair. 'Yes, Toby, they are pretty nice. I guess we'd better get the camera and take some photos of them, eh?'

When Son of Saratoga departed Cheshunt, he left a legacy behind him: four Cheshunt mares were in foal.

'One for each week of his stay and one for spare,' as Kendrick put it. After all, as he had added, 'there was many a slip 'tween cup and lip.'

Max worded it slightly differently: 'Pity I didn't have any more mares in season!'

But all went well: it was as if Son of Saratoga's coming had blessed Cheshunt with some badly needed good fortune. 'Morgan Luck,' as it would come to be called at Cheshunt, had arrived with Son of Saratoga. Eleven months later four beautiful foals were born.

From that time onwards, Morgan blood ran in the veins of many of the Cheshunt horses, and the strong family interest in the Morgan breed, which Kendrick Tenny had kindled, flourished.

Blue Mountain Mist, always known as Blue, was a pretty blue roan mare, a brumby Welsh pony cross. Her filly foal by Son of Saratoga was named Saratoga Mist but she was called Misty from the beginning.

Stella, leaning on the gate, gazed admiringly at the lovely Misty. She never tired of hearing about Kendrick Tenny and Son of Saratoga.

In the neighbouring smaller home paddock, the two younger mares thundered down the length of the fence-line yet again. The noise and vibrations made by galloping horse hoofs pounding on the turf never ceased to amaze her. A voice spoke just behind her:

> *"Half a league, half a league,*
> *Half a league onward,*
> *All in the valley of Death*
> *Rode the six hundred.*
> *'Forward, the Light Brigade!*

Charge for the guns!' he said.
Into the valley of Death
Rode the six hundred."

'If those two girls can make such a racket, just imagine what the mighty six hundred must have sounded like as they rode into the valley of Death. That was Tennyson, sis, and Mum's after you, you'd better getting moving or you'll miss the school bus.'

'Damn! Okay, thanks, Toby.'

'Good to see you back to normal again. This place is far too quiet when you're confined to barracks! I'd watch that lingo in front of the parents if I were you!'

Stella pulled a face at her brother before reluctantly heading towards the farmhouse. Toby was right about one thing: it was good to be back to the normal routine. At the beginning of the month she had been taken ill with what the doctors said was a viral sickness of some kind. One of the usual winter 'flu bugs they had told her mother, probably doing the rounds. No, there was nothing to worry about, it was only the 'flu. She had been feverish and shaky for about ten days and only too thankful to be safely tucked up in bed, sleeping most of the time, black Sambo at her side. His purr was comforting during her waking hours. Another week had passed before she was strong enough to return to school. She had been back at school for a week now and today was Monday, the beginning of the last week in August.

Stella slipped into the house via the laundry door, leaving her boots on the wide verandah. She washed vigorously in the laundry, after shedding warm jacket, scarf, woollen beanie, long woollen socks and gloves. These late winter mornings were always the coldest of all.

'Come on, Stella, no time to dawdle this morning.' Her mother set a bowl of steaming hot porridge on the kitchen table.

'I'm going to ride both Desert Star and Star of Bethlehem after school,' Stella told her mother as she helped herself generously to cinnamon, sugar and milk.

Kirsty smiled at her daughter. 'So long as the evening doesn't close in too early, you should manage it. Eat up, now!'

While she ate her breakfast, the girl looked contentedly about her. The big farmhouse kitchen was a good place to be at any time and all the family called it the heart of the home. It opened into what town people might call a dining room but at Cheshunt, it was inaccurately named the kitchen extension. She loved the round dark wooden table covered with the blue checked cloth and the huge wooden dresser which took up almost an entire wall, reached nearly to the ceiling, and was home to an incredible assortment of items. She revelled in the warmth radiating from the stove, warmth which had nurtured many an orphaned lamb and kitten, snug in a straw filled box pushed hard up against the stove's solid side. Sambo was purring from under the table, seated on one of the chairs. The girl hated to leave the happy, homely kitchen.

Teeth were brushed and a comb dragged through the thick chestnut curls which were then firmly restrained into two plaits. White socks, white long-sleeved blouse with the school crest on the pocket, and well-made navy blue slacks were donned. Collecting her school pullover from under the bed, she gave it a good shake to remove any dust before dumping her heavy school bag by the front door. She just had to collect her lunch and put on her black lace-up shoes.

'Stella, hurry up!' her mother called from the laundry.

She raced back to the kitchen, shoes in hand, and plumped down on one of the blue vinyl upholstered kitchen chairs. The sturdy black shoes were slipped on, laced up tightly and double knotted. Then she stood up.

Something was wrong. Her legs didn't seem to be working properly. She fell back into the chair. She tried again. She still couldn't get up. Putting both hands on the seat of the chair on either side of her, she pushed hard. For a long second she stood balanced on both feet before something gave way. For the third time she fell back into the chair. She tried one more time, making a grab for the back of the chair as soon as she was on her feet. Her legs, unable to hold her, crumpled, and Stella, unbalanced by her grab for the chair-back, fell to the hard floor. Slowly, she partly crawled and partly climbed back onto the chair.

'Stella —' her mother was suddenly standing in front of her, '— why are you just sitting there? You'll miss the bus at this rate! Get a move on, girl, for goodness sakes!'

Two grey eyes stared up at Kirsty Richards, who saw that her daughter's face was chalk white.

'Stella?' Her voice was worried now. She knelt in front of her daughter.

'Mum,' the child spoke in a rigidly controlled voice, 'I don't seem able to stand up properly. My legs feel sort of funny, as if they don't really belong to me.'

Chapter Three: 'It's only the 'flu!'

Stella gazed at the walls of the small hospital ward with a stony face. To her fury she had been placed in a single room attached to the children's ward. She was pleased about the children's ward: at age sixteen she could easily have been sent to an adult ward. It was being alone that she hated so much and it made no sense. Why on earth couldn't they have put her in the main children's ward, in the big room?

She hated this room. It had nothing. No personality, no colour. Plain bare walls painted in a depressing shade of blue-grey with a plain white ceiling. The walls bore no pictures, no photographs, no drawings. Nothing. They were a complete blank.

Nothing hung from the ceiling, not a gently twirling mobile nor a small distracting toy swinging from its ribbon. She wondered about that. Surely it wouldn't have taken much effort or expense to brighten up the room a little?

The one window was securely netted; could not be opened and, on the outside, was protected by ugly, curved iron bars. Those bars made her feel like the prisoner she knew herself to be. Whilst she understood their necessity, she wondered if there wasn't some other means of obtaining the same end, something far less obvious.

Her window overlooked an inner courtyard. It was paved with a small circular pool in the middle. A statue carved from some kind of white stone rose from the centre of the pool, and water fell like gentle feathers from statue to pool. It had become Stella's sole aspect of visual pleasure. She had always loved fountains and waterfalls.

Stella felt cold and uncomfortable in the white hospital gown she had been requested to keep on following tests performed earlier in the day. There would be more tests shortly, she had been told, so there was no point in changing back into her pyjamas yet. It wouldn't be long, maybe half an hour or so. That had been three hours ago, thought Stella crossly, checking her wrist-watch.

She tugged a warm cardigan from her bedside locker and pulled it around her shoulders. In the past weeks her entire world had been turned upside down.

In the beginning Stella didn't realise what was happening. This was just another of the doctor's stupid old viral infections, just like the 'flu bug they said she'd had a couple of weeks earlier. It would run its course and she would be fine soon, just like last time.

Yes, she had joint pain, especially in her legs. Her knees, ankles, hips and wrists were hot, swollen and red. She always felt weak and tired, often hot and sweaty. She tossed and turned most of the night, unable to sleep due to the pain and her inability to get comfortable. She would sink into a restless doze just before dawn, waking up so stiff she could barely roll over in bed, soaking wet and shaking with cold. She always limped badly now, some days worse than others. Sometimes she couldn't hobble to the bathroom without grabbing on to pieces of furniture, walls — anything sturdy enough to give her support and balance.

All she wished to do was to stay in bed, but she soon found that if she stayed in the same position for more than a few hours the stiffness and pain only increased. So she would struggle out of bed, shuffle out to the kitchen for a drink of water, then shuffle back to bed again.

Doctor Charles Mason, the elderly family doctor who had been watching over the Richards family for more than twenty years, began paying twice weekly calls. One of the few doctors who still did regular rounds, Charles Mason did not like what he was seeing. Painkilling drugs were prescribed and no diagnosis was made. He told Kirsty Richards to let the girl rest as much as possible and gave no indication as to how long this situation would last. Blood for testing, quite a lot of blood, was taken and sent off to the laboratories.

Every morning, Kirsty would help her daughter get settled in the bathroom, filling the tub with soothing warm water and bubble bath. Peeling sweat-sodden pyjamas off the child, stripping saturated sheets from the bed, the mother was appalled at the volume of fluids the girl was losing. These had to be replaced by drinks containing the necessary sugars and salts. Totally exhausted by her bath, a very unsteady Stella would be helped into clean, loose, cotton track pants and tee shirt, and escorted back to bed. Her painful limbs supported by pillows, she would sink into a deep sleep, often not waking until noon. She would usually be at her best during the afternoon and Kirsty would tuck her up on the old sofa in the kitchen-extension-cum-dining-room, Sambo at her side. Some days she would settle with a book, usually an English set book. All other school work had been banned for the present. Kirsty noticed that Stella winced at sudden loud noises and that the radio appeared to bother her. Like the rest of the family, Stella's interest in television was practically non-existent. Three months could easily pass without the set being switched on. Other days Stella would lie with a pile of old horse magazines, listlessly turning the pages, smiling with pleased recognition when she saw a familiar face, equine or otherwise. Time now had practically no meaning for her and she hardly seemed aware that days had turned to weeks and those weeks were now passing. Her appetite was dwindling and Kirsty was hard pressed to coax the girl to eat.

An increasingly worried Kirsty attacked the doctor:

'Surely all those tests must have thrown up *something*?' she demanded.

'Mrs Max, apart from showing she's a touch anaemic, they didn't.' He hesitated for a moment. 'I am afraid she will have to go into hospital for a few days. I want to arrange some X-rays and MRI scans, as well as a number of other tests, and I also want her looked at by several different doctors. They will be checking for congenital defects, possible fractures, deficiency in certain minerals such as calcium, any growths, lumps or tumours or other abnormalities.'

'That rules out our local hospital, doesn't it?'

'Yes, I'm afraid it means a trip to Sydney but we've really got no choice.'

'Doesn't that mean a visit to some sort of specialist first? You can't directly admit her to a Sydney hospital, can you?'

'Now, Mrs Max, you leave medical procedure and politics to me. A colleague of mine runs an outpatient clinic at the hospital I'm thinking of. I can arrange for Stella to be directly admitted to the hospital through him — all on the same day. That will make it much easier on both you and your daughter. I'll give him a call and sort something out with him. My secretary will get on to you as soon as we've got something arranged.'

Three days later Stella was admitted to hospital.

'May I come in?' a gentle voice spoke from the doorway.

Startled, Stella looked up. A woman was regarding her through kindly blue eyes. She wore no uniform of any sort and no identifying badge was pinned to the front of her fawn jumper. Most unusually, she waited for Stella's consent before entering the small room: most people bustled in with an officious air, as if they owned the place.

The woman looked much older than Stella's mother. She had short grey hair, was of medium height and her figure was nicely plump, which Stella found very appealing. She could not stand skinny mothers or grandmothers. Her dark brown skirt was well-cut and contrasted pleasantly with the fawn jumper, to the left breast of which was pinned a twinkling cat brooch. In one hand she carried a small cane basket by its handle.

'Hello,' Stella spoke shyly.

'May I sit down?'

'Of course.'

The woman seated herself on the sole chair in the room, the cane basket on her lap. 'My name is Mrs Walker and I belong to a group called Hospital Helpers.' Seeing that the child was listening with obvious interest, she continued:

'My day is Thursday and I have been coming to this hospital every Thursday for over a year now. Each week the ward sister selects one or two patients whom she feels might like a visitor for a short while. Today she chose you.' With a smile, Mrs Walker put the cane basket on the bed.

Stella stared at the woman, eyes wide with surprise, before stammering, 'Th-th-thank you very much.'

The little basket of neatly woven cane was wrapped in clear cellophane and finished with a beautifully tied red ribbon bow. Filled with six or seven small objects, it provided the sole note of colour in the drab little room. Stella flushed with pleasure, unable to lift her eyes from the vivid scarlet. One trembling finger gently touched the thick, rich satin bow. Observing the tears in the girls' eyes, Mrs Walker kept talking:

'There's quite a few members in our group, although many of

them are unable to actually visit the hospital, so they help from home by making all the little items in our baskets. We've got some wonderfully talented people, you know. One man is a double amputee — lost both his legs — and he is very gifted at woodcarving. He has a small shed in the back of his garden and spends hours working there most days. He makes the carved wooden animals for our baskets. Then one lady works with dried flowers — she grows them herself, dries them then makes beautiful cards and book-marks. The lavender she grows is used to fill lavender bags which are sewn by another of our group. You get the idea?'

'What other people do you have?'

'Well, there's a lady who has to be very careful of her heart; has to live very quietly and can't do much housework. Lives with her daughter. Her particular talent is crochet. Her daughter buys plain white face washers and the mother crochets pretty lace edging all around them. She also makes crocheted toys for babies and small children. Then we have a couple,' she said smiling, 'real characters they are. Bill — he refuses to be addressed by his surname — his hobby has always been calligraphy. Since retirement —' She broke off, seeing the puzzled expression on the girl's face.

'Calligraphy? It is a decorative form of handwriting, a true art and extremely difficult to do. Bill makes labels for the jars of homemade cinnamon-sugar popcorn which are his wife's speciality. It's yummy popcorn, that I can tell you!' Mrs Walker ended with a laugh.

So many of the hospital patients she saw did not wish to talk but wanted to listen. The ward sisters were usually astute in selecting who needed a kindly visitor, a change in direction of thought or a distraction. She wondered what was wrong with this child but knew it was highly unlikely she would ever be told. The rules pertaining to privacy of information were tightening further every day.

'Where do you live?' the girl was shyly asking.

'Rose Bay, near Bondi,' Mrs Walker explained. 'When are you going to open that basket?'

Scarlet with embarrassment, Stella explained:

'I was kind of saving it for tonight. My Mum brought me down from the country on Monday but she had to go back home yesterday. I think she will be back tomorrow to take me home — at least I hope so.' She bit her lip. 'I've got some more tests this afternoon so I thought it might be nice to open the basket later on. If you don't mind, that is?' she finished anxiously.

This speech had revealed far more than Stella would have believed possible.

'My dear,' Mrs Walker answered gently, 'you must open and enjoy it whenever you wish.'

The ward sister entered the room, followed by two white-clad wardsmen.

'Right, they're waiting for you, Stella.' The sister put the clipboard of notes on the bed.

One wardsman went to the head of the bed, shut off the brakes on each of the two wheels, and grasped the headboard in large, capable hands.

'My basket!' Stella panicked, picking it up.

'I'll make sure it's safe, Stella — don't worry child.' Sister took the basket from the shaking hands and placed it on the broad window-sill. 'Now, lie down quietly like a good girl.'

Stella obliged and Sister firmly pulled up the sides of the bed and locked them into place. The second wardsman was now at the foot of the bed and shutting off the two sets of wheel brakes. Together, the two men began maneuvering the bed, working with deceptive casualness, towards the doorway.

'Goodbye, Mrs Walker and thank you for the nice basket.' Stella stuck a hand through the protective bars and waved frantically.

'Goodbye, Stella. It's been delightful meeting you.'

'See you when you come back, child, and don't fret over your basket. It will be perfectly safe.'

Stella lay quietly as the wardsmen wheeled her down the long corridor towards the lifts. Everything looked so different from this angle.

'Warm enough?' the man at the head of the bed asked her.

'Yes, thanks.'

'It can get a bit cold waiting around downstairs so ask for another blanket if you need it,' the second man told her.

'Why aren't I going on a trolley?' she asked suddenly.

'Much easier to keep you in your bed. Far less painful for you,' she was told.

They arrived at the lifts and the second wardsmen pressed the button. The wait was relatively short.

'Okay, love, bit of a bumpy ride now but it won't be for long.' The first wardsman pushed the head of the bed towards the open lift doors.

His partner winked at Stella. 'Keep your hands inside those bars, young lady. We don't want to bang against anything.'

She hastily checked her hands before realising he was gently teasing her. Relaxing a little, Stella pulled a face at him.

Mrs Walker left the hospital and made her way down to the car park. She had paid a visit to another patient after Stella, a long term patient whose family never visited her. One saw some dreadfully sad things during these visits.

As she slid her keys into the ignition of her Volkswagen Golf, she recalled the words of the head sister on the children's ward:

'I'm a bit worried about this child. Country girl from a big farm — never had a day's illness in her life — spent most of her time on horseback, I gather ...' Here she had sighed.

'What is it, Sister?'

'I shouldn't be telling you this, what with all the paranoia over patient privacy rules these days — lot of rubbish if you ask me — but I know you're a discreet soul ...' Again she hesitated.

'That I am, but what is it that bothers you about this child?'

'To sum up, lack of diagnosis. Yes, I know, from one point of view it could be said to be early days yet, but it's not really. The weeks are ticking by and none of the tests show anything except slight anaemia — not unusual at her age — and signs of mild infection. Not only is this child suffering a great deal of pain, her body is changing as you look at it.'

'But a medical diagnosis will be found, surely?'

'Yes, in the end it probably will be but it could take a very long time, possibly years.'

Mrs Walker had gazed at the sister in dismay. 'What happens in the meantime?'

The other woman shrugged. 'Treat the symptoms and keep on looking for an answer. One of the big problems we face in this modern era is far too much reliance on tests, many of which are not really accurate. For example, take juvenile rheumatoid arthritis. An antibody known as the rheumatoid factor can be, and often is, found in children with juvenile rheumatoid arthritis. However, the absence of the rheumatoid factor does not mean that JRA, as we call it, can be ruled out. Far too many medicos are inclined to treat the test results as gospel truth. I've nursed a number of children on this ward who tested negative for every possible JRA test — again, it is the same thing — a number of things *may* be present in the blood of JRA children but not necessarily are. Eventually, it was grudgingly admitted that JRA *could* be a possibility but that there was no real proof. Unfortunately, some doctors are very reluctant to admit to having made a mistaken diagnosis.'

'Did you mention JRA, as you call it, because you think Stella may have that condition?' Mrs Walker had asked with interest.

'I chose it as an example because it is so often wrongly diagnosed and sometimes never diagnosed at all. It is quite extraordinary but somehow, people just associate all forms of arthritis with the elderly. Explaining to young parents, for example, that their two-year-old has probably got JRA can be quite a task. It's a shocking thing to see in very small children or babies.'

'But do you think Stella may have it?' she had persisted, perhaps unwisely.

'I think it is one of the more likely possibilities and I've said far too much.'

It was late in the evening before Stella was returned to her room on the children's ward. She was very tired and the tears were not far away. The technicians had been very kind and handled her as gently as possible but, inevitably, they had hurt her. Her swollen limbs and ceaseless joint pain made every form of movement torture. Sister took immediate charge.

'Nurse, two blankets from the hot-cupboard, please!'

Numerous tablets were administered to Stella and she was slipped out of the white gown and cardigan and back into pyjamas. Then she was wrapped in the heavenly soothing warmth of those wonderful blankets. Tears slid down her face: tears of relief, exhaustion and pain.

'It's all right, child, those tablets will take effect very soon.' Sister skillfully adjusted the pillows supporting the girl's legs before pulling the nurse's call buzzer within Stella's reach.

Stella lay still in the quiet, darkening room. The corridor lights, reflected in the shining linoleum of the little room's floor, threw a golden pathway to the window sill. The little cane basket stood there on the broad sill, its scarlet ribbon a brave beacon of colour and hope. She fell asleep, the ghost of a smile on her face.

Chapter Four: Telopea speciosissima

The owls were hooting softly, calling to one another and swooping in and out the barn. This barn was their haven, with its lofty rafters stretching between the high walls. Plenty of rodents were naturally attracted to the bales of neatly stacked hay and straw. The back barn, as it was always called at Cheshunt, held Max Richards' reserve stock of hay and straw. The Lucerne hay came from Canowindra; the best meadow hay from both the Orange and Goulburn districts, and the straw, well, that came from wherever Max could get the best deals.

The barn stood just below the brow of the hill, situated low enough to be protected from the worst of the weather, but within easy distance of the rough access track which wound part of the way across the top of the ridge. The scene had a stark and haunting beauty if one were of a mind to see it.

A sole human was creeping across the hillside. The moon shone silver and bright, making use of the hooded torch unnecessary. The human almost wished he hadn't bothered with the torch he carried, but it was too late now, and he might need it later.

The huge barn would guide him, he had been told: he couldn't miss it. It was his locator beacon, Dean had said. Once he had the barn in his sights, all he had to do was climb to the hilltop and start going down the other side. That was where he would find the waratah flowers, according to Dean. They were all over that slope. It was easy enough to remember: barn one side, waratahs on the other side. Dean had rather nastily added that even an idiot like him should be able to retain that small amount of information in his thick skull.

Sean didn't really understand the importance of the red flowers, but during the past five weeks he had learned that it was best not to think too much and not to ask questions. He did what he was told to do. If he didn't, Dean and Dieter could get mean and Sean had the bruises as proof. Dean had said that people in the cities, like Sydney, paid real good cash for these flowers. His job, a very important one, he had been told, was to get into this place where the waratahs grew and cut some samples. It appeared that the potential buyers wanted to be sure that Dean and Dieter could deliver what they had promised.

Sean had been ordered to get as many sample flowers as he could stuff into a sack and carry. The small knapsack on his back held a clean sack and a small pair of sharp-bladed secateurs — the essential tools needed for the job. Sean had somehow imagined the plants to be in neat rows like they were in the parks of Sydney. He had never envisioned stumbling about a tree covered hillside, almost smashing his toes on sandstone slabs.

Something swooped low, almost brushing his shoulder, causing Sean to jump with fright. A small cry escaped his lips as he tripped and stumbled. He made a desperate attempt to save himself but his ankle caught against the remains of a burned out log and he fell hard to the ground. He lay where he fell, breathing hard and fighting back the tears. The torch had flown from his hand and crashed against a sandstone slab before disappearing into a patch of undergrowth. The owl who had been the cause of his scare hooted loudly in the distance. Sean knew it was laughing at his plight.

It was many minutes before the boy finally sat up, bruised and shaken. Fortunately, the black knapsack still remained attached to his back. Sniffing violently in an attempt to banish the last of his tears, he was almost overwhelmed by a scent from his now seemingly distant childhood. All those times he had been sick with bronchitis, his mother had made up a big bowl of hot water and added some stuff from a large glass bottle. An inhalation, that's what she'd called it. The liquid poured from the bottle had given off a wonderful scent, very strong and powerful, but wonderful. Why could he smell that same sort of scent now? The image of his mother's face appeared before him: her warm smile, the blue eyes which always appeared to be peeping out from under her thick brown fringe, the tiny scar below her right ear left by a broken glass door …

Fresh tears filled his eyes as he painfully struggled to his feet and continued on his mission. One day soon he must find a way of escape.

Two weeks' stay in the Sydney-based hospital had not produced a diagnosis of Stella's medical condition. Slightly frustrated, the doctors had prescribed various medications, including cortico-steroids, to treat the symptoms. Rather to Kirsty's surprise they were proving remarkably successful, possibly too successful. The reduction in the pain levels was quite astonishing and Stella perked up enormously.

Two days after returning home, Stella had talked of going back to school soon. Kirsty had suggested two weeks at home, during which time Stella could begin catching up on the lost ground of missed classes. A telephone call to Koolkuna High School had produced positive results. Stella was now busy with work sheets, essays and assignments.

'How are the waratahs this year?' Stella looked across at her father. The two of them were sharing the quietness of Max's study, working at opposite ends of the massive wooden desk. Outside, a gentle rain was softly falling through the night.

Max, busy with the never-ending paperwork that was part of owning and managing a farm, looked up from his mass of papers. 'What inspired that question?'

'Not really sure. Just suddenly thought of it —' a shadow briefly crossed her face, '— and I guess it's a while since I've been out to the back barn.'

'What say we pay it a visit tomorrow and you can see for yourself? Time I checked the hay supplies, anyway. It's a date!'

'It's a date, Dad.' She smiled at her father and returned to staring blankly at the guidelines of her, as yet unstarted, history assignment.

'Having trouble?'

'Well, a little —'

'What's your set task?'

'We have to write an essay, Dad, on a person who lived during the Victorian era, between 1837 and 1901, it says here. We can't choose obviously famous people like Florence Nightingale, Lord Shaftesbury, Charles Dickens or Charles Darwin, unless we are really desperate, the teacher said. I've got no idea who to write about and am fast getting desperate.'

Max looked thoughtfully at his daughter. 'Been quite clever, your teacher,' he spoke meditatively. 'I'd say he's after the personal angle. All of you have ancestors who would fit in that category, Stella, unless there is a country restriction.'

Checking the guidelines for what seemed liked the fiftieth time, Stella shook her head. 'No, there doesn't seem to be.'

'Well, what could be easier? Choose an ancestor who fits within that time frame.'

'But I don't know anything about any of them,' wailed Stella.

With a sigh, Max pushed his papers aside and leaned back comfortably in his chair. 'Listen and take notes, Stella, because I am only telling you this once. The research you will have to do for yourself.'

Hastily snatching up a pencil and her rough notebook, the girl sat back to listen.

'Have you ever heard of Major General Charles Gordon of Khartoum? No? Well, we're talking about 1884 and 1885, so make a note of those dates. In 1884 the British government ordered General Gordon to Khartoum in the Sudan to evacuate Egyptian military forces. After his arrival, the city came under siege from the Mahdists, also called the Dervish Army — you can look this up in the encyclopaedia for background detail. My great-great uncle, your great-great-great uncle, was part of the Camel Corp sent out in an attempt to rescue General Gordon.'

'What was his name?' asked the breathless female descendant of the Camel Corp private.

'Private Tobias Charles Richards,' replied that soldier's great-great nephew. 'He kept a diary of his army years but his real interest was the camels. The diary told of poorly fitting saddles, badly adjusted and overloaded packsaddles and how the camel's backs would be rubbed raw —'

'Those poor camels!' burst fiercely from Stella in high indignation.

'He wrote of treating the camel sores with a mixture of tar and animal fats, probably an early equivalent of the Stockholm tar used today. He didn't think much of the care given to some of the camels so he stepped in where possible.'

Stella, busy with her notebook, learned that four camels were needed to carry the apparatus pertaining to a five-barrelled Gardner gun. She heard that the camels were not supposed to be used as cover or protection against the enemy but sometimes inevitably were. She learned that camels could kick in all directions, unlike horses; that her great-great-great uncle had been considered not too dusty a marksman; that General Gordon had been martyred, killed in the January of 1885, at Khartoum.

'Why not call your essay Diary of a Camel Corps Private?' Max suggested.

It was a beautiful spring day as the two riders headed out to the back barn. Casper walked eagerly along the track, his neat grey ears pricked and alert, his neck arched. He was a combination of Welsh Mountain pony and Dartmoor pony blood, a beautiful animal looking much younger than his years. He was Toby's childhood pony, Max having sternly forbidden Stella any younger or friskier mount. Thrilled to be back on a pony after her long weeks of illness and pain, Stella acquiesced without a murmur. Max was astride his beloved Misty, always his mount for what he regarded as pleasure jaunts.

Cheshunt had been blessed with the beautiful native gift of the waratah shrub, *Telopea speciosissima,* for as far back as anyone could remember. The eastern slope, falling gently away from the main ridge, was home to the majority of the erect shrubs although they could be found in several other locations on the farm.

The plants flourished in the well-drained, sandy soil of the eastern slope, enjoying the morning sun. They shared the hillside with the native eucalypt trees, whose dusty green leaves provided a perfect foil for the blazing colour of the spring blooming waratahs.

The slender stemmed shrubs seldom grew much above three meters in height, sometimes much less. The sandstone slabs which dotted the eastern slope helped protect the plants from any strong winds; they also protected the roots.

Because the eastern slope could not be seen from any public road, the waratahs had been well protected from unscrupulous people whose one idea was to make money from the blooms. Such persons waited for the shrubs to burst into flower in the spring then went to enormous lengths to cut the beautiful crimson, pink and very rarely, white blooms, complete with their long straight stems and dark green leaves.

The waratahs always found a ready sale in the big cities, especially at the beginning and finish of the spring flowering season when availability of the blooms was limited.

Last year, when the magnificent domed flowers first announced the arrival of their season with their usual splendid splashes of bright colour, Max Richards had received a telephone call from his neighbour, David Fairchild.

'Max, I would appreciate an hour of your time — now, if possible.'

Bellara lay adjacent to Cheshunt's western boundary and had been in the Fairchild family for generations. The name Bellara, an aboriginal word meaning good place, had been chosen in 1921 by David Fairchild's grandfather, James Fairchild, on his return from the horrors of the Western Front. Built from local sandstone blocks quarried on the property, the Fairchild homestead featured tall narrow windows, squat chimneys and a wide, welcoming verandah. On his arrival, Max was greeted by Mike, David Fairchild's black and white border collie.

'Well, here I am, David. Now what's the problem?'

'We'll go to the packing shed,' his friend and neighbour spoke quietly but with a certain grimness.

Bellara prided itself on its diversity and one of its activities was producing a range of flowers for the markets. It was to the coolness of the long flower-packing shed that the two men now walked. The waratah grew naturally at Bellara, as at Cheshunt. Both Max Richards and David Fairchild were protective of the beautiful plants, refusing to market them commercially on a regular basis. Both men had occasional exceptions to this rule: if a shrub blew down or had to be removed for some reason they would send the blooms to the markets, but only then.

Within the cool darkness of the packing shed, David led Max to a long bench. Max let out an exclamation of dismay as he bent over the blooms, some of which were bruised and broken.

'What gives, David?'

'Very early this morning Mike gave the alarm. You know how keen his hearing is and what a grand watch dog he makes?'

Max nodded as he continued to examine the long-stemmed waratahs laid out along the bench.

'Alwyn suspected the waratahs immediately and headed right up to the hill, complete with his rifle. He's a bloody good shot, though as his father I shouldn't say so. He saw two blokes cutting the blooms and fired a couple of rounds over their heads — scared the dickens out of them. They dropped everything and ran for their lives. We're not as lucky as you people at Cheshunt: our waratahs are in sight of the road.' David sighed and waved his hand at the blooms on the bench. 'Here are the spoils collected by Alwyn. The buggers can't have been at it too long or there'd be more flowers. Alwyn is sure he got everything and I believe him.'

Max measured the stem lengths with eyes and hands. 'Getting nice long stem lengths I see.'

'Looks like it. Market price is directly related to stem length and all these are well over eighty centimetres. No curves in them either — all nice and straight. Either they knew what they were doing or they were told exactly what to do.'

'I see your visitors really did drop everything when they ran.' Max looked at two pairs of sharp-bladed secateurs and two large cool boxes for flower transport.

'I'd say the cool boxes means the blooms were headed straight for the markets,' said David, picking up a large crimson bloom.

'What will you do?' asked Max.

'Put up a sign saying the waratahs are protected by savage dogs and men with guns,' snapped David. 'What else can I do? There's little use reporting it to the police — although I will do that anyway. Bill at the station is a good bloke but there's not much he can do. We all know that perhaps ninety-five percent of all waratah flowers sold at the big markets are taken direct from the native bush or stolen from properties like ours where they grow naturally in their original surroundings. This, of course, is because they are almost impossible to grow as a crop where man wants them to grow. Got minds of their own have *Telopea speciosissima* and I admire them for it. Even if you and I, Max, planted dozens of young seedlings, the chances are they would fail. They're fragile babies with a tendency to every imaginable disease. They like to grow naturally where they choose to grow — and who can blame them?'

Max sighed as he gently touched a snowy white flower, now partially bruised and bent. 'She's a beauty — have you got many of the white shrubs, David?'

'Six, I think.'

'Nice. We've got three at last check.'

'Now we know the bastards are about you'd better keep an eye out on your place, Max. Let me know if anything happens and we might combine forces.'

Max, riding along with Stella in the spring sunshine, remembered all this. In spite of David Fairchild's warning, Cheshunt had been fortunate last year as regards their waratahs. Perhaps young Alwyn Fairchild had frightened the thieves off because Bellara had been troubled no more either.

Stella was lost in a dream of bliss. All that terrible pain had almost gone — it was only bad in the early mornings now, when she first awoke and it still took her a while to get moving properly. But still, compared to what had gone before, well, there was no comparison. She revelled in Casper's eager paces and in the pure joy of being astride a pony again.

'Can those legs of yours handle a canter?' Max asked his daughter.

'Daddy!'

'Just checking, just checking. You've bounced back unbelievably quickly, you know.' A frown momentarily crossed his face as he spoke the last sentence: something bothered him about his daughter's almost miraculous recovery from pain and illness. It was too quick to be true. Things didn't work that way; didn't happen like that. Irritated, he pushed the intruding thought away and allowed Misty to break to a canter in wake of Casper and Stella. The elder states-mare of Cheshunt flew across the grass, eager to catch her juniors.

The grassy ride led to the access track which topped the main ridge. Below them, on the eastern side of the slope, a blaze of crimson colour greeted them. The riders reined their horses to a halt.

'Wow, Dad ...' Stella spoke softly. 'Has Mum seen them this year?'

'She's hardly had a chance, child,' Max spoke drily. 'We'll have to try and change that.'

'They are so beautiful, it would be impossible to ever tire of them. Dad, look, there's a pink one in bloom, down there.'

'Can you remember what *Telopea speciosissima* means, child?'

'Beautiful, showy and seen from afar.'

'They pretty well named themselves, didn't they?' Max gazed down the slope with approval.

'Those sharp leaves suit the flowers,' observed Stella thoughtfully. 'They kind of make the right sort of setting for the bright colour of the flowers. Christmas colours, red and green.'

'We'll go down a bit closer.' Max's legs closed against Misty's warm sides, encouraging her to move down the hillside. 'Watch out for the sandstone slabs in the undergrowth.'

The two horses picked their way slowly down the top quarter of the slope, their riders halting when they reached the closest group of waratah shrubs.

'They love the sandy soil, don't they?' Stella eyed a bloom covered shrub of two meters tall with grave satisfaction.

'That's the main reason they only grow in certain areas on Cheshunt,' agreed her father.

'I can't find the white one.' Stella stood in her stirrups and turned her head in every direction possible.

'Down there, see? Behind that big, burned out log. That's how I always find it.'

'It's funny how our three white bushes are at three separate locations. They're very rare, aren't they?'

'Extremely rare.' Max dismounted and handed his reins to Stella.

He examined the closest few shrubs, checking the leaves, stems and flowers.

'We get better flowers on our plants than some people do,' Stella spoke proudly.

Max laughed. 'No credit to us, Stella, I'm afraid. It's a lot to do with the balance between sun and shade. The right amount of shade tends to produce higher quality blooms whilst too much sunlight can burn and brown them. They need the right balance and the partial shade they receive from the eucalypts here seems to suit them.'

Stella waited patiently whilst her father completed his inspection. Both horses bent their heads to snatch at the odd bite of undergrowth.

'Nothing much to eat there,' the girl chided the pair affectionately. She heard a sudden exclamation from her father as he suddenly bent in the undergrowth.

'What is it, Dad?' she called.

'Just a minute,' was the terse reply.

She watched as he hunted about in the rough grass and weeds surrounding several of the blooming shrubs. He then paid close attention to certain of the stems. Finally, a grim expression on his face, Max walked towards her, something grasped in his right hand.

'We've had a visitor.' As he spoke, he displayed a pair of secateurs, small, but very sharp-bladed. From his pocket he withdrew a small and battered pen knife.

'Oh, Dad!' Stella cried out in dismay.

'I can see about a dozen places where the blooms have been cleanly cut off on long stems. Always a dead giveaway. You still doing okay there?'

'I'm fine, Dad.' She hesitated. 'What do you think made him leave the clippers and knife?'

'Got frightened or ran out of time.' Max remounted Misty.

'Ran out of time?'

'Might have been dropped off to collect samples by his handler,' Max spoke in disgust. 'The handler plays safe, tells some kid to grab the samples or else, and that he'd better be ready for pick-up at a set time or he'll be left stranded out here. Often happens like that with the amateur thieves.'

'Dad! You sound almost sorry for the thief!' Stella was indignant.

'Child, I'd like nothing better than to see the handler jailed for a lengthy period of time, not just for stealing our flowers but for making use of some kid whose down and out — if it happened that way. Now, for the barn.'

Ten minutes later the riders reined in within the shadow of the huge back barn. Stella stumbled as she dismounted and only her father's swift action prevented her from crashing to the ground. Max had been keeping alert for such a happening: this speedy recovery (in his mind he was calling it a speedy *so-called* recovery) of Stella's still bothered him. His strong arms gently lowered her to the ground close to a sturdy stump.

'Thanks, Dad,' his daughter spoke breathlessly. 'I'm fine, really. I think my riding muscles are a bit out of practice.' She leaned back against the rough bark of the old stump and closed her eyes.

The horses were hung up to a handy gum tree which had been used for that purpose for as long as Stella could remember.

'I won't be long. Try and flex those leg muscles a little if you can manage it.'

On entering the vast cavern known as the back barn, Max cast an eagle eye for signs of intruders. Cigarettes were a very real danger in hay barns. A still burning cigarette carelessly cast aside, or worse still, deliberately planted, could reduce a year's supply of hay to ashes in hours. He could find no trace of any cigarette stubs. Still, that didn't mean that there were none to find. It was impossible to check every inch of a barn this size, especially when it was stacked more than half full. Somehow he rather doubted that the waratah thief had entered this barn — there was no need for it. Casting such thoughts aside, Max turned his attention to his hay stocks and began counting bales.

Stella, leaning against her stump, watched as a flock of small honeyeaters flew overhead. She knew they were heading straight for the nectar-laden waratah blooms on the eastern slope. Where waratah nectar was concerned, the little birds were almost insatiable in the brief flowering season. She could hear her father's boots on the wooden flooring of the barn echoing in the half-empty vastness. Slowly, she began flexing her ankles, wriggling her toes and stretching her calves. Ouch — that last hurt. She still felt pretty good — it was when she had dismounted from Casper that her legs didn't seem able to support her weight very well. If Dad hadn't been so quick — oh well, she hadn't ridden for ages and her riding muscles had gotten a bit stale through lack of use, that was all — nothing to make a big deal about. It was high time she got to her feet. Slowly and carefully, using her stump for support, Stella stood up. Yes, that was all right. Still with one hand on the stump, she tentatively took a step. Yes, no trouble there. Another pace forward, still gripping the stump. Still going fine. Perhaps she'd better walk around the stump to make sure before letting go, use it as her central support — kind of like lunging a pony. The thought made her grin broadly. Three steps — four — five — six — seven — they were very small steps. Eight — she was still going strong — nine — ten — and eleven. She'd done it! Releasing hold of the stump, she triumphantly stood alone. How curious that such a trivial activity should make her feel so proud. Slowly but with increasing confidence she made her way to the barn.

'I love the smell of hay and straw, Dad.' Stella, her nose pointed in the air, sniffed ecstatically.

'You look like a rabbit,' Max laughed down at her from a stack of bales. 'I'm almost done here.'

'Is everything all right?'

'Fine. We've been getting through our hay supplies quicker than expected lately. As you know, we have to keep a decent supply in reserve stock because it is getting harder and harder to get top quality lucerne hay. As for meadow hay, well, that is becoming scarcer than hen's teeth. All the best hay, along with goodness knows what else, is going for export, mainly to Saudi Arabia where they are prepared to pay pretty much anything for it.' He paused, sighed and continued, 'You know most of this, Stella. Well, I needed to see exactly what we have stocked up here in the back barn. We're fine in the main barn but we can't afford to run low overall.'

'Have we got enough?'

'More than enough but one has to keep looking ahead. You remember all the trouble we had getting meadow hay last time? It took months before I could get a truckload across from the Coopers at Orange. Most of the high quality hay crops are pre-sold for export.' Max jotted some figures down in the small spiral notebook which resided permanently in his breast pocket, and jumped down from the bales.

'I wish I could still do that.' His daughter eyed him wistfully.

'You will again, don't you worry.' Max reassuringly passed an arm about Stella's shoulders, resolutely ignoring that nasty little imp (speedy so-called recovery!) pecking away at his brain.

Stella made no objection when lifted to her saddle by Max.

Aware that they were homeward bound, Misty and Casper eagerly headed back to the top of the main ridge, where they paused. Just below them on the western slope was the back barn. Nearly the whole of the eastern slope was dotted with splashes of brilliant crimson colour. The eastern slope gradually flattened away into a narrow strip of land adjoining the river.

'Goodbye, *Telopea speciosissima*,' called Stella. 'We'll bring Mum to see you very soon.'

At these words the icy fingers of Max's imp gave an extra hard nip and Max felt himself flinch.

Chapter Five: 'I told you so!'

The cup fell to the floor splashing hot tea in its wake.

'Sorry,' whispered a voice that sounded nothing at all like Stella's. Her hands gripped at the edge of the table, dragging the cloth askew. The saucer joined the cup on the floor, followed by a small plate.

Max, glancing across the table, watched in mounting horror as his daughter's face appeared to swell.

'Stella?'

He was answered by a loud breathing noise and an attempt at speech. Round red weals were breaking out across her face and neck. She made feeble flapping movements with her hands. A half-full glass of pineapple juice was knocked over on the now wrinkled cloth.

Leaping to his feet, Max bellowed for Kirsty. He was lifting Stella from her chair when Kirsty appeared from the laundry.

'Kirsty! It's Stella. Look at her!'

Seconds were all Kirsty needed. 'Get her flat on the floor,' she ordered, her fingers on her daughter's wrist. The pulse was weak and rapid.

'I'll call the ambulance,' Max, white-faced, touched Stella's damp forehead then stood up.

On the floor, Stella retched and wheezed, the rash on her face and neck spreading and strengthening.

'No, Max, the ambulance will take too long. Get the Pajero ready — it'll be much quicker to take her ourselves.'

Max left at a run.

Kirsty, kneeling by her daughter, spoke quietly: 'Stella, can you hear me, darling?'

A heavy nod was followed by an almost indecipherable, 'Yes, Mummy.' Terrified grey eyes looked up at Kirsty.

'Listen to me, Stella. I know you feel very bad right now but it's going to be all right. Daddy's getting the car and we are taking you to see Doctor Mason.'

Another heavy nod was accompanied by a slight lessening of panic in the grey eyes.

Kirsty heard the Pajero brake violently at the front door.

'Max, carry Stella to the car and lie her flat. I must ring the doctor.'

'Why?'

'For God's sake, shut up and just do as I say!' For the first time Kirsty's professional nursing calm snapped. She ran to the telephone.

Kirsty had an extremely short talk with Doctor Mason before grabbing Stella's medications and two blankets and running for the car. The engine was already turning over as Kirsty slid into the back seat beside her daughter. Max had driven ten car lengths before Kirsty managed to shut her door.

'I know she's going to die, Kirsty.' Max was pushing the Pajero faster and faster. He almost clipped one of the massive wooden posts at the front gate as he turned left onto the rough gravel road. He took the next corner on two wheels.

'It won't be much help if you kill us all on the road,' retorted his wife tartly. She deftly covered her daughter with one of the light blankets. A thin pillow was supporting the girl's head.

'Do you want me to stop?'

'No, I can manage.' Kirsty checked Stella's pulse again.

'Did you get the doctor?'

'Yes, they'll be waiting for us.'

'They?'

'Doctor Mason and Sister Braddock.'

'What did he say?'

'To do exactly what we're doing.' Kirsty had no intention of repeating the doctor's injunction for haste.

Max now had his hand on the horn and was sounding it with everything he'd got. They had reached the small wooden bridge at Lunchtime Crossing. Two vehicles were parked in the middle of the old bridge, completely blocking the road. The drivers were having a casual talk, windows wound down, car engines idling. Max swore as he made the sharp turn onto the bridge.

'It's that bloody old fool Jason Constable,' he growled, roughly winding down his own window, 'and his clot of a son-in-law. Should be working, not holding a ruddy mother's meeting on a public right of way!'

Alerted by the blasting horn and the determined pace of the approaching Pajero, the bridge obstructers were already moving their cars. Both men raised their hands in greeting as the Richards family shot past. Max ignored the salutation but Kirsty called out her thanks from the fast departing vehicle. She caught a glimpse of two startled faces gaping after them and they were gone from her sight.

They were climbing the tightly twisting road up from the narrow river valley now. This road had been carved through the native bush generations ago and today that same bushland was virtually untouched by time or progress. They passed a lay-by in which a stone watering trough proudly reposed, a relic from the horse and buggy era. A blur of movement shot across the road barely missing the massive bull bars on the front of the Pajero. A large kangaroo had jumped down from the high bank on the right, landing in the road. Several more bounds and the marsupial vanished into the bush on the lower side of the gorge.

'That was close,' breathed Kirsty in relief, 'and so quick. They always seem to come out of nowhere.'

Her husband grunted in reply. They rounded the next corner to be met by a massive blackbutt tree lying across the road.

'Oh no!' Kirsty clenched her fists in frustration.

'Hang on, Kirsty — it's not as bad as it looks.' Max nudged the Pajero right up close to the fallen tree.

The blackbutt had been cut in two at the thinner end and that section had then been rolled aside, leaving just enough room for a narrow vehicle to pass through. Max, now forced by necessity to drive with caution, edged the Pajero up to the gap. The steering wheel was turned hard to the left and the car inched forward, branches and leaves from the fallen tree whipping at her flanks. The capable hands gripping the steering wheel swung it back to the right. It was like going through a gate that was only a small part opened. Displeased at the vehicle's passing, a last leafy branch swiped malevolently across the windscreen and they were through. Max put his foot down on the accelerator and the car picked up pace.

They would be at the main road very soon. Kirsty could see the top of the tall water tower now, distinct and white, above the native forest. It stood at the top of the gorge. Just a few minutes more of the rough road and sharp bends. *Please, please, God, let it be all right! Please look after my daughter. God, please!*

'What's the matter with Stella? What on earth has happened?' demanded Max, pushing the Pajero up a steep bank to overtake on the left hand side of the unsealed road.

'I don't really know, Max,' Kirsty temporised, one hand at her daughter's wrist.

Stella was lying across almost the full length of the back seat, her knees partially drawn up. As Kirsty watched with anxious eyes, the girl retched, appeared to try to struggle to a sitting position and suddenly fell back, unconscious.

The car shot across the road with a violent swerve. The road, which had only been receiving intermittent attention as Max had watched his daughter through the rear vision mirror for increasing periods, now received none at all. He let out a low cry:

'She's dead! Kirsty, she's dead!

Kirsty lost her temper:

'Pull yourself together and stop behaving like a wimp!' she snapped. 'If you can't drive more safely you'd better let me take the wheel. I'm thoroughly ashamed of you, Max Richards!'

An electrically charged silence filled the vehicle as Max stared at the road ahead, his lips tightly closed. Kirsty sent up a silent prayer as Koolkuna came in to sight.

Something was biting the back of her hand. It must be one of those horrid ants from the big wooden post at the front gate. She tried to brush the nasty thing away with her other hand but somehow it was too much effort. A voice spoke and she felt something touch the bitten hand. Nice — a kind person was killing that beastly ant for her. She tried to smile, to thank the good person. She remembered no more.

Stella lay quietly taking in her situation. Why was she wearing a funny mask on her face? It was annoying but she let it be for the present. She looked down at her left hand — so that was why it felt a bit sore. Some sort of needle thing was stuck right into her hand. Her eyes followed the slender clear line which ran from the needle to a glass bottle of fluid hooked to a pole at the back of her bed. She was lying in a cool white room containing three hospital beds and appeared to be the only patient. Through a large square window a small, neatly fenced yard was visible.

'Strawberry clover,' said Stella in a muffled voice, plucking at the elastic holding the oxygen mask in place. Released, it fell on the bed, giving out a steady hissing sound.

'What did you say?' A tall woman with immaculately groomed short grey hair got up from the desk where she had been writing.

'Strawberry clover,' repeated Stella, pointing to the window. 'You've got strawberry clover in your yard. Too much is bad for horses — you must only let them have a few mouthfuls sometimes, for a treat. Hello, Sister Braddock.'

'Hello, Stella,' smiled the nursing sister who had known the Richards family since before Stella was born. 'How do you feel now?' She deftly attached a blood pressure cuff to her patient's right upper arm. 'Quiet till I get a reading please.'

Stella lay still and considered how she felt. Her face felt a bit strange and swollen. She was very cold. Her throat was a bit rusty and thick. She could see a funny rash on the top of her chest where her blouse had been unbuttoned. Apart from that, she felt pretty much as usual. All this was relayed to Sister Braddock shortly.

'Your blood pressure's coming back up nicely,' was all Sister would say on that front as she neatly wound up the rubber tubing. She next replaced the blanket covering Stella with a heavenly warm cellular blanket, pale primrose in colour.

'Mummy and Daddy?' Always in times of stress, trouble or strong emotion, Stella returned to those childhood names for her parents.

'They stayed to make sure you were all right before Doctor Mason ordered them off home. I will call them in a minute to let them know that you're properly awake and talking about feeding horses. That must mean you're almost back to usual status.' The kindly light blue eyes twinkled at the girl.

'Sister, what happened?'

'How much do you remember? Don't think too hard, just let your mind drift back.'

'Daddy and I were sitting at the breakfast table, later than usual because it was Sunday. Mummy wasn't there — she had finished and was in the laundry putting washing in to soak for Monday, I think. I took all my tablets — I have to take about six different sorts ever since my legs got funny — and Daddy made us both a second cup of tea. I just picked up the cup to start drinking the tea when I felt as if I couldn't breathe properly. My throat got sort of thick. It gets a bit vague after that. I kept wanting to be sick, I think, but nothing would come up. I was lying on the kitchen floor — then I was in the car — Mummy shouted at Daddy — he was driving too fast — something about a kangaroo — I got bitten on my left hand by an ant, and I woke up here. It's all kind of mixed up in a sort of dream. What happened to me, Sister?'

'You had a very severe allergic reaction,' explained Sister Braddock.

'To what?'

'One of your medications. Doctor Mason will explain everything to you and your parents later on. I must call your parents now as I promised.'

'When can I go home?'

'Later this afternoon.' The elderly doctor had entered the room. 'Well, Miss Stella, you certainly livened up Sunday morning for everybody, didn't you?'

Despite the warmth of the day, a chilly silence reigned supreme at Cheshunt. Too much had happened in too short a period of time. It had been a very near thing with Stella as Doctor Mason had told them: the child had nearly died from a violent allergic reaction to the corticosteroids. She had been saved by prompt action, cardiopulmonary resuscitation and injected adrenaline. Yes, the doctor was aware she had been on these corticosteroids for some weeks — had been started on them in hospital — he had the full report from the hospital doctors. Some allergic reactions worked like that — in an accumulative fashion. There would be no visible reaction for weeks or months and suddenly the threshold danger point was reached. They had been extremely lucky this time and, of course, that was the end of the corticosteroids for Stella. He, personally, did not like using corticosteroids, especially on children. Many doctors disagreed with him on this but there it was — he disliked the drugs — avoided prescribing them whenever possible. Kirsty, quite wrongly as it were, felt she heard the ring of blame directed at herself and was accordingly racked with guilt. She had trained as a nurse, albeit over thirty years ago, and therefore should have known or found out more about what had been prescribed for Stella.

Max was thoroughly ashamed of himself, knowing how poorly he had coped with a genuine life-threatening emergency. They had nearly lost their only surviving daughter, for Christ's sake! His mind flew to those four radiata pine trees—four children dead in infancy — three girls and one boy. He shook his head as if to brush away those thoughts. Kirsty had been magnificent — done all that was right — never lost her cool — had even remembered to grab all the child's tablets, for goodness sake! Panic and fear had driven all calmness and thought from him. Yes, admit it! He had panicked, driven like a madman, nearly killed them all a good half-dozen times — behaved like a complete imbecile. In spite of all this, one part of Max acknowledged the fact that he had always been bothered by Stella's almost miraculous, swift deliverance from crippling pain. In his experience of life, things just did not work out that way. Max's inner imp, that nasty little fellow, was saying, 'I told you so!'

Alcohol was almost unknown at Cheshunt. Cecil Lewis Richards, Max's father, had been much too fond of his drink, especially during the second half of his life. Cheshunt had deteriorated accordingly. Martha Rose Richards, Max's mother, had lost two babies during delivery, the somewhat doubtful assistance of an alcoholic doctor contributing little to their chances of survival. So no, alcohol was seldom to be found at Cheshunt.

Practically thrown out of the surgery by the doctor, his daughter's face haunted him as Max Richards drove very slowly home. Kirsty sat silently next to him. She spoke once:

'She's going to be all right, Max.'

'I know, Kirsty,' he blinked rapidly several times. 'I know.'

Their emotions were too raw for conversation. The drive seemed endless. When they finally turned through the wide gateway at Cheshunt, Kirsty spoke again.

'Where's Toby today?

'What?'

'Where's Toby today?'

'Over at Bellara. He and young Alwyn Fairchild had some scheme on — something to do with the western boundary, I think.'

Max stopped the Pajero close to the house and Kirsty wearily got out. She felt as if a year had passed since breakfast, yet a glance at her wrist-watch told her it was not much past midday. Mindful of Doctor Mason's private instructions, she headed straight for her kitchen pantry. Hidden on the very top shelf and at the very back (behind rows of glass baby bottles now used for feeding orphaned lambs) was an unopened bottle of Chatelle Napoleon French brandy. With the maroon, gold and cream-coloured carton tucked firmly under one arm, Kirsty was climbing down from the kitchen chair needed to access the top shelf just as Max entered the house. She prepared for battle.

'Doctor Mason told me to take you straight back home and get a good dose of brandy down you.'

'Where did that stuff come from, Kirsty?' He sounded weary, resigned, rather than angry.

'You remember that nice couple with the bay standardbred — we helped them out that day when he panicked in the float — it came from them.'

'That was ages ago.'

'Early last year 'cos it happened at Blacktown Show.'

Max eyed the attractive carton suspiciously, shrugged his broad shoulders and took two glasses from the kitchen dresser. Kirsty sank into a shabby bean bag of vast proportions. A familiar sound from the laundry heralded Sambo's entrance via the cat flap. Stella's adored black cat was in search of his young mistress. Sambo eyed with interest the mess of broken china and spilt tea decorating the kitchen floor.

'I must clean all that up,' Kirsty spoke listlessly.

'It can wait.' Max, unaccustomed to such tasks, was clumsily opening the Chatelle Napoleon.

Sambo reached out an inquisitive paw and touched a piece of Stella's broken cup. The piece rolled over and Sambo retreated. He then walked over to Kirsty, decided she was temporarily an acceptable substitute for his missing mistress, and jumped onto her lap.

She took the glass tumbler which Max held out. It was perhaps one-fifth full of the amber fluid.

'Sip it very slowly,' ordered her partner. Taking his own glass he sat in the old wooden rocking chair.

Seeing Max gently rocking, glass in hand, only confirmed the strangeness of this atrocious day. He never sat down unless it was to eat a meal, work at the farm ledgers or attend to business papers — things of that nature. He was one of those people who, without rush or haste, was always quietly busy, moving from one task to the next with no fuss or bother. She never recalled ever seeing him sit in the rocking chair before.

Kirsty's mind was a jagged kaleidoscope of images. Stella, her face swelling up as Kirsty watched, that rash spreading down her neck to her chest. The terrified grey eyes asking as clear as the spoken word: *'Am I going to die?'* A bottle of corticosteroid tablets, tablets which had been taken twice a day for several weeks. Flashes from that crazy drive to Koolkuna and a fast moving kangaroo. Stella collapsing into unconsciousness as they neared Koolkuna. Max almost attacking Doctor Mason, shaking him and shouting at him to save their daughter. Herself trying to pull Max away from the doctor. The doctor coolly and quickly assessing Max before giving him a solid slap across the face. Max standing still, blinking, shocked, the imprint of the doctor's hand clear on his left cheek.

She and Max sitting together in the surgery waiting room, Max frightened for Stella and ashamed of himself. Today she had witnessed a Max she had never seen before and this only added to her bewilderment.

The telephone shrilled loudly. The second trill had barely begun before the receiver was snatched from the wall by a shaking hand. Kirsty spoke very little and listened intently before slowly replacing the receiver and turning to her husband.

'She's awake and talking. She's telling Sister Braddock that too much strawberry clover is bad for horses. Oh Max — Max — Max —' Bursting into tears, Kirsty flung herself into her husband's waiting arms.

'When can we go and get her?' he spoke in muffled tones, his lips pressed against the top of Kirsty's head as she clung tightly to his chest.

'They said not before four.'

'That gives us almost two hours.' Max led her towards their bedroom at the far end of the house.

Chapter Six: Sean Stevens

The telephone shrilled loudly at the police station. It was answered by Sergeant Bill Stroud. The call was short and to the point. Sergeant Stroud's eyebrows rose as he listened. He replaced the receiver, his mouth pursed in a soundless whistle. Now what did David Fairchild *and* Max Richards want to see him about?

The two men arrived together at midday. Sergeant Stroud greeted them with a warm handshake and led the way to his small office.

'Now, gentlemen, what can I do for you? You sounded a bit concerned when you called.' He nodded at David Fairchild.

Max looked at his longtime friend and neighbor. 'You start and I'll chip in where necessary.'

'Right.' David paused for a moment as he collected his thoughts and decided the best way to begin. 'We had a visitor at Bellara last night.'

'Unwanted, I presume?'

'Oh, yes, most definitely unwanted.'

'Right, what's the full story?' The Sergeant produced his notebook.

David eyed it uneasily. 'Is that really necessary at this stage?'

Sergeant Stroud raised his eyebrows. 'Like that, is it? We'll leave the notetaking for now, then. Let's have the story — you've got me curious.'

David Fairchild began his narrative:

'Last night, my boy Alwyn and Toby, Max's boy, went out after rabbits on our place. Took their rifles and our dog, Mike, and headed up into the hills. Both boys are very good shots and careful, as you know.'

The Sergeant nodded: he did know it. In his position in this rural area, you quickly learned who was to be trusted with a rifle and who wasn't.

'Boys were out a couple of hours before they'd had enough. They were walking home on the track which runs across the bottom of our waratah slope when Mike suddenly took off. He found this kid — a boy — scared the living daylights out of him, so Alwyn said — kid of about fourteen. Kid said he was looking for something in the undergrowth close to the waratahs. Wouldn't say too much at first but insisted he'd lost something under 'the big flowers'. Also seemed to think he was on Cheshunt. When told he was on Bellara the kid burst into tears. Seemed to break him up totally. He kept saying, 'Dieter will kill me!' Toby and Alwyn did the only possible thing — brought him back to Bellara. Boy was cold, hungry and scared out of his wits. Turned him over to my head nurseryman for the night — good chap with a nice kind wife — live in the sandstone cottage at the end of our lane. This morning the kid was only too eager to talk — it all came pouring out — not a nice story at all. His name is Sean Stevens, by the way. He seems scared to death of someone called Dean Lucas.'

The story David Fairchild now told was not an unusual one and it made Sergeant Bill Stroud both angry and sad.

Sean's mother, Rhonda Stevens, had been banished from the family home when it became obvious she was carrying her boyfriend's child. The boyfriend had long since disappeared.

Rhonda's parents, pillars of their local church, could not allow their Christian charity to extend to their daughter; after all, what would the congregation and the church council think? Rhonda Stevens left the small country town in which she had lived all of her sixteen years and travelled to Sydney.

With little money, no friends or contacts and heavily pregnant, the choices open to her were virtually non-existent. If Rhonda would agree to give up her as yet unborn child for adoption, life could be made somewhat easier for her. Some so-called charitable institutions applied pressure to the young girl, urging her to do 'what was best for the child.' Stubbornly, she refused. Despite rising unemployment, she managed to find work for a few hours each day in a small cafe, largely due to the pity felt for her by the female owner. She earned enough to pay the rent of a small room in a boarding house. She got one good meal a day at the cafe and ate little else. Three weeks before Sean was born, Rhonda was approached by the woman who ran the boarding house. The woman was well aware of the girl's plight. What she thought of Rhonda's parents had best be left unsaid.

Unlike many people, Bronwyn Vaughan knew all about the single parenting pension introduced the by the Whitlam government. Her cousin, who worked for the St Vincent de Paul Society, provided the essentials for the coming baby. In other words, Bronwyn Vaughan took Rhonda Stevens completely under her wing.

The baby boy, when he came, was not strong; the young mother spent anxious days coping with croup and bronchitis. They now shared a larger room on the ground floor, close to the laundry room and easier for prams. The room had a small annex which once curtained off, made a perfect place for baby Sean's cot. Rhonda was delighted.

The rent stayed the same. Besides caring for her baby, Rhonda helped as much as she could in the boarding house. There was certainly always plenty to do — Bronwyn Vaughan catered especially for country people who came to Sydney to work or study. Some people lived there for years.

And so the years ticked by. When he was five Sean began attending the local primary school. At Bronwyn Vaughan's suggestion, Rhonda started attending technical college three days a week to obtain her Higher School Certificate. She enjoyed the study but was always eager to return to both her son and the boarding house.

The boarding house was truly home and haven to both Rhonda and Sean Stevens. They both loved Bronwyn Vaughan: to Sean she was a second mother or an adored aunt. Sean grew taller and stronger and loved helping the man who did all the outside yard work. They painted the garage together. Rhonda went back to technical college two days a week and trained as a stenographer. She also worked hard at the boarding house, much harder than Bronwyn Vaughan liked. But Rhonda would not be stopped: she knew how much she owed to that good woman who had probably saved her from the streets. Debts had to be paid.

Sean lost his mother when he was eleven years old. Rhonda Stevens was one of seventeen people killed when a train ploughed into a bus at an outer Sydney railway station. That brave flame of light was gone from the lives of Sean Stevens and Bronwyn Vaughan.

Sean grew even closer to Aunt Bronwyn as he'd always called her. She said little but in a hundred different ways showed him that this was, and always would be, his home. He grew quieter and more thoughtful, for the first time wondering why he seemed to have no other family. Other boys had grandparents, cousins and uncles. Why didn't he? He asked Aunt Bronwyn. He now heard for the first time how his mother had arrived at the boarding house before he was born, unwanted by her parents and her son's father. Bronwyn Vaughan told him the whole story, not dramatically nor tragically, but quietly stated the facts. In succeeding talks she told him about his mother — how brave and strong she she'd always been — never giving up, however tough life got. He'd always loved his mother but now a pride in how she'd managed to survive was ignited within him.

He started at high school and, after the first uneasy months, settled in well, showing a decided aptitude for science. He also showed promise in cricket as a batsman. One morning he was surprised to find that his aunt was not busy in the boarding house kitchen, supervising the cooking and serving of breakfast as usual. John, the English cockney breakfast cook, said he'd not seen her that morning. The savoury aromas of frying bacon and simmering baked beans followed Sean as he flew down the steep, narrow stone steps to the single-bedroom basement flat where his aunt lived. The sturdy oak door was locked, but the almost ground level, circular window, was open, covered with a wire screen.

It was the work of seconds for Sean's pen knife to cut through the screen. The small pen knife had been given to him on his eleventh birthday by his mother. She'd had his initials engraved on the shield, S.V.S for Sean Vaughan Stevens. It was his most precious procession. He found his aunt still in bed, lying peacefully on her side. According to the doctor, she had been dead for some hours. Death was due to a heart attack.

Still reeling from the shock of this second loss in just over two years, Sean never really understood what followed. Like many people, Bronwyn Vaughan had made no will so she died intestate. It appeared that her only living relation was a brother residing in Wales, on the opposite side of the globe. Thirty years ago, on the eve of Bronwyn's departure for Australia, there had been a bitter quarrel between the brother and sister.

Telling her brother she devoutly wished never to set eyes on him again in this life or the next, she left Wales for good. Her parting shot had been that she hoped the platinum blonde he intended to marry would be the ruination of him. The estrangement had lasted until her death.

Bronwyn Vaughan's solicitor was aghast at the situation. For more than twenty years he had practically begged his client to make a will. Her reply had always been the same: she had no intention of leaving this world till she was ready. If he insisted on pursuing the topic she would be forced to find another solicitor. Mr Merriman knew when to accept defeat. Now he was resolutely determined to do his best for his deceased client, that poor little lad and that white elephant of a boarding house. As so often with an intestate deceased estate, the situation was complex and would take some time to bring to a satisfactory conclusion.

The few employees at the boarding house tried to keep the place operating. They had been devoted to Bronwyn Vaughan and the boarding house was their home. But all knew that change was inevitable: one by one the guests began looking for alternative accommodation and, in the privacy of their own rooms, the staff started reading the job vacancy columns.

What happened next was most unfortunate. Passing the office door one day, Sean heard voices. The door had slipped from its latch and was ajar. Sean heard his name spoken. He stopped to listen:

'— will not allow the boy to come under the control of the state's child welfare system.'

'— entitled to any money … fight you on that —'

'— avoid the courts but it may not be possible. I suggest —'

'— foster the boy out —'

'— fully intend to do the best for the lad but do agree —'

'— once this place has been sold —'

'— may not be a quick process —'

Sean waited to hear no more. Heart racing, he fled the boarding house, running down to the harbour front. Nobody wanted him! They were going to get rid of him! He knew all about fostering — that movie one night in the television room — cruel foster parents — boy was beaten — didn't get enough food — slept on a thin mattress on the floor of the attic. The boy at school who had once spent time with mean foster-parents, had arrived at school one morning with his face so beaten that he was unable to open one eye, then had suddenly disappeared from the school. The thoughts ripped through his terrified mind, robbing him of all sense and reason. He had lost his mother, then his aunt. Now he was going to lose the only place he had ever called home.

Sean left the boarding house the following morning. With him he took as many of his clothes as he could stuff into his knapsack, his pen knife, a small framed photograph and the contents of the petty cash box. He was reported missing within twenty-four hours of his departure so the instinct which had warned him to get away from Sydney was proven correct.

It was on the train heading west that he met Dean Lucas. Dean Lucas was a nasty piece of humanity who fed on the weaknesses of people much younger than himself. Within thirty minutes of this meeting Sean had confided his situation to the man. Dean was alighting at Lithgow to change trains. By the time the station was reached he had persuaded Sean to join forces. The two left the train together. They had a lengthy wait at the country station on the western fringe of the Blue Mountains — trains were few and far between on the small branch line which ran to the north.

Night was closing in when they reached the tiny station at Koolkuna. An older man driving a beat up old kombi van was waiting for Dean. Sean hung back awkwardly while an urgent whispered conversation took place between the two men. The older man nodded and turned to Sean:

'Hello, son, you're welcome, I'm sure. My name's Dieter.'

Sean climbed into the front seat of the kombi. Dieter took the wheel and Dean sat close to the door. Sean felt trapped in the middle. He didn't know why but he was beginning to feel frightened of his new friends. The two hour long drive over mainly unsealed roads finally ended. The beam of the kombi's headlights revealed an old shack surrounded by native bush. A frozen hand gripped Sean's heart. What had he done?

The Lucas family kept themselves to themselves; did as little work as possible and avoided all contact with authority, especially the law. Using a youngster like Sean to steal waratahs for them was right up their street; the kid could be sent in alone and if he got caught, well, he carried the can. Being a kid, the chances were strong he would not be too harshly treated. Kids could be very useful once you had a firm hold over them. Hot tears were scalding down his icy face as, rucksack in hand, Sean stumbled over the rough ground towards the open door of the shack and his new life.

Five miserable weeks crawled by. He longed to run away but where would he go? Running away the first time had landed him in this mess. Dieter and Dean told him he was officially listed as missing and the police were looking for him, which only terrified him further. He was taken out at night with the Lucas men to learn the tricks of the trade. Some nights Dieter would drive the battered old kombi many hours till a selected property was reached. Sheds and barns located a long distance from the homestead were always the targets. Small tools, spare parts for machinery, small cans of diesel fuel, fencing materials, farming chemicals and tins of paint were just some of the items that were loaded into the kombi van.

Then came the night he was taken out to Cheshunt to collect waratah samples. It was not until late the following day that he discovered his treasured pen knife was missing. Frantically the boy searched every corner of the tiny, bare bedroom that he slept in. Then he remembered the previous night — yes — he definitely recalled feeling the knife's comforting familiar presence in his pocket as he crept across that hillside. A sudden twinge from his bruised ankle provided further aid to Sean's memory. That fall — the owl had scared him badly — he had stumbled and dropped the torch. That must have been when the knife had slipped from his pocket. He had to get it back! The last birthday present his mother had given him! Swallowing hard, his head dropped to his hands. He must think hard — there just *had* to be some way of getting his pen knife back.

It took Sean several days to work out a plan of action and another two weeks to implement it. He knew he mustn't show too much haste to get back to that farm with the red flowers.

He had been late back to the pick-up place that night — time had been lost searching for the broken torch. Dean had been angry at having to wait. Sean had managed to find the torch, but in his rush back up and then down the hill, had somehow lost the secateurs as well as his pen knife. Both Dieter and Dean had been furious — not at the actual loss of the secateurs — they had a dozen stolen pairs hidden in the shed — but at the evidence of trespass and theft. Sean was now able to turn this to his advantage.

Choosing his time carefully, the boy approached Dieter. Dean was safely away with the kombi on 'business' and Dieter was much easier going when his son was absent. They had also pulled off a highly satisfactory job the previous night, managing to steal a small, almost new generator from a locked shed. It was the work of moments to unscrew the door hinges and Dieter had almost chuckled with delight at the ease of the operation.

'We'll be able to get over a grand for that generator, me boy,' he told Sean. 'That was quite a night.'

'Dieter,' Sean spoke up, 'I feel bad about leaving those clipper things at the place with the red flowers.'

The man frowned slightly. 'Never good to leave things lying round — dead giveaway you've been there.'

Sean hung his head. 'I know, sir.'

'Not too good if someone finds them, you see.'

'I could go back and look for them.' Half statement, half question, the words hung in the air.

'What's that? What did you say?'

'I could go back and look for them, sir.' Sean swallowed hard and forced out the next words. 'You've been so good to me, sir. I don't want to let you down.'

Dieter looked sharply at the boy. He was finding his own son a bit annoying of late. Too many bright ideas, not content to listen to his old dad who had been in the game all his life. Sneering at his old fashioned ways — no respect for his elders — not like this nice lad. Dean would not be back till late tomorrow …

Dieter made up his mind: 'Okay boy, I'll drive you out there tonight. We'll take the ute.'

'I won't let you down, Dieter.'

It was just past ten that night when Sean was dropped off at Cheshunt, at the western boundary adjoining Bellara.

'Two hours, boy, and don't keep me waiting,' Dieter told him.

'And make sure you come back to this same spot. And don't lose that torch!'

The old ute had long vanished in a cloud of dust when Sean realised something was wrong. He couldn't see the big barn which had guided him so well on his previous visit. Fighting back the tears, he climbed over the tightly strained wire fence, tearing his jeans in the process. Perhaps the barn was over that hill. He began walking.

Very soon all sense of direction was lost. He couldn't find that barn anywhere. He climbed over another wire fence, crossed an open paddock, then yet another of those tight wire fences that seemed to delight in tearing clothes and skin loomed ahead. He climbed it, at the cost of a shirt sleeve and a scratched arm. Now he was walking up a slope.

Suddenly the bushes with the red flowers were in front of him. With a huge sigh of relief he sank to the ground. He had found the place at last! A few minutes to catch his breath and he would begin his hunt for the treasured pen knife. He *had* to find it.

Sean had no idea he was on Bellara, not Cheshunt. Dean had always been in charge of the waratah thefts and, totally unintentionally, Dieter had dropped Sean off at the wrong place. The boy was found just before midnight by Mike, the Fairchild's border collie.

There was a long silence in the small room when David Fairchild finally finished his story. Sergeant Bill Stroud had pricked up his ears a number of times during the narrative. He now went to a large, grey filing cabinet which stood in one corner, removed a manila folder and placed it on his desk.

'Persons reported missing within the last three months,' he explained to the two other men. He opened the file and, withdrawing a large sheet of paper, slid it across his desk.

'Oh, Lord,' whispered David Fairchild.

The photograph under the word 'Missing' showed a happy, healthy, well-nourished boy of thirteen, smiling at the camera. It was obviously a school portrait: the boy wore a neatly ironed shirt and a striped tie. He had big blue eyes and dark brown hair, cut very short.

'Sean Vaughan Stevens,' said the Sergeant. 'Been missing for just over seven weeks. So he's been out at the Lucas dump, poor little lad —' He shook his head before taking another paper from the file.

Max Richards cleared his throat. 'He's in pretty bad shape, Sergeant. He's been knocked around quite a lot by the look of him — thin as a rail — scared to hell — especially of Dean Lucas.'

'I'll get those Lucases for this,' the Sergeant spoke with forceful calm.

'They'll be long gone by now,' Max said coolly.

'About young Sean?' David broke in.

'Yes, David, I know what you're asking. The boy can stay with you, at least for the moment. I know he's in kind and safe hands.'

'Don't you dare let him fall into the hands of the child welfare people,' growled Max, pushing back his chair.

'Now, Max, they do have their uses —' The policeman stood up.

'Do you know who reported him missing?' David asked.

The Sergeant checked the second paper he had taken from the file. 'Merriman and Merriman — they're Sydney solicitors — representing Bronwyn Vaughan, the boy's adopted aunt. I'll get on to them at once.'

Chapter Seven: Vignettes

Stella was reading Marguerite Henry's *Justin Morgan Had a Horse*, the book sent to Toby by Mr Kendrick Tenny so long ago. She lay curled up in the sitting room on the battered old divan which the family used as a sofa, Sambo purring contentedly at her side. Her face and neck had gradually returned to their usual shape and size. The angry red weals covering her face, neck, chest and shoulders had faded to pale pink and hardly itched at all. She was aware still of a slight tightness in her chest — it hurt a bit to breathe — but it improved a little more with each passing day. Most of the previous Sunday now appeared as a vague dream to Stella. She dropped the book as the screen door slammed shut behind her father.

'Dad, what's going to happen about that boy, Sean?'

'He's safe at Bellara for the present, Stella. It will probably take a while for the legal boys to sort everything out.'

'I'd like to meet him, Dad.' Stella looked up at Max eagerly.

'I'll take you with me next time I go over to Bellara.'

— *TWO* —

In a first floor bedroom of the homestead at Bellara, a young woman stood brushing her hair. The mahogany framed cheval glass had belonged to Deswyn's great grandmother and reflected a damsel of medium height with a nicely rounded, distinctly feminine shape. The damsel had a thick creamy skin which many a young lady would have died for, large blue eyes fringed with long, dark lashes and very dark red hair, which when unrestrained, fell in thick, rippling waves below her shoulder blades.

Deswyn Fairchild was twenty-seven. She had been mistress of Bellara since the death of her mother nine years ago.

Automatically she began quickly twisting the rich red tresses into a simple chignon. She paused, remembering that Toby Richards was expected at Bellara this morning. The ghost of a smile tugged at her full lips as she began plaiting her hair into an elegant French braid.

— THREE —

David Fairchild stood on the wide back verandah of the homestead, greatly enjoying the scene in front of him. Clifford Martin, his elderly head nurseryman, had lived and worked on Bellara for nearly forty years. Cliff had a new young helper who dogged his every step. The third member of the trio was Mike, the black and white border collie, who was delighted to have a new playmate.

Cliff was working at the wooden table which stood outside the small greenhouse. As David watched, Sean vanished into the greenhouse, reappearing almost immediately with an armload of seed trays. Mike, who had been stretched out in the warmth of the spring sunshine, arose from his place of slumber close to the table, and padded after Sean, never allowing more than a few feet to separate the two.

It was Sean's third day on Bellara and even in that brief time, the change in the lad was quite remarkable. Remembering the shock he had felt on seeing the photograph in the police station, barely recognisable as the thin, dirty, terrified, bruised and beaten child found amidst his waratahs, David experienced a sudden spurt of anger.

— FOUR —

Audrey Martin was busy doing her morning house work. How good it felt to have a youngster in the home again. One hand touched the tiny gold cross at her neck. *Mother of God, please keep the child safe. Please let him stay here with us.*

— FIVE —

Sergeant Bill Stroud drove down the long track which led to Bellara homestead. He'd always liked those two giant wagon wheels which flanked the front gates. Rather a nice touch.

The visit paid to the Lucas shack had not been a total waste of time. As he had suspected, the Lucases themselves were long gone. The old ute, just about falling to pieces, was still there but the kombi van was absent. Evidence of stolen goods still remained in the old shed — obviously they hadn't been able to take everything with them. In a small, meanly furnished bedroom, the Sergeant had found a rucksack, a small pile of boy's rumpled clothing, a pair of sturdy leather school shoes and, hidden beneath the thin mattress, a framed photograph.

Pulling up in front of the homestead, Bill Stroud gave two cheerful toots on the horn.

— SIX —

Sean felt safe so long as he stayed close to these nice people. Mike made him feel safe, too. He had his treasured pen knife back, returned to him with a kindly smile by Mr Richards. Sean had stammered out an apology for stealing Mr Richards' flowers and the apology had been accepted with grave courtesy. Somehow, Sean felt better after that and his heart had lightened a little.

Mr Martin had produced some mineral oil, a bottle of rubbing alcohol and a handful of clean rags and shown Sean how to properly clean and care for his knife. Sean's heart had filled with pride when Mr Martin had assured him that his knife was a very good one.

'Lad, could you fetch me a bag of seed labels? You'll find them on the top shelf just inside the door.'

Sean grinned as Mike lumbered to his feet and padded after him. He bent to gently fondle the silky ears.

'It's hardly worth your effort, old boy.'

— *SEVEN* —

Toby Richards cantered Serenade along the well-trodden bridle path towards the western boundary. For more than seventy years the Richards and Fairchild families had ridden back and forth between Cheshunt and Bellara. He was hardly aware of the beauty of the late October morning. The face and form of a young woman had taken possession of his mind.

— *EIGHT* —

Alwyn Fairchild was struggling with the wire strainers. He swore under his breath, not that there was anyone to hear. Whoever had invented wire strainers had not thought too much about the poor devils needing to strain the bottom strand of sheep fencing!

Once that wire was strained taut, he paused in his labours for a moment. Removing his broad-brimmed felt hat, the young man rubbed vigorously at his sweat-soaked hair. The same very dark red as that of his twin sister, Alwyn's hair was always kept militarily short.

He was worried about his twin.

— *NINE* —

In the Phillip Street offices of Merriman and Merriman, a serious discussion was underway.

'This whole business is most irregular,' Mr Ephraim Merriman, the senior partner of Merriman and Merriman, spoke in a dry, thin voice.

'We did impress upon her the importance of making a will,' Mr Aaron Merriman said drily.

'Quite so, quite so.'

'I wonder if the brother will put up much of a fight for a share of the goods?' Mr Jonathan Merriman cheerfully queried.

Both his elders frowned at him. It was this distinct lack of seriousness, this lack of reverence for anything legal, which had prevented Mr Jonathan Merriman's name from being added to the brass plate in the foyer of the Phillip Street office building. Young Jonathan (he was forty-two) was definitely considered too frivolous in approach and attitude by both his grandfather and his uncle, to as yet aspire to the august heights of being the third name on the brass plate.

'In my experience,' Mr Ephraim spoke even more drily than usual, 'most people like money.'

'Those people — what's their name? Fairchild? — who found the boy. Can't the boy stay there? Seems the ideal solution to me. Sell that boarding house for a tidy sum (just look at the location — prime harbour frontage — should get a fortune for it), put the money in trust for the boy — the Fairchilds can adopt him — at the very least they could foster him but it's always best to steer clear of the child welfare bunch — don't want them sticking their noses in all the time. Some of the trust money can be paid to the Fairchilds for expenses and so forth. Don't see why a brother the old girl hadn't exchanged a word with in more than thirty years should come in for a windfall.' Mr Jonathan leaned back in his chair, very pleased with this simple solution. In his mind's eye he could already see a new brass plate (larger and grander) in the downstairs foyer, elegantly engraved with the names Merriman, Merriman and Merriman.

Chapter Eight: 'People like you shouldn't be allowed —'

She had been admitted to a different hospital this time, but it was still in Sydney and a long way from home.

Stella gazed thoughtfully at her legs. Her right leg was slightly turned inwards to the left, as if trying to reach out to its fellow leg. They had given her something for pain a short while ago so she didn't feel too bad. Of course, she knew the pain would come back: it always did.

Ever since the corticosteroids had been stopped, the pain had been steadily increasing again. Joint pain, in her knees, ankles, hips and wrists: hot, swollen, red and painful. Her movements were becoming more laboured and clumsy all the time. Some days she had falls, times when her legs just seemed to give way beneath her. She was learning to be very wary of falls. Broken bones, so she had been told, were the very last thing she needed. So it was back to limping and hobbling her way along, gripping at anything sturdy enough to provide that vital support. It was almost automatic now to always be checking ahead to make sure support was available to aid her progress along a chosen route.

Things that had once seemed too trivial to even rate a thought now reared up in importance. Such stupid things, such silly things too ...

Having a bath, for example — what normal sixteen year old ever paused to ponder over the difficulties that such a simple activity entailed?

To Stella's resentful and somewhat understandably biased eye, the bathroom at home now resembled nothing so much as a display room of appliances for disabled people. But the day had come when not only was her father required to lift her into and out of the bath, but she could no longer always support herself. Shining chrome grab rails were screwed firmly to the two walls adjacent to the tub; a safety device resembling the shape of an upside-down U was clamped tightly to the side of the bath; an adjustable shower seat able to stand within the bath was purchased, and two large rubber mats of the suction grip type — they were always placed within the tub itself — were obtained.

Then there was going down steps which Stella found much worse than ascending the said stairs. Clinging to any available railing, she would place her left leg (which she now called her 'good leg') on the desired step before slowly and carefully dragging the right leg down to join it. A short period for regaining her balance and catching her breath, a readjustment in position of the hands gripping the rails, and the whole process had to be repeated till the next step was gained. If the staircase was devoid of railings she was forced to resort to sitting on her bottom and descending by that method beloved by two-year-olds. But she was not two years old …

She was getting so incredibly clumsy, always dropping things. Her hands and fingers had lost much of their pre-illness dexterity. She recalled a horse show and an open 'Good Hands' class in which both adults and children had competed. To her amazement she had won the class. She must have been about twelve. She had been riding dear old Casper that day — one of his last shows before his retirement from competition. Her mind drifted away to home, her beloved Cheshunt, and the horses. Perhaps the doctors would let her go home very soon …

Then there was this business of people bumping into her. Whoever would have imagined something like that could matter so much? With most people, the contact was purely accidental and nearly always followed by distress and an apology. But some people had not been so nice. She remembered the first time she had met hostility:

'People like you shouldn't be allowed to clutter up public places,' the elegantly suited young woman had stared angrily at Stella. 'Why can't you stay at home or better still, in some place for useless people!'

Barely comprehending what she was hearing, Stella lay on the pathway where the woman's hurried passing shove had placed her, trembling and shaken from her unexpected fall.

'I suppose you need assistance in getting up,' the woman spoke disdainfully, as if Stella was an unpleasant specimen of humanity to whom she was now forced to do her duty. She took a step towards Stella.

'Don't bother,' the quiet but steely voice came from a bespectacled young man wheeling a bicycle. Leaning his cycle against a nearby tree, he knelt by Stella. 'Just take it steady for a moment and I'll help you when you feel ready to move. There's no hurry at all.'

He had been so kind, she recalled; helped her up and to a handy park bench; asked if he should call someone, if she needed medical help. She'd explained that her mother would be along in the car very shortly, that she, Stella, should have been more careful around people. She would always remember his reply:

'It was not your fault. I was just behind you and saw the whole thing. That female was rushing along talking on one of those new-fangled portable phone things. Damned things are luxury items for city executives, if you ask me. Ugly, heavy-looking brutes, aren't they? Must weigh a ton! I heard what she said to you.' He'd hesitated. 'Look, you must never pay any attention to those sort of people, you know. Most people are pretty okay but there's always a few bad apples in the barrel. People like her don't mean anything in this world. The people who count are those who battle against the odds all the time. I don't know what's wrong with you but I was following behind you quite a way — long enough to see you're suffering pretty badly with those legs. Don't ever take any notice of mean and cruel comments — ignore — if you can't ignore — rise above it — if you can't do that, get plain angry and let it out. But don't let it bring you down.'

He'd asked if he should stay till her mother came but she'd thanked him and shaken her head. Reclaiming his bicycle, he'd regained the path and eventually turned out of the park gate. She'd never seen him again.

She was learning the slow and bitter lesson that less than perfect health was socially unacceptable to some people. Illness and disability just did not fit in with modern living in a so-called civilised, advanced and enlightened country like Australia. They were ranked with old age. She remembered hearing the parents of a school friend talking to her own parents one day. They'd openly admitted that they were not prepared to look after Mrs Devery's elderly mother; they were far too busy with work, with their social life, with their trips abroad. No, it wasn't a financial thing — the old girl was perfectly prepared to pay her way and more — and anyway, they were not exactly short of money — but it was the bother of the whole business. Old people were such a bore, such a bother to have around. No, there was nothing the matter with the old lady, she was just plain old. Later in the day, she'd heard her mother say to her father in the dry voice she always used at such times:

'It doesn't seem to have occurred to Paul and Lizzie Devery that they too will one day be old and unwanted. Nemesis does happen, you know.'

Then there were clothes …

The only clothes that Stella ever displayed the slightest interest in were riding clothes. Even then it was only to approve what her mother produced for the various classes at different horse events. Stella wore shorts and shirts in the summer, jeans and shirts in the winter and jodhpurs as often as possible. Feminine frills and flounces were highly impractical on a farm — anyway, she detested all forms of female frippery. Clothes were something you pulled on in a hurry in the morning and threw off in equal haste at night. Or they used to be …

Many parts of Stella's body were now swollen, painful, stiff and rash covered. She couldn't bear anything tight or even firm — everything had to be loose and easy to manage. Her feet couldn't fit into any of her shoes. She went barefoot where possible, at other times borrowing footwear from her family. When her rashes reduced her to tears, she wore a loose cotton robe her mother had bought especially.

Stella sighed and picked up her book. Until her illness, Stella had seldom had time for any reading other than that required for school. It wasn't that she disliked reading but a day held only so many hours and when you spent most of those hours on horseback or working on the farm, reading took a back seat. Since the coming of her sickness she had begun to regard books in a rather different light. Each one was a portal to a voyage of discovery, and during that voyage it was possible to escape from a world which had become a frightening, painful and uncertain place.

Stella was currently delving into *The Crown of Success* or *Four Heads to Furnish* and thoroughly enjoying every page. First published in 1889, this Victorian gem was written by A.L.O.E. (A Lady of England) otherwise known as Charlotte Maria Tucker. Deswyn Fairchild had discovered it within an old trunk that had belonged to her great grandmother. It was illustrated with four delightful colour plates and Stella spent much time studying these.

Her troubled world receded as she followed the struggles of Dame Desley's four children: lively Dick, vain Matty, lazy Lubin and lame Nelly. Their mentor was the solemn yet kindly Mr Learning who imbibed paper and ink for breakfast. Stella had never read an allegorical tale before and she was charmed by the cleverness and imagination of the writer. She read of Mrs Sewing who sold both Plain-work and Fancy-work plants; of the magic purses of Time given to each of the children; of the cunningness of the boy called Pride and the silliness of Miss Folly; of visits to the famous bazar of Grammar, to the shop of Mr Reading and to the workshops of Messrs. Arithmetic and Mathematics; of the beautiful bird Content who was Nelly's loved companion. Each character, each adventure, gave a little colour to Stella's day.

'Stella?'

She had been so absorbed in *The Crown of Success* that she had failed to hear two people enter the room.

'Stella, here's Doctor Bredon to see you,' Sister Andrews, head of the ward, spoke kindly.

'Hello, Doctor.'

'Good afternoon, Stella. What's that you're reading?' Doctor Bredon was a man of somewhat vast proportions. He stood well over six feet tall and his rotundness always reminded his young patient of an apple barrel whose hoops were feeling the strain.

Stella held out the book. *'The Crown of Success,'* she spoke shyly.

'Bless my boots, child. I didn't know you modern youngsters read such old fashioned books. Must date back to the Victorian era, eh?'

Stella felt mildly indignant. 'I like it very much,' she spoke with a touch of defiance.

'Good for you, child. Now, about you. Been on the telephone to Doctor Mason today and had a long chat about you. I think we can let you go home tomorrow. We'll see how you get on with this new lot of tablets, see if they keep things under control a bit better. Sister here has already called your mother — with that long distance to come we wanted to give her at least a bit of notice — pleased to be going home, eh?'

'Oh yes!' The heartfelt words were accompanied by a wide beaming smile.

'Sister, I've written up a good supply of calcium supplements for Stella to take home. She should have been on them months ago. Could you make sure the order goes down to pharmacy tonight? Then all the medicines can be given to her mother together. I'll need to see Mrs Richards before Stella leaves us. Can you arrange that as well please?'

It was with a joyful heart Stella watched the two adults leave the room. The very thought of going home caused her spirits to soar. Renewed hope came bubbling up from within.

Chapter Nine: Old Dan

Kirsty gently closed her heels against Serenade's gleaming bay sides and urged him into a smooth canter. They flew along the bridle path. It wasn't often these days that Kirsty was able to be in the saddle; now she realised how much she missed it. The light rain, little more than a mist, fell in a silent silver curtain. It was just Kirsty and Serenade, the two of them alone together and nobody else in sight. She revelled in the joy of the moment. All the twists and turns in the road, all the potholes, the sudden gaps in the path of the trail that was called Life, were forgotten for the moment.

The Anglo-Arab's hooves thudded along the leaf-strewn path; the animal was enjoying the outing as much as his rider. The air was laden with the wonderful scent of the scribbly gums, *Eucalyptus haemastoma*. Kirsty especially loved the areas where the bridle path wound through the natural bush. She took note of several fallen logs which would be fun to jump when she returned later. Jumping with full saddle bags was not always the wisest, especially when one was carrying food.

She patted the bay gelding a trifle wistfully, wishing it were possible for her to ride out more. Serenade was a beautiful animal, what she called a lady's ride. You didn't often hear the term, lady's hack, much these days, more's the pity, thought Kirsty. The one essential quality that typified a lady's hack was impeccable manners. That was why Serenade had been selected to be trained to carry a sidesaddle.

Kirsty had often wished that horses played a more vital role in everyday life. As a child she had listened spellbound whilst her grandfather spoke of the last days of the horse and carriage era in his native England.

Kirsty had had her usual early morning start with Stella. They now had a morning routine established which worked well for both of them, but it had taken a lot of trial and error to get to this point. Getting Stella up and organised for the day ahead was a lengthy process involving much time, patience and organisation. Stella's first tablets were taken dead on five every morning — until they had partially alleviated the severity of the joint pain and inflammation, the child could not get out of bed. Kirsty hadn't liked the look of those lymph nodes this morning; they were terribly swollen. The child was also mildly feverish, breathless and sensitive to noise.

About ninety minutes after the first tablets of the day, Kirsty had helped her daughter to the bathroom, settling her in a warm, muscle-relaxing bath. She had then stripped the soaking bed and made it up with fresh linen before helping Stella out of the bath and wrapping her in a huge towelling robe. They had long learned that this was the simplest method of drying a painful body. Kirsty had laid out Stella's loose clothing in her room and by a combination of sitting on the edge of her bed and clinging to the bedpost, Stella had slowly donned each garment. The thick chestnut curls were then brushed out and loosely tied on the top of her head with a scrunchie so as to keep them out of the way. All this activity invariably left the child exhausted, shaking and desperate for a return to bed. As usual, Stella's morning appetite had been virtually non-existent and Kirsty had to resort to one of what Toby called 'Mum's secret magic nourishment potions.' This morning it had been mashed banana, milk and natural yoghurt with spoonfuls of Sustagen Hospital Formula added (Doctor Mason's suggestion). Kirsty had poured the mixture into a large, safety-lidded, plastic travelling mug with thick handles. These mugs had become essential, thanks to Stella's hands which were now swollen and lacking in much of their previous co-ordination. Kirsty knew it would take her daughter most of the morning to drink all the 'magic potion' but that was all right. Much better for the nourishment to go in slowly and stay down.

Toby had firmly told his mother that he would be working near the house this morning. He'd promised Dad to overhaul that chainsaw which had developed a stubborn inclination to jam; he'd bring the damned thing over to the workshop behind the house, that way he could keep an eye on his sister. Knowing that once Stella had settled to rest, she would probably sleep for most of the morning, Kirsty had gratefully accepted her son's suggestion. A last quick glance around the partly closed bedroom door had revealed a very drowsy daughter and an equally drowsy Sambo.

Kirsty arrived at the stables to find that Toby had bridled and saddled Serenade and was waiting to see her mounted.

'Thanks, Toby.'

He finished adjusting the strap of a saddlebag and looked up at her.

'Enjoy your ride, Mum. You need a break away from looking after Stella.'

'Toby, if I'm not back by eleven, her next dose of tablets is on the little blue tray on the kitchen dresser.'

'Right.' He patted the bulging saddlebag appreciatively. 'Looks like Old Dan is in for a right treat.'

'He'd live on tinned beans, billy tea and damper if he had his way.'

'Nothing wrong with that,' her big son grinned up at her.

'I'll remember that, my lad,' Kirsty retorted, gathering up her reins.

Riding across the larger of the two home paddocks, Kirsty's mind was occupied with her daughter. There was still no official diagnosis but Doctor Mason had told Kirsty it was now being treated as a systemic inflammatory disease. It was a case of treating the symptoms as much as possible, looking for the combination of medications which helped the most and continuing the search for an accurate diagnosis. Kirsty was beginning to feel very tired …

She turned Serenade onto the track which led to the bush. Kirsty loved the towering creamy columns of the forest giants, the mountain blue gums (*Eucalyptus deanei*). They stood like sentinels guarding and protecting the smaller trees: the prickly-leaved paperbark (*Melaleuca styphelioides*), the sunshine wattle (*Acacia terminalis*) and the hardy juniper-leaf grevillea (*Grevillea juniperina*). She saw a New Holland honeyeater hopefully searching for a late-flowering grevillea. Once she reached the scribbly gums, she would treat herself and Serenade to a brief canter. They'd taken it pretty steady most of the way because of those blasted eggs. Never mind, there was always the return trip, then she'd really let Serenade fly.

Always clad in khaki moleskins, khaki long sleeved shirt, elastic sided boots and broad-brimmed felt hat, Old Dan had been resident on Cheshunt long before Kirsty first arrived as a new bride.

Kirsty smiled to herself. How long ago it seemed now. That girl who had been the very young newlywed Kirsty Richards seemed to belong to another time, another world.

After their arrival at Cheshunt, Max, very proud of his new young bride, had taken her over as much of the property as it was possible to manage in a single day. Not even allowing her time to unpack, he had two horses saddled and waiting before she had a chance to do more than glance quickly at all the rooms in the old farmhouse. Max had told her that her new home was sorely in need of a woman's touch as it had been many years since his mother had died.

That day, if she recollected correctly, she had ridden a quiet, well-mannered little bay mare, called, most appropriately, Lady. Max was taking no chances with this newest and most precious of his possessions. Clad in jeans, yellow shirt and elastic-sided boots, she had gaily ridden at her new husband's side, trotting along the bush tracks, cantering across the wide paddocks.

'We're going to see Old Dan now,' Max had told her. 'He'd never forgive me if he didn't get to meet you on your very first day.'

'Who's Old Dan?' she'd asked with interest.

'It's quite a tale,' Max spoke soberly. 'When Dad came home from the War in 1946, he brought Old Dan with him. I was only ten but I can still remember it so clearly. Mum and I were at the station — Mum had white gloves and a dark blue snood thing — funny how one remembers details like that. We had been waiting for ages — the train was very late — the Fairchilds were there as well, waiting for David's Dad. The train came in. After Dad had stopped hugging Mum and me, he beckoned to this chap who had been standing quietly a short distance away — we hadn't even noticed him — and said to Mum: 'Rose, I'd like to introduce you to Dan. He saved my life on Crete. He's coming to live with us.' Mum didn't so much as blink an eyelid.'

Kirsty had listened entranced to the unfolding tale.

'Of course Mum had got the house all shining and spotless for Dad's homecoming — she'd been cleaning, scrubbing, dusting, polishing and washing for weeks. She politely offered Old Dan the best spare bedroom — he equally politely refused it. Said he preferred do doss down on the verandah if that was no trouble to the missus. He'd just lay out his army bedroll and that would do him fine. It didn't take him long to find the hut down near Brackens Bend. The hut was made back in my granddad's day — it's a solid enough place — the men used our own sandstone quarried here on

Cheshunt to build it — but nobody had lived there for years. Things had been let go a bit during the war years and the hut had been more or less forgotten. One morning, Mum was working in the garden when Old Dan approached her, complete with all his belongings rolled up in his army kit bag.

'Why Dan, you're not leaving us?'

'Thanks, missus, for taking me in and making me feel welcome. I won't be troublin' you much in future, ma'am. I'll be right comfy in the hut. It's best for me and best for your man and you. The boss says he can use another man on the place and I'd say he's right. It's a tidy size of a place you've got here, takes a lot of work to keep it running right and proper. I'm not so dusty with the stock meself, missus — can turn a hand to most things that come my way — daresay I can make meself useful.'

'But Dan, what about cooking and food?'

Much amused, Dan replied, 'I can fend for meself, missus, don't you be frettin' now. Grew up in the Channel Country of Central Western Queensland, near Birdsville. You soon learn to look after yerself in the Channel Country.'

Mother was still expressing her concerns when up rolls Dad on horseback, leading another saddled horse and a sturdy old gelding we used as a packhorse.

'Said your few words to the wife? Good, we'll load up old Clyde here and be on our way.'

Max paused in his story for a moment, 'he's been here since 1946, hardly been off the place.' His voice changed, 'To be honest, Kirsty, I don't know how Cheshunt would have managed without him. Things got pretty rough after Dad came home from the War.'

She'd reached out a slender, strong young arm and gently touched the hand that rested so casually on his right thigh. Their mounts touched noses, exchanging equine confidences.

'Don't tell me if it bothers you, Max.'

'No, it's okay.' He smiled at his new bride. 'Mum was expecting a baby — must have gotten pregnant the night Dad came home, by the dates. The baby — it was a little girl — died during delivery.'

Kirsty let out a tiny cry.

'Dad wasted no time in getting Mum pregnant again. Mum wasn't too well during this pregnancy and Dad started drinking a bit. Not much, just a bit — but it was the beginning of him turning to the bottle when anything went wrong. The second little girl also died during her birth.'

'Oh Max.' Kirsty's eyes filled with tears. 'Not both of them?'

'Years later I learned that the doddery old doctor who attended Mum during both deliveries was an alcoholic who should have been struck off the medical books decades earlier. The War caused a shortage of doctors and this being a remote district, well, country folks tend to put up with things. Of course, Mum should have been sent to one of the Base hospitals for the births but Dad wasn't the type to consider something like that. Mum didn't recover from the birth — got very sick — they called it postpartum infection. She died within the week.'

'How old were you?' asked Kirsty softly.

'Twelve.'

'And your father? How did he manage?'

Max gave a short laugh. 'He didn't. That was when he really got stuck into the drinking.'

'But who looked after things? Cared for you? Cooked? Washed, ironed? Got you off to school? Saw you did your homework? All that sort of thing. Who did the million and one things needed to be done every day?'

'Cheshunt would have fallen apart if it hadn't been for Old Dan. The day after we buried Mum, Old Dan moved back onto the verandah, complete with bedroll. Refused to have a room in the house. He could manage Dad when the drinking got out of control. Then the Fairchilds — you haven't met them yet, of course — our nearest neighbours — Bellara marches with Cheshunt on our western boundary — stepped in. They were horrified at what was happening. They loved Mum — most people did. David's parents took a pretty strong line with Dad about me. I was sent to school down in Sydney with David. It was a relief to get away from Cheshunt, I can tell you.' He paused for a moment.

Kirsty was too appalled to speak. They were now riding through a forest of mountain blue gums. The smooth columns reminded her of the vast pipe organ at the Sydney Town Hall.

'I was seventeen and in my final year at school when Dad died. I wish I could say I felt sorry but I didn't. I was only four when he went away to the War and the man who came back was a total stranger. I would hear Mum crying at night, and during that last year when she was pregnant again she was always so tired and pale.

'Ever since Dad died I've been trying to get the place back on its feet again but it's going to be a long haul. Now I've found the perfect partner to help me.' He smiled at Kirsty. 'It was a wonderful place in my grandparent's day, Kirsty, and I'm going to try to get it that way again if it kills me.'

Emerging from the bush, they turned onto a track which crested a slope. For the first time, Kirsty could see the shining curve of a river.

'What a beautiful view.' Kirsty gazed appreciatively at the scene spread out below her, '… like something from *Alice*.'

'Who's Alice?'

'Alice from Looking Glass country.'

'What are you talking about?' demanded a bemused Max.

'Max Richards, haven't you ever heard of *Alice in Wonderland* and *Alice Through the Looking Glass?*'

'Vaguely, I think, but what the devil have they got to do with anything?'

Kirsty shook with laughter. 'Oh, Max, you are funny! In *Alice Through the Looking Glass,* Alice sees all the land below her divided into squares like a chessboard. It looks a bit like that from up here. What's the name of your river, by the way?'

'It's part of the Cudgegong River which eventually merges with the Macquarie River. That curve is known as Brackens Bend — no, I don't know who Bracken was. Old Dan's hut is on that slope across the river, overlooking the Bend. We'll need to cross the river at Brackens Bridge.'

The horses made their way down the long trail which negotiated what Kirsty now called the chessboard fields. They disturbed a small mob of kangaroos and paused to watch as the marsupials bounded away to the bush. At Brackens Bridge the two riders dismounted.

'We always lead horses over this bridge,' Max explained, leading the way onto the old but sturdy structure.

'I'm not surprised.' Kirsty eyed the rough, log-like timbers and massive iron bolts with interest. She patted Lady encouragingly and led her onto the centre of the narrow span. There were no railings and the bridge was barely wide enough to allow the passage of a single vehicle. The horses' iron-shod hoofs echoed against the solid hardwood; now and then, contact with an iron bolt created a loud clang. Below, the river tumbled and splashed, swirling around the support pillars.

'Must have had a fair bit of rain in the mountains,' Max scrutinised the rushing water thoughtfully.

Kirsty would never forget her first sight of Old Dan standing in front of the sandstone hut. She saw a man of perhaps fifty years, not above middle height, lean and sinewy. His khaki-covered shoulders were broad. Startlingly vivid blue eyes gazed out calmly upon the world. His face, like his hands, was deeply tanned by sun and wind. His dark brown hair was now streaked with grey. In his arms he cradled a blue heeler pup.

Max swung himself down from his saddle. 'Dan! It's grand to see you again! I've brought the new missus to meet you!'

Old Dan gently put the pup on the grass and accepted Max's handshake. He looked up at Kirsty still mounted on Lady and touched his hat.

'Hello, Dan.' Kirsty smiled. 'Max has told me so much about you. It's wonderful to meet you at last.'

'High time the Boss had a wife.'

'I'll agree with that.' Max grinned. 'How've things been, Dan?'

'Pretty fair, Boss. Time you were back. Land needs its owner.'

'Heck, I've only been gone one week,' protested Max. 'Surely a man's allowed a few days with his new wife?'

Old Dan snorted and picked up the pup.

'What a beautiful little pup,' said Kirsty. 'What's her name?'

'He's a dog pup. Name's Bluey.'

'It would be,' laughed Max.

'It's a right, sensible name for a sensible little critter. He's a good little chap.'

'Glad you've got a companion, Dan.'

'We got trouble with the northern bore, Boss. Windmill sails snapped in the high winds two days back. Think somethin's jammed down below, too.'

'Thanks, Dan. I'll get onto it right away. Do you need any supplies for the present?'

'No, Boss, I'm fine. Mayhap next time someone's out this way they could fetch along a brush for Bluey here. Not got a brush in the place and the little chap needs one.'

'I'll see to it, Dan,' Kirsty promised.

'Well, Dan, we'll leave you in peace and be on our way.' Max mounted his horse.

'It was a pleasure to meet you and Bluey.' Kirsty patted Lady's bay neck and smiled at Old Dan.

'Little Missus.' He touched his hat again and nodded. Little Bluey gave a small yap as the pup's owner turned to Max:

'Boss, 'tis plain as the nose on your face that you've got two ladies now. They fit together right proper.'

How pleased Max had been at this sign of approval which, coming from Old Dan, felt like a benediction.

'That was a long conversation for Old Dan,' Max had assured Kirsty on the ride home. 'He's never been one to use three words if one will do the job.'

With a mischievous grin he explained why Old Dan always wore long sleeved shirts: 'He's got a tattoo above his left elbow. The name Betty in red letters surrounded by a heart!'

Kirsty burst out laughing.

'He really likes you.' Her new husband gave her a fond glance. 'To call you the Little Missus was the ultimate sign of approval. Dan always called my mother the Missus,' he finished with a sigh.

'You really loved her, didn't you?' Kirsty ventured.

'Yes, Kirsty, I did.'

'Max?'

'Yes?'

'Why is he called Old Dan? He's not old.'

'I don't really know.' Max rubbed his head in puzzlement. 'He's just always been known as Old Dan. Even in the army — so my Dad said — perhaps that's where he got the name?'

'Funny.'

'Nicknames are funny,' Max shrugged.

'It's not really a nickname, Max.'

'What d'you call it then?'

'More like a sobriquet,' said Kirsty.

'And what in the name of heaven is that?'

'Fancy word for a nickname!'

'Kirsty! You little —'

Before he could finish Kirsty had flicked him with her whip and pushed Lady to a fast canter. Max tore after her in pursuit.

Kirsty came back to the present as the misty rain lifted. The sun was struggling to break through the low clouds and get a grip on the day. She was now negotiating the chessboard fields and mentally checked the contents of her saddlebags. One small fruit cake, homemade of course and a special family recipe handed down to Kirsty by her mother; a piece of well-cooked corned beef; tea, tinned milk — those small tins really added weight to her saddlebags — two tins of sardines, six fresh eggs carefully packed in dry rice and a slab of Old Dan's favourite gingerbread, freshly made and gloriously sticky. Her thoughts drifted away to the man she was going to visit.

How stubbornly he refused to allow Max to either patch up the hut or modernise it in any way.

'You keep all those new-fangled notions for your own place and leave a simple fella like me to enjoy me own bit of space in peace,' he growled at Max. 'That's the trouble with the world today, everybody always wantin' to change everythin' all the time.'

With a touch of laughter in his voice, Max had pointed out that putting on a new roof once in twenty years or so, could hardly be termed rushing around changing things.

Old Dan had remained obdurate. As Max had admitted to Kirsty, the walls of the hut were solid enough, having being constructed from the local sandstone. The same could hardly be said of the roof, made from corrugated iron, which by now rather resembled a patchwork quilt. From that point of view, it was fortunate they were so far from the sea: the salt would have made very short work of Old Dan's roof a long time ago.

It was one of Cheshunt's best kept secrets who actually helped Old Dan patch up his roof. He could easily manage the work himself but as to where the actual materials came from, well, that was quite a mystery. But every so often another piece of corrugated iron in yet another colour would appear on the roof of the hut. Kirsty had often said it would make the pioneer ladies who excelled in patchwork quilts, proud. The list of possible good Samaritan providers was strictly limited and each denied any knowledge of who could possibly be delivering sheets of iron to Old Dan. Old Dan greatly enjoyed his little game with the Boss and no one had any intention of giving away his secret and spoiling the mystery. It had become a traditional Cheshunt joke.

'I see the Invisible Roof Man has been on his rounds again,' Max would say, eyeing yet another neat patch of newly attached iron, and shaking his head.

Old Dan disliked modern civilisation and had found a niche which pretty well enabled him to ignore its very existence. He had no desire to be anywhere other than where he was and many years could pass without him leaving Cheshunt. The last time had been to the hospital.

Toby, aged twelve, on riding out to visit his friend, had been met by a frantically barking Bluey, a short distance from the hut. The faithful blue heeler, now a very old dog, had guided Toby to his fallen master: he was lying unconscious next to the stump where he chopped his fire wood, the sharp-bladed axe fallen at his side. Toby, putting his heels to his horse as never before, had ridden hell for leather for his mother.

It was at times like these that Kirsty was so thankful for her nursing training. She suspected there was little time to waste and she had been correct: Old Dan's appendix ruptured in the helicopter, on the way to hospital. If they hadn't already been in the air, the doctor had grimly told Kirsty, he very much doubted if they could have saved him.

Old Dan had undergone emergency surgery, hovered between life and death for several days. He greatly surprised everybody, except those who knew him, by clinging to life with a tenacity that could only be expected of such an obstinate bugger, as Max had privately told the operating surgeon. In spite of this, recovery had been very slow and the surgeon had kept him in hospital for six weeks.

On release from hospital, the surgeon had flatly told Kirsty that Old Dan would need proper care for another month, maybe longer, and he could not return to his solitary life at the old hut. Too feeble to utter more than token protest, Old Dan had been established on a divan bed on the screened verandah of Cheshunt for four weeks, his faithful old dog at his side. From there he could see and hear what was happening on his beloved Cheshunt.

One morning when Kirsty was busy dealing with the produce of the three mulberry trees, Old Dan had spoken to Max:

'Boss, don't think I haven't appreciated all you and the Little Missus have done for me but I gotta get back under me own steam again. I need to get back to me own place.'

Max totally understood. 'I'm riding out that way later today and I'll see what shape your place is in after all this time.'

Old Dan had fired up immediately. 'I don't need you takin' this chance to pretty up the old place. It'll be just fine as it is. It doesn't need any of your fancy touches.'

'Dan, you've been away for ten weeks! At the very least someone will have to check you haven't been overrun with rats and every other sort of critter.'

'Old Bluey here will soon sort that lot out.' The thin and slightly tremulous hand gently fondled the pointed ears. He looked up at the younger man. 'All right, I don't want to make a fuss — can't stand people who make a fuss — you go and take a look at the place, but remember, I'd like to go back soon.' He sank back on the upright, excessively uncomfortable wooden chair he always insisted on using. It was a very old piece of furniture, and had been earmarked by Kirsty for the junk shed, a large and airy timber construction next to the workshop.

Kirsty had removed the chair to the verandah for Toby to later carry down to the junk shed. The next time she had seen the chair, Old Dan was sitting on it.

Two days later, following a thorough scrubbing of every available surface, the old hut was ready and awaiting its tenant. Max knew exactly how far he could allow his eager team doing cleaning detail to go. Curtains would have promptly been torn down and used for more practical purposes, as well Kirsty knew, so she settled for a checked tablecloth, six tea towels (the tattered relics she threw on the fire made her shake her head), a potholder (a new innovation for Old Dan but after first scoffing at it he had grudgingly come to admit its usefulness), two blankets and two pillows (he could say all he liked but he was still far from well and would probably use them) and a good supply of food.

There were two choices of transport: some would say neither were suitable for a man recovering from serious abdominal surgery, thought Max Richards ruefully as he considered his options. The old utility truck with its four wheeled drive would be able to traverse the rough ground which led to the hut; it was a good solid vehicle, old fashioned with no frills and designed as a work horse. However, its complete lack of any decent form of suspension meant that its occupants got shaken around like peas in a jar.

No, it would have to be horseback. Max would mount Old Dan on Tom, a steady gelding who knew how to take care of his rider and made a pretty good job of it too. The two men would ride out this afternoon, taking it nice and easy and the old man should be okay.

Expecting trouble from Kirsty, Max had rather hesitantly told her of his proposed plan. Looking a touch thoughtful she had nodded in agreement. Clearly, his surprise must have shown on his face because Kirsty had laughed and playfully flicked him with the tea towel she was holding.

'Of course I knew it was the only possible way to get poor Old Dan back to his beloved hut. You know, underneath that facade he's a real darling. I shall miss him.'

Max grinned. 'Obviously you haven't got enough to do. I could change that.'

Kirsty ignored him. 'Max, could we get that old chair out to the hut? He loves it so much.'

'Sure,' Max agreed 'Ned's driving out ahead of us this afternoon with Old Dan's things and he can chuck the chair in the back.'

Ned was one of the Cheshunt men.

Old Dan had always been considered a bit of a misogynist locally, although it was admitted that both Rose Richards and young Kirsty Richards had won a warm corner of his heart. He had never had much time for women, considering most of them to be the cause of trouble and upset amid their menfolk. They aroused wild passions in the younger chaps which led to the young 'uns getting unsettled, neglecting their work, drinking too much, fighting and sometimes behaving stupidly with guns. One thing was certain: he had loved Rose Richards, the Missus, and now he loved Kirsty Richards, the Little Missus. He would protect her with his life, if need be.

Kirsty dismounted to cross Brackens Bridge and led Serenade across. She could see smoke rising from the tall chimney of the sandstone hut. Good! She could do with a mug of tea and an hour in the peaceful serenity of Old Dan's company. Out here, life moved at a much slower pace and she felt so very weary. She was forced to admit that this illness of Stella's was taking a heavy toll on her. If only a diagnosis could be found! If only a definite treatment could be found! In her heart she knew the child was getting worse although much of the time she refused to admit this, even to herself. Dear Old Dan! Perhaps for a short while she could forget this endless, gnawing responsibility and worry that was eating away at her normal vitality and love of life.

Chapter Ten: Kirsty Carey

Kirsty stood gazing up at the night sky. She loved the peace, the tranquility and the *hugeness* of the night-time sky. She found the two pointers, alpha Centauri and beta Centauri, then the Southern Cross. When she was a child, her father used to take her out at night-time and, pointing up at the Milky Way, explain its magic for her. Later, her new husband, Max, had shown the same fascination with constellations, galaxies and solar systems. He too loved to tell Kirsty facts relating to space, planets, comets, celestial objects and astronomy as a whole.

Kirsty appreciated the quiet serenity that came with the night on a farm. The bustle and most of the noise of the day was gone. She was a long way from the home of her childhood.

Her childhood. Those two words always conjured up the beautiful hymn written by William S. Pitts so long ago. Her grandmother would play the piano and the children would gather round her and sing:

> *There's a church in the valley by the wildwood,*
> *No lovelier spot in the dale,*
> *No place is so dear to my childhood,*
> *As the little brown church in the vale.*
> *Come to the church in the wildwood,*
> *Oh, come to the church in the dale,*
> *No spot is so dear to my childhood,*
> *As the little brown church in the vale.*

Kirsty Carey had grown up in a tiny bush community hundreds

of miles away from Cheshunt. Her father, Joshua Carey, was the local blacksmith. Even then, the term *farrier* was starting to replace the word *blacksmith*, but Kirsty's father had been the real thing: a master who crafted and created things from iron and steel. His forge had been known throughout the vast surrounding hinterland and people came from far and wide to have Joshua Carey shoe their horses and attend to their welding needs.

Kirsty's mother had been christened Estelle Alexandra Mary but was always known as Alex. She had trained as a nurse before her marriage to Joshua Carey. She had fallen pregnant with Kirsty within weeks of the two-day honeymoon and Kirsty had been followed by Peter, Charles, Phillip and Brian.

Joshua Carey may have been a superb craftsman but he was a poor businessman. Alex, on arriving back from her honeymoon, had discovered a chaotic mess in what was meant to be the little office of her new home. Joshua, it seemed, never bothered too much about people paying or not. They would pay when they could, he assured his new bride; she was not to trouble her pretty little head about things like that.

Alex may have been pretty but, fortunately for both of them, she was also possessed of a vast stock of common sense. Putting aside all plans of making the necessary feminine changes to the sturdy but very plain cottage, Alex immediately got busy in the minute office.

She soon discovered that some of her husband's customers had not paid him for over two years. He kept track with a rough sort of day book. Each time he did business with a customer, it was jotted down in an exercise book, if he remembered to do so. It did not take Alex very long to determine that it was always the same people who never got around to paying.

The young bride bided her time, knowing she would have to move carefully in such a close-knit bush community. As a newcomer, she had no wish to rock the boat, alienate people and lose her husband customers. She and Joshua had to live here: it was their home and their livelihood. But at the same time, it was not right, this business of people not paying Joshua what they owed. She called it stealing, but only when speaking to herself.

As a young newlywed and a newcomer to the small community, Alex attracted much attention. As was customary in such places, she was invited to a number of 'ladies only' gatherings: morning teas, a luncheon and a shower welcome. Shower welcomes were a speciality of the bush, each guest bringing along a small gift to help the bride in her new home. Alex received tray cloths, pillow cases, a table cloth and table mats, all made by hand and beautifully embroidered. Bush ladies were very talented with their needles. Alex was entranced by some milk jug covers, hand crocheted in radiating wheel patterns and edged with glass beads.

It was at these gatherings she began to learn about the community. By putting a judicious question here and there and by listening more than she talked, Alex began to form an idea of the people in the district. Three names consistently showed up in her husband's day book: McGregor, MacIntosh and Kershaw. Other names appeared now and then but it was these three Alex was worried about. Between them, they owed Joshua a considerable amount of money.

When the young matron hostessing the shower welcome mentioned the name Angus McGregor in a disparaging tone, Alex's ears pricked up. She listened as a chorus of feminine voices agreed with their hostess on the subject of Angus McGregor before putting forth a tentative query.

'Who is Angus McGregor?'

A dozen voices tried to tell her at once. Their hostess silenced them with a regal gesture before taking the floor.

Angus McGregor, it appeared, was the meanest Scotsman alive, well, certainly the meanest person within a hundred miles. He paid his bills about once every two years or so, only when threats of the law were brought against him. Alex learned that in this district people were very reluctant to stir up trouble against each other, and that the menfolk especially tended to let things slide. So long as there was food on the table and clothes on their backs they wouldn't press for unpaid bills. They would get paid, sooner or later, and they always did, didn't they?

The women didn't see it in the same light at all. It was they who had to purchase groceries at the general store and clothe the family. However skilled they were at sewing, at making things over, at creating a meal from a few soup bones and garden vegetables, they did require money for some things. Children's shoes were always a bone of contention in growing families, and that was only one item.

Alex learned that Fergus MacIntosh was Angus McGregor's brother-in-law. He always followed Angus's lead, being a weak and mealy-mouthed character. When Angus left his bills unpaid, Fergus followed suit. It was never necessary to set the law on Fergus, he hastily paid up the moment Angus was targeted for debt recovery.

Alex returned from her welcome shower in a thoughtful frame of mind. The name Kershaw hadn't arisen but she had enough to think over for the present. Joshua, very much enveloped in the glow that comes to newly married men who are deeply in love with their wives, was only too pleased that Alex had dropped the subject of outstanding bills. He liked a quiet life, living at peace amidst his friends and neighbours. There was no need to go looking for trouble.

Looking at Alex, clad in her pretty flowered frock, topped by the huge straw hat and finished with pink ribbons, Joshua felt humble. He knew he had been incredibly lucky to wed his Alex — she was a cut above him all right, properly educated and with her full nursing certificate. He had left school at thirteen to help support the family after his father had died.

Ten days following the welcome shower, Alex was out riding. Her aim was twofold: she wanted to take some magazines to one of her new friends, who had wistfully commented on the lack of fresh reading material in the community. She would combine the magazine drop off with an exploration of some of the area, most of which was still new and strange to her.

Joshua owned a fat skewbald gelding, taken, although he would never tell Alex, in partial payment of an unpaid debt. Joshua actually got much the better part of the deal: the skewbald, a sturdy mixture of brumby, Dartmoor and Welsh pony blood, was the perfect family general equine, able and willing to do everything asked of him. His name was Cisco.

When Alex found out Cisco's history, as she inevitably did (Alex would always find out everything, her family would soon come to realise), she only laughed and gave Joshua a hug.

'This time you got the best end of the deal,' she told him.

She and her mount were still getting to know one another so Alex took things at a steady pace. It was a hot afternoon and the bush had the drowsy feel it always had on such afternoons. The magazines, along with two paperbacked books were tucked away in her saddlebag. Alex walked and trotted Cisco along the track, enjoying herself despite the heat. Noticing that bush flies were irritating Cisco, she pulled him up next to a young eucalypt tree. She broke off two large twigs, well covered with the sweetly smelling leaves and tucked the twigs into Cisco's browband. The sturdy gelding nodded his head in seeming appreciation and Alex laughed and patted him.

She delivered the magazines and books, which were received

with cries of delight and appreciation, to her new friend, Betty Kaplan, but declined a pressing invitation to stay for a while. Alex explained, a tad untruthfully, that she had other errands to do and, truthfully, that Betty was first on her list. She stayed mounted on Cisco's back and the two young matrons talked at Betty's front gate. Betty brought her a cool drink of water which Alex drank gratefully.

After bidding her friend farewell, Alex decided to stop at the general store. No sooner had she reined in Cisco than Mr Bowen, the proprietor, waddled out to greet her.

'Good afternoon, Mrs Carey. How are you today? It's a hot afternoon for you to be out and about! I just came out to tell you that the sewing fabric you asked me to get in has arrived. I don't suppose you'll be wantin' to take it with you today, on horseback, now will you?'

Alex's face lit up. 'Oh thank you, Mr Bowen. Yes, I have been waiting for that.' She looked doubtfully at her saddlebag. 'Would it fit in here?'

'Surely would, Mrs Carey, surely would. You just wait a while and I'll fix it up proper for you, so no nasty leather dressing gets on that fine new fabric.'

Alex smiled as she watched the kindly old man waddle back into his store. Most people in her new community were so kind and helpful, why did there always have to be a few bad apples to spoil the barrel, so to speak? For a moment she dwelt resentfully upon the topic of Mr Angus McGregor. If he could be brought into line, so to speak, his brother-in-law would obviously follow suit. It must be possible to do *something*.

Heavy footsteps on the wooden floorboards heralded the return of Mr Bowen with Alex's parcel.

'Don't worry, it's well protected,' he assured her. 'I wrapped it in two sheets of fine tissue paper, two sheets of brown paper, a sheet of that thick white paper I keep for the bacon, and two sheets of newspaper.' Proudly he handed the parcel up to her.

'I can see you've taken a great deal of trouble.' Alex thanked him, tucking the said parcel away in her saddlebag.

The stout old man watched young Mrs Carey ride off down the road. She turned in her saddle to wave. She was a real nice young lady, and a proper lady, too. God knows how that young slow-top, Joshua Carey, had managed to snare her. Not that he had anything against young Carey but this girl he had married, why she must have had her choice of dozens of young fellows. Shaking his head, Mr Bowen returned to the comparative coolness of his store and thankfully sank onto a convenient barrel.

Just past the small cluster of dwellings which comprised the village section, there was a small hillock. The first people who moved into the area had deliberately chosen to build their homes in the shelter of the tree covered hillock. Alex turned Cisco onto the track which led to the peak. Her aim was to get a general idea of the surrounding countryside.

As she rode along, Alex's mind was busy with Betty's problem concerning lack of fresh reading materials. Surely something could be done about that, even if only in a small way. Alex knew the closest public library was well over one hundred miles away, and most of those miles were over rough tracks, bad roads and seasonally washed away temporary bridges. In other words, plain inaccessible. There must be some way of starting a local lending library, mused Alex. She began making a mental list of those of her new friends whom she thought just might be interested in such a scheme.

Alex and Cisco reached the top of the hillock and paused for breath. On looking all around her, Alex was able to work out her bearings, to a pretty good extent. She'd always had what her grandmother called a 'good bump of locality.' The village was immediately below, to the south-east, and she could make out her husband's forge a mile to the south. The two bedroom cottage she was in the process of improving lay a short distance from the forge.

The track she had ridden up seemed to continue down the opposite side of the hillock, to the north-west. If she followed it, then circled around to the left, she should sooner or later arrive back home. Most of the countryside within a couple of miles of the hillock was partially cleared, native bushland. Here and there, a small area had been completely cleared and given over to stock. A few smaller zones of tilled earth gave proof of hopes for future crops.

She put her heels gently to Cisco's plump skewbald sides and put her proposed plan into action. At the base of the hillock the narrow track widened out into a dusty road leading to several farms. Alex kept to the verge as much as possible, keenly taking note of her surroundings. The third farm appeared to be rather luxurious for these parts, with a large house, timber rail fences that had actually been painted where they fronted the road, several horses, which Alex immediately recognised as thoroughbred, and a very new looking utility truck parked close to the house. Alex's finely marked eyebrows rose: this place was definitely different from the usual run of things around here. She rather wondered about that …

Alex noticed a woman on the front verandah of the big house but she was too far away to notice any details. A few hundred yards on the road gave out, turning into a bridle path and Alex halted. From her observations atop the hillock, Alex hoped that if she now followed this bridle path to the south, it should lead her back home. The ride had taken her quite some distance and, much as she had enjoyed it, she would be glad to reach home again. She thought Cisco would be pleased to reach his cool stable, and gave him a consoling pat. She then checked that the eucalypt twigs with their scented leaves were still fixed firmly to his browband before riding on.

Sometime later they stopped again, delighted to find the shadow of a large barn thrown across their path. Alex lightly dismounted and loosened Cisco's girths. He gave an exaggerated sigh of relief and began to pick at odd clumps of grass. It always amused Alex how horses could use those huge teeth and large mouth so delicately, wrinkling up their muzzles as they fastidiously checked out possible edibles.

It was quiet enough for Cisco's eating to appear unusually loud. It was then that Alex became aware of different, strange sounds which appeared to be coming from the direction of the barn. The barn had a doorway opening onto the bridle path; it was through here the sounds were being emitted. Puzzled, the young matron concentrated on the noises, figuratively cocking her ears, so to speak. Cisco stopped munching which enabled Alex's ears to sharpen still further.

Suddenly her pretty young face flooded bright scarlet with embarrassment and shame. She had only been married some weeks and she knew exactly what those sounds implied. The barn's inhabitants must have been very close to the doorway because not only could Alex hear far more than she wished, of the passionate encounter obviously taking place, she could also hear their words:

'Damn, there's someone out there,' a male voice spoke. 'Sure I heard a horse just then.'

'Oh, let them be, Mac, darlin', come on, we need to finish what we started,' from a female voice.

'It won't do to get caught, not for a man in my position.'

'Speakin' of a man in your position, Mac, your best position is right inside of me.'

'You're a little trollop!'

'It don't seem to bother you none, Mac, not that I noticed.'

'Suppose Fanny ever caught on? She would try and divorce me, by God.'

'Shouldn't think you got too much to fret over, Mac. It's a man's world out there and as far I can see, them divorce laws come down hard on the womenfolk, even when 'tis the man to blame.' Was there a touch of bitterness in the feisty sounding voice?

A reluctant chuckle was followed by, 'You're quite a sharp little filly for a strumpet, girl, I must say.'

'Ta for nothin', big boy.'

'Don't you ever worry about Don catching on to your little games?'

'Nope. I got that boy just where I want him. I can handle Don all right, don't you worry your head about that.'

'I sure don't want Fanny getting wind of our little capers.'

'You scared of her or somethin'?'

'I don't want to lose her money.'

Alex, who had stood spellbound listening to this fascinating conversation, now hastily tightened Cisco's girths and swung herself into the saddle. She had been far from silent with her swift movements and all conversation in the barn abruptly halted. As she adjusted her reins, in preparation to making a hasty departure down the bridle path, a figure appeared in the doorway of the barn. Alex raised her head and her eyes met a pair of piercing blue ones, set in a sunburned, craggy face. The man looked to be of middle age with grizzled hair and was strongly built. His arm and shoulder muscles were those of a man who had performed hard physical labour from his earliest years. Of the girl or woman who was his companion in passion, there was no sign.

The man and Alex locked eyes for a long moment. Much later, Alex was to wonder if her thoughts had shown on her face that day: she rather thought so. She turned Cisco quickly, put her heels to his sides and sped down the bridle path at a swift canter. She did not look back.

The community was not especially surprised when Mr Angus McGregor, followed of course by his brother-in-law, Fergus MacIntosh, paid all his outstanding bills the following week. They were just downright relieved; after all, it was about that time again, more than two years since the last settlement. It did, however, take the community a long time to realise that Angus McGregor had paid up, for the very first time, without being taken to the law. In the end the menfolk never did quite believe it — they thought someone was just being too shy or bashful to admit it was they who had sued for recovery of outstanding debts. The women thought otherwise.

'That old so and so has never paid anyone anything in his life unless he was scared of something,' declared Betty Kaplan.

'You're right, Betty. There's something strange happened to old McGregor,' agreed Dotty Monk, who had hostessed Alex's welcome shower.

However the community was stunned when a bare six months later, Angus McGregor again paid his bills. Even the men admitted it was a tad unusual. The women snorted at their men's slowness and got busy.

'Girls, I think some person might just have gotten a hold on Angus,' Dotty Monk, the undisputed leader of the young matrons, spoke up.

'Sure seems that way,' agreed Audrey Miller, a pretty redhead expecting her first baby any day.

'Blackmail, you mean?' eagerly proposed flighty Rose Grant.

'Not really *blackmail*, Rosie,' demurred Betty Kaplan. 'More like he's been caught with his hand in the till someplace, and that that someone will keep quiet so long as Angus pays his bills.'

'Sounds just like blackmail to me,' sniffed Rose, keen to retaliate what she considered a snubbing.

'Perhaps he's just had a change of heart?' suggested Alex, quietly knitting in her corner.

The uproar was immediate.

'Oh Alex, after twenty odd years of stringing people along? He was doing the same thing to my Dad when I was hardly out of rompers.'

'Alex, no, that guy hasn't got a heart.'

'No, Alex, something must have happened and I wish I knew what.'

'And obviously it's happened in the last six months or so. It's just over half a year since he made that previous payment without the debt collector being called in.'

'Okay, girls,' laughed Audrey, 'what has been new around here about six months ago, or mayhap a touch longer?'

'Alex joined us,' cried out Rose. 'She's the newest person in the place for ages and ages. Perhaps she's got something to do with it.'

The young matrons all laughed at the very idea of Alex Carey having anything to do with Angus McGregor. In her cane basket chair, glad to be seated in a corner, Alex flushed very slightly and wished her friends would change the subject. It wasn't as if she had actually done anything at all. How could she ever have imagined the outcome of that ride on that hot afternoon when she and Cisco had stopped by the shade of an unknown barn?

She had fled from the scene, her mind in turmoil. Alex had no idea who either of the participants were, having only been in the district some weeks. She had heard the name Mac and automatically assumed it was a diminutive of a Christian name. Once home, she didn't mention the incident to Joshua, instinctively sensing it was better not. One never quite knew, here in this isolated bush community so many years behind the times, how the men would react.

The following week, when Angus McGregor (and Fergus MacIntosh) had paid their long outstanding bills, Alex never connected the events. How could she? She had no idea who Angus McGregor actually was, never having met him or had him pointed out to her as Angus McGregor. Why should she presume a man enjoying some obviously illicit passion in a barn should be Angus McGregor?

It took some months for Alex to gradually join up the links in the chain. One day she was introduced to Mrs Fanny McGregor, a dark woman with unhappy eyes, who was far too beautifully and expensively dressed for the bush. Alex next learned that the luxurious looking farm with the only painted wooden rail fences in the district belonged to Angus McGregor, or rather, to Fanny McGregor, so most folks thought. But it was not until Angus paid his bills for the second time within a mere six month period that the answer literally stared Alex in the face.

She was working in the small office affixed to the rear of the house one morning when there was a brisk rapping at the front door. Someone, thought Alex, half irritated, was certainly giving Joshua's beautifully crafted horseshoe door knocker some heavy use.

'Oh, ma'am, if you please,' the young girl who helped Alex in the house three mornings a week, stood in the office doorway, wide-eyed.

'What is it, Doreen?'

'It's that Mr McGregor, the one that don't pay his bills. He wants to see you, ma'am.'

'Thank you, Doreen. Show him in, please.'

'Show him in here, ma'am?'

'Yes, Doreen. Bring him here to the office.'

With a sigh, Alex set aside the accounts, which were definitely in a much improved state of order since her arrival on the scene, and stood up. As she smoothed out the skirts of her frock, she wondered about her unexpected visitor. So she was finally going to meet Mr Angus McGregor.

'The missus is in her office.' Doreen's means of announcing the visitor's arrival made Alex's lips twitch involuntarily.

She turned to the doorway and found herself staring straight into the piercing blue eyes of the man from the barn.

'Good morning, Mrs Carey.' He already had his wide-brimmed felt hat in his hand.

'Good morning,' Alex spoke quietly and politely.

'I have come to pay my account,' he spoke with surprising dignity and produced a fat leather wallet from his back pocket.

Alex nodded. 'Please take a chair whilst I make you out a receipt,' she told him.

Alex was extremely puzzled. Most people just gave Joshua the money at the forge when they came in with another job for him. It was rare for a customer to bother to come across to the house. She sat at her table whilst Mr McGregor counted out the money to her. Alex checked the money, locked it away in an iron cashbox and wrote out a receipt in her neat, clear handwriting.

'Thank you, Mr McGregor.' She handed him the receipt and stood up.

'Mrs Carey —'

'Yes, Mr McGregor?'

'Mrs Carey —' he tried again.

'Yes, what is it, Mr McGregor?'

'Damnation,' he almost shouted, 'stop saying my name like that, can't you!'

His face had reddened. Sweat was breaking across the sunburned face and he ran trembling, work roughened fingers through grizzled hair.

Bewildered, Alex stared at him. 'I'm very sorry, Mr McGre —'

'Don't DO that, woman!' he bellowed.

Alex stood silent.

'All right, what is it you want from me? Tell me.'

'I am very sorry but I really don't understand you.' She was troubled now.

'What do you *want* from me?'

Alex began to understand. He wanted to buy her silence. Rage began to simmer inside her.

'All I want from you, Mr McGregor, is for you to leave my home as soon as possible.' She wanted this man gone from her home. He tainted the sweetness of the air.

He tried again at the front door. 'Mrs Carey, if my wife found out —'

She felt nothing but contempt although she didn't show it.

'Goodbye, Mr McGregor.'

Before she shut the door, he made one final appeal. 'Are you sure you don't need something?'

Alex held herself erect and spoke with dignity that was not untinged with compassion. 'Mr McGregor, I do assure you that you have nothing at all to fear from me.' She closed the door.

He never believed her of course, for people always assume that they will be treated as they treat others.

Totally unrelated to the McGregor/MacIntosh debt problem, now seemingly solved, we must not forget Billy Kershaw. His was the third name Alex had noted in Joshua's day book. Shortly after Angus McGregor's visit to Alex, young Billy Kershaw's body was found in the rather appropriately named Lost Creek. He had shot himself, leaving no letter.

This was the community into which Kirsty, the first of Joshua's and Alex's children, was born. As the eldest child and the only girl with four younger brothers, Kirsty could have had a very difficult and confining existence, but for her mother. Alex would not allow Kirsty to become handmaiden to the boys, an extra pair of hands in the house tending to the needs of the male sex, as so often happened in such families. Alex had seen too much of that. So Kirsty had her daily tasks, none of which caused her to pander to her brothers. They were trained to take care of Kirsty.

Joshua, thrilled that his Alex had presented him with the sturdy sons so essential to a bush blacksmith and craftsman, nevertheless regarded Kirsty as his special darling. Alex in miniature, she had the same mop of black curls and the same beautiful brown eyes as her mother.

In the small and seldom used parlour of the Carey home, a portrait hung on the wall. It had been taken by a travelling bush photographer at Joshua's proud insistence, when Kirsty was a year old. It was a charming study and Joshua beamed with pride each time his eyes fell upon the picture of his two beautiful ladies, as he always called them. Alex, her dark curls firmly restrained and neatly twisted into a chignon, was wearing a dark, short sleeved frock sprinkled with dots and finished with a white collar and cuffs. Round her neck hung a fine chain, its tiny heart nestled at Alex's throat. Both were gold although the photograph didn't show this. It was, of course, a black and white portrait. Alex held Kirsty on her lap. The child wore a light-coloured, short sleeved, smocked frock, short white socks, sturdy shoes with straps and a white butterfly bow adorned her hair. It was clear that a great deal of time and effort had gone into the creating of this picture, both by the photographer and the adult sitter. Having a photograph taken was a very special occasion and the preparations made within the bush community, when it was known that the bush photographer was on his way, were considerable.

Kirsty's early years were very much confined to the community. She helped her mother in the house and garden, much preferring the latter to the former. She rode and groomed Cisco from her third year. She did tasks for her father, especially when they involved taking messages on horseback. She attended the small bush school which was situated on the big, cleared lot, just up from Mr Bowen's general store. She played with her brothers, especially Peter who was closest in age to Kirsty and the most like her in character. Together, she and Peter kept Charles, Phillip and Brian in line.

When Kirsty was twelve, she was sent to school in Sydney, a feat which would have proven impossible without Alex's much older maiden sister. Kirsty boarded with her aunt in a northern suburb, and attended daily the nearby Saint Brigid's Anglican School for Girls. The transition was not easy, with Kirsty returning home to the bush only during the school holidays.

Her intense love of books and reading came from her mother. Alex had founded the community's library in a corner of her tiny office. Alex had coaxed Joshua into making and erecting some shelves and her library had commenced business with two dozen books and a box of magazines. How proudly those original twenty-four volumes had stood upon their new shelves.

School had been followed by nursing training, a vocation Kirsty had shown leanings toward since she were quite small. Joshua and Alex were very proud of their daughter's acceptance into a good Sydney-based hospital. Some of other bush community parents were surprised: to them, a grown daughter, especially when she was the only daughter in the family, should be at home helping her parents. But they hadn't really approved of Kirsty's smart city education either, although nothing was ever said.

Kirsty had loved her nursing from the very first day. Before long she had also grown very attached to Sydney and felt at home there. On their days off, she and a few friends — fellow trainee nurses — would explore new areas and return again and again to favourite locations.

They swam at the beaches of Bondi and Maroubra, enjoying the ride on the electric tram of the Maroubra Beach line. They walked through the lips of the giant Smile into the tawdry magic of Luna Park to ride the big dipper, the Ferris wheel, and the ghost train. They took ferry rides to Manly and explored the Corso before enjoying newspaper-wrapped fish and chips on the beach. They explored the cobbled streets of The Rocks, learning something of its colourful history. It surprised the young nurses to learn that bubonic plague had broken out in 1900, affecting Darling Harbour, Surry Hills and other areas, as well as The Rocks.

Like many citizens of Sydney, they followed the ongoing saga of the Sydney Opera House project. The girls had been at school when, in December 1955, the international design competition for a Sydney Opera House was announced. It had been won by the Danish architect Jørn Utzon, one of more than two hundred and thirty entrants. The girls also remembered July 1957, when the New South Wales State Parliament had allocated £3,500,000 of public money for the creation of the Opera House. Their parents and teachers had been quite vocal on the subject. The Opera House project was sometimes called 'the state treasurer's worst nightmare'.

They walked across the famous Bridge, that iconic Sydney landmark. They paid a visit to Taronga Park Zoo (free entry tickets given to them by the social director of the nurse's home). They picnicked in the Royal Botanic Gardens and spent hours in the Art Gallery of New South Wales. They attended services at both St Andrews's Cathedral and St Mary's Cathedral, greatly admiring the intricate gothic revival architecture of both churches.

In short, during their four years, they enjoyed themselves using the minimum amount of money, often little more than bus, train, tram or ferry fares. They laughed together as they rode the Red Rattlers, often strap-hanging in the crowded peak hours. It was grand to be young, healthy and training to be a nurse in a Sydney-based hospital.

It had been on Bondi Beach that Kirsty had first met Max. Max, who had recently come of legal age, was reluctantly spending time in Sydney at the gentle suggestion of Mr Fairchild, and the much more pointed requests of both Max's solicitor and bank manager. There were matters, it seemed, that necessitated Max's presence in Sydney. Come Saturday afternoon and Max was tired out with all the legal and financial ramifications of inheriting a large property from an alcoholic father. Returning to the modest boarding establishment where he was staying, Max collected a pair of old shorts, his bath towel and a novel. He would spend the afternoon on Bondi Beach and forget all about the heavy stuff clogging up his brain. He needed to do something different.

Max enjoyed a long swim in the surf before he retreated to the warm sand and his bath towel. He buttoned up his long sleeved shirt and pulled *A Town Like Alice* from his rucksack. Forty minutes later Max looked up from his book and idly scanned the beach. *A Town Like Alice* dropped to the sand, unheeded. A girl was just emerging from the surf.

His gaze was first captured by the blue and white striped bikini which clung to a figure that was slim but curved in all the right places. Max detested skinny women. Woman should look feminine and sexy, not like emaciated boys, for goodness sake. The top half of the bikini was certainly nicely filled. The girl had long, lightly tanned legs with strong thighs and slender, well-shaped feet. He raised his eyes to her face and his heart turned over. Large, warm brown eyes shone in an oval shaped face. A mass of black curls was pulled back into a pony tail, which swung between her shoulder blades. She carried herself with unconscious pride, standing tall and holding her neat, square shoulders well back. Max thought she looked taller than average, perhaps around five feet nine or ten inches. The girl walked along the sand past Max. Watching the swing of her neat bikini-clad hips, Max felt a sudden longing.

The girl stopped about seventy feet north of Max and dropped to her knees. She seemed to be rummaging in a brightly-coloured sort of bag but it was too far for Max to see clearly. As he strained his eyes yearningly, the girl stood up and dried herself vigorously with a large towel. Then she pulled what appeared to be a vivid yellow tee shirt over her head before sitting down on the sand.

Kirsty hadn't even seen the tall, broad-shouldered young man whose eyes followed her so yearningly. Her mind was fully occupied with the dying woman on her current ward. Kirsty had just finished her ten day stint on Verity ward and today was the first of her four days off. She had felt the need to get away from the hospital, the nurse's home and the whole hospital precinct.

Conflicting thoughts had battled in Kirsty's head on the bus ride to the beach. She much regretted the gradual closure of the tram lines in Sydney; today, only a few lines still remained in operation. As the bus rumbled along the streets, Kirsty thought resentfully of what the sister tutors all said about emotional involvement with patients:

'A nurse must never become too close to her patients. Any form of emotional attachment must be stopped before it starts.' Those words had been drummed into the young nurses' heads from their very first day in the school of nursing.

For the past ten days Kirsty had been caring for a young woman her own age who was in the final stages of pancreatic cancer. Frances Jacobs and Kirsty had hit it off immediately, quickly becoming friends. Checking on her patients for the last time before going off duty yesterday afternoon, Kirsty had bent to hug Frances.

'I'll see you in four days, Fran. I'm on the early shift Wednesday.'

'Are you doing anything special?' the thin-faced girl with the huge eyes smiled up at her.

'Just catching up with the usual washing, ironing and a bit of shopping. Can I do anything for you?'

Fran had shaken her head. 'No. Nice of you to ask, but I don't need anything.'

'Take care, Fran, and give the staff hell!'

Fran had laughed up at Kirsty but something in her patient's eyes had bothered the young nurse. It had haunted Kirsty through a restless night. She needed to get away for the day and Bondi Beach was just the ticket. The washing, ironing and shopping could all go hang for the present.

The long swim in the foamy surf helped clear her heavy head and she felt slightly more cheerful. But she was always aware of Fran's eyes laughing up at her. Even her second-hand copy of *Steamboat Gothic* by Frances Parkinson Keyes couldn't hold Kirsty's attention for long. Normally she was riveted to each page of the novel which was by one of her favourite writers. Irritably Kirsty pushed the book aside and lay face down on the warm sand, her head pillowed on her arms. Perhaps she could catch up on a bit of sleep.

'H-h-hello, w-would you like to come for a walk along the beach?' It had taken Max ninety minutes to pluck up the courage to approach the girl lying on the sand.

It took some thirty-odd seconds before Kirsty realised the words were addressed to her. In that time, Max had cursed himself for a fool a dozen times over.

Kirsty lifted her head and gazed into a pair of steady, serious blue eyes. Afterwards, she was never able to explain why she had answered this total stranger the way she had.

'Yes, I would like that very much, thanks.' And with those words, she had scrambled to her feet.

'I'm Max Richards, by the way.'

'Kirsty Carey.'

That had been the beginning.

Still gazing at the night-time sky at Cheshunt, Kirsty came back to the present with a sigh. The screen door banged and Max appeared on the verandah.

'Kirsty?'

'Over near the hydrangeas,' she called back.

'What on earth are you doing out here at this hour?'

'Enjoying some peace and quiet.'

'It's nearly midnight, woman. Come on, bed.' He put an arm around her shoulders and gently pulled her towards the house.

'Stella?'

'Fast asleep, as you should be.'

'Okay, just give me a few minutes.'

Fifteen minutes later Kirsty lay on her side, Max's arm thrown protectively about her. She was almost asleep when her mind flew back to Bondi and the day she had met Max. She had told him all about Fran Jacobs. He had listened quietly, asking an occasional question and radiating a solid, dependable, sympathetic presence.

When Kirsty had returned to Verity ward, early on the Wednesday morning, she had been greeted by an empty bed in Fran's room. Frances Jacobs had slipped away from life very early on Monday morning.

Chapter Eleven: Declaration of Independence

Stella had chosen her time with great care. She had been planning this for some weeks now, plotting her strategy with attention that almost rivalled that of the generals who had planned the D Day landings in 1944.

To have any chance of success, a number of factors had to fall into place on the same day. Patience was a virtue Stella was gradually and resentfully learning to acquire. She had bided her time patiently, knowing her chance would come.

Her father was away for several days, something to do with a new breed of cattle being developed — they were called Lowline, she thought. He had an uncanny knack of sensing when his daughter was up to something so she had breathed a somewhat guilty sigh of relief when he had departed Cheshunt at sunup, exactly as planned.

She knew that Toby was working in the chessboard fields, along with Old Dan, Ned and some of the men. They wouldn't reappear till after sundown, barring accidents. Toby always worked hard alongside the Cheshunt men, never shirking any task however difficult, dirty, dangerous or monotonous.

Mum was the biggest problem. Ever since this stupid illness, Mum hated leaving her daughter completely alone for any length of time. Stella reckoned she would need at least three hours to manage what she intended.

The telephone call came at midday. Kirsty Richards, in the process of taking down the exceedingly dirty curtains in her husband's study, cursed mildly and dropped the armful of striped chintz on the floor.

'Kirsty?' It was Max's voice.

'Goodness, Max, why aren't you gazing at lovely Lowline ladies?'

'Kirsty, I need you to go and see the livestock agents for me — as soon as possible, I'm afraid. Wally Luceno knows all about it and is expecting you.'

'It can't wait?'

'Sorry, Kirsty, it's very important and must be done as soon as possible.'

'Okay. I'll go immediately.'

'Thanks, love, and sorry.' Max ended the call.

'Damn!' Kirsty eyed the pile of curtains ruefully. 'So much for you lot!'

The slow, uneven shuffling sounds which heralded her daughter's approach could be heard as Stella made her way towards her father's study. Dragging her right leg — now decidedly more than slightly twisted inwards — across the floor, Stella appeared in the doorway.

'What's up, Mum?'

'I've got to go into Koolkuna to see the livestock agents for Dad. Top priority, so I'm told.'

Kirsty had barely turned out the front gate before her daughter, taking several deep breaths to steady herself, went to work. Trying to hurry would be her downfall, as she well knew.

Several days earlier Stella had coaxed her father into moving Casper much closer to the house. She had pointed out that if she couldn't ride, at least she could enjoy having a pony close enough for her to pat. Max Richards had raised no objection, especially as Casper had put on too much weight with the spring grass, and the white pony was now installed in one of the house yards, as they were called. The four house yards were more like very small paddocks: roomy, sturdily fenced and usually well grassed over. Casper, to his disgust was given the one yard which was sparsely covered with short, rough grass. He did not approve of Max's edict that small, elderly ponies with a tendency to hoof problems must be restricted from eating too much rich feed.

Once on the verandah Stella tugged on an old pair of her father's riding boots. Her own boots could no longer fit her swollen feet and ankles, but her father's boots, helped by a pair of extra thick woollen socks, fitted snugly. Stella grimaced at the large boots then pushed the thought away. She had more important things to do.

Using the verandah posts as support, Stella painstakingly shuffled to the northern end of the house. Halting to catch her breath, she eyed the distance to the first of the house yards from where Casper was now eyeing her with great interest. There was no help for it, she would have to crawl along the grass — it was safest and probably quickest in the long run. The ten metres seemed to go on forever and, not for the first time since her illness had reduced her to these lengths, Stella empathised with babies learning to crawl and walk.

Finally, sweat pouring down her scarlet face, hands scratched and dirty, and knees bruised and sore, the traveller arrived at her destination. Panting, she collapsed in the grass against the fence. A velvety nose touched her wet hair and two huge, wise brown eyes looked down upon her.

'Made it, Casper darling,' gasped Stella. 'Just give me a moment.'

Whilst she waited for her breathlessness to decrease, her trembling fingers slowly unwrapped a barley sugar tugged from her shorts pocket. Once her chest had stopped heaving, Stella slipped the sweet into her mouth. She needed the sugar in her system.

As soon as she had recovered from her exertions, Stella used the sturdy fence rails to clamber awkwardly to her feet. A few wobbling paces brought her to the yard gate and she gratefully felt the smooth, rounded, galvanised piping beneath her fingers. Stage one was almost complete.

Once Stella was inside the yard with Casper, she laboriously unwound what appeared to be two ropes from around her waist. In reality, they were two lead ropes with snap-link swivel clip attachments. Casper rubbed his head gently against her arm and Stella clipped the first lead rope to the brass ring on the nearside of the headcollar's noseband.

Obeying the command, 'stand', the white pony stood still as a rock whilst Stella clipped the second lead rope to the brass ring on the offside of the noseband. She then knotted the free ends of the two lead ropes together, creating a basic set of reins. Stage one was now achieved.

By far the most difficult part of the operation had now been reached. Stella had to get herself on Casper's snowy white back. Less than a year ago a light spring from her agile feet would have seen Stella mounted in a trice. Or she might have vaulted on over Casper's tail, he being one of the few Cheshunt horses to allow this. Today, it would be a difficult, demanding and painful challenge.

Patient and good as Casper was, Stella felt dubious about leaving him untied while she scrambled inelegantly onto his back. Unknotting one of the pieces of baling twine always looped around the top rail of the yard fence, she threaded it through the brass tie ring on the chin-piece of Casper's headcollar then tied it with a quick release knot to a second loop of baling twine which was firmly secured to the rail. Then she took a deep breath: now for the hard part.

It was only when Stella attempted to climb the wooden rail fence that she realised she couldn't do it. She was unable to make her legs move in the necessary positions. It was a physical impossibility. Tears of disappointment were followed by tears of rage and frustration. She *had* to get up on Casper by herself just to prove to herself she could still do some things independently. She was on a mission and there was no turning back.

Stella looked about her in search of inspiration. The verandah! That was it! The northern end of the front verandah was only two steps up from ground level but the southern end was a very different matter. If she could persuade Casper to stand next to the verandah at the right place, she should be able to just slide onto his back from the verandah floor. Flushed with delight, she got to work immediately, dimly realising that all this was taking a great deal longer than she had anticipated.

With no support available Stella was again reduced to using hands and knees to return to the verandah. One hand kept a tenuous grip on the lead rope reins as Casper dawdled beside her, dropping his head to grab a mouthful of grass when the going got too slow. The summer sun beat down relentlessly, unusually hot for early December. Her left knee met a stone resulting in a yelp from Stella. A thistle brushed against the soft skin of her inner thighs and she swore, using a word that was decidedly unladylike. Her tee shirt clung to her wet body and her eyes filled with salt-laden perspiration. Only stubbornness and determination kept her moving. Finally the northern end of the verandah was reached and she crumpled in a heap at the base of the two steps.

Ten minutes later the moistness of a rough but gentle tongue caused Stella to open her eyes. Her vision was filled with a soft, white muzzle and an enormous tongue. Casper was licking her face.

Stella gently pushed him away with one hand. Enough was enough. Sitting up, she took Casper's reins in one hand before pushing herself up onto the bottom step, backwards. Then the second step was negotiated and she was back on the northern end of the verandah. Casper was tied to the closest verandah upright whilst Stella shakily took stock of her situation. She fumbled in her pocket for another barley sugar before using the upright to clamber to her feet. Three unsteady paces took her to the water barrel which collected rainwater from the roof. Grabbing one of plastic mugs which were always hooked over the barrel's rim, Stella filled it half full and sipped it down slowly. Water! There was nothing in the world so good to drink as fresh rainwater! She half-filled the mug a second time before sinking into the shabby old divan which stood nearby. Casper looked at her enquiringly.

She allowed herself a short time for recovery, too long would only allow her muscles to stiffen up after all their unaccustomed use and abuse. At least she had plenty of support on the verandah enabling her to stay on her feet. Stella didn't call the actions her feet and legs made to get from place to place, walking.

Forcing herself back on her feet, she limped towards Casper. Once untied, she led him south along the verandah, Casper on the grass, herself on the actual verandah. When his back was the same level as the tiled verandah floor, Stella halted. That looked about right.

'Casper, stand!' she commanded crisply.

The pony gazed up at her wonderingly but obeyed the order. Stella dropped the reins and trusted to hope. There was no way she could manage both the reins and getting on his back together, not from this height and angle. With a groan she used the closest upright to assist her in sitting down close to the verandah edge. One part of her was wondering why the devil she had started all this in the first place.

With great difficulty Stella awkwardly got herself kneeling on her good knee, the left one. She grabbed Casper's long white mane with both hands and pulled as hard as she could. He stiffened, became aware of the impending change and stood rock still, ready to receive his young mistress. Stella dragged the twisted right leg off the edge of the verandah and across Casper's back. Her upper body fell forward onto the pony's neck and her left leg scraped along the verandah floor before sliding down Casper's flank. Stella grabbed the rope reins before pushing herself into an upright position.

'Good boy, Casper,' she gasped out, patting the silky neck.

It took a long minute or two for her to realise that she had actually achieved by far the most difficult part of her plan. She was flooded with a wonderful sense of triumph and achievement. She was actually sitting on Casper's back and she had done it alone.

As Stella implemented stage three of her plan, a surge of guilt rushed over her. She felt she could always, at a pinch, explain why she had done what she had, up to this point. But now she was stretching the boundaries beyond common sense and reason and well she knew it. She reassured herself that she would be back home before anyone ever knew she had been away and, pushing aside any self-reproach, turned Casper in the direction of the bridle path leading to the western boundary.

Neat white ears pricked and alert, neck arched, Casper walked out eagerly. It always annoyed Stella when people said there was no such colour as pure white in horses. Casper was as white as a friendly ghost, hence his name of course.

As the commanding generals of D Day could have told Stella, troops can run on their adrenaline for a certain period of time after all other resources have been used up. But powerful as that adrenaline surge is, it only lasts for a limited time and once both resources and adrenaline have been utilised, the body says 'enough', and will grind to a halt. Stella had been extremely profligate of her resources that day and the adrenaline surge which had got her this far was fast burning out. She was approaching the end of her body's capabilities.

The sun burned down upon her, hot and relentless. In the excitement and intensity of her planning she had totally forgotten her broad-brimmed Akubra. One hand gripped feebly at the rope reins, the other was twisted through a lock of Casper's mane. Casper, well aware that all was not as it should be with his young rider, now walked carefully along the track. Stella's much abused and tormented leg muscles were screaming their protest. The usual smells of summer penetrated her nostrils: Eucalyptus haemastoma, radiata pine, sunshine wattle (*Acacia terminalis*) and the scent of warm pony. Her body swayed on the pony's broad back and her eyes were partly closed. She could barely remember what she was doing nor why she was doing it. Dimly she was aware of the golden ring of bell-birds close by.

Images drifted before her: the little girl who had always to be tied in to her wheelchair to stop her from falling out. She had been born with a very serious case of something called spina bifida and was paralysed from the waist down. Judith, her name had been — the same name as her cousin — and she and Stella had met in hospital. A nurse had privately told Stella that Judith would always be wheelchair bound. The eleven-year-old child had liked to propel her chair into the older girl's room and talk with her. She had told Stella that she lived with her Mum in a small unit quite close to the hospital, that she had three brothers, all younger and that Dad had walked out one day and never come back.

Stella saw the features of another girl, not yet of high school age, who had been a permanent patient of the hospital. Stella didn't understand what was wrong with her, only that it was something that had kept her lying in a hospital bed for almost two years. This girl belonged to a very large family who kept a family/friends visiting roster. They worked it so that there was nearly always someone with the child. Stella would see the different relatives coming and going in the next room at all hours. Sometimes one would stop to say hello to Stella. They were always smiling and cheerful which had been totally beyond Stella's comprehension.

The faces danced before her. The world was full of people suffering from illnesses that were not their own fault. Who decided who should be healthy and who should not? Why should some people be chosen, like numbers in a ballot, to be healthy? Huge numerals floated before her, then faces followed by more numerals. Just as a vast number six descended from the clouds and perched itself comfortably between Casper's white ears, Stella slipped into unconsciousness.

Reliable and steady as Casper was, he could hardly be expected to ignore a large goanna sitting immovably in his path. He stopped rather abruptly; his young mistress slid from the pony's warm back and landed in a crumpled heap in the centre of the track. The goanna, a trifle peeved at having his peace disturbed, vanished into the surrounding shrubbery.

Casper, a wise and experienced equine, did not like it when things were wrong, and today a great deal was wrong. He bent his neck and gently blew at his mistress's cheek. Her damp chestnut curls quivered at the touch of his breath.

For many years now, Bellara had not been an equine-based property like Cheshunt but horses were still considered the most practical means of doing certain things, even in the 1990s. Currently, four horses called Bellara home. About the time that Casper met up with the goanna, two of the Bellara equines were nearing Cheshunt, having carried their riders from the western boundary.

Sean Stevens was in a state of quiet bliss as he rode along the narrow bridle path. Terrified that this new life might be snatched away from him at any moment, Sean liked to stay close to these kindly, capable people who seemed able to protect him from the horrors that life could throw up. During the past few weeks Miss Deswyn had been teaching him to ride on Susie, her own childhood pony. Yesterday she had decreed that he was ready to manage the ride from Bellara to Cheshunt.

'Good idea,' David Fairchild agreed. 'Sean can come with me tomorrow.'

Proudly riding behind David Fairchild, Sean tried to remember all that Miss Deswyn had taught him. She had recited a sort of poem which helped:

Keep your head and heart up
Keep your hands and heels down,
Your legs keep close to your horse's sides
Your elbows keep close to your own.

She had also found a box of books in Bellara's attic, books belonging to her twin in his boyhood. The books now reposed importantly on a shelf in Sean's bedroom at the Martin's cottage. Among them had been Margaret Clarke's *Care of the Australian Horse and Pony*. Sean had slowly and reverently turned the pages of this Australian bible of equine matters, hoping to expand his knowledge as quickly as possible. Sean leant forward to pat Susie's warm chestnut neck, praying that this new and wonderful life wouldn't be suddenly snatched away from him.

'Good Lord!' David Fairchild, rounding a sharp bend in the track, reined in Crusader abruptly.

Sean, lost in a dream and forgetting all his riding lessons, almost allowed Susie to canon into the huge appaloosa gelding's massive quarters. Susie indignantly flung her head high in the air and pivoted on her hindlegs, almost unseating Sean.

David Fairchild swung himself to the ground and, reins looped over his arm, strode over to the body huddled on the ground. A white pony standing close by whickered a quiet greeting.

'Sean, take Crusader and Susie and tie them up to those tree branches over there. Remember what Deswyn taught you about 'hanging up' horses now.'

'Do you know who it is?'

'It's young Stella Richards and dear old Casper.' The man frowned as he bent over the girl.

'The girl who has been sick?'

'Yes, can you get my water flask from my saddle please, Sean?'

David Fairchild tugged a relatively clean handkerchief from his pocket and soaked it with cool water from the flask. Then he gently wiped Stella's hot face all over.

Sean picked up Casper's rope reins and eyed the headcollar with awe. 'She was riding with no saddle or bridle.'

Stella's eyelids flickered and a pair of grey eyes stared up David Fairchild and Sean.

'Stella?' The man's fingers felt for her wrist. 'Stella, do you know who I am?'

'Mr Fairchild,' a voice whispered.

Water was poured into the lid of the flask and held to the girl's lips. She drank slowly at first and then greedily.

'Hey, steady on, not too fast,' her rescuer protested.

'Casper?' the voice demanded.

'He's fine, young lady. Stayed with you by the looks of things.'

The tight little face softened slightly and the grey eyes looked up lovingly at the white pony. A shaking hand pushed away damp chestnut curls from her face.

'I'm not sure what's happened here but I don't think you're hurt at all, Stella. However, we need to get you into the shade so you will allow me to pick you up and settle you under that tree near the horses over there. No arguments, okay?'

Looking at the kindly, understanding, somewhat quizzical face of the man, Stella's inward resentment, rebelliousness and misery eased a little. Tears filled her eyes as she nodded her assent.

Propped up against the trunk of the wattle tree, Stella felt unutterably weary. More tears spilled down her grubby face but she was just too sore, tired and miserable to care. Guilt also overwhelmed her.

The shrewd eyes of David Fairchild observed the child. He had a pretty fair idea of what had happened this morning at Cheshunt. The important thing now was to get Stella home as quickly and safely as possible. His quick mind ran through the possible options before he called Sean over from the horses.

'I'll need a lot of help from you, son, to get this young lady back home. I'm going to put her up on Crusader and hold her in front of me but you'll have to lead Casper from Susie. Think you can do it?'

Sean swallowed hard before answering, 'Yes, sir.'

'Good lad.'

Stella was lifted into Crusader's saddle then David Fairchild led the huge appaloosa over to the grassy bank, where he easily got up behind Stella. One arm held the child securely in place whilst he managed the reins with the other hand.

'You lead the way,' he told Sean, who was already mounted on Susie, Casper's rope reins held in his right hand. 'Just follow that path till you come to the gate.'

Chapter Twelve: Hertfordshire to New South Wales

'Why is your place called Cheshunt?' Sean Stevens slotted together two pieces of the puzzle's edge before glancing up at Stella.

'It's historical,' explained the girl. 'My Dad's grandparents, I think it was, came to Australia from a place called Cheshunt in England.'

'How long ago?' The boy added another piece to the jigsaw.

'About 1905 or 1906.'

'Wow.' Sean looked impressed.

'If you're really interested you need Dad or Toby on the subject. They're the family historians.' Stella gingerly rearranged her aching limbs on the old sofa. It was forty-eight hours since her ride on Casper and she felt as if she had been beaten all over with a giant baseball bat.

Kirsty Richards had said very little about Stella's adventure. It was perhaps fortunate that David Fairchild's group had arrived back at the farmhouse bare minutes ahead of Kirsty thus sparing her the anxiety of a missing daughter. Toby had also not wasted words but he had bluntly told his young sister exactly what he thought of her. It had not been flattering.

'That cat sure loves you.' Sean reached out a finger to stroke Sambo, who, as usual, lay curled up beside his adored mistress. 'How old is he?'

'Six. Dad found him early one morning — he had been dumped as a tiny kitten — next to our front gate. Aren't people beasts?'

'Some people are,' the boy spoke so quietly that Stella could hardly hear him.

The pair worked in companionable silence for a while.

'Hi kids, you've sure chosen the best place on a hot day.' Toby entered the screened-off section of the verandah. He grinned down at the two heads, one chestnut and one very dark brown.

'Toby, can you tell us about Cheshunt in England and how our people first came to be here, on our own Cheshunt in Australia?'

'Why the sudden interest, little sister?' Toby raised his eyebrows.

'Sean was asking about it and I suddenly realised I don't really know much about our history.'

'Fair enough.' Toby sank into a basket chair which had definitely seen better days. His eyes caught slight movement at the base of the shade-cloth screen. 'We've got a visitor, kids. Look!'

'That's only Ajax,' Stella spoke dismissively.

Sean, however, was intrigued. 'What is it?'

'Ajax, the blue-tongued lizard,' explained Toby.

Sean gazed in fascination at the reptile which appeared to be a survivor from the dinosaur age. It had a big head, a long body ending in a neatly tapering tail, very short legs with small feet and was coloured grey and brown in broad stripes. The verandah tiles were each one square foot and the lizard occupied almost two tiles. Sambo eyed Ajax balefully.

'How does he get on with Sambo and Jasper?' Jasper, an Australian Kelpie, was Max's tireless working dog.

Toby and Stella laughed.

'Ajax rules the roost,' Toby assured Sean. 'They both have a healthy respect for him. Blue-tongues have quite a bite — they latch on and won't let go — but only when they feel threatened.'

'They're omnivores,' added Stella. 'Ajax loves dog and cat food as well as Mum's strawberry plants, especially the tiny strawberries. We have to make sure he's not around when we feed Jasper. Sambo's fed indoors.'

'Can you pick him up?'

'You can, but he doesn't really like it. Prefers to be on terra firma. Can't say that I blame him.'

As they watched, Ajax thoroughly investigated the base of the screening, poking his nose up against the green fabric at various places.

'Some blue-tongues can regrow their tails if they get damaged in a fight or accident,' Stella told Sean.

'Mainly the younger ones,' put in Toby.

Sean absorbed the information, his eyes following the reptile. He would ask Miss Deswyn where he could find a book about lizards like this one. One part of him longed to gently pick up Ajax for a closer look but Sean's own experiences had taught him to respect the freedom and rights of all living creatures. Wise beyond his years, he was content to observe from afar.

'Toby, you were going to tell us about Cheshunt,' Stella reminded her brother.

'Right.' Toby collected his thoughts for a moment. 'Here goes. Our people — the Richards side of the family, that is — lived in what used to be the ancient parish of Cheshunt in Hertfordshire, near the River Lea. They were small farming folk mainly — dairy — making butter and cheese — some grew corn and barley — there was a flourishing brewing industry needing the barley — and some folk produced hides for the leather and tanning industry. The parish of Cheshunt, as well as much of Hertfordshire, was renowned for agriculture during the 1700s and the first half of the 1800s. But industrialisation and the expansion of the railways brought great change, forcing the decline of farming. Commerce and industrial enterprise took over from agriculture and many farming people were unhappy with this. This was one reason why so many folk emigrated from the United Kingdom, often coming out here to Australia. Dad's grandparents, Robert and Eleanor Richards, left Cheshunt in Hertfordshire in 1904. Many girls born in the Cheshunt district were given the name of Eleanor. Do you know why, Estelle Eleanor Richards?'

'Uh, something to do with the Eleanor Cross?'

'Right. One of the Eleanor Crosses can be found at Waltham Cross near Waltham Abbey. It used to actually be within the parish of Cheshunt but the parish and district boundaries have been changed several times and I don't know anything about the new boundaries.'

'What are the Eleanor Crosses?' Sean spoke shyly.

'Queen Eleanor of Castile was the wife of the Plantagenet king, Edward the First, also known as Edward Longshanks. We're talking about the thirteenth century, Sean. After she died near Lincoln, her funeral procession had to travel to Westminster Abbey. At each of the overnight resting places — there were twelve — a stone cross was erected, on the orders of the King.'

'What about the encyclopaedia?' suggested Stella, whose interest in her second name had been stirred for possibly the first time in sixteen years.

'Fair enough,' agreed her brother. 'No, Stella, stay put. I'll get it.'

A few minutes later the trio were pouring over the thick volume.

'Wow, they're not just stone crosses — they're more like temples or monuments with all that carving.' Stella peered at the small illustrations. 'I do wish the pictures were bigger but you get the idea.'

'It says only three are left fully standing,' Sean was slowly reading the small print, 'Geddington, Waltham Cross and Hardingstone, but remains of the crosses can be seen at some of the other resting places.'

'The one at Geddington is over twelve metres high.' Stella's eyes widened.

'Not exactly pocket sized,' agreed her brother.

'A number of replicas also exist, most of which were built during the Victorian era.'

'Listen to this about Charing, the last resting place of the funeral procession of Queen Eleanor of Castile, before Westminster Abbey. The original cross was located in Whitehall and destroyed during the Civil War. The replacement cross was created in 1865 and stands in the forecourt of Charing Cross Station today. And look, there's a map of the journey, showing all the resting places.' Stella laid a finger on the simple chart.

'The Queen died in 1290,' Sean put in. 'Why was the King called Edward Longshanks?'

'Good question, Sean. He was unusually tall with very long arms and legs. Shanks is another word for legs.'

Sean closed the encyclopaedia and carefully placed it on the old iron table, next to the jigsaw puzzle. Toby, amused at the interest shown by the youngsters, returned to his narrative.

'So we have Dad's grandparents, Robert and Eleanor, leaving England in 1904. They were very young, by the way — both were under twenty. They had only been married a few months before boarding the *R.M.S. Orontes* for Australia — before you ask, R.M.S.

means Royal Mail Ship — and they arrived in Fremantle in Western Australia in November 1904. We are really fortunate that several of our ancestors kept diaries and Eleanor Richards kept quite a detailed account of the voyage. Dad's got the diaries locked away, hang on a moment —'

Toby was back within minutes and placed two items on the iron table. Two heads promptly bent to look.

A black and white photographic image of a single-funnelled steamship was printed on thick, cream-coloured card. The card was quite large, slightly smaller than quarto size. Written beneath was the inscription:

The Orient-Pacific Line RMS Orontes, 1902 Fairfield Shipping Co, Glasgow.

Built for the Orient Line, maiden voyage 24 October 1902, London to Australia. Displacement 9,028 gross tons, speed 18 knots, twin screws, two masts, one funnel.

Words of faded blue ink filled the reverse of the card:

28 September 1904: Departed Tilbury Docks in the Port of London yesterday. Have been at sea almost 24 hours. They say the voyage will take around 45 days so we expect to land at Fremantle on 10 November. Robert paid 104 pounds for our two berth stateroom in second class. The space seems very small at first but I expect we will get used to it. We are fortunate to have a porthole with curtains. Some people have inside staterooms with no porthole at all. A poor woman, Mary, with a sick baby came into 'our' part of the ship today. She was looking for help for her baby, but the ship's doctor appeared to be drunk. I took her into our stateroom and did what I could. Being the eldest of eleven children has taught me something about baby care. The baby did seem a little more settled when Mary left and I made Mary promise to return tomorrow. Apparently third class passengers are not meant to mix with the other classes, so the steward told me. That sort of thing makes me so angry. I will try to find a doctor among the passengers.

Five faces gazed out of the photograph which was printed on very thick card and about the same size as the picture of the ship. A young woman sat clad in the garb of the early Edwardian era: high necked blouse with leg-o-mutton sleeves, skirt with close fitting waistband flaring in graceful folds to the floor and a broad-brimmed hat of straw finished with a wide ribbon around the crown. Two young men dressed in close, tapered trousers, shortish jackets, neatly buttoned vests, medium-high collared shirts and boots stood behind the young woman, one with his hand protectively on the woman's chair, the other man slightly apart from the couple. A tiny boy in a sailor suit stood in front of his father whilst a baby girl sat on her mother's lap, bare footed below a white, frilled frock.

Written on the back in the same hand as the ship card were the words: *Robert, Eleanor, James, Roy and Esther, Cheshunt, New South Wales, Australia November 1908. Four years in Australia.*

'Who was James?' queried Stella.

'Robert's brother who came out to Australia on the same ship.'

'1908,' the girl spoke thoughtfully. 'When was grandfather born?'

'1910. The family records show that he was the fourth child born to Robert and Eleanor.'

'What happened to James?' asked Sean.

'If grandfather was the fourth child, why did he inherit Cheshunt?' demanded Stella.

Toby laughed. 'Whoa, youngsters, slow down. Family history, especially with large families and second marriages, gets exceedingly complicated. Let's keep it simple today and just cover the basics. So in November 1904, Robert and Eleanor, along with Robert's brother James, arrived in Australia. First stop was Fremantle —

nearly all the immigration ships made Fremantle their first port of call. One week later Robert, Eleanor and James disembarked from the *R.M.S. Orontes* at Sydney. By the middle of the following year they had found their way north-west to this area and had purchased land — this land, Cheshunt, which is our home today.'

'And James?' prompted Sean.

'He helped Robert and Eleanor get Cheshunt off the ground — damned hard backbreaking work in those days — volunteered during the First World War and never came back. He was killed at Ypres in Belgium, at Passchendaele. Never married.'

'And Robert and Eleanor's children?' Stella spoke soberly.

'They had six all up which was quite modest for those days. Dad's father was the fourth, as I said before.' Here Toby hesitated. He was only too well aware of the damage done to Cheshunt by his grandfather. Max rarely spoke of his father but when he did, it was with bitterness. Toby had worked long and hard beside Max to turn Cheshunt around; knew that after his return from the Second World War, his grandfather, Cecil Lewis Richards had allowed Cheshunt to deteriorate while he had retreated into the world of the alcoholic. Toby had no intention of telling certain chapters of family history to these youngsters — he'd pretty much covered all the relevant basics, anyhow.

'How come you know so much?' Sean looked at Toby in awe.

'He's always been a history nut,' Stella piped up. 'He spends ages reading all the old diaries and family papers.'

'We've been jolly lucky that so many of the papers and books survived.'

'You were going to tell us about Robert and Eleanor's children,' Stella reminded him.

'As I said, they had six, but several died during childhood,' Toby responded flatly.

Stella recognised both the tone of voice and facial expression which meant the subject was closed.

'So that's how your people came to be here and why your place is called Cheshunt.' Sean carefully picked up the picture of the ship. 'Must have been some incredible voyage.'

'I'd like to read the diary that great grandmother Eleanor wrote on the ship,' Stella said meditatively. 'Her writing seems quite easy to read.' She sighed and eased her body into a more comfortable position on the sofa.

Toby glanced at her, noted the white face, the dark shadows under the eyes and the tight lines of pain around the mouth. He stood up.

'Sean, would you mind taking that encyclopaedia and those photographs back inside? Just put them on the kitchen table for now. Too much sunlight is bad for old documents and pictures.'

As soon as Sean was out of hearing, Toby bent to his sister.

'Pain getting pretty rough, eh?'

She nodded resignedly, biting her bottom lip hard.

'Come on, tablets and bed.' He helped her to her feet.

'Toby,' his name was spoken beseechingly, '… will I always be like this — a useless cripple?'

It was as if an icy arrow had pierced his heart. His mind was flooded with images of Stella in a wheelchair, of her whole body as twisted as that poor, terrible right leg had gradually become, of an active young life destroyed by pain and malfunction. With an effort he resolutely thrust the thoughts aside.

'Of course you won't, baby sister. I promise you that with my whole heart. It will all come right very soon.' In an exceedingly rare gesture he kissed the top of her head. There was no other answer he could have possibly given.

Chapter Thirteen: An Unexpected Gift

It was late at night when the meeting broke up. Some lingered to chat but Toby Richards was not of their number. He needed to check over a couple of sick animals before his day was finished. His hand was on the old ute's door when a voice hailed him:

'Wait a minute, Toby. What's the hurry?'

'Sorry, Alwyn, but I've got to get moving. Got two patients in the sickbay.'

The other young man nodded in understanding. 'Right, I won't keep you but I've got a delivery for you —'

Eyebrows raised, Toby leaned against the ute as Alwyn dashed away. Koolkuna Produce Barn and Farm Supplies had put on a good show tonight. The special feature had been native vegetation laws and the possible changes to these laws. Both the local and state governments had been represented, as well as a regional environment group. The discussion had been positive, informative and interesting, as well as good-humoured. This wasn't always the case.

Toby grinned to himself in recollection of a former meeting:

The new president of the Koolkuna District Farmers association had shown eagerness to accept speakers with new and different ideas. When approached by representatives of a recently formed group who claimed great interest in protecting the environment, the president had happily booked them for the following monthly meeting. In his enthusiasm and naiveté, the president had neglected to check both the new group's agenda and proposed presentation, although the group's name, *Perfect Planet,* should have sent out a warning beacon. The opening words of the group's first speaker had sent hostile waves around the room: '*All clearing and burning of land is not only completely unnecessary but is a criminal act against our planet. Are YOU committing this atrocity? Are YOU free from blame?*'

Within ten minutes total chaos reigned. The people from *Perfect Planet* had been hustled out the back entrance to the accompaniment of pithy verbal castigation and catcalls. The president barely summed up the courage to return to face his outraged fellow members, some of whom were demanding his immediate resignation for letting the enemy in.

'Have you even considered what could happen if ignorant morons like that ever get some power?' a furiously angry farmer had bellowed at the president.

'— and here we are!' Alwyn's reappearance jerked Toby back to the present. 'From Deswyn, for your mum. She said there's a note inside — oh — and treat it reasonably carefully. Don't put a sack of feed on top of it.'

'Idiot!' Toby carefully took the cardboard box from his friend. 'Nothing alive inside, I trust?'

'Nope.'

'Tell your sister it will be safely delivered,' Toby opened the ute and gently placed the box on the passenger seat.

It was very late when he finally arrived home to a sleeping house, the injured horse and ailing ewe now comfortably settled for the night. One verandah lamp had been left switched on for him and he quietly let himself in by the laundry door before depositing Deswyn's box on the kitchen dresser. His mother couldn't fail to see it there when she took the mugs down for early morning tea. He was asleep the moment his head touched the pillow, too tired even to dream of a beautiful woman with dark red, rippling hair.

The following day dawned wet and the increased humidity had upped the ante on Stella's ability to cope with her pain-racked body. She looked up from the book she had not been reading. Her mother had just entered her bedroom.

'You can't possibly see to read in this dim light, child.'

'I'm not really reading, Mum, just lying here. Listen to Sambo, he sounds like a combustion engine.' She caressed her adored cat with swollen yet gentle fingers.

Kirsty noted the listlessness in the young voice and the whiteness of her face.

'Why not come out in the sitting room? We can settle you on the sofa for a while. A change of scenery never hurts. What were you not reading, by the way?'

Stella gave a faint grin and slowly and awkwardly began the process involved in getting up from her bed. 'Nothing very exciting, just one of my set school books. Emma.'

'Jane Austin. Well I'm glad that you're still expected to read the classics at school.' Kirsty grinned at her daughter. 'How do you like it?'

'Mmmmnnn, I've only got halfway through the first chapter. So far —' Stella wrinkled her pretty nose.

'— and that's as far as you feel like reading,' finished Kirsty.

Stella burst out laughing which effectively halted her getting-up-from-her-bed process. 'Don't make me laugh, Mum, or I'll never make it up.'

Sambo, indignant at having his peaceful slumber so rudely disturbed, gave his usual plaintive meow and gazed reproachfully at his young mistress, his green eyes glowing emerald in the dimness of the room. His long, thick black tail gave a tentative twitch or two but his heart wasn't really in it.

'He'll follow you out within ten minutes,' observed Kirsty. She kept an unobtrusive eye on the progress of her daughter, who slowly, painfully, taking one careful step after another, made her way out to the sitting room. Stella's hands grasped at both walls and furniture to balance her unsteady steps.

Stella was breathless when she finally collapsed onto the battered old divan. Sure enough, by the time she had recovered and settled herself comfortably, a somewhat disgruntled Sambo was padding across the sitting room floor.

Kirsty returned to her daughter's bedroom to strip the bed. Stooping to retrieve a number of objects from beneath the bed, she noticed a crumpled sheet of paper which had somehow got wedged beneath a heavy, wooden bed leg. It was entitled *Worksheet for Jane Austen's Emma*. Kirsty read the first question: *Discuss the relationship between Emma Woodhouse and Harriet Smith. Did Harriet benefit at all from Emma's friendship? Would Harriet have been better without Emma's friendship?*

Kirsty's eyebrows rose as she studied the sheet. She foresaw struggles ahead. Although strongly approving of the classics, she often felt that those who selected the set English books for New South Wales high school students needed a good kick. Wryly, she recollected that fateful term during Toby's high school years when a deluded English teacher had dropped *Catch 22* on a class of incredulous sixteen-year-olds. It had not actually been a set book but the teacher had misguidedly decided it would benefit her advanced English class. Even Toby, an avid reader and excellent student, had rebelled.

'Mum, I'm not reading that rubbish about men falling in love with each other!' he had exclaimed, dropping the thick paperback on the kitchen table.

Toby's entire class had refused to read *Catch 22*. The class had been asked to write an essay about the novel and one of Toby's enterprising friends had written: *school students should not be expected to read such crap. It is a complete waste of time.*

The short-sighted teacher had raged and ranted at the class, failed just about everyone and taken the single paragraph written by Toby's friend to the headmaster. Nobody was ever quite sure what happened in the headmaster's office but suddenly all the copies of *Catch 22* were taken up by the head of the English department, the class was given nice new editions of Orwell's *1984*, and Toby's friend became the class hero. Still, today, the words *Catch 22* produced a burst of laughter from Toby.

Kirsty smoothed out the crumpled worksheet as best she could before laying it on Stella's desk. For perhaps the tenth time she mentally recalled the wording of Deswyn Fairchild's note:

Dear Mrs Richards,

Please don't think I am trying to butt in or interfere in any way but I wondered if Stella could possibly make use of this. It is about a year old and proved very helpful to my aunt. I believe that many people find them extremely beneficial but they do not work for everyone. It seems to depend on the medical condition being treated as well as the person's physiology. But the great thing is, if it cannot help Stella, it certainly cannot harm her.

Kindest regards,

Deswyn Fairchild

Kirsty had opened the box earlier that morning, stared in bewilderment at the medley of contents and sat down with the instruction manual. Slowly and carefully she learned about

Transcutaneous Electrical Nerve Stimulation being used to control and manage severe pain.

The device was called a TENS machine. Insulated wires ending in flat paddles ran from a small, battery operated control box. The paddles were attached to the skin by use of a sticky gel and the control unit sent out small electrical impulses. The settings were controlled by the user. Despite Kirsty's first impressions, it appeared amazingly simple to operate.

Kirsty's first reaction had been sheer rage. In the eight months of Stella's illness why had this never been even suggested, let alone tried? What the blazes did all the doctors and hospital people think they were playing at? Okay, this TENS thing probably wouldn't work but they had to keep looking for solutions; they had to try and keep on trying. If Stella's pain couldn't be brought under better control, the girl would soon be completely crippled, a mass of twisted, distorted limbs. Didn't these medical idiots have any idea what it was like to watch your own child suffer from pain day after day, night after night, with no end in sight?

Her second reaction had been to get started immediately: attach the machine to Stella and see what happened. Long after that day, she was to wonder what had held her back. Was it the fear that the TENS machine would bring no relief to Stella? Fear that here was yet another possible solution that worked for some people but not for her daughter? So many hopes had been built upon and had come crashing down.

This had been followed by caution. Perhaps it would be best to wait and talk this over with Max. But Max was away from home, looking at sheep on a run near Euabalong and not expected back till the day after tomorrow at the earliest. She silently cursed Max and his Merino sheep, along with the recent announcement by the Australian Government of the suspension of the Wool Reserve

Price Scheme.

Next had come the urge to call Deswyn. Kirsty's hand had already been reaching for the telephone when she paused. What, after all, could the younger woman tell her that she hadn't written in the note? A long discussion on the pros and cons of TENS machines would serve no use. The thing would either help Stella or it would not. The ball was totally in Kirsty's court and she was baulking the issue. Deswyn had more than done her part.

Again the desire for Max's counsel had almost overwhelmed her. But Max was not here: probably at this very moment he was running expert hands over a fine Merino ewe, assessing her quality. Kirsty had the telephone number of the sheep run hosting his visit but it had long been understood between them that she never called him except in dire emergencies.

Kirsty had mechanically performed her usual morning tasks, her mind stubbornly returning to the TENS machine. Now she stood in Stella's bedroom, staring out as the late summer rain continued to stream down. It certainly was late summer rain as tomorrow would be the first day of autumn. The part of her that was countrywoman born and bred thought of the dams, the dry paddocks, and the thirsty gardens. Every few points made such a difference when you lived on the land. This would certainly put some life into her poor hydrangeas. So many English immigrants had planted a hydrangea walk in their new Australian bush gardens and Max's grandmother had been no exception. Kirsty had come to love the shrubs with their huge, beautiful, showy blooms in varying shades of blue. She stood for a few minutes longer, revelling in the sound and sight of the rain. For a moment she felt a longing to go outside and just stand there, soaking up the gift from the heavens till she was saturated all through by the cleansing drops. Kirsty laughed at herself — but still — fresh water truly was the lifeblood of existence.

She was roused from her abstraction by the dining room clock striking eleven. Slowly her eyes travelled around her daughter's bedroom, a veritable temple to Equus caballus, the horse. One photographic enlargement showed a beautiful black mare ridden by a happy, healthy, laughing girl. It had been taken ten months ago at the Royal. Something within Kirsty snapped.

'What is that thing, Mum?'

Kirsty, looking down at her daughter on the divan bed, saw that *Emma* had been replaced by *The Morgan Horse* magazine which Kendrick Tenny still sent over regularly. Kendrick Tenny was a very old man now, still living on his farm in Vermont. The farm was managed by his son-in-law and grandson but Kendrick's word was still law in all things that mattered.

'It's called a TENS machine.' Kirsty put the open box on the sturdy mahogany coffee table next to the divan.

'TENS machine?'

'Transcutaneous Electrical Nerve Stimulation.'

'Golly, what a mouthful. What does it do?'

'It might help you a bit with pain control.' Kirsty was very careful not to build up her daughter's hopes too much.

Stella's expression brightened and she looked up at her mother expectantly.

'You'll have to help me,' Kirsty continued. 'We're both learning together here. You can start by moving that cat out of the way. We need your legs unencumbered by furry obstacles.'

Sambo, whose purr currently resembled the sound of a gently bubbling kettle not quite on the boil, was displeased at being disturbed. He leapt down to the floor and watched the proceedings balefully from a short distance.

'Good job you're wearing shorts. Makes things easier.' Kirsty skillfully rearranged the pillows beneath Stella's legs.

The girl watched with interest as Kirsty fitted the wired paddles to the control box and tested them against her own palm.

'What can you feel?'

'A very mild sort of tingling. Quite pleasant.' Kirsty experimented with the control dials.

Under the keen eyes of Stella and Sambo, Kirsty switched the machine off and applied a clear gel to the four paddles at the end of the wires. She then gave Stella the control unit while she placed two paddles on each of her daughter's legs, attaching them each side of the lower thigh, about four inches above the knee.

'I'm not sure they'll stay in place if I don't keep perfectly still, Mum.'

'Soon fix that. Just keep still for now.'

Kirsty returned with several bandages, two of which she used to secure the paddles firmly in place.

'That should do the trick.' She tied off the second bandage neatly.

'It feels fine, Mum.' Stella carefully moved her left leg a little.

Kirsty rechecked the instruction manual. 'We'll start you off with thirty minutes on a low setting. Slow and steady seems the way to go.'

'Like the tortoise beat the hare, right?'

Hearing the hope in her daughter's voice, seeing the barely controlled eager expectation in her daughter's face, Kirsty sent up a plea. *Please God, please God, make this work for her. Please make it work for my beautiful daughter who doesn't deserve this suffering.*

'Pass me the control box, Stella.'

Kirsty checked the settings and switched the small machine on.

'Can you feel anything yet?'

Stella shook her head.

'I'll turn it up very slowly. Make sure you tell me as soon as you feel something.'

Sambo chose that precise moment to jump back up to rejoin his young mistress. Only swift action by Kirsty prevented furry paws and insulated wires getting tangled. Sambo was banished via the front door.

'Let's try this one more time.' Kirsty picked up the control box again.

'Where did you get it from?'

'Get what?'

'This machine. I can feel it now.' Stella stared fixedly at her legs as if she should be able to actually see something happening.

'Strong or faint?'

'Only just — it's barely there.'

'We'll leave it like that for the first time. Hare and tortoise, remember? Thirty minutes starting from now.' Kirsty checked her watch.

'Where did the machine come from?'

'Deswyn Fairchild sent it over. It belonged to her aunt. Toby brought it back from the Farmers meeting last night.'

'Ah,' Stella spoke thoughtfully.

'What is it, child?'

'Nothing, Mum.' She settled herself as comfortably as possible against her pillows. Not for the world would Stella disclose what she truly believed to be a secret known only to herself.

Kirsty put the control box on the coffee table. If this actually worked (and it probably wouldn't) she would have to create some means of attaching the device to Stella's clothing. Perhaps a special sort of pocket which could be pinned to whatever her daughter was wearing.

Returning to check Stella some fifteen minutes later, Kirsty paused and stood quietly. *The Morgan Horse* had slipped to the floor and Sambo was again curled up next to his mistress, his bubbling purr resumed. Stella was sound asleep, but was there a very slight tinge of colour in her cheeks, an easing of the tightness around her mouth, a barely perceptible lessening of the rigidity in her legs?

Kirsty told herself that it was quite ludicrous to imagine she could see any change in Stella. She gave herself a firm mental shake and returned to the kitchen.

Chapter Fourteen: Toby Richards

Toby was riding home on Jester. The bay colt, now three and a half years of age, was fulfilling his earlier promise. Misty, Jester's dam, was half Morgan, half brumby Welsh pony cross, her sire having been Son of Saratoga. Max Richards had sent Misty (whose official designation was Saratoga Mist) to the best Morgan stallion in the state so the resultant foal, Jester, was three-quarters Morgan.

Jester (officially designated as Saratoga Jolly Jester) was showing all the characteristics of the Morgan breed. His coat, a rich mahogany bay, was perfect foil to the growing black waterfall of a mane and the high set tail. His well-defined head sat upon an upright, strongly arched neck. The powerful, compact body was short backed with well-muscled hindquarters and chest. He stood proudly on strong, clean legs which bore no white markings. Best of all in Toby's eyes, the colt possessed intelligence, stamina and a good temperament.

Toby had been three months shy of twelve when he'd been sent to school down in Sydney, the same Jesuit school his father had attended. Before that he had attended the one-roomed bush school at the Crossroads, complete with its single, dedicated teacher, water tank on a wooden stand and fifteen children aged between four and twelve. He had ridden the five mile distance twice a day on his pony, Casper.

The teacher, city born and bred, must have been a remarkable person. As well as showing youngsters barely able to grip a pencil between chubby fingers the first steps in reading and writing and preparing older students for high school, he had to deal with issues that were definitely not covered at teachers college, nor met at the larger urban schools. His early days at the Crossroads had been an education of the sort not found in the text books.

One boy rolled up to school complete with the family milking cow.

'She be in my charge,' he had laconically explained. 'You got better grazing in this schoolyard than us got back home. Me old man said if I gotta waste time gettin' some schoolin' then Daisy here best get some good of it. We ain't got much land.' He affectionally rubbed the placid cow behind one ear before adding, 'She'd soon keep the grass down for you, mister.'

A girl arrived with a toddler clasped to one hip. The rucksack on her back held both her school books and the infant's requirements for the day.

'Mum's sick,' she told the teacher, 'and there's no one to look after Jack. He won't be a bother, I promise. I'll just fence off a corner of the verandah for him and put down his blanket and toys.'

'Is your mother very ill?' asked the teacher.

'Cancer,' replied the girl stoically. 'Dad shot through as soon as he knew she was dying. We won't be seeing him again, that's for sure.'

Little Jack had indeed played quietly in his corner, been attended to at recess and during the luncheon hour and slept peacefully throughout the hot afternoon.

One small girl didn't bring anything to eat for recess or luncheon. An older girl, one arm protectively around the smaller child's thin shoulders, enlightened the teacher:

'It's not her fault, sir. Her mum's a bit out of it some days.'

The teacher had given the little girl his own lunch. He soon discovered that Mum took refuge in the gin bottle when life got too much for her, which was pretty well all the time.

One morning most of the older children were absent. When he had asked if anyone knew why, he was stared at in amazement.

'Fruit picking,' piped up a small girl with dark red plaits: one Deswyn Fairchild.

'Fruit picking?'

'Yes, sir. They started picking on Saturday,' explained the girl's twin brother. 'We're not allowed to go,' he added in a grieved tone of voice.

'For how long will they be away?'

The class had been thoroughly bewildered by this stupid question. Didn't this teacher know *anything?*

''Till it's all picked,' Deswyn told him kindly.

'I didn't know children picked fruit,' he offered weakly.

'Yep. They go with their mums an' dads,' another boy spoke up. 'Kids can help in tons of ways. When parents let them,' he ended gloomily.

There was a general nod of agreement. Some of the children exchanged rueful glances of understanding.

The teacher, one Mr Neil Moffat, quickly grasped the fact that a long spell of drought brought its own issues. School had just started one morning when he thought he heard the sounds of bleating, a sort of soft baa-baa baa-ing noise.

He cast a sharp glance around the classroom but the dozen children present were industriously copying from the blackboard. No child wore the overly innocent expression which belied trouble.

He took a deep breath and pulled himself together. He really must stop imagining things. Since he had come to the Crossroads his once clear-cut way of thinking had somehow been dimmed. Now he appeared to be hearing invisible sheep.

Returning to the blackboard, Mr Moffat began writing up that week's list of spelling words for his middle group of pupils. He had soon learned the best way to work with a class of mixed ages was to divide the blackboard into three sections. He chalked the words *address* and *breathe* on the painted board and was halfway through *calendar,* when his stick of chalk snapped and fell to the floor in pieces. Bending to collect the scattered fragments, he thought he felt slight movement in the wooden floor boards. Ignoring this ridiculous suspicion, Mr Moffat dropped the chalk fragments in the small bin, picked up a new stick of chalk from the ledge and completed the word *calendar.*

Consider, disappear and *extreme* had been added to the list before the floor boards moved again, this time accompanied by that faint baa-baa baa-ing sound. Resolutely the teacher continued to work and *grammar, height, island* and *knowledge* made their chalky appearance in the centre section of the blackboard. This time he definitely felt movement beneath his feet. Walking over to the closest window, Mr Moffat let out a startled gasp. Twelve heads turned to look up at him, mild enquiry on their faces.

'The schoolyard appears to be full of *sheep!*' spluttered Teacher.

Mr Moffat was quite correct in his surmise. Neatly corralled by the schoolyard fence, a mass of woolly backs, dirty white in colour, heads bent, intent on busily cropping the lush grass, had appeared to have taken possession. The children all stood up to see.

'Your Uncle Jim's let the sheep out again,' Alwyn Fairchild pointed out to the boy sitting next to him: one Stuart Buckley.

Stuart nodded stoically and began packing away his school

books.

'No feed at your place?' asked Toby Richards sympathetically.

Stuart shook his head. 'The bush fires went right through our place and now they've been followed by this long drought. I know Uncle Jim shouldn't really keep doing it but we've got a lot of sheep to feed. He waits till Dad and Grandpa aren't around and lets them out. Old Darkie will be by the gate keeping an eye on them. He can always be trusted with the flock. He's a grand old dog.'

Compassionate nods came from around the room. These children knew all about drought and the appalling ramifications that accompanied it. Young as they were they had all seen animals slowly lose their plump healthy condition, become little more than covered skeletons and eventually die a slow and painful death. Good owners and true stockmen almost always stepped in with a gun before matters reached these lengths but inevitably, especially on the larger properties, occasional tragedies happened. Life in the Australian rural areas could be cruel and the children learned this very early in life.

'I'll tell Dad,' Deswyn Fairchild spoke quietly.

Stuart's head shot up proudly. 'We don't need charity, Desi.'

The girl with the red plaits touched the boy's hand. 'No, but friends can help each other, can't they?'

Stuart bit his lip as he stared at the pretty girl with the serious eyes who understood so well. Finally he spoke gruffly: 'Thanks, Desi,' before returning to tidying away his books.

'What are you doing, Stuart?' Mr Moffat, who had unobtrusively taken in every word exchanged by the children, now asked.

'I'll have to take the sheep back home, sir,' the boy stood up.

The teacher looked at his schoolyard full of woolly backs. The circular iron water tank stood on a low wooden stand from beneath which now protruded dozens of woolly rumps. Over by the open gateway he saw a black and white dog, seemingly relaxed and resting. Mr Moffat had little doubt that any movement of the sheep towards the gateway would bring instant reaction from the animal, which he presumed was a border collie. The man's lips twitched involuntarily as again he thought of his city life and training. How would his colleagues from the inner west and inner southern suburbs of Sydney cope with such a situation?

He would have liked to have assured the boy that the sheep could remain but knew this was impossible. Perhaps he could make the best of both worlds for now.

'Sit down, Stuart. You can take them home at lunchtime.'

'Thank you, sir.' The boy reseated himself wearing a big smile. A whole morning of grazing in that lush schoolyard was really something. But he would have to make Uncle Jim understand that this mustn't happen again.

'Before we return to our spelling, Stuart, what breed of sheep are these?'

'Corriedale, sir,' Stuart spoke proudly.

'I thought all sheep had horns but I see these ones don't.'

An amused ripple ran around the room. Mr Moffat didn't seem to know *anything*.

'Not the Corriedale breed, sir,' said Stuart politely yet firmly.

Mr Moffat picked up his stick of chalk and the spelling lesson was resumed.

The little school at the Crossroads also brought with it some memorial educational encounters of the sort only to be found in a rural bush district. Responsible adults took steps to ensure their children understood that actions had consequences, especially where guns were concerned.

One afternoon a jeep pulled up behind the school. A man clad in the official working clothes of the New South Wales Forestry appeared at the open door of the classroom. Snugly nestled against his left shoulder was a small grey koala.

'That's my Uncle Rob,' whispered a small girl to her desk-mate, 'with Aunt Lucy.'

'Who?'

'Aunt Lucy, of course,' was the hissed reply.

'Who's Aunt Lucy?'

'The baby koala, you clot.'

'Why's she called Aunt Lucy?'

'Paddington's Aunt Lucy, of course.'

'Koalas are not bears,' stated the desk-mate with disapproval.

The forestry ranger's niece looked daggers at her friend. This, she considered, was hitting below the belt. Koalas *looked* like bears so why shouldn't they be named after bears? *Of course* she knew they weren't bears, everyone did, didn't they? About to retaliate with a suitably withering riposte, she was beaten to the post by her teacher.

'Silence!' bellowed Mr Moffat, glaring at the two culprits.

Lips twitching as he discretely observed his small niece, the forestry ranger, one Mr Rob Carr, entered the classroom and shook hands with Mr Moffat. Mr Moffat told his pupils to leave their desks and sit on the floor at the front of the room, close to Mr Carr and his small furry friend.

Despite their rural bush lives, few of the children had ever seen a koala as close as this. They gazed at the small marsupial with delight and wonder, exclaiming at the thick, ash grey fur, the large fluffy, soft ears, the black knob of a nose, the small, black button shaped eyes, the white furred rump and the appealing expression.

Whilst Mr Carr talked, holding the class entranced, the teacher busied himself at the blackboard transcribing the ranger's words. Aunt Lucy gazed benignly at the children, enchanting them with her serious expression, her five-fingered front paws clutching firmly to her protector's shirt.

The ranger explained that koalas were extremely finicky eaters. When feeding an orphan such as Aunt Lucy it was essential to find eucalyptus leaves not contaminated with pollutants or poisonous chemicals. Eucalyptus, high in water and low in energy or calories, formed the sole source of nutrition for the koala, who needed to sleep as much as twenty hours a day.

A wave of anger reverberated around the room as Mr Carr told how he had found the young koala joey still clinging to her dead mother's back. Visiting thrill seekers had shot the adult mother, finding her ideal target practice for their new rifles. The joey was about nine months old and fortunately had been found almost immediately after her mother's death.

Aunt Lucy's story resulted in hisses and muttered expletives from the boys and cheeks wet with tears from the girls. The lesson had been well and truly learnt, driven home with a sure hand.

Mr Moffat soon learnt that education was not always regarded with a friendly eye by rural families. A boy of eleven could, in many ways, do a man's job on the farm and some parents had no intention of allowing their sons to remain in school until the age of fifteen as New South Wales legislation decreed.

Despite the differing views of education, these country children had a pride in their land that he had found missing in the city schools. Each morning the fresh young voices sang *God Save the*

Queen as if they truly meant it. There was no shuffling of feet or whispered asides, no nudging of neighbours or giggling. They stood tall, backs straight, heads high, eyes bright and clear.

One of the weekly highlights was the singing program on ABC radio. After lunch Mr Moffat, whose tiny cottage was across the lane from the school, would carefully transport his treasured radio to the classroom, where songs would be learned that would travel with these children all their lives. The young voices sang out clear and sweet and the strains of Australian folk songs would reach any who might be passing the Crossroads at that hour. *The Dying Stockman, Travelling Down the Castlereagh, Botany Bay, Waltzing Matilda, The Queensland Drover* and *Click Go the Shears* were perhaps the traditional Australian country favourites, yet many other songs were taught and loved. It was a very catholic selection: the Irish ballad, *The Gypsy Rover;* the Negro spiritual, *Dem Bones,* which was sung with such enthusiasm and gusto; the Scottish song called *Football Crazy* and translated from Spanish, *Señor Don Gato* and his cat: all these and more became part of the children's repertoire for the annual school concert.

The idea of a high school at Koolkuna had not yet even been thought of when three very nervous youngsters left for Sydney by train, accompanied by Mrs Ifanna Fairchild. Deswyn definitely thought she was getting the worst of the deal.

'It's okay for you two.' She glared at her twin brother and Toby Richards who were sitting in the two seats opposite. 'At least you know each other. I won't know anyone at all!' She gave her new school hat a vicious twist with restless fingers.

'Please stop mauling that hat, Deswyn, and put it back on your head where it belongs.'

Hearing the note of steel in her mother's voice, Deswyn obeyed, albeit as reluctantly as she dared.

'Cheer up, Des, we'll be able to visit,' Toby said encouragingly. He turned to Mrs Fairchild. 'We will, won't we? Be able to visit Des?'

She smiled and nodded. Content for the moment, the three children settled back in their seats with books.

Ifanna Fairchild was seriously worried. This was the first time the twins had ever been separated for more than a day. Both children were taking it hard although neither said much. There was another thing: back at Cheshunt, Kirsty Richards was pregnant again. As the train steadily moved towards Sydney, Ifanna could not help but be aware that major changes were taking place in both families.

Toby's steadfastness was a major part of his character: what couldn't be cured must be endured, and as quietly as possible. People who thought his quietness indicated a lack of courage soon realised their mistake — Toby could fight for what he believed in.

The twins, physically as similar as fraternal twins could be, were inseparable and very dissimilar in character. Deswyn was quick to react, talkative and had a vivid imagination. Alwyn always thought long and hard before he spoke, never talked unless strictly necessary and had no imagination whatsoever. Both had the temper so often associated with red hair. Deswyn lost her temper quickly and often, then forgot all about it ten minutes later. Alwyn's rages would build very slowly over time, climaxing in wild outbursts which left him distressed for many days afterwards. This would happen perhaps twice a year.

Each child's entrance to boarding school was typical of that young person. Whilst unpacking his small case in his dormitory, Toby took out a framed photograph of his mother on Son of Saratoga and placed it carefully on his half of the chest of drawers.

'Who is that?' demanded a boy, gaping at the lovely woman on the magnificent Morgan horse.

'My mother.'

'Liar!' said the boy, who was commencing his second term and therefore felt entitled to throw his weight around so far as the new boys were concerned.

Toby looked at the boy steadily. Very few people realised exactly what Toby's mother meant to him. She was more than a mother: she was a person to be cherished, loved and most of all, protected.

'Liar!' the boy said again, louder.

Toby looked at the photograph and then back at the boy.

'That babe isn't your mum!' sneered the boy.

The boy never saw the blow that knocked him to the floor. The second punch was administered by Alwyn, not in anger but in a sense of justice, fair play and loyalty. Toby sat on his adversary's chest and Alwyn on his legs. Their dormitory mates watched in awe.

'That lady is my mother. You don't call her babe,' Toby stated calmly.

A pair of frightened, pale blue eyes stared up at him. Beneath the bravado, like all bullies, this boy was a coward.

'Understand?' demanded Toby.

'Y-y-yes.'

'And don't call me a liar.'

'N-n-no.'

'Get up,' Toby ordered, rolling off the boy's chest.

Alwyn got to his feet in a leisurely manner, rubbing his hands on his shorts, as if to rid them of something distasteful. Grins were exchanged among the watching boys. The grins changed to reluctant respect when Toby thrust out his hand out to his foe.

'Shake?'

With a look that combined disbelief, shame and admiration, the boy responded:

'Shake.'

It was at least three weeks later when Alwyn spoke to Toby:

'You know Molony — the chap we had a spot of bother with on the first day?'

'Yes, what about him?'

'I think he's all right.'

'Take you this long to decide?' Toby grinned.

'Well, I like to be sure about things — take my own time.'

'Idiot!' His friend gave him a friendly buffet. 'Let's go look at the cricket field. The first eleven are practising.'

Several miles away Deswyn was also unpacking her small night bag. At the moment she was alone in her four bed dormitory at her new school. Soberly she looked at the writing case her mother had given her as a parting gift. Like her mother, the little compendium combined practical with pretty and lacked nothing. Envelopes and writing-paper that matched, postcards, a sheet of ten cent stamps, a biro pen and two lead pencils, all fitted neatly in a leather folder. The folder was pale blue with the outline of a golden horse stamped in one corner. Tears filled Deswyn's eyes as one finger gently stroked the stamped horse; she thought of dear chestnut Susie back at Bellara. Approaching footsteps warned her and stopped the tears from becoming a flow. Hastily she rubbed at her eyes with the hem of her very new school frock. Three people entered the dormitory.

Deswyn recognised the lady who had welcomed her and her mother earlier and shown them to this room. Her name was Miss Milford. She spoke to Deswyn:

'Deswyn, this is another new girl, Donna Elliott,' and then turned to the smartly dressed, pleasant looking elderly woman accompanying her.

'Mrs Elliott, Deswyn comes from the country out beyond the Blue Mountains, near Koolkuna. She had a long train journey to get here.'

Mrs Elliott looked at Deswyn with interest and smiled. 'What a huge adventure for you, Deswyn. You must tell Donna about the country. She's always lived in Sydney.'

Deswyn looked at the third member of the trio. She saw a girl about her own height with a warm olive skin, high cheek bones, full lips, enormous brown eyes and masses of thick black hair. Her hair was severely restrained in two tight plaits but appeared to be fighting its bonds. If left to its own pleasure it would riot in all directions. The eyes of the two girls met.

'Hello, Deswyn.'

'Hello, Donna.'

They smiled awkwardly at each other.

'You two girls will have this room to yourselves for the first week or two,' said Miss Milford. She explained: 'Christine came down with mumps three days ago, much to her poor mother's annoyance.' She smiled and continued, '… and Karen broke her collarbone last week. She's having a pretty bad time of it, I'm afraid. I gather she's most upset because it has ruined her summer's tennis!'

'Is she a very keen player?' asked Mrs Elliott.

'Indeed she is, and a very good one at that. She has been our junior school champion for the past three years. Karen would spend every moment of the day out on the tennis courts if it were allowed.'

Deswyn wondered if she would be expected to play tennis. Never having held a racquet in her life, she sincerely hoped not.

Some hours later two small girls lay awake. The pretty blue floral curtains had been pulled across the two windows but it was not yet fully dark. Daylight saving was now in its third year in New South Wales.

'Did you want to come here?' Deswyn couldn't stand the silence any longer.

'I don't really know,' replied the other girl.

'What do you mean?' demanded Deswyn, sitting bolt upright in her bed.

'It sounds silly, I know, but you see, I had to go somewhere and I suppose this place could be okay.'

'Why did you have to come to boarding school if you live in Sydney? Are your Mum and Dad going away?'

There was quite a lengthy pause before Donna spoke in a tight little voice:

'My mother died two years ago. That was my grandmother who came with me today. My father has just married again —' the small voice became unsteady and hesitated, '— and she doesn't like me very much — his new wife — so they decided to send me away to school. Grandmother — she's Dad's mother — doesn't like Michelle either — she's the new wife. Grandmother wants me to go and live with her but Dad and Michelle won't agree. They're afraid about what people might say. Grandmother chose this school so it's sure not to be too bad. My mother —' here the voice faltered again. 'My mother was so beautiful and so kind — she came from Italy.'

Deswyn listened in mounting horror. As Donna finished speaking, Deswyn bounded out of bed and shot across the room, throwing her arms around the other girl. Normally loquacious, Deswyn searched desperately for something comforting to say to this poor, unwanted girl. Suddenly she had a brainwave:

'Do you speak Italian?' she demanded.

The other girl nodded through the tears which were now silently falling.

'Say something in Italian then,' ordered Deswyn.

'Penso che possiamo ese amici.'

'What does that mean?' Deswyn sounded awed.

'I think we can be friends,' replied Donna, smiling through her tears.

The two girls hugged each other.

By the time Deswyn, Alwyn and Toby returned home for the August school holidays, all three had accepted life at boarding school in their own way. It was a very special holiday, that August, for in July, Kirsty Richards had been safely delivered at full term of an extremely lively, healthy, baby girl. On the last Sunday of the holidays, Estelle Eleanor Richards was christened in the tiny, sandstone church at the Crossroads.

Saint Paul's Anglican Church at the Crossroads dated back to 1849. Its walls were twenty inches thick, keeping out the heat on the hottest days in summer and the steeply pitched roof was slate. What fascinated the children was the tiny bell tower mounted on the western end of the nave roof. Made from sandstone, it was a bell tower reduced to its simplest form: a bell cote or housing from which the bell hung.

An English visitor might have found something incongruous in the setting: a bare, dry paddock not yet recovered from a drought-stricken winter, a scattering of native gum trees and a fence of rusty barbed wire straggling between parched wooden posts. A cattle grid had been laid between the gate posts.

It was cool and dark inside the church, the gothic arched windows allowing little natural light to enter. The rich colours of the memorial window to Martha Rose Richards dimly cast their light upon Martha's grandson. Toby stood proudly beside his mother in the front pew of the cantoris side, his mind very much fixed on the present. In front of him, baby Estelle slept peacefully in her well sprung English pram.

The Fairchild family were seated across the aisle in the second pew of the decani side. Deswyn was annoyed because she could not see the octagonal baptismal font, located as it was at the west end of the church and so behind her back. She had lingered by it on entering the church, gently running a finger across the intricately carved sandstone until a sharp nudge between her shoulder blades had moved her on. She would deal with her brother later, she fumed silently. Aware of her mother's reproving gaze, Deswyn hastily picked up her prayer book.

Toby reined in Jester and leaned down to unhook the chain which secured the five-barred gate leading to the fire trail. He had enjoyed his time with Old Dan, glad that today's work had taken him in the direction of Brackens Bend. Toby had grinned ruefully as Old Dan recollected the past:

'You were pretty put out when the Boss first told you about that college place.'

'Yes, I know, Dan. Bloody fool, wasn't I?'

Toby had been frankly appalled at his father's gentle but firm insistence on agricultural college. He had been counting the days until he could leave school and join his father and the men on Cheshunt, determined to prove to both them and himself that he could do a real man's work on the land. He had tried to explain this to his father only to receive the following reply:

'Son, you will be of far more use to me and to Cheshunt with the thorough training and schooling a good agricultural college can give you. To succeed on the land today it is essential to combine both tradition and new ideas, to get the right balance and to get the balance right. Call it investing in the future if you like. Experience of farming in another state will only add to your knowledge.'

'Another state?' This was getting worse by the minute! Good grief, the next thing the old man would suggest sending him to South America! After six years at a Sydney boarding school all he wanted to do was stay at home and work on the land, the land that was in his blood.

'Yes, there's a very good place near Adelaide, not far from Gawler where they do all the eventing. That should interest you, even if the thought of agricultural and horticultural studies doesn't at this moment,' his father had finished drily.

Outwardly he had complied with Max's wishes but inwardly he was rebellious. Hoping for a touch of sympathy Toby had ridden out to see Old Dan.

'Looks as if I'm going to be sent away to college, Dan.'

The man had looked sharply at him. 'Feelin' sorry for ourselves, are we?'

Toby flushed a deep scarlet, something which had not happened for years. He suddenly felt very small, younger even than the baby sister twelve years his junior.

'Are ye thinking of yerself or Cheshunt?' The vivid blue eyes had stared out accusingly.

'I can't see why we need to change things,' the boy spoke in a low voice. 'Cheshunt is just fine as it is now. Mum and Dad have made it perfect.'

'Lad, for anything in life to succeed there's gotta be some change. Mayhap on the land more than any place else. Nothing stands still. It's not so easy to make a good living from nor but sheep and cattle, not anymore it isn't. It's the folks who give a few acres to this and a few acres to that — still keepin' on the stock, to be sure, if ye must — but lookin' to other ways and means. Some of those folks that put a bare ten acres under olives are making a rare killin' from them. Garlic's another, then there's those funny lookin' mushrooms at the Sayer place over the range — they started in a very small way and are now supplyin' half the Sydney fancy eat joints. But a man's gotta know what he's at. No use puttin' down olives where the soil's bad for 'em, now is it? Nor garlic or frilly mushrooms where the blighters won't grow, eh? *That's* why the Boss wants you all up to date with these things. Change has to come but in the right way.' The old man shrugged. 'I dunno, it's a fair heavy load to put on the green shoulders of a lad like yourself. The Boss is asking a lot of you — dunno if it ain't be a tad too much.'

Inwardly chuckling, Old Dan added more water to the billycan over the hot coals. From the corner of his eye he watched as the boy stiffened. Old Dan saw the shoulders — they were already broad and well-muscled for a youngster that age — jerk back. The head shot up and the jaw tightened. For a long moment, fire burned in the brown eyes as they glared at the man whose entire world was Cheshunt and the Richards family. Then young Toby relaxed and laughed.

'Dan! You old devil! You said that on purpose!'

Old Dan carefully added a few gum leaves to the billycan.

Toby stared into the dwindling fire. His nostrils twitched appreciatively as the aromatic smell from the billycan reached him.

Beside the sandstone hut was a small yard. It had been painstakingly constructed from split logs and, like all Old Dan's work, was solid, neat and practical. At this moment the yard housed the mare that Toby was riding that day. The chestnut mare was a half-bred Morgan, legacy of that famous visit to Cheshunt by Kendrick Tenny and Son of Saratoga when Toby had been seven years old. Her proper name was Lady Arietta but for workaday purposes she was known as Etta.

Etta stood peacefully in a corner of the yard, her silky nose buried in the contents of a hay-net. The hay-net was the product of Old Dan's nimble fingers, woven from nylon baling twine during the long winter evenings. The mare stamped a hoof and gave a quiet whicker of contentment.

The boy spoke abruptly:

'My dad had a pretty hard time when he was my age, didn't he?'

The older man slowly removed the makings of a cigarette from the breast pocket of his long-sleeved khaki shirt. A single rectangular sheet of rice paper was withdrawn from the tiny envelope packet. The small tin with rounded corners supplied the necessary pinch of richly smelling tobacco. Calmly and deliberately the paper was filled with tobacco, cradled and rolled between dexterous fingers and moistened with a quick lick from the tongue. The completed cigarette was then eyed with satisfaction before being held to the hot coals and slid between the waiting lips.

'Did he tell ye that?' The blue eyes were quizzical. A thin ribbon of blue-grey cigarette smoke curled skywards.

Toby looked indignant at the mere suggestion: 'Dan, you know he didn't! Dad would never say anything like that.'

The man who had returned from the hell-hole of the Second World War with Cecil Lewis Richards in 1946, who had known three generations of Richards males better than they knew themselves, looked steadily at the youngest of them. This boy had the right stuff in him; he would make a proper man someday and that day was not that far off. The Boss was right about this college stunt and, if he knew the Boss, college was not the only surprise waiting for young Toby down the track.

Old Dan was well aware of what the boy must have heard locally about his grandparents and his dad. There were plenty of clacking tongues running loose, especially among the womenfolk and as for that General Store, Mrs Underwood exchanged a bit of gossip with every sale she made over her counter. A pound of frozen peas would be accompanied by:

'… and the way that poor lady died was right cruel. Such things ought not to be allowed. If it hadn't been for that husband of hers, not to mention that doctor, Martha Rose Richards would still be alive today, I shouldn't wonder. Should have been struck off, he should. Would have been too, if it hadn't been for the War.'

A ball of twine might get the purchaser:

'… and that child was barely twelve when his mother died and look what he had for a father! Never the same since he came home from the War. That's when the drinking took over.'

And the fortunate buyer of machine-knitted woollen work socks would be honoured by:

'A youngster of seventeen, still at school he was, down in Sydney. Left with no parents and all that great property to manage. Don't know how in the world he managed it, I don't.'

Old Dan strongly disapproved of women in general and

especially Mrs Underwood and her cronies. Such a look of disgust momentarily crossed his face that Toby waited in trepidation for the blast. It never came.

'Your dad had a fair bad time for a while but tis not my place to be telling' ye about it. He'll tell ye when he's fair and ready. Pay no mind to that old biddy at the General Store, not her nor her like. Talk helps no-one. Go to that fancy college place and mind you do it with the right spirit and no chip on ye shoulder.'

Toby's three years at the South Australian agricultural college had been followed by eighteen months hard work as a station hand in the Northern Territory.

'Hard labour,' Toby ruefully called it.

'Knocked all the airy-fairy nonsense out of ye and brought ye down to size by teachin' ye a bit about real life,' was how Old Dan put it.

Ifanna Fairchild, godmother to Stella, had died during Toby's second year at college. The reins of Bellara quietly passed into the eighteen-year-old hands of Ifanna and David's daughter, Deswyn, and remained there ever since.

Toby, riding homeward on Jester, reached down and patted the hot bay neck.

Chapter Fifteen: Koolkuna High School

Stella lay on what was generally known as Stella's Couch in the school sickbay of Koolkuna High School. The school sickbay was actually comprised of two rooms: there was the small room with a single bed in which Stella now lay and a larger room with three beds, divided by curtains. She switched on the TENS machine and waited for the now familiar tingle to *find itself*, as she called it. Once that happened she could regulate the pulse rate and set the timer for thirty minutes.

Life had definitely changed since the arrival of the TENS machine. Max summed it up most succinctly if not with total accuracy:

'No sixteen-year-old would be prepared to put up with that rigmarole of telephone wires swinging all over the place, not to mention all those idiotic questions thrown at her by thoughtless nincompoops — asking if she is listening to the radio indeed! — unless she derived a great deal of assistance from it.'

The wired paddles did not swing all over the place — they were neatly bandaged into place every morning by Kirsty, remaining so until late in the afternoon. The neat pocket which Kirsty had cleverly contrived for the control unit was unobtrusively pinned to Stella's clothing.

Several weeks after the introduction of the TENS machine Stella asked to return to school. Somewhat dubiously Max paid a visit to Koolkuna High and laid his cards on the table. The result of a fairly short but serious talk with the assistant principal had been almost too good to be true. In short, the man told Max that as long as Stella showed up at school, the school would do the rest. *In fact,* the assistant principal had suggested, *why not get her started tomorrow morning? After all, Stella has already missed a great many weeks of schooling and year eleven is a vitally important year in her education.*

Max had agreed and shaken hands warmly with the assistant principal, keeping his many doubts to himself. On returning to Cheshunt, Kirsty received the news with restrained hope, Stella with delight.

The school exceeded all expectations. Stella attended classes where possible. When she could no longer sit upright in her special chair or when the pain levels rose beyond control, one of the male teachers would carry her to the sickbay. *Stella's Couch,* as the sickbay bed which had been permanently allocated to her came to be called, became her base at the school. Teachers would work with her in sickbay, in their rare free half hours. Friends would bring their work to the sickbay and help Stella catch up on the many weeks of lessons she had missed. More than half her school time was spent in this room.

The situation at Koolkuna High was complicated by the fact it was built on a split-level plan; there were stairs everywhere and they were *narrow* stairs. As far as was practical the teachers kept Stella to the ground floor. When this was not possible she was carried up and down the stairs. One senior teacher laughingly joked to Stella that his fitness level had never been better. With all the weight carrying up and down the stairs she was forcing him to do, he was actually developing some muscles.

This happy, positive and helpful approach to Stella was the hallmark of the teachers at Koolkuna High. The sole standout was a female teacher, who, for no discernible reason, developed a decided hostility to the partially crippled girl.

There were many days when Stella never left her sickbay bed, yet it was still much better for her to be at school learning what she could. The assistant principal had been most positive on that point. Other days were better and Stella slowly limped her way around a small part of the school, one hand always grasping for the security of a wall or railing, struggling on to her next destination and always attached to her TENS machine. She quickly learnt to snap at people who mistook the TENS machine for a radio. Explanations were tiresome and took too much of her precious energy and if people were so stupid as to confuse the two, well they didn't jolly well deserve a polite response.

Stella sighed and gingerly manoeuvred onto her left side, easing the pressure on her right leg. It had been one of her very tough days and she probably would have been better off at home. Right now she longed for the comforting familiarity of her own room and bed. She also wanted her mother quite badly. Mum was always able to make things seem easier to manage; she always knew what was needed at any given time.

Stella got through first period English pretty well but it was during second period Geography that the pain levels started to rise. Nerolee Turner, seated next to Stella, immediately noted her friend's stress and, whispering, suggested she leave the class. Stella, shaking her head, quickly returned a negative reply. She would wait till the class was over. Miss Erin Butler, the young teacher conducting the class, quickly caught on to the problem. Moving to her young pupil's side she spoke quietly and with compassion:

'Stella, would you like to go to sickbay?'

The girl looked up at her with such obvious pain in those beautiful grey eyes that the teacher had been forced to take a grip on herself to avoid showing her distress.

'Nerolee, Mr Ellingham is teaching two rooms down. Would you please tell him that Stella Richards need some help. He'll know what you mean.'

Nerolee, only too pleased to be given a legitimate excuse to leave the much detested grid references, compass points and keys of map reading, gave her friend a sympathetic glance and sped off in search of Mr Ellingham.

Miss Butler quietly assisted Stella to pack up the things on her desk. Nerolee then returned to the room, Mr Ellingham hard on her heels. The two teachers exchanged a few brief words then Mr Ellingham picked Stella up and carried her to the sickbay. Ordered to do so by Miss Butler, Nerolee followed with Stella's school bag.

'Do you want me to call your mother, Stella?' Mr Ellingham asked, once his burden had been carefully deposited upon the sickbay bed.

'No, thanks, I think I'll be fine,' had been her rather wavering reply.

'Can I get you anything or do anything to help you? What about pain killers?'

'I've got my own stuff, thank you sir.'

'I'll check in with you at the end of the period.' He smiled at her and left the room.

Nerolee, who had been hovering in the background, now covered Stella with the small blanket folded at the foot of the bed. 'Do you need a hand with painkillers, Stella?'

Rather wearily the girl on the bed shook her head. 'I can't have anything for a while yet, Nerolee, but thanks anyway. You could get me a drink of water.'

Delighted to be of use, Nerolee went into the adjoining room which contained a small kitchen at one end.

'Look, I know you don't like her but shouldn't I get the first aid teacher?' Nerolee returned with the glass of water.

'Don't you dare!'

'But mightn't she be able to help in some way?'

'No, she might not! She's utterly useless! You're much better help than she is.'

'But Stella,' Nerolee hesitated, not wishing to upset her friend, 'you don't look very well. Your face is chalk white and your neck is a bit swollen.'

Stella gave a small smile. 'How would she be able to help with that? Do stop fussing and if you dare go and find Mrs Munnings I will never speak to you again!'

'All right, all right, but what about calling your mum like Mr Ellingham suggested?'

'Maybe in a while but I'll see how things settle down. The TENS should help.'

'If there is nothing more I can do for you I guess I had better get back to class,' Nerolee spoke with extreme reluctance.

'I could try and think of something more, if you like.' Stella looked up at her friend, the shadow of a twinkle in the weary eyes.

Nerolee chuckled and carried Stella's school bag close to the bed. 'You might need something from your bag in a while.'

Stella half sat up. 'Just as well you said that. My history assignment is due today and history is next period, the last period before recess. Could you give it in to Mr Keane for me?'

'Sure thing.' Nerolee lifted the bag. 'Do you want me to find it?'

'Please do. It's in a bright red folder and should stand out a mile. At least, I hope I haven't forgotten it and left it at home.'

Nerolee, poking around in the school bag, quickly found the vivid scarlet folder. 'All's well, here it is.' She put the folder on the bed and after restoring some order to the school bag, closed it again.

'Thanks, Nerolee, I do appreciate it. A lot of work went into the wretched assignment.'

'I can see that by the thickness of the folder,' said her friend ruefully. 'I just about managed to do the minimum amount demanded by our dear Mr Keane. What did you do it on, by the way?'

'Oliver Cromwell, the case for and against. What about you?'

'Ugh,' Nerolee wrinkled her nose. 'Trust you to do a tough one. I did Queen Anne.'

'Well, that's no pushover.' Stella settled herself more easily on the narrow bed.

'I'll come and see you at recess,' Nerolee promised, moving in the direction of the doorway.

'Great, and thanks for everything.' Stella gave her a little wave.

Stella glanced at her wrist-watch. It was a quarter to eleven. She must have dosed off for a while because she had never noticed Mr Ellingham's return to check on her and she knew he would have kept his word. Her class would be in the middle of history with Mr Keane right now. She hoped Nerolee had remembered to give her assignment in.

Stella had rather enjoyed that assignment. She had been horrified at the execution of King Charles I in 1649 and rather appalled when reading details of the English Civil War and England's years as a republic. She had found it very difficult to come up with a case in favour of the Lord Protector, not to mention his so-called clean living wreckers, but had struggled on, doing her best to see the story from both sides of the coin. She was rather hoping that Mr Keane, who tended to be somewhat merciless with the marking of his assignments, would rate it highly.

She stretched her legs out carefully, one at a time, leaving the more painful of the two till last. She felt slightly better after her sleep and the TENS machine had helped a little but the pain level was still very bad. Her next round of tablets was due at eleven: she took them at six hourly intervals. She rather expected a small flurry of visitors when the recess bell rang at eleven and she was to be proven correct in those expectations.

First to arrive was Mrs Munnings. Mrs Munnings, who actually taught economics, also held the prerequisite first aid certificates needed by at least one teacher in any school. Although admittedly an excellent economics teacher, she lacked that necessary *something* required by those who cared for the injured or sick. It was perhaps rather fortunate that Doctor Mason's surgery happened to be situated at no very great distance from the school. This meant that Mrs Munnings' first aid skills were seldom called upon to do more than apply an adhesive dressing to a small cut or supply a couple of Panadol for a bad headache. The good lady certainly meant well and tried her hardest but her ministrations tended to be avoided by all and sundry.

'Ah, Stella,' she announced on arrival at the sickbay, 'having yet another bad day, I see. You do seem to have a lot of them.'

'Yes, Mrs Munnings,' Stella spoke softly.

'I should imagine it must bother you a good deal, all these classes you miss,' the teacher continued. 'After all, this is a very important time for you, being your first year in senior.'

Stella stayed silent.

'But of course, one must always try and remain cheerful at all times and look on the bright side of things. There is always a bright side, you know, my dear. Every cloud has a silver lining.'

Stella stayed silent.

'I think, when one is in the situation you find yourself in, it is a good thing to remember that there are always people much worse off than you,' Mrs Munnings went on, obviously having no idea of the effect her words were having on Stella. 'Only last week I was reading about a young girl who is paraplegic as the result of a car accident. She will be in a wheel chair for the rest of her life. She was about your age, I think —'

'Mrs Munnings, do you possibly think you could fill this for me?' Stella interrupted, holding out the now empty glass that Nerolee had filled earlier. 'I have to take my medications.' Stella felt her control slipping and too much more of Mrs Munnings might well result in a well-aimed and preferably extremely heavy text book being thrown at the teacher.

'Certainly, my dear.'

Mrs Munnings had just returned with the glass of water, when, to Stella's unspeakable relief, Mr Ellingham walked in.

'Ah, Stella, I have been attempting to call your mother with no success, I'm afraid.'

Stella, slowly sipping at the water, thought for a long moment. Mrs Munnings murmured something about Stella having no need of her now that her favourite helper had arrived and slipped away.

'She might even be here in Koolkuna, Mr Ellingham. I think she said something this morning about needing to go to the produce barn — and, once she's come all the way in, she always does lots of other things as well.'

'I think you'd be better off at home, don't you? I know how

much you hate being fussed over, but you don't look very well today. I don't think there's much chance of you getting back to class, do you?'

A sudden desire for home, her own bed, the comforting knitted patchwork quilt made by her grandmother, Sambo, a soothing massage from her mother's skilled and gentle hands, the air redolent of baby oil and sorbolene cream, the wonderful warmth of hot water bottles and most of all, her mother's comforting presence, overcame Stella. Unable to speak for the moment, she stared up at the understanding teacher, her lips quivering.

'Fine, I think that's clear. Ah, here comes your old comrade in deeds both good and bad.' This last was spoken in a lighter tone as Nerolee appeared in the doorway. 'Nerolee, I am going to try and locate Stella's mum. You seem to be well laden with tasty goodies — buying up the school canteen, I see! You may stay here with Stella till her mother arrives — and yes, before you ask, that does mean beyond recess.' Withdrawing from his breast pocket an elegant silver-coloured pen and a small notebook, he quickly wrote a few words on a page torn from the notebook and gave the page to Nerolee. 'An explanation for any teacher who questions you remaining up here.'

'Thank you, sir,' both girls chorused.

'Stella, where do you suggest your mother is most likely to be found? Produce barn, post office, Doctor Mason, chemist shop or livestock agent?'

The two open mouths that gaped at Mr Ellingham as if he were some magical genie caused him much amusement. 'I gather I got it right,' he said drily.

As he left the sickbay he heard the incredulous tones of Nerolee Turner: 'But Stella, how on earth could he possibly know which places your mother would be? Do you think they have some sort of spy system in place?'

This caused him to chuckle so much that he was asked to explain himself to Mrs Laura Kelly, who met him on the staircase. That stern preceptress of English was much diverted at the notion of a spy system keeping track of pupils' parents.

'What we do need is a tracking system to keep check on all the children,' she opined with a laugh.

Back in the sickbay, Nerolee assured her friend that her much-laboured-over history assignment was now safely in the hands of Mr Keane, as was her own, she added somewhat ruefully. She then urged upon Stella a packet of crisps, a chocolate topped doughnut, a muesli bar and a carton of orange juice, all of which were rejected by the invalid, albeit with much thanks.

'I forgot to have breakfast,' Nerolee explained, spreading out this tempting repast on the little table beside the bed.

Stella, knowing her friend's ways, merely smiled at her. Stella also wondered if Mr Ellingham would be able to locate her mother or if he would miss her altogether. The sound of approaching footsteps heralded the possibility of another visitor and sure enough, a girl wearing large spectacles and with a thick plait of light brown hair reaching between her shoulder blades, entered the room.

'Goodness me, are you two having a picnic?' she raised her eyebrows.

'Only me,' Nerolee hastily swallowed a mouthful of doughnut. 'Stella's not up to it.'

The girl turned blue eyes upon Stella. 'Sorry you're having a bad time,' she said kindly. 'Mr Conning sent this for you — I think it's that special worksheet he's giving us in double maths after recess. He asked me to tell you to do the worksheet when you feel up to it — no hurry or anything.' She held out what looked like several foolscap sheets neatly folded in half.

'Thanks, Annette.' Stella hauled herself up onto one elbow. 'Could you just slip it into my school bag — yes, that's it, there.'

'Have a crisp, Annette?' Nerolee hospitably waved the cellophane packet at her.

'Thanks.' The visitor helped herself and smiled at Stella. 'You're going home, I hear?'

'Yes, I hope so — Mr Ellingham's trying to find my mother now.'

'He's one of the best, isn't he? I won't bother you any longer, Stella, and I hope things settle down a bit soon.'

'Thanks for bringing the maths sheet,' Stella called after her and received a friendly wave in return.

The smell of food from Nerolee's picnic was beginning to nauseate Stella and she had a distinct yearning for solitude. People were so kind and they meant so well and they tried so hard to be helpful — well, some of them did at any rate —

A gentle suggestion that Stella would be just fine on her own till her mother came, and that perhaps Nerolee should return to class when recess ended met with an indignant response. Her friend considered she had been entrusted with Stella's care until the arrival of her mother and she was not going to desert her. Stella, who was fast wishing her school friends at the opposite end of the earth, merely nodded wordlessly. She closed her eyes and waited for the recently swallowed painkillers to kick in.

Mr Steve Ellingham grabbed young Sean Stevens and made a beeline for Koolkuna's sole shopping and business street. Much quicker to do it this way.

It was Sean who located Kirsty Richards in Koolkuna Produce

Barn and Farm Supplies.

'Hi, Mrs Richards, we've been looking for you.' The big blue eyes smiled up at Kirsty. For the thousandth time she marvelled at the miracle wrought by her neighbours on Bellara. They had literally given this boy his life back. The legal side of things appeared to be progressing favourably — very slowly, of course — always the way with legal matters, especially when they reached beyond Australia — but at least they *were* progressing. Sean considered Bellara home and Kirsty knew that any attempts to change this state of affairs would result in definite trouble and possible tragedy.

'Hi, Sean. Is it Stella?'

The boy nodded gravely. 'Mr Ellingham tried to call you at home but Stella said you'd be here in Koolkuna. We've got to meet up with Mr Ellingham at the post office. I think Stella needs to go home.'

'Then it's just as well you found me so quickly,' said Kirsty cheerfully.

Within minutes she was at the school, car parked immediately below the sickbay, and following Steve Ellingham up the stairs.

'Mrs Richards, what on earth are you doing here? Not enough to do out at Cheshunt?' Mrs Kelly, one of Stella's favourite and most supportive teachers, stopped dead in her tracks at the sight of Kirsty.

Kirsty laughed. She had always liked and admired this sturdy, direct, down to earth, matter of fact woman, who had a heart of gold hidden not too deeply behind a gruff exterior.

'Stella needs to come home.'

The other woman nodded in understanding. 'She does have a rough time, doesn't she? Look, I know it's not easy for any of you but you did the right thing in sending her back to school. The mere fact of her being in the scholastic environment makes a massive amount of difference.' The thoughtful eyes met Kirsty's and she moved a step closer, touching the other woman lightly on the shoulder. 'She's a great kid, Mrs Richards, and you should be very proud of her. I know we are, here at school. Sorry, I have to run; my junior English class is waiting on me.' The head of the English department continued down the stairs.

A minute later Kirsty stood in the sickbay gazing down at her sleeping daughter. Nerolee had been unceremoniously dispatched to class by Steve Ellingham who now spoke softly to Kirsty:

'I'll carry her down to your car, Mrs Richards, when you're both ready.'

'I think we'll take her as she is, still asleep. Just let me check her wires.'

He watched with interest as Kirsty Richards carefully separated her daughter's swollen fingers from what appeared to be a mass of insulated wiring. He would have liked to ask more but now was not the time. Kirsty nodded to him and he deftly lifted the girl, one arm beneath her shoulders, the other under her knees. Her head was supported safely against his shoulder. She didn't wake.

Stella did not wake until she was back in her own room at Cheshunt. She lay across the back seat of the Pajero, wrapped in her blanket, her head on the two pillows which Kirsty always kept there. A pain-racked morning followed by the relief of painkilling medication had done its job only too well.

During the drive home Kirsty's thoughts were busy. She recalled the surprise of a friend, Pamela, who could hardly believe that Stella was accepted by the local state high school in the child's semi-crippled condition. Pamela, on hearing all Kirsty had to tell about Koolkuna High, assured her that Stella would not have been accepted, let alone heartily welcomed, at the school her own children currently attended. That school would have referred Stella to a school for children with disabilities, refusing her admittance. Kirsty found this very hard to believe but it did at least reinforce how amazingly fortunate they had been with Koolkuna. She also hoped that Stella would never hear this little anecdote but knew it was a vain wish; somehow, Stella always heard the unpleasant stories relating to disability and illness.

Chapter Sixteen: Birth of a New Idea

Many hundreds of miles away from Cheshunt, Mrs Alex Carey sat in the old wooden rocking chair on the front verandah of the small, sturdy cottage that Joshua Carey had first taken her as his pretty, young bride. Alex's once-black curls, neatly restrained by a hairnet, were now silvery white in colour but the beautiful brown eyes, the same eyes she had passed down to her daughter Kirsty, still sparkled with warm colour and interest in life.

Kirsty liked to gently tease her mother by telling her that William Shakespeare's words, *age cannot wither her, nor custom stale her infinite variety,* might have been written for her. Alex would spiritedly reply that she did not yet consider herself aged and that if Kirsty had to quote from Shakespeare, she might do better than Antony and Cleopatra, of which she had no very great opinion.

Alex's hands were busy as always, the knitting needles working briskly and smoothly. Betty Kaplan was expecting her first great grandchild. Having met as very young, newly married women, she and Betty had now been close friends for well over fifty years. The matinée jacket Alex was knitting would form part of a layette for that much wanted baby, the soft white wool being ideal for the purpose.

Raising her eyes from the small sleeve steadily growing on her needles, Alex eyed her daughter-in-law with restrained approval. Much as she loved this bush community which had so warmly welcomed her long ago, Alex was pleased that none of her children had married within that community. She had extremely firm ideas on breeding, both in people and animals and believed in the introduction of new blood. It kept the family line strong.

Nora was a good girl. She was married to Charles, the third of Alex's five children and the second of her four sons. It was Charles who had inherited the talent of his father Joshua Carey, that master craftsmen of iron and steel. It was also Charles who had first thought of the stirrup.

It had all begun with a letter from Kirsty. She was a regular correspondent and wrote to her mother almost every week. Words flowed easily from Kirsty's pen:

'.. and you know, of course how much the horses have always been part of Stella's life. If only we could get her riding again for just a short time on her better days but it has proven very difficult. Dear old Casper is a perfect angel — so good and patient — but that is not the problem.

Stella's right leg is now so twisted that it is impossible for her to make any use of the stirrup irons. Her wonderful balance in the saddle has completely vanished and even the use of a wide strap around Casper's neck makes no difference. She clings desperately to the pommel, her whole body trembling, the tears pouring down her face. She longs to be in the saddle yet is terrified and bewildered by the strangeness of this different body which has taken on a life of its own. It doesn't belong to her anymore, refusing to obey her commands.

We tried again yesterday — at Stella's insistence — I knew I should have put my foot down but there it is. One always hopes, doesn't one? She hadn't been on Casper's back more than a few minutes when the twisted right leg locked into spasm. Stella let out a cry and groped wildly in the air, her face was chalk white and she fell forward onto Casper's neck. Apart from a slight flick of one ear, Casper didn't move a muscle. Max lifted Stella whilst I took charge of the bad leg and between us we got her resting on the grass. The whole leg is so swollen and distorted, especially around the knee and ankle joints.

Gentle massage, heat and support bandages settled things down again and she slept for the most of the afternoon. I was in the kitchen preparing dinner when a muffled sort of crash came from the direction of our young lady's bedroom. En route to investigate I was almost flattened by Sambo, bristling with indignation, his tail resembling a newly purchased bottle brush of exceptional high quality. It takes quite a lot to separate him from his adored mistress, as you know.

I was met by a missile whizzing past my nose, obviously the second ball in the over. It had been flung across the room with a throw that would have not disgraced Dennis Lillee on a good day. Your granddaughter was sitting up in bed, fists clenched, eyes blazing, two bright splotches of colour flaring on her otherwise ashen cheeks.

'Mum! Look at this!' she could barely choke out the words.

I picked up the missile and its counterpart: two very new and very expensive hardcover books.

'Are these what Cousin Lindsey sent you?'

She nodded, tears sparkling.

Mum, you just should have seen those books. Both were about children restricted to wheelchairs through accident or illness. The author took the line that this was a form of punishment and the children had got their just deserts. Mum — it was not only cruel — it was sick and dangerous. Perfectly normal kids being handed out a form of so-called divine justice.

In the end I took them to bed and kept Max awake half the night reading him select excerpts. It was abundantly clear the author's knowledge of crippled or restricted children had come from television soap operas, if it had come from anywhere at all. Why can't people stick to writing about what they know and understand?

It appears that Stella actually struggled her way through the first book in its entity, before bowling it through space. She didn't get past page five of its partner.

It took a long time to calm her down. This morning Stella gleefully ripped the books to pieces. It took her ages — those poor little hands are so puffy and sore — but between two pairs of scissors and a little help from me, the task was finally completed. It was definitely an act of catharsis.

As you can see, all in all, yesterday was not one of Stella's better days.'

This letter was read out loud by Alex after the usual Sunday dinner at which Nora and Charles were always present. They had retired to the small room at the rear of the cottage, the room which had been Alex's office for so many years and was now a comfortably furnished withdrawing room for the family. The walls were so thickly papered with family portraits of every imaginable type and size that it was almost impossible to see the colour or pattern of the wallpaper underneath.

Joshua's hand reached for his pipe and tobacco pouch. He sat in the aptly named grandfather chair which proudly dominated the small room. His five children and their families had clubbed together to buy the chair for his eightieth birthday. Made from mahogany, upholstered with dark green velvet, it was a very superior article of furniture indeed and he was secretly highly gratified with it. He quietly absorbed the words of his daughter's letter. He would speak when ready.

Alex, having returned Kirsty's letter to its envelope, now picked up her knitting. She wished to complete the winter waistcoat she was making for Joshua. After that she was planning a layette for Betty Kaplan's eagerly awaited first great grandchild.

It was Nora who spoke first. 'I wish there was something we do to help them at Cheshunt.'

She sat with Charles on the compact little sofa, hands clasped around her knees, face thoughtful and rather sad.

'Lindsey always was an idiot,' Charles spoke calmly, removing a small sketchpad and pencil from the breast pocket of his shirt.

There were sounds of general agreement from the family.

'Good for Kirsty, getting Stella to wreck those damned books,'

Charles continued.

Joshua blew a little cloud of smoke towards the ceiling. His eyes twinkled as they saw the sketchpad and pencil in his son's hands. As he watched, the pencil began to move swiftly across a page.

Sketch after sketch came into being under Charles' clever fingers. Like his father, he was a creator. He would pause, scribble a few cryptic calculations beneath a drawing then the fingers would fly again.

The evening was a short one and just before nine the younger couple rose to leave. Their home was a very brief walk down the road, across the lane from the forge. Charles tucked away his sketchpad and turned to wish his father goodnight.

'Come up with something for that poor girl, have you?'

'I'm not sure yet but, maybe — I'll have to try some things out at the forge. Too early to tell.'

'I'll be interested to see what you have in mind, son.'

Charles grinned affectionately at his father. 'If it comes off, I'll call it the Twisted Stirrup!'

Down at the forge, Charles was bent over his workbench. A pair of hands slipped over his eyes and a bright young voice spoke:

> *'Old Tubal Cain was a man of might,*
> *In the days when earth was young;*
> *By the fierce red light of his furnace bright,*
> *The strokes of his hammer rung:*
> *And he lifted high his brawny hand*
> *On the iron glowing clear,*
> *Till the sparks rushed out in scarlet showers,*
> *As he fashioned the sword and the spear.*

And he said: 'Hurrah for my handiwork!
Hurrah for the spear and the sword!
Hurrah for the hand that shall wield them well,
For he shall be king and lord.'

'I hardly see myself as Tubal Cain,' said Charles drily.

The hands were removed and Charles looked up at his daughter Judy. At seventeen she was very like her mother Nora: small and sturdy, dark hair worn very short, changeable hazel eyes which could move from brown to green in an instant, a decided chin and a huge smile which would unexpectedly flash out, bathing you in its warmth. She had a temper which blazed out just as unexpectedly. She was also as bright as a button with a passion for poetry and the classics. Charles had found her reading Dickens when she was barely eleven years old.

'Perhaps you'd prefer some Longfellow.' Judy paused, threw a grin at her father and began:

'Under a spreading chestnut-tree
The village smithy stands;
The smith, a mighty man is he,
With large and sinewy hands;
And the muscles of his brawny arms
Are strong as iron bands.
His hair is crisp and black and long,
His face is like the tan;
His brow is wet with honest sweat,
He earns whate'er he can,
And looks the whole world in the face,
For he owes not any man.'

'There appears to be plenty of poetry about blacksmiths.' Charles' lips twitched. He found it hard not to be amused by this daughter.

'Oh, there is Dad, there is.' Judy flung herself onto the wooden seat of a dilapidated dining chair which had long been relegated to the forge. One of the half-grown, plump kittens who called the forge home rushed across to her and was gently lifted onto her lap.

'Without wishing to be rude, Judy-girl, what can I do for you?'

'Stella.'

'Ah.'

'Will you and Grandfather be able to help her at all?'

'We're doing our best, child.'

'What exactly are you trying to make?'

'A stirrup iron that has the flexibility and shape needed for that bad leg but is still strong enough to provide the essential support.'

'Very difficult?'

'Very difficult,' he confirmed.

'Is it a first?'

'There's nothing out there in the marketplace so far as we can tell.'

'Will you patent it?'

Charles raised his eyebrows. 'How about waiting to see if we can come up with something before worrying about patents?'

'Are you experimenting with different mixes of metals?'

'Yes. Your grandfather is the real expert there — his working knowledge of metallurgy is much greater than mine.'

'Support, flexibility and shape,' mused Judy, one finger absentmindedly stroking the purring kitten.

'That's about it, Judy-girl.'

'I guess need truly *is* the mother of all invention.'

'History would agree with you,' Charles nodded.

Judy jumped up, still holding the kitten, her chin jutting even more determinedly than usual.

'I know you'll come up with something, Dad. I just know you will.' A kiss was planted on the top of her father's head and she was gone, pausing only to return the kitten to the wicker basket he shared with his brother and sister.

It was many weeks before Judy, almost bursting with pride, carried the extremely precious parcel to what had once been Mr Bowen's general store. A large sign proclaimed *Warren's Retail Outlet* and along with certain modern amenities, the store now boasted a post office section. Some people said it was just as well for Mr Warren that Mr Bowen had been cremated, as the so-called modernisation of his beloved general store would have most definitely resulted in some ghostly haunting appearances had he been buried in the local churchyard. The locals knew that those who are cremated cannot return to haunt.

Giving birth to anything is a painful and protracted experience. Anything worthwhile — and many a thing not so worthwhile — is born of blood, sweat and tears. Charles had no idea if his creation would be of any use to his niece. He could only wait for word from Cheshunt.

Chapter Seventeen: Gerry King

The girl with the attractive freckles adorning her strained white face clung desperately to the young woman.

'Please, please, Bev, don't let them start in here! I just can't take any more of it.'

The woman with the wonderful fat plait of strawberry blonde hair bent and hugged the girl on the bed. 'Doctor Coulthart knows the score, Gerry and I've spoken to the senior sister here tonight — had a word with your special nurse as well. Everything should be fine.'

'I can't stand any more of the fighting, Bev. It does something to me — hurts my head.' An unsteady hand rubbed at the temples.

'I know, love, I really do.'

'They sit one each side of my bed and fight across me, Bev. That's all they do. If I try to say anything they shout at me to shut up. It's kind of strange — they don't want to talk *with* me — but it's like they have to have me there with them, looking on while they fight. It's like being caught between two animals fighting about who gets to eat the prize — and I'm the prize.'

There was a brief pause; the girl swallowed hard and reached a trembling hand to a tumbler of water on the bedside locker.

'On Monday,' she continued, 'it was worse than usual. One of the hospital helper people came round in the morning and gave me some magazines and a puzzle book. She was nice — didn't make dumb comments or ask stupid questions. Mum and Dad came in later — the magazines were on the locker — the top one had a big picture of a speed boat on the cover. Mum went ballistic. She grabbed the magazine and started shouting at Dad — told him everything was his fault for buying the boat — no-one else had wanted the wretched thing. She kept saying this funny word — ergo, I think, or eego, would that be it, sis? That buying the boat was all about Dad's ergo or eego.'

'I think you mean ego.'

'What does it mean?'

'Mum meant that Dad got the boat to make himself look good to other people.'

'Like wanting to show Mr and Mrs Vorderman — to show them he's got a bigger and better boat than they do?'

'That's it.'

'But just because he got a fancier boat doesn't mean he knows more about boats and water sports than the Vordermans.'

'You've got it in a nutshell, girl. He doesn't. What happened next?'

'Dad snatched at the magazine and Mum held on to it. It was rather funny in a strange sort of way — a kind of magazine tug-a-war across my bed. They each had about half of it. Mum tugged and Dad pulled — Mum tugged some more — so did Dad — the glue in the spine must have been some sort of super super glue — it held for ages.'

Perched on the hard and uncomfortable chair close to the bed, Beverly listened quietly, her thoughtful eyes fixed on the girl's face.

'At last the poor magazine tore in two — Mum fell right across my bed —'

The elder sister momentarily closed her eyes.

'No, it's fine, honestly — she didn't hurt me — she didn't fall *there*. Really, sis, it wasn't a problem.'

Beverly nodded wordlessly. It was all she could manage.

'Dad laughed when Mum fell — big mistake, that. Mum threw her part of the magazine at his head — missed by a mile. Dad laughed again. Mum went back to that ergo word — sorry — ego thing again. A lot of it was kind of hard to follow — I couldn't make it out. But she said Dad just wished to be better than Mr Vorderman. She went on a lot about boats and w-water-s-skiing — w-w-water-s-skiing —' Here the voice became tremulous, quivered, paused, gathered strength and continued:

'That award Mr Vorderman's got for saving someone — you know the one I mean — he won't ever talk about it but Mrs Vorderman showed it to me and Angela when we were kids. She keeps it safely hidden in her desk 'cos Mr Vorderman won't let her stick it up on the wall. You *must* have heard about it, sis?'

Beverly felt cold and sick. She was suddenly sure she knew where this one was going. Inwardly she cursed her parents to the devil and beyond.

'Mum started talking all about that. She said that Mr Vorderman got his award for saving that boy from drowning — he put his life in danger to save a child's l-life —' Here again the voice faltered, shook, hesitated and the eyes that had been fixed on her sister's face dropped.

'And then?' came the quiet prompt.

'She told Dad he was the opposite of Mr Vorderman in every way. That all he ever wanted to do was show off — to try to impress people — to pretend he was a man when he was a mouse. I didn't get that thing about mice. What have animals got to do with it? But that's what she said. Dad tried to interrupt but Mum shouted him down. *'Mr Vorderman saves children, you d-destroy c-children. Look what you did to m-my d-d-daughter!'* S-she kept r-repeating it in a s-sort of rhyme — over and over again. Then she started on again about boats and w-w-water-skiing — and the d-dangers of p-p-propellers … oh Bev — those awful, awful propellers. I still have nightmares about the b-blades coming at me. They get closer and closer — huge c-chopping b-blades — they're hunting for me. I'm frozen in place — I c-can't get away.'

The young woman rose, took the damp washer from its rail on the side of the locker and carefully wiped the tears and sweat from the girl's face. The restless hands plucked ceaselessly at the cellular blanket.

'Then the sister came in. She t-t-told M-M-Mum and Dad t-to leave, at once. They were still fighting as they left — I could hear them — well, 'twas mostly Mum — as they went all the way down the corridor to the lifts.'

Beverly took the unquiet hands within her own, holding them captive until their restless butterfly movements were stilled.

'B-Bev, you don't know what it was like when they had gone. The room was all quiet and peaceful again, like something mean and bad had gone away. Oh, Bev, is it horrid of me to feel like that about Mum and Dad?'

'No darling, it is not horrid of you at all. You couldn't be horrid if you tried. You are a good and beautiful girl.'

'They won't come to visit me again, will they?'

'No, they won't. Doctor Coulthart has banned all visitors except me and Fabian.'

Beverly felt the taut body of the girl relax; heard the relief in the voice when she next spoke:

'You will come as often as you can?'

'I will come every day, so long as baby doesn't object.'

'I wish I could see her,' Gerry spoke wistfully. She adored her little niece, the four month old Olivia, but Beverly disapproved of bringing a healthy young baby on a visit to a germ-ridden hospital.

'I know, love, but it shouldn't be too long this time. Doctor Coulthart thinks you'll be out in about ten days, maybe even earlier. Your room's all ready and waiting. You'll probably get sick of all the baby-sitting we've got planned for you. I hope you're going to be a good aunt and do some knitting.'

'I can't knit,' protested Gerry.

Relieved to keep the subject away from their parents, Beverley pursued this new topic with enthusiasm.

'That's no problem,' she spoke briskly. 'I can easily teach you. Olivia will be delighted to have something knitted by her favourite aunt. We'll start tomorrow.'

Gerry managed a watery giggle.

After Beverly had gone, Gerry lay on the hospital bed and stared unseeingly out the barred window. Evening was closing in, a wet and stormy night lay ahead but Gerry was completely unaware of it. Dinner arrived and only the kindness of the ward maid persuaded her to at least taste each dish. To her astonishment, she found she was hungry and vegetable soup, macaroni cheese and apple crumble were consumed with amazing ease. The ward maid smiled her approval as she collected the empty tray.

'"Tis a wee bit lonesome for you in here, I'll be thinking. Sister tells me you'll be having a roommate soon, lassie. Later tonight, so I'm told.'

It was much later and the quiet room was discreetly lit by the small hooded night-light. Gerry cautiously manoeuvred her body into an easier position. Her mind was restless, looking back down the years.

Mum and Dad had been happy then, no shouting or horrid name-calling. Gerry and her three sisters had always loved the water — they lived in a beachside town south of Sydney. Doreen and Angela, the middle sisters, loved snorkelling in the shallow lagoons and inlets, while she and Bev had preferred swimming in the surf. A quartet of water-babies, their mother had laughingly called them.

Gerry had been fourteen when she and her sisters all learned to water-ski, thanks to the kindness and generosity of their friends and neighbours, Axel and Hetty Vorderman. The Vordermans had no children of their own and delighted in teaching the local youngsters to canoe, kayak and water-ski.

The accident happened one year ago, on a Sunday family day. She had just turned sixteen. Dad — as always — was driving his new boat. She was water-skiing and Doreen was spotting for her. Thanks to the training by Mr Vorderman, the girls were always scrupulous about spotting — although Dad rather scoffed about it.

No one was ever able to say exactly what happened but Dad seemed to lose control of the boat. The boat went straight over Gerry, the propeller blades slicing her left leg from mid-thigh to ankle. The leg had to be amputated above the knee.

She had been in and out of various hospitals and clinics for the past year.

Mum had never forgiven Dad; had started divorce proceedings within weeks of the accident.

Gerry remembered the words of her adored eldest sister, words that had not been intended for Gerry's ears as she tried to explain things to some cousins from Sydney:

'… that huge lottery win was just about the worst thing that could have happened to Dad. Much against the advice of all our water skiing friends he decided to buy a speed boat. Naturally, Dad, being Dad, it had to be the newest, smartest, fanciest boat — complete with all the trimmings — and oh boy — boats can sure have a stack of fancy fittings when some sucker like Dad gets in the hands of an eager-beaver snake-oil salesman. I reckon that guy must have laughed all the way to the bank. As you might well imagine, the poor Vordermans nearly had a fit — they have been around boats for generations and know their stuff.

Dad was featured on the front page of our local newspaper — huge colour photo — beaming with pride, standing next to the new boat. He was written up as 'our newest boat expert'. I always thought the editor was being rather tongue in cheek with that one.

Trying to persuade Dad that ownership of a smart new speed boat didn't instantly qualify him as an expert was a lost cause. It wasn't too bad to start with because he nearly always took Mr Vorderman out with him — the poor man did a supreme job of work in trying to educate Dad about power boats in general and safety issues in particular — explained what was required and how to go about it. I also think Dad was genuinely afraid of making a fool of himself in the beginning. Unfortunately he soon got over that — you know how hasty and reckless he can be — he always know best — thinks everything will turn out just fine — says precautions and safety are a waste of time.'

Gerry heard the quiet but unmistakable sound of curtains being pulled around the dividing rails separating the two beds. She welcomed the interruption to her tumultuous thoughts. Being alone gave her too much time to think.

Chapter Eighteen: 'Is your Mum nice?'

Although she had learnt not to dwell on it, never would Stella forget that visit to what was supposed to be a speciality clinic for people with her kind of illness. It had been one of the first few places they had tried in Sydney. She hadn't liked the place from the moment they arrived.

Her mother had been asked to fill out what appeared to be dozens of forms full of seemingly meaningless questions. Stella could understand that a basic history of her condition was required but many of the questions were ridiculous. She had been mortally offended to be asked if she could be pregnant, although her mother appeared to understand the reasons behind that query, at least.

After an endless wait, they had been directed to a small room and Stella had been told to take all her clothes off, with the exception of her knickers, and to don a thin cotton robe. The robe, which opened all the way down the back and was only kept in place by tapes at the neck, stopped well above her knees. It was a freezing cold day and the room had no form of heating. Stella, very ill, frightened, in severe pain and barely able to hobble, began to cry quietly.

Stella could tell that her mother was not pleased with their reception at the clinic, although she had said little. Kirsty comforted and reassured her daughter, assisting her to partially re-dress over the robe. The thick woollen cardigan, hand-knitted by her beloved grandmother had provided special warmth, along with happy memories of its creator.

When, after an interminable wait, the medical assistant had finally returned, that woman had been most displeased.

'I thought I told you to get undressed and get into a robe,' she snapped, eyeing Stella's cardigan, tracksuit pants and fluffy socks with disfavour.

Her mother spoke up. 'I told my daughter to put those things on after she got dressed in the robe,' she said quietly, one hand reassuringly on Stella's shoulder. 'This room is excessively cold.'

The medical assistant mumbled something inaudible before asking Stella to come with her then moved towards the door. When she realised that the figure stumbling along behind her was not alone, she spoke abruptly:

'No, not you, Mrs Richards. We only need your daughter, and she'd better get those clothes off.'

'Mum!' Stella omitted the single, spontaneous cry for help without being aware she had done so.

'It's all right, Stella,' her mother spoke quietly, soothingly, as she so often did to young or frightened animals at home. Then she faced the medical assistant.

'I will not leave my daughter, please understand this. I can also help her slip those few garments off when we get where we're meant to be going. Is that perfectly clear? She is absolutely freezing, and so am I for that matter.'

The medical assistant gaped at her mother, clearly not used to meeting opposition. She hesitated, 'Well —'

'I could speak to someone else but, considering our reception here so far, I would be far more inclined to take my daughter home again.' Her mother used what the family always called her 'regal, English heritage voice', and Stella could feel a tiny bubble of warmth well up inside her. *Good old Mum, you just couldn't get anyone better when the going got rough.* She squeezed her mother's hand in appreciation.

The room to which the now cowed assistant led them, looked, to Stella's overwrought mind, like a torture chamber from the Elizabethan era. She would later admit she had possibly exaggerated a trifle.

The assistant told Stella to get up on a strange looking sort of bed. It was covered in black vinyl and very high off the floor. Her mother, now assisting Stella to remove the cardigan, tracksuit pants and fluffy socks, spoke up:

'It's much too high for my daughter. Hasn't it got a control which lowers it? It must have, I'm sure.'

Casting an unfriendly glance at this superior, stuck-up woman who kept challenging her authority, the medical assistant operated the foot pedal which controlled the height of the diagnostic bed. She then left the room, leaving Mrs Richards to assist her daughter awkwardly onto the bed.

A few minutes later, a shortish, tubby, bald man bounded into the room. He was clad in a white tunic and trousers. Stella hated him on sight.

'So how's life treating you, young lady? It's great to be young, isn't it?' He rubbed his hands gleefully together.

Stella, staring at him stonily, could not believe her ears. She noticed that her mother stiffened, rather like her favourite mare when she was alerted to possible danger.

'Now we mustn't let these little problems get us down too much, must we? I always tell my patients they will feel much better if they remember the world is full of people much worse off than they are. Helps every time. Now, what do you say to that?'

Kirsty Richards, only too well aware that anything her daughter might possibly say would be unprintable, hastily intervened. 'Doctor, perhaps we could start the tests?'

How she would later regret those words!

'In a hurry, are we?' the doctor said playfully. 'Ah well, I do recollect you have travelled a bit of a distance to see me. My reputation preceded me, I see. Well, well, it's grand to have a bit of fame.'

Kirsty could not believe what she was hearing. By now, her only wish was to get the tests completed as quickly as possible and get both Stella and herself out of there.

As Kirsty later confessed to Max, she knew in her heart she should have taken Stella away within minutes of first seeing the doctor. She was held back by the burning desire to try to help her daughter: they still had no idea what was happening to her poor, swollen, pain-racked body; they were fumbling around in the dark. No-one had yet suggested a proper diagnosis, let alone come close to any form of treatment or cure. The family was desperate, turning this way and that in their quest for answers.

Kirsty would never in her life forget what followed. It would be many a month before Stella would allow herself to be touched by another doctor. Kirsty was starting to doubt whether this man they were seeing was properly qualified in the necessary field, but she supposed he could have been. You get good and bad people in every walk of life.

Telling Kirsty that he needed to test her daughter's range of mobility to see how limited that range now was, he seized Stella's right leg, the bad one, and pulled it hard.

The single scream emitted by her daughter was not actually very loud — Stella had never been inclined to loud noises — but it was one of pure agony. Hot scalding tears were silently pouring down her face.

Kirsty sprang to the doctor's side. 'What do you think you are doing?' she demanded hotly.

Surprised, the man stood back. 'It's bound to hurt a little, you know,' he tried to soothe her.

'Hurt a little! The child is in torment! Surely you can see that?'

'Now, now, my dear.' He patted her on the shoulder, 'Don't fuss so. I can see you're one of those over-anxious mothers. Doesn't do your daughter any good, you know, being like that.'

Before Kirsty could recover from both her fury and indignation, the doctor had swiftly taken hold of the same leg again, this time twisting it in another direction.

Stella's second scream came at the exact moment that Kirsty grabbed the doctor by the shoulder. 'You bastard! You fucking bastard! You belong with the Spanish Inquisition! Get away from my daughter! Get away from her! I forbid you to lay another hand on her. If you touch my daughter again you will be sorry for the consequences!' She pushed roughly past him to where Stella lay, now quietly whimpering like a tortured puppy.

Kirsty was so shaking with rage that it took a moment before she could speak with the gentle firmness her daughter needed. Wordlessly, she stepped to the small hand basin attached to the wall, soaked her clean handkerchief in cold water and tenderly wiped Stella's face. One damp hand reached out, clutching pitifully at her mother's skirt.

Taking a deep breath, she spoke slowly in the direction of the doctor. 'You will kindly get me a wheelchair and get your receptionist to call for a taxi. Now, this instant, if you please.'

'But my dear lady, there is no need —'

'Did you or did you not hear what I just said?' she demanded, her voice rising dangerously.

The doctor left the room without another word.

Speaking softly, using deft and gentle movements, Kirsty stripped the hated gown from Stella and dressed her. The girl was trembling so much she was unable to offer much assistance.

The wheelchair arrived, pushed by a young nurse who looked worried. 'Can I help in any way?' she asked Kirsty.

'Just give me a hand to get my daughter settled in the chair please.'

Supported on either side, Stella was skillfully swung into the wheelchair.

'I'll help you outside. You've got a taxi waiting, haven't you?' the young nurse looked at Kirsty.

'Thank you, yes. I hope we have a taxi waiting. I certainly asked for one.'

Stella was wheeled from the room which now represented a nightmare to her, straight past the reception desk where accounts were usually settled, and out onto the busy city street. The taxi was waiting and the driver, on seeing the wheelchair, leapt from the driving seat. He was a big, brawny man, middle-aged with a kindly face. He spoke to Kirsty, obviously the leader of the small group.

'If you will allow me, ma'am, I can simply lift the little lady in the cab. She looks as if she's been in the wars good and proper, she does.'

Kirsty glanced at Stella and, receiving a nod, warmly thanked the thoughtful cabbie. His whole demeanour was like a breath of fresh, pure air after the shambles that had been the medical clinic. He managed his youthful burden with the ease and skill of one long accustomed to such things. Stella was deftly laid across the back seat of the cab.

'I'm afraid she'll have to wear a seatbelt,' the cabbie spoke apologetically.

'Oh, we're old hands at this,' Kirsty smiled. She helped ease her daughter into a sitting position, but with her legs still lying along the back seat. The left hand seat belt was pulled on, adjusted and safely buckled. The cabbie produced two small sofa pillows from the boot.

'Would these be of any assistance? I always carry a few bits and pieces.'

Kirsty gratefully accepted the pillows, putting one behind Stella's shoulders and the other under her right knee.

'We all right to go?' enquired the cabbie.

'Just one minute please,' Kirsty told him. She turned to the young nurse who stood on the sidewalk, her hands on the wheelchair. 'Thank you for your help.' She hesitated for a second and then spoke again. 'Look, I know you probably think it's none of my business but I am going to make a suggestion: find another job. Get yourself out of that place.'

The young nurse looked troubled but she said nothing. Her eyes dropped to the pavement.

Kirsty continued, 'I can see by your badge that you have your proper nursing training from a good hospital. They're screaming out for trained nurses all over the place. Find a better job and get clear of that place before there's trouble.'

Kirsty smiled at the nurse, nodded and got into the taxi, taking the front seat next to the driver. The cab was just waiting to pull out into the crowded traffic lane when she heard a frantic tapping on her window. Kirsty struggled with the unwieldy handle and finally managed to open the glass a few inches.

'Thanks for the advice, I'll take it.' The nurse spoke loudly against the roar of the traffic, stepped back from cab, smiled and waved.

'Where are we heading for, ma'am?' the burley cabbie asked.

Kirsty named their hotel and twisted round to check that Stella was all right in the back. Stella's eyes were closed, her head resting against the back of the seat. The pain killing tablets administered prior to leaving the hotel this morning would have well and truly kicked in by now. Exhausted from all the upset, Kirsty settled back for what would be a fairly long drive through the teeming city streets.

Once back at the hotel, the kindly cabbie insisted on carrying Stella inside, depositing her gently on a large sofa in the reception lounge. Assisted by Kirsty, Stella managed to stumble the short distance to the lift. Returning to their fifth floor suite felt like entering a haven of safety. The earlier trauma seemed to have occurred in another time and place, not a mere ninety minutes earlier in the same city, albeit a different part of it.

It took Kirsty an hour to sort Stella out. The girl's expressive grey eyes, ringed with dark circles of pain, stress and fatigue, never left her mother's face. Apart from uttering the gentle commands which allowed Kirsty to tend her daughter, she spoke only once.

'I am extremely sorry, Stella, for what happened this morning. I should have done more research on that clinic before taking you there.' She closed her lips tightly.

'It's not your fault, Mummy,' the tired voice spoke, one hand reaching for her mother.

Once Stella had been showered and assisted to dress in light loose garments, she was only too grateful to retire to bed. Kirsty refused to give the poor limbs their usual gentle massage: after this morning's manhandling, they must be left strictly alone. She made up the two hot water bottles, without which they never travelled anywhere, and covered her daughter with a light blanket. Bending to kiss her daughter lightly on her forehead, she was somewhat startled when two slightly shaky arms reached up in a hug.

'I love you, Mummy.'

'Love you too, darling. Got any reading material handy?'

'Oh yes. I brought three books and some horse magazines with me.'

'Good. I'll be in the other room.'

Stella woke an hour later. She was not happy. Every muscle felt stiff, her leg and hip joints were more swollen than was usual. Numerous rashes had suddenly reappeared on her face, arms and chest; she was nauseous and she felt hot and miserable. All she wanted was her mother, who could always make things bearable.

Stella looked down at her legs, the right one supported by the usual collection of pillows. The cellular blanket was most unusual, a soft, delicate pink. She had never seen one of that colour before. It was strange how much the little things mattered nowadays.

She wondered why that dreadful day at the clinic had come to mind. It had been ages since she'd even thought of it.

Her right leg was grossly swollen and twisted, and in a desperate effort to reach the other leg, had achieved the almost unbelievable angle of ninety-two degrees. This amazing phenomenon had been photographed by medical students and professors alike, greatly to Stella's disgust.

'Hello,' the voice came from behind the curtain separating the two beds. 'Do you mind if we pull this thing back?'

'Feel free,' offered Stella.

'How mobile are you?'

'Pretty pathetic at the present,' returned Stella, glaring at her legs.

'Just give me a moment, will you.'

Some interesting thumps and bumps were followed by the jerky drawing back of the curtain. Standing lightly between a pair of crutches was a tall girl of about Stella's own age. The two eyed each other appraisingly.

'Stella Richards.'

'I'm Gerry King. Welcome to my castle. It's good to have company.'

'Thanks. Don't you hate these awful barred windows?' demanded Stella. 'I was here last year but in the next room.'

'Snap! I was here last year too, and in a single room. Nearly went bats.'

The two exchanged a comradely grin.

Gerry firmly tied the curtain in place before carefully making her way back to her bed. A few adroit movements and she was back in bed, crutches neatly together on their special hook, within safe and easy reach.

'My sister's coming in later,' Gerry spoke proudly. 'She said something about teaching me to knit but I don't know if she really means it. She's got a new baby girl.'

'So you're an aunt? What's the baby called?'

'Olivia. She's four months old.'

'You must knit something for Olivia,' urged Stella. 'It'd be an aunty sort of thing to do.'

'Yes, that's what my sister said. Can you knit at all?'

Stella shook her head before asking if Gerry's sister would bring baby Olivia in to visit.

'No way. Says healthy new babies don't belong in hospitals — too many germs are bad for them.'

'Shame — I'd love to see Olivia — but I think your sister's right,' Stella spoke judiciously.

Gerry flushed warmly. 'She's a darling,' she said unsteadily.

'I might ask Mum about learning to knit,' said Stella thoughtfully, 'she will be in this afternoon.'

'Is your mum nice?' The blurted out words were almost shocking in their directness.

'What?' Stella gaped at the other girl.

'Is your mum nice and kind?'

Stella managed to collect her wits before replying: 'She's a darling! The bestest mum in the whole world!'

'My mum's divorcing my dad because of this,' the other girl jerked her head down towards what remained of her left leg. 'She says he tried to destroy me!'

Stella stared at her, aghast.

Chapter Nineteen: 'They come as a pair'

Do not be frightened,
everyone is still here,
I know you are scared,
and the future is not clear.
I also know you are strong,
and God is on your side.
That you have a powerful will,
and a heart full of pride.
With a rough journey ahead,
your strengths will show.
Upon conquering these feats,
a new energy will flow.
So try not to worry,
everything is going to be fine.
God will smile upon you,
and your soul will shine.
So when you claim victory,
and this path is put aside
Your friends will be here,
and God as your guide.

The poem scripted in Judy's careful hand was enclosed in the parcel. The parcel was waiting for Stella when she arrived back from hospital.

Curled up on the old divan in the sitting room, a delighted Sambo purring lustily at her side, she looked at her family with contentment and appreciation. Since befriending Gerry King in hospital, Stella now viewed her family from a slightly different perspective.

'Don't forget to open your parcel.' Her mother nodded at the coffee table pulled up close to the divan. The parcel stood there, waiting and expectant.

'I won't.' One hand gently massaged Sambo's cheek bone. 'It's just that it's so good to be home again. I'm enjoying things — taking them nice and slowly — letting all the niceness sort of soak in, if you know what I mean.'

'We understand, kid.' Toby dragged up a sturdy old footstool of the type called pouffe and sat his tall, lean frame down upon it. He looked affectionately at his baby sister.

Max, who rarely sat down unless it was absolutely unavoidable, was most untypically seated on a kitchen chair. He had reversed it and was leaning his folded arms on the back.

'It's got Uncle Charles' name on the back,' Stella sounded surprised. She began tearing at the thick brown paper. 'How funny. Why would he send me a parcel, I wonder? Aunt Nora usually sends things for birthdays and special occasions, and Judy, of course. Perhaps it's meant for you, Mum, 'cos you're his sister?'

'I doubt it,' the said sister spoke drily.

Underneath the brown paper was a box, tightly tied with thin baling twine.

'Here …' Toby removed his treasured folding pocket knife from the leather pouch on his belt.

Stella shook her head at the knife. 'You do it please, Toby. I'm too clumsy with my hands — I'll only cut myself or do something stupid.'

'Not stupid, but very sensible,' the young man spoke brusquely. He cut the baling twine with a sharp snap.

Sambo chose that moment to pounce on a large piece of torn brown paper and shot across the floor.

'Cat on a toboggan,' laughed Stella.

The box, shaped like a large boot box, had a fitted lid. The lid was firmly sealed to the box with very wide, sticky packing tape.

'Someone went to a lot of trouble,' commented Max.

'It certainly wouldn't have been Charles,' responded that gentleman's sister. 'Nora or young Judy, I should think.'

Toby deftly sliced through all the tape. Stella took off the lid to reveal lots of balls of crumpled newspaper.

'Fish around,' suggested Toby with a grin.

'Carefully,' warned his mother.

Her family watching (Sambo had abandoned snow sports and now chased a ball of crumpled newspaper), Stella put her swollen hand into the box and poked about.

'Any luck?' asked her father.

Her face changed as the hand grasped a hard object. It seemed strangely familiar and yet different. Quickly, using both hands, she drew the item from its wrappings. It stood there, in all its glory, a stirrup iron, but not quite a stirrup iron. She lifted it, held it in her hands.

'That looks rather special,' Max said quietly.

She looked up, eyes shining. 'Dad, do you think —' and was afraid to say more.

'I don't think that Uncle Charles would have sent it without a very good reason,' said Toby soberly.

'Try the rest of the box,' suggested Kirsty.

Further exploration discovered a second stirrup iron nestled amidst the newspaper balls. The bottom of the box held two envelopes. The first held an enclosure from her uncle.

My dear niece,

I was never one for fine nor fancy words. That talent lies with my daughter. I will keep this brief and to the point.

Your Grandfather Carey and I have made this stirrup iron for you. We call it the Twisted Stirrup. You will soon find out why.

We hope it may be of some help to you, child. You must promise to use it for no more than five minutes a day for the first week. During the second week, you may extend that to ten minutes a day.

Like most stirrups, they come as a pair. Please use them as a pair.

I remain your affectionate

Uncle Charles

Stella sat bolt upright, a Twisted Stirrup in each hand, her uncle's open letter in her lap. Two bright spots of colour burned on either cheek. With awe she looked from one hand to the next, up at her family and back to what she held in each hand.

'Charles always was a clever sort of chap,' Max acknowledged. 'He's like your Dad, Kirsty.'

Kirsty laughed. 'He was the only one of the boys to inherit any of Dad's talent with iron and steel,' she agreed. 'It used to drive Dad round the bend when we were kids. He used to say, *'Four boys and only one with that touch of steel in him.'* It showed up pretty early too. Charles was tagging in Dad's footsteps as soon as he could walk, always trying to go down to the forge. Mum never had to worry if Charles went missing — sure as eggs he'd be down at the forge, getting in the men's way. I should know — it was always me who had to go and fetch him home.'

Toby reached out and touched one of the stirrups. 'They've done a neat job,' he said admiringly.

The second envelope held the poem from Judy and a short letter.

Stella read the beautiful poem out loud, her voice faltering, wavering and uneven. She came to the final words with tears in her eyes:

'So when you claim victory,
and this path is put aside
Your friends will be here
and God as your guide.'

'That Judy is one gifted youngster,' Kirsty spoke softly, breaking the silence which had followed Stella's reading.

'She's a good kid,' Max spoke gruffly.

Stella swallowed hard, scrubbed at her eyes with a non too clean handkerchief and thought of Gerry King. Perhaps she could send a copy of this beautiful poem to her new friend: she'd have to ask Mum about it later. She and Gerry had promised faithfully to keep in regular contact. Stella reached for the letter which had accompanied Judy's poem. Scribbled untidily on a piece of foolscap notepaper, that young woman had written:

Dearest Stella,

You should know that Dad and Grandfather Carey worked their butts off for many weeks to come up with this thing for you. They just wouldn't let it go. Talk about burning the candle at both ends — they just never stopped.

Sorry you've been in hospital again. Do hope the Twisted Stirrup is a rousing success. I just know it will be. Dad and Grandfather Carey — well, their stuff is always the greatest. They're the best!

I wanted them to take out a patent on the Twisted Stirrup but they don't seem interested.

Send us a letter when you get a chance. We don't hear that much from you these days.

Judy

P.S. No need to tell Dad that I told you they worked their butts off. But you'd know that anyway. You're not stupid.

Chapter Twenty: A Winter's Day

If an observer were to take up abode in a secluded position not far from the sharp bend where Stella had been rescued by David Fairchild and Sean Stevens, he would have noticed that the track between Cheshunt and Bellara was unusually busy that day. The activity had begun early.

The frost was crisp on the ground when the first person passed the hidden observer: Toby Richards. Moving at a steady trot, he was riding one horse, leading another. He was headed for Brackens Bridge and Old Dan.

Old Dan's elderly mare had recently been found dead in her paddock one morning. The old man had collected shovel, pickaxe and crowbar from his small shed and gone to work. His girl would be buried where she had fallen and he would do the burying.

The old man would have undoubtedly dropped dead beside his beloved mare if Max hadn't ridden into the paddock within the hour.

'Dan! What in the blazes do you think you're doing?' a furious Max had demanded, '… trying to kill yourself?'

'She's got to be buried at once, Boss,' came the dogged reply.

'I know, Dan, and I'm sorry about old Strawberry. She was a grand mare.'

'That she was, Boss. I'm right glad ye didn't bring the Little Missus with ye today. Tis no sight for a lady.'

Max could only agree but forbore from saying so.

'Dan, please, let me bring the tractor in. We'll get her in the ground much quicker.'

There was a long silence. The old man looked at his mare and at the small amount of digging he had managed to do. Very slowly he laid down the shovel and collected his hat from a fence post.

'She would appreciate what you've done, Dan,' Max said gently.

The vivid blue eyes which had not dimmed with the passing years rested upon the mare. He had covered her with two horse blankets.

Today, riding towards Brackens Bridge and the old sandstone hut, Toby had no idea of his reception. He hoped that dear old Etta would quickly earn a warm place in the old man's heart. His father had said the two would be good for one another.

Soon after Toby had ridden away down the frosty track, hoofs coming quickly in the opposite direction sounded in the clear morning air. Sean Stevens, now quite at home on the little chestnut mare, Susie, was bound for Cheshunt with a message.

Sean delivered his message, paused for refreshment in the Cheshunt kitchen and was soon riding back for Bellara.

'Something's up at Cheshunt,' he announced mysteriously.

'What do you mean?' asked David Fairchild in surprise.

'I think it's to do with Stella.'

David exchanged glances with his daughter.

'She's kind of excited,' Sean tried to explain. 'It's like she thinks something good might be going to happen but she's afraid it might not happen after all.'

'What did she say?' prompted Deswyn encouragingly.

'Oh, she didn't actually *say* anything — not about that, I mean.'

'Did you see Mrs Richards?'

'Yep. She gave me some beaut gingerbread and a glass of milk. It was funny — she seemed a bit like Stella — sort of excited but afraid at the same time. Only she didn't show it as much as Stella did.'

Unable to make anything of all of this, David changed the subject.

'Well, you said that Max is ready for those new shorthorns, Sean, so we'll move them right away. With Mike along, we won't have much to do, you and I. Between us we should be able to stop any wanderers wishing to go bush. It's a small herd anyway.'

Mike, David Fairchild's faithful black and white border collie, heard his name and lifted his head.

Sean beamed his approval. There was nothing he loved more than being on horseback, helping Mr Fairchild with the cattle. Sean had no idea that both Bellara and Cheshunt were already becoming rarities within their time: he would have been horrified to learn that many farms and stations used motor cycles when mustering or moving cattle and sheep.

The twenty shorthorns were slowly and safely escorted along the track from Bellara to Cheshunt. The roan and red beasts were docile and good natured, showing little inclination to go bush.

Max, mounted on Serenade, was waiting above the sharp bend in the track, Jasper in close attendance.

'They're to go into the small paddock beyond the Five Acre,' he explained.

David reined in Crusader and turned to Max, eyes twinkling. 'What say we pair of oldies let the youngsters do all the work? I'm sure young Sean here can manage this little bunch.'

'How about it, Sean? Can you put the shorthorns in that paddock over there?'

'Yes, sir!' The boy turned scarlet, thrilled to be given the responsibility but scared that he would get it all wrong.

The two men were not worried, knowing that Mike and Jasper would not let matters go awry. With the exception of opening and closing the heavy gates, the dogs could easily have done this task themselves.

'You know, David, you've done wonders with the boy.' Max watched critically as Sean slowly got the small herd moving again, making no attempt to hurry the cattle.

'Not really.' The other man shook his head. 'The credit should go to the boy himself and the people who brought him up — his mother, and that woman from the boarding house place — Bronwyn Vaughan. They must have been good people.'

The men watched as Sean struggled with the first of the gates. The shorthorns were held in check by the two dogs while Sean dismounted Susie and grappled with the five-barred wooden gate. The gate finally swung open and stayed there, held by its massive weight. Quickly, Sean remounted and helped the dogs move the herd through the opening.

'Makes a lot of unnecessary work for himself.' David shook his head.

'Come on, David, he's doing fine. He'll learn soon enough. Needs a few more of these small jobs, but by himself.'

'He's certainly a trier.' David grinned ruefully.

Sean had dismounted Susie again, shut the gate and remounted. Now they had to cross the paddock known as the Five Acre and deal with another heavy wooden gate to reach their final destination.

'Any word on those Lucas bastards?' asked Max suddenly.

'Talked to Bill Stroud only last week. They appear to have vanished off the face of the earth. The sergeant says they'll show eventually — alive or dead. People usually do. I don't know,' he rubbed his chin thoughtfully, 'maybe I'm imagining things but why do I get the feeling Bill Stroud's not telling all he knows?'

Max shrugged. 'Probably isn't. Maybe he's got a line on them and doesn't want anyone butting in.' The eyes of the two men met.

The Five Acre had excellent grazing, as yet barely touched by the early winter frosts, and the shorthorns were quick to take advantage of this. It was amazing how rapidly they spread out across the pasture.

Sean was dismayed. It had been easy enough to keep the herd together on the track through the bush and he had been feeling quite proud of himself. Now he had forgotten what he should do. He was sure the cattle were all laughing at him.

A nudge at his stirrup iron caused him to look down. It was Mike's familiar black and white face, trying to tell him something.

'Oh Mike, I can't remember what to do.' Despairingly, he waved a hand at the grazing shorthorns.

Mike gave a small bark and sped off. As Sean watched in amazement, the border collie worked neatly and efficiently to bring the recalcitrant animals back into a tight group.

'Thanks, Mike.' Sean breathed a huge sigh of relief.

Sean and Mike got the herd moving in the direction of the final gate on the far side of the Five Acre. Jasper, who had taken advantage of Sean's inexperience to enjoy the glorious delights of chasing a rabbit, pursued the said rabbit until it disappeared down a hole.

Sean dismounted from Susie, pushed the heavy wooden gate wide open but this time held it open. How he wished he could manage these gates from the saddle. Mr Fairchild and Mr Richards made it look so easy. But Mike was already guiding, pushing, encouraging and nudging the shorthorns through the opening. The boy counted them through as he had been taught and watched as they spread out, heads already bent to the grass. He led the little chestnut mare back through the gate, closed it, pulled the chain over the hook and remounted Susie for what seemed like the fiftieth time that morning.

'You're a grand boy, Mike,' he spoke in heartfelt tones.

Jasper gave up watch on the rabbit hole and rejoined them, tail wagging.

'And you were no help at all,' scolded Sean, but then he sighed. 'I guess it was my fault for not knowing what signals to give you but I still think you played me up.'

It was early in the clear winter afternoon when the observer once more saw activity on the track. Once again it was a meeting place.

The two horses arrived first. Max Richards on Serenade was leading Casper. Casper walked eagerly along the track, his neat grey ears pricked and alert, his neck arched. He was bridled with his usual simple egg-butt snaffle with short sporting reins and wore a thick neck-strap. The stirrup irons had been run up the leathers and hung just below the saddle skirts, the leathers threaded through them. The irons were like no stirrup irons the observer had ever seen.

The vehicle came next, crawling slowly along the track. Obliging and versatile as the Pajero was, Kirsty had no wish to jolt or jar Stella, who sat beside her in the front seat for this short ride from the house.

Stella was dressed in warm Damart pants which had become a vital item in her cooler weather wardrobe, a cotton roll-neck skivvy under a hand-knitted woollen vest (courtesy of Grandma Carey) and a pair of her father's work socks. On her right foot she wore one of Max's riding boots, on her left foot, one of Toby's. Her face wore a huge smile.

Rather than have this first ride with the Twisted Stirrups in the yards, it had been decided to make an outing of it. Five minutes would vanish quickly anywhere but spent on the bush track just beyond the larger home paddock would make it seem special. Since her illness, Stella's heart often ached with longing for the bush.

Serenade, much to his disgust, was hung up to a wattle tree. Kirsty rubbed his nose and scratched him behind the ears.

'Sorry, boy, it won't be for long. Today is Stella's and Casper's time. I'll get a ride on you again very soon, promise.'

'Kirsty, stop fussing over that horse and come and give us a hand,' yelled Max impatiently.

Stella, who was levering herself out of the Pajero, giggled.

'Just check the length of those stirrup leathers, will you, Kirsty — they should be about right.'

'Arm length check,' Stella held out one arm, whilst keeping a firm grip on the frame of the Pajero's door with the other.

'I'd say yours are a tad shorter than mine.' Kirsty eyed their two arms held next to each other.

Kirsty checked the stirrup leather on the nearside, shortened it by a single hole and repeated the exercise on the offside.

'Should be fine, Max.'

She helped her daughter across the uneven ground to where Casper was patiently standing.

'Stella girl — I am going to pick you up and put you on Casper's back. Don't try to find the stirrups. Just get your balance in the saddle. Use the neck-strap — don't be proud. Kirsty, hold Casper so he doesn't move — not that I think he would, but just to be sure. Ready, Stella?'

Max picked up his daughter and, with some assistance from Kirsty who gently manoeuvred the difficult right leg, guiding it across Casper's rump and safely over to his offside, quickly had her in the saddle.

Kirsty devoutly hoped that the support bandages which Stella wore would prevent any return of the agonising leg spasms.

'When does the five minutes start?' asked Stella anxiously.

'When both feet are in the Twisted Stirrups.' Max gently inserted his daughter's left foot into the nearside iron.

'How does that feel?'

'Fine ...' She looked down at her left foot. '... but this leg's not that much of a problem, Dad.'

'We've got to start somewhere.' He grinned up at her.

Kirsty held the second stirrup out a little from the saddle, turning it to the correct angle.

'Stella, we're going to bring the iron to you. Keep that leg where it feels all right and we'll fit the stirrup around your foot. Don't you try and do anything now. Right?'

Stella nodded, the grey eyes intent on the stirrup in her mother's hands. She watched as the oddly shaped item was slipped past her toes and under the ball of her foot. Then her mother's hands were removed.

'Can I walk a bit?' She was gathering up the reins.

'Just up the track to the wattle tree and back for now.'

'What do you think?' Kirsty stood very close to her husband, her eyes never leaving the retreating form of her daughter.

Max shrugged, a habit which never failed to annoy Kirsty, but she held her peace for now. 'Only time will tell.'

'Do you understand how it's supposed to work?'

'I think so. Somehow, Charles and your Dad have given it a certain amount of pliability, bendiness if you like, without compromising support. Instead of forcing the foot and whole lower leg into a position the legs can't cope with, it sort of guides them. Most stirrups today are stainless steel and while that does a great job for most people, it is totally unforgiving on legs like Stella's. She needs the support and she needs the 'give' factor. Too much stretchability would be worse than useless, and rigid, unforgiving support is just as bad. Has to be a combination of support and 'give', you see.'

Kirsty nodded in understanding.

Stella had reached the wattle tree. Obediently she turned Casper. It was a perfect early winter afternoon along the edge of the bush, but she could not keep her eyes from continuously returning to her right stirrup. Her foot, clad in her father's riding boot, felt almost caressed by the kindly, guiding stirrup.

During that short ride she felt almost invincible.

Why then, the observer wondered, did the girl's face crumple as she was lifted down from the white pony? She had seemed almost ecstatic such a short while ago. Now the tears were pouring down her face and she was clinging to the woman. The woman led the girl away to the vehicle, tucking her up in the front passenger seat. The man had ridden away on the bay horse, leading the white pony and the woman had driven the vehicle slowly up the track.

Chapter Twenty-one: Diagnosis

When Kirsty needed to sort out her thoughts she often retreated to the paved hydrangea walk. At this time of year there were no large, mop-headed blooms in their unique shades of blue, but the long established shrubs provided an air of stability, permanence and peace. Thyme had been planted between the apricot-coloured bricks of the walk and each step Kirsty took crushed some of the leaves of the perennial evergreen herb, releasing its aromatic scent. Her nostrils quivered appreciatively.

It was called juvenile rheumatoid arthritis. At long last the official diagnosis had been formally given by the so-called medical specialists and the so-called medical experts, although Kirsty had long been sure in her own mind, as had Dr Mason and one or two of his wiser colleagues.

'The tests for the rheumatoid factor and ANA came back negative again. Despite this, I am still sure she has some form of juvenile rheumatoid arthritis. I have seen this before in many other youngsters,' Dr Mason had told Kirsty many months ago.

'ANA is antinuclear antibodies, right?'

'Been doing some research, I see. Yes, that's right. It is done for a number of reasons, checking for autoimmune disorders is one. The ANA test can show up positive in juvenile arthritis but in my experience, it often doesn't.'

'And the rheumatoid factor?'

'It's the same thing. The rheumatoid factor *may* be found in children with juvenile rheumatoid arthritis — in some cases it is. But it is by no means *always* present. You know, Kirsty, far too much reliance is placed upon all these tests.'

'Then why bother doing them?' Kirsty had snapped, tired to the bone and fed to the teeth with the whole medical profession.

'I wonder that myself at times.' The elderly doctor looked kindly at her. 'Try not to worry so much, child.'

Stooping to pat Sambo who had surprisingly followed her to the hydrangea walk, Kirsty thought of her daughter. Before the illness, Stella, a tall girl, had stood straight as a young sapling, all five feet ten inches of her. Her sturdy limbs had been tanned and strong from long hours spent outside and she always ran everywhere, never walked. But now —

Stella's joints, especially in her legs, were hugely swollen. The lymph nodes in her neck were also often swollen. All her movements were stiff and jerky, sometimes clumsy and uncontrolled. Her range of motion was greatly restricted and she walked haltingly with small, unsteady steps. Her skin, no longer clear and healthy, was covered in numerous rashes. Continual pain and restricted movement had caused the wide shoulders to hunch forward in a protective and defensive posture. Her entire body was swollen and much irritated by any clothing that was not loose and light. A firm waistband could reduce her to tears. She was often hot and sweaty, at times feverish; always tired and weary.

They faced a huge problem: Stella's body did not respond to any of the drugs usually prescribed for juvenile rheumatoid arthritis. The search for the right drug or combination of drugs was proving to be a long and heartbreaking affair.

Most of these drugs operated in an accumulative fashion. It usually took between four to six weeks, sometimes longer, to determine if each drug worked or not. During those weeks, which slowly ticked over into months, the child still had to live through each day and night, her life dominated by pain.

'I'm afraid it's not going to be easy,' the eminent rheumatologist had admitted. 'Your daughter appears to be one of those rare children on whom the usual medications have no effect. We are going to have to keep trying different things. It's going to take time.'

Ideally, Stella had to be kept as active as was reasonably possible, and so the fight went on: treat the symptoms, try to keep the pain under enough control to allow a certain amount of daily activity. For always, hovering just out of sight but not out of mind was the fear: use those legs or one day you won't be able to use them. It takes a short space of time for muscle atrophy to take hold and cripple an active person.

The TENS machine helped control the pain more than anything. Stella, now expert at managing the compact device, used it a number of times each day.

Kirsty felt as if she were doing battle against an evil foe. Out there somewhere there had to be the right answer to her daughter's illness. It had to be found and she, Kirsty, the child's mother, had the responsibility of finding it. She would visit every bloody doctor in Australia, if need be.

Later that day, she watched Stella and Casper in the small home paddock, her eyes wet. Stella had now been promoted to ten minutes with the Twisted Stirrups.

Kirsty hadn't been at all surprised at her daughter's sudden collapse that first magical day she had tried the Twisted Stirrups: she had been expecting it. Too much had happened in too short a time and the backlash was inevitable. The collapse had been emotional rather than physical: this wonderful stirrup seemed almost too good to be true. Yes, it had worked today but perhaps it wouldn't tomorrow. It was like having a brief taste of heaven and fearing you wouldn't be admitted again the following day.

Stella had ridden the promised five minutes for six days, her legs appearing to adapt fairly easily to the Twisted Stirrups. At her mother's insistence, there had been no riding on the seventh day. Stella had demurred.

'No athlete trains every day of the week,' said Kirsty, settling the matter.

Stella was now intent on making the most of the ten minutes allowed her. She had learnt during these past ten days how to make every few seconds in the saddle count. She could not afford to waste even a single second of this precious time.

'It's made all the difference in the world to her.' Toby came up and stood beside his mother.

Together they watched as Casper broke into a trot for a dozen strides before his rider brought him back to a walk.

'I think dear Casper's enjoying the regular work again,' Toby observed with a grin.

Chapter Twenty-two: The Kite Festival

It was her sheer helplessness that was the worst part. Stella gazed down at the twisted, distorted, swollen, painful limbs that were her legs. She was wearing loose fitting blue shorts with a white cotton tee shirt and sitting on the beach. A wide-brimmed straw hat in a pretty shade of carnation pink protected her face. No member of the Richards family went anywhere without a hat; it was one of her father's most inflexible rules.

Yesterday, Stella and her parents had made the long drive from Cheshunt to Sydney for the monthly visit to the eminent rheumatologist. Her mother had suggested they spend a few hours at the beach before making the journey home later today.

Stella was struggling badly today with the turmoil raging inside her head. It had all begun yesterday afternoon at the rheumatologist's clinic. She had been sitting in the award-winning designer-decorated waiting room at the end of the visit whilst her parents had their usual private talk with the specialist. Stella detested her condition being discussed within her presence and had begged her parents to deal with the doctors as much as humanly possible.

Suddenly and silently, the closed door leading to the private surgery had opened a fraction, thanks to the faulty door catch. *So much for award-winning designer-decorated waiting rooms belonging to fancy doctors who can't even make sure they have solid door catches,* had been Stella's first scornful thought. She even had a small private chuckle with herself. Tough, practical with everything in good working order and no fancy frills was the way of things at Cheshunt. She looked with scorn at the expensively framed piece of modern art on the waiting room wall, wondering if it was meant to be hung upside down. Were those white fluffy things clouds in a purple sky or sheep in a purple field?

She could hear the soft murmur of her mother's gentle voice and the deeper tones spoken by her father, and again, smiled to herself. In spite of everything, she knew she was very lucky in her parents. Look at poor Gerry King!

Her mind flew to Gerry, now living with her eldest sister in the Sydney suburb of Epping. It was Stella's turn to write to her friend. She would fill pages telling of life at Cheshunt, of which Gerry could never get enough.

It was exactly at this moment that the loud voice of the rheumatologist boomed out those unforgivable and unforgettable words which were clearly heard by Stella.

'— considering all the circumstances of the situation, I would seriously advise you to consider a wheelchair or, at the very least, a walking frame. It would be a lot easier on you and to be honest, I seriously doubt if she will ever walk properly again. Might be an idea to start getting the child used to the idea of a more restricted life.'

Then the door was gently closed and Stella knew her mother would have seen the door slightly ajar and moved swiftly to deal with it. She closed her eyes and let her body fall more deeply into the well-cushioned chair. She felt cold and sick.

It had been a late appointment and it was dark by the time Max Richards had driven his wife and daughter through the busy city traffic to their hotel. Stella had spoken very little but this was not unusual following the much-hated medical appointments. Kirsty and Max knew that something was very wrong but they knew better than to try to ask questions. Their daughter would tell them in her own way and in her own time. Stella could never be pushed.

'Dinner from room service, I think,' Max announced as he assisted his daughter to settle on the sofa in their hotel room.

'There might even be something worth watching on the television,' his wife added, covering Stella with a warm but light blanket. Television was rarely watched at Cheshunt and not just because the reception was poor on the sole available channel.

Stella's distress had been soothed by the quiet family evening. She enjoyed her dinner, a delicious omelet with salad followed by fresh fruit salad. Eaten in front of the television, the meal was followed by a shower and her usual muscle massage and leg exercises. The long drive from Cheshunt, followed by the stresses of the medical visit, had tired her out and she slept unusually well.

The beach visit had been proposed by Kirsty in the hope that Stella would break her silence on what was so clearly upsetting her. She had always been like this: any prompting, however gentle, would only shut the door even tighter. And speaking of doors, thought Kirsty, her lips tightening, just exactly how much of that moronic doctor's speech had been heard by Stella? Kirsty was starting to dread the very words, medical specialist. They would probably do much better with a good, old fashioned witch doctor or medicine man!

The gentle curve of Bondi Beach stretched out in front of Stella. Her father was parking the car, which by necessity, was some distance away. Her mother had slipped across the road behind the beach, saying she would not be long. For the moment, Stella was alone and trying to bring some order to the chaos of her thoughts.

Three things that oaf of a rheumatologist had said were flashing through her mind like neon alarm beacons. A wheelchair! Stella gritted her teeth and bit her lip hard. Never, never, never! She would crawl inch by inch across the ground before she would be forced into one of those things. She would roll across the floor if necessary but she would *not* be confined to a wheelchair! And as for a walking frame … the very thought made her anger boil up again.

What exactly had the doctor said? Something like: *it would so much easier on you,* meaning her parents and family. This was a remark that worried her. She was well aware how much of her parents' time and resources were needed to look after her properly. Her father worried about how tired her mother got sometimes: Mum was not nearly as strong as she pretended to be and even Stella could see that Mum was getting thinner every passing month.

Then there was money: she was fast learning that it was a fact of life that being ill was an expensive business. Monthly trips to Sydney with accommodation at the motel — her tablets and other medications, some of which were unbelievably expensive — all the many and varied medical tests and scans — hospital and clinic visits — the list went on and on. One day Stella had accidentally seen on her father's study desk his account books. He had been balancing the medical accounts and she had felt sick when she saw some of the totals. When she tried to speak of it to him, her father had gently but firmly informed her it was his responsibility and none of her business. Somehow, she had never quite been able to banish those amounts from her mind. Some of the figures ran into thousands of dollars.

The third of the doctor's remarks felt as if it were burnt in to her brain in capital letters: *DON'T KNOW IF SHE WILL EVER WALK PROPERLY AGAIN.* Another section of her mind was consumed with rage against a door that had come ajar and also against the rheumatologist whose surgery the door was in.

Frozen spikes of fear were jabbing at her brain: *wheelchair, won't walk again, wheelchair, won't walk again, wheelchair, won't walk again.* The words beat an endless rhythm: *wheelchair, won't walk again, wheelchair, won't walk again.* Hot tears filled the big grey eyes and slid down her cheeks as she stared stonily out to sea.

'Stella?' A hand gently touched her shoulder and her mother was standing beside her. Kirsty Richards slipped a small carton of ice cold milk into the cool box before settling on the blanket beside her daughter.

'I forgot the milk this morning at the hotel. I have remembered everything else, I hope.'

Max Richards whistled quietly to himself as he strode along the promenade at Bondi Beach. This place always brought back memories. He and Kirsty had spent their honeymoon here: two crazy country kids. A smile broke across his tanned faced as he recalled Kirsty in that blue and white striped bikini. How she had loved the surf.

Max was suddenly jerked back from the past to the present. Just ahead, a woman was struggling with a light wheelchair which held a small girl of about ten years old. She obviously wished to take the child and the chair down on to the sand. The pair had halted at the bottom of the ramp leading down from the promenade; the small front wheels of the chair were just touching the dry sand of the beach. The woman seemed uncertain what to do next.

'May I give you a hand?' Max stopped beside the woman and took off the broad-brimmed felt hat without which he was rarely seen.

The small dark woman smiled up at him uncertainly, one hand on the child's shoulder.

'Thank you very much. I would like to get Alison on to the beach but I think the wheels will sink into this soft sand.'

'Would Alison allow me to carry her whilst you manage the

chair?' Max smiled down at the fair-haired child.

A pair of serious blue eyes returned his look for a moment before she nodded assent.

With deft and gentle movements, Max picked up Alison in his strong arms and held her close to his chest. The small head with its two stiff plaits lay trustingly against Max's shoulder. Two large net bows of bright crimson ribbon tied off the ends of both plaits. The splashes of vivid colour reminded Max of the waratahs at home.

'This is so kind of you,' the woman spoke shyly. She collapsed the light wheelchair with the deft practiced movements that spelled frequent use. 'Please just park us any place that is convenient for you.'

'My wife and daughter are over there on that red and blue blanket.' Max nodded his head in the general direction of Kirsty and Stella. 'What about a nice spot not too far from us?'

'That would be just fine. How old is your daughter?'

'Stella turned seventeen in July.'

'What a pretty name. You don't often hear it these days.'

'Short for Estelle and named after her grandmother.'

'Estelle is a lovely name, too. Does she like her name?'

'Oh yes,' laughed Max, 'she does indeed. Stella has always been extremely close to the grandmother she was named for; she is very like her in character, too, and is very proud to bear her name.' He stopped about five or six meters behind where his wife and daughter were sitting gazing out at the Tasman Sea. 'Will this be all right for you?'

'Perfect thanks.' The dark haired woman quickly set the wheelchair on the sand and rummaged in her bulging shoulder bag. From its depths she withdrew a very large beach towel which she spread out on the flat sand.

'Here, on that towel?' asked Max.

'Yes please,' nodded the woman.

Alison clung to Max Richards as he gently lowered her to the towel. He was careful to support the child in a sitting position till she found her balance, using her small hands to settle herself. Something in the competent way she managed her restricted body suggested a long term condition: Alison was very used to this.

No-one looking at Max Richards would have had the slightest idea of the raw fury that was raging behind the pleasant facade. Here was yet another child whose life must be sheer hell. Why on earth did these things have to happen to children? He hoped that the woman and child had some decent support behind them. And where was that child's father? Why wasn't he here helping his wife and daughter when they needed it? Frowning slightly, he watched as the woman withdrew what appeared to be a misshapen bundle of stiff fabric from her full shoulder bag.

Alison must have studying his face because the child gave a small laugh as her mother put her lips to a nozzle projecting from one corner of the bundle.

'That's my pillow,' she explained. 'Mummy has to blow it up. I can't do it myself yet, but I will be able to one day soon.'

'I'm sure you will, Alison.' Max smiled at both mother and daughter. He politely made his farewells, receiving heartfelt thanks in return. Making his way across the few meters of sand to his family, a small but clear voice reached his ears:

'Wasn't he a nice man, Mummy? I wish we had a daddy like that.'

Mother and daughter sat very close together taking in the panorama that was Bondi Beach in early September.

Lace edged white ruffles of foam topped waves of emerald green, sapphire blue and aquamarine. Bright red and yellow flags designating the safest swimming areas flapped gently in the breeze. A few gaily-coloured beach umbrellas with their vivid quartered segments sheltered babies and anxiously hovering new parents. Children with plastic buckets and spades were busily at work on sandcastles — some of the completed constructions were quite miraculous in their attention to detail.

'I wonder why there are so many people flying kites?' wondered Kirsty.

'The Kite Festival,' said a voice behind them.

'Of course, I had completely forgotten.' Kirsty smiled up at her husband.

'What's the Kite Festival?' Stella asked listlessly.

'It's an annual event where people who love flying kites come to Bondi. I think it started back in the late 1970s. It's always held at the beginning of September, if I remember correctly, which is probably why there are so many kites today. Look at that beauty.' Max pointed to an elegant Chinese dragon of bright scarlet and gold.

'The Chinese first invented kite flying,' continued Kirsty. 'The earliest kites go back a very long time and I believe they were created out of silk and bamboo.'

'Didn't the Chinese first discover silk and the silkworm?' Max could see that his daughter was now listening intently although she was saying little.

'The Chinese were using silk from the silkworm four thousand years ago. They are a very clever people and they make beautiful kites.' Kirsty gazed up at the sky as she spoke. 'Look, another

Chinese dragon.'

'It must take a lot of silkworms to make enough silk for a kite,' Stella spoke up.

'It must,' her mother agreed.

'Those box kites always interest me, from an aerodynamic point of view,' began Max.

Both his ladies groaned and Stella let out a small giggle.

'Well, if nobody's interested …' Max pretended to be hurt, which drew a further giggle from his daughter.

'Darling, of course we're interested.' Kirsty patted him on the shoulder soothingly. 'Please continue. Actually, I do know what you mean,' she added. 'One wonders how they ever get off the ground. I can see how all the other kites, those basic diamond shaped ones like we had as kids, for instance, and the newer windsocks and even the dragons would be able to fly but I never could work out the secret behind box kites.'

A windsock flew above the little family, trailing rainbow-coloured ribbons which fluttered in the breeze. The light blue sky created the perfect backdrop for the riot of colourful motley.

'There must be nearly a hundred of them,' exclaimed Kirsty.

'Ahem, if I may continue about box kites —'

Stella giggled again and some of the tension in her body eased a little.

'The important aerodynamic factors are the actual angle of the line which connects the person to the kite and the tension in that line. Put them together with the wind factor and that is what makes your kite fly. Remember, it is always the wind that causes uplift and no wind equals no kite in the air. It is the shape of the box kite which allows the wind to give it a strong uplift and that is why box kites tend to be able to fly higher than other kites, in the right hands, of course.'

Kirsty, having understood about half of this little speech, nodded wisely. Stella's interest was piqued and she began asking her father more about kites and kite flying. After fifteen minutes of this, Max jumped up, spoke a quick word in Kirsty's ear, and headed for the promenade.

All this kite talk had jerked his memory and he suddenly recalled passing a small kiosk displaying kites for sale. He found it quickly enough, set up on the grassy area behind the promenade. Kites of every imaginable shape and colour were strung across the top the kiosk. The front counter was piled high with clear plastic bags, each containing the makings of a simple, but colourful diamond shaped kite. A flurry of windsocks fluttered from the two vertical poles on either side of the front counter. A large flower pot was crammed with windmills-on-a-stick for smaller children to enjoy. Max quickly purchased a bag holding the makings of a small, vividly hued, diamond kite. The proprietor of the stall assured him that the bag held everything: the kite, the struts, the tail and plenty of line wound around an easy-to-hold handle.

'There you go, kiddo.' Max handed Stella the plastic bag. 'See what you can do with that.'

'You help me, Dad.'

Kirsty watched, amused and relieved. That dreadful frozen look had vanished from Stella's face and she appeared genuinely interested in what her father was both telling and showing her. Together they constructed the simple diamond: it was electric blue with a huge yellow, happy smiley face on the front.

'What say I'll try it out to see how well it flies and then you can give it a go?' Max suggested.

'But I won't be able to run along the sand like those people.' Stella nodded to where several teenagers were tearing along the wet sand, trying to force their kites into the air.

'You won't need to, trust me. Those kids are only fooling about anyway. Just give me a few minutes.'

Max took a bearing of the wind, making rather a song and dance of it when he saw it made his daughter smile. He frowned at her, wriggled his eyebrows and ostentatiously licked a finger and raised it to the wind. Then he turned ninety degrees and tested the wind again. Stella was racked with laughter by now.

He is a real darling, thought Kirsty. *How many men would be as good to his family as Max is? Most of the chaps I hear about usually beat a hasty retreat at the first signs of trouble, especially when it relates to long term illness. They just don't seem able to cope with it. If they don't run away, then they resort to drink. But when you do get a man who is able to deal with it, he doesn't just do okay, he manages brilliantly.*

Max, who now had the kite in the air, continued to joke. He took several steps backwards, pretended to fall down in the sand and then actually did fall over a hidden tuft of beach grass. The kite slowly fluttered down on top of him.

Stella was laughing so much that she fell on her side, dropping to the blanket, tears of mirth streaming down her face. Kirsty too shook with laughter and suddenly wondered when the three of them had last enjoyed what she called 'a good family laughter session'. It had been far too long …

Alison and her mother were also enjoying the antics. Alison's serious blue eyes followed the kite but they also followed Max Richards. Kirsty, who never missed anything, had already observed the lonely little couple. Her warm heart bled for them.

Max, who always knew when enough was enough, ended his

clowning well before his audience grew tired of it. He concentrated on getting the little 'happy kite', as he called it, flying properly. The wind had increased and he was able to keep it flying, once it was aloft, with very little walking or running. He was pretty sure, if he found the correct location in relation to the wind, that Stella would be able to guide the line for a short time, once the kite was in the air and fairly stable.

It was at times like these that it was really driven home to Max how restricted children like Stella and Alison were. Most youngsters walked and ran and played and climbed and swam without even pausing to think. Children shouldn't have to think of such things. Childhood was supposed to be a time of lightheartedness, not pain, illness and restriction. Almost angrily he shook his head, trying to thrust away his thoughts.

Max explained his plan to his family: he would get the kite flying where the uplift was good then hand it over to Kirsty. It was her responsibility, he told her sternly, to keep it aloft. Her lips quivered with the beginnings of a grin but she held her peace. He would then assist Stella to where her mother should still have the kite in the air — this was said with a firm glare in the direction of his wife. Providing the winds cooperated and with just a tad of luck Stella would get her turn at flying the kite. He would support and balance her whilst she concentrated on the kite.

This ingenious plan was put into action. *Well,* thought Kirsty with a private chuckle, *whatever else happened they were providing entertainment for other beach goers, especially that little girl over there. And it had certainly brought plenty of smiles to Stella's face. To be honest, I think Max is genuinely enjoying himself.*

Stella, standing braced and supported by her father some minutes later, felt the joyous tug of the kite string as the happy-faced blue diamond literally reached for the sky. She felt the sense of freedom, the wind blowing her curls and cooling her skin whilst her eyes followed the kite she was actually controlling. Images from the film *Mary Poppins* danced through her mind; they moved in time with the kite dancing in the sky. A sudden gust of wind lifted the kite higher and Stella, one hand gently guided by that of her father, was able to direct it still. The tail, decorated with blue and yellow bows, streamed out gaily, prancing, curvetting and curling. A pair of small hands clapped enthusiastically.

Too soon it was over and down, down, down came the kite, swooping towards the ground. Stella, exhilarated but exhausted, wobbled, fell against her father and was gently lowered to the sand. Part of the tail fluttered close to her before coming to a final rest. She smiled and softly fingered one of the yellow bows. For the first time since arriving at the beach Stella began to look around her and take real notice of the people. The clapping she had vaguely heard must have come from that little girl sitting with her mother: they were the only people close enough. Stella raised her right hand and waved gaily to the pair.

Chapter Twenty-three: Morgan Luck Promise

The Pajero was fifteen minutes short of the Blue Mountains town of Lithgow when the dam finally broke.

'Mummy, I don't care what that doctor says, I will never use a wheelchair!' The explosive words were followed by their daughter's head pushing between the two front seats, her arms tightly clutching the said seats for support.

Max swore beneath his breath and kept his eyes firmly fixed on the road.

'So you heard what that idiot said yesterday? I thought so,' Kirsty spoke casually.

'Mummy, you won't make me use a wheelchair, even if it does make things much easier for you?'

Kirsty's soul burned with an anger she barely knew she was capable of. She wished she lived in the days when hanging, drawing and quartering was an acceptable form of punishment. What immense satisfaction she would feel from witnessing the spectacle: seeing a certain eminent rheumatologist drawn on a hurdle to his place of execution in the front of a jeering crowd then hanged by the neck till he was almost dead, to be then cut down by willing and helpful assistants and whilst still alive, his body cut into four pieces thus to be dealt with at the King's pleasure. For the first time in her life she understood the cruel desire to hurt, to do harm, to strike out and wound.

'Mummy?'

'No, darling, we will never make you use a wheelchair, not ever.' The effort to speak slowly and gently was so physically intense that her arms and legs trembled.

'Would it make things easier for you?'

By God in Heaven she would make this bastard pay for what he had done to her daughter. She quietly took two deep breaths and again spoke carefully and slowly:

'Of course not. Doctors often make very stupid suggestions.'

'But, Mummy, it takes so long for me to get really short distances and sometimes I have to be helped to walk or even carried. Wouldn't it make it a lot easier for you and Daddy, for the teachers at school, if I was in a wheelchair?'

Kirsty closed her eyes. So he had done this to her daughter, made her feel she owed her family something, made her think she was a burden to them. She would kill this maniac of a doctor; she would get him struck off the medical council; have him stripped of every damned qualification; burn down his bloody fancy home in some expensive, upmarket Sydney suburb, no doubt, she would —

'Mummy?'

'No, darling, it would not make it easier at all,' Kirsty said gently.

'Are you sure?'

'Yes, darling.'

'Really sure?'

'Really sure.'

'That's good 'cos I really hate wheelchairs. I don't want ever to have to use one. But if it would help you and Daddy — make things not so hard on you —' the young voice faltered to a trembling halt.

'No, darling, it would not help us at all.' Kirsty reached a hand out and touched a finger to the swollen face just behind her own. The finger was seized by a hot hand; the hot hand found the mother's hand and clutched it desperately.

Max cleared his throat and spoke.

'We're just about to reach our usual pull up spot. I believe it is over the next hill. I don't know about anyone else but I could use a good strong cuppa.'

Stella lay back on the brightly checked blanket and looked up at her parents. She remembered that blanket from her earliest agricultural shows and outings: it always accompanied the family everywhere they travelled by car. It had a permanent home in the Pajero. Four pillows supported her: two behind her head and two beneath her right knee. Within easy reach sat a large, safety-lidded, plastic travelling mug with thick handles, partially filled with hot, sweet tea. It had been a long time now since she had been able to use 'normal' cups and mugs with safety. She didn't need burns to be added to her list of problems.

'Stella,' the mother's voice was gentle and soft, 'what else did you hear in that waiting room? Somehow I don't think you've quite told us all of it.'

'Did you truly mean that about the wheelchair? About it not making things easier for you?'

'Stella,' Max's serious eyes met those of his daughter, 'when has your mother ever lied to you about anything?'

The blue eyes held the grey eyes till the girl's shoulders relaxed. She gave a little sigh.

'I'm sorry, Dad, but —'

'Yes?'

'It's just that I don't — don't —'

'Don't what?'

'Don't find it easy to trust adults anymore!' The rushed words were followed by a storm of tears.

Kirsty breathed a silent sigh of relief. The dam had finally burst. With Stella one just never knew. The girl was capable of holding things within for weeks, even months, greatly to her own detriment and often to that of her family. A certain incident from the child's early school years came to mind.

Stella had been in her fourth year at the little school at the Crossroads when the first winds of change were felt. The first female teacher arrived. Prior to this, it had been considered extremely unwise to send women teachers to certain single teacher bush schools but the age of women's liberation, independence and as some would say, outright stupidity had arrived.

Trouble began early. For no apparent reason, it appeared that Miss Michelle Griffiths had developed an immediate antipathy to the young Stella Richards. The dislike had been returned in spades. However, instead of telling her family what was happening at school, Stella had bided her time, amassed her resources and declared war on the teacher.

Nobody ever quite understood how Stella first discovered that something to do with horses made Miss Griffiths 'go all funny'. Her eyes would get red, swollen and watery; she would get breathless; she sneezed a lot; her nose wouldn't stop running and she got red rashes on her arms. Quietly chuckling to herself, Stella went to work, aided by a band of young faithfuls.

Five naughty youngsters asked seemingly innocent questions to carefully selected adults and learnt some interesting facts. If a person 'went all funny' because of horses, it didn't actually need the presence of a horse to cause this strange phenomena, and anyway, Miss Griffiths wouldn't go within a mile of any equine being. Items that had been in regular contact with horses could cause the same fascinating symptoms: rugs, blankets, brushes, bandages and the like.

'We can't exakerly put a horse rug on her desk,' pointed out one of Stella's followers.

'Nor a dandy brush or stable bandages,' added another youngster sadly. 'Shame, really.'

'How 'bout an old saddle cloth? She mighten' know what it's for. Might think it's a floor rug or somethink?' was one bright suggestion.

'What about horsehair from the inside of rugs and the brushes?' suggested one hopeful.

'You've got it!' Stella beamed at the last speaker. 'Now, all of you, gather round and listen … this is what we'll do.'

Five youngsters showed an unusual willingness to assist their elders with animal chores the following morning before school. Five sets of busy little hands carefully and industriously removed horsehair from horse brushes, from saddle cloths, from inside New Zealand rugs, from light cotton show sheets and from articles of clothing. They had been extremely fortunate with the timing: it was an unusually warm spring after an equally unusually cold winter and all the livestock were shedding hair on everything they touched. Gleeful chuckles were suppressed as bundles of thick horsehair in every imaginable colour were stuffed into old feed bags, which were then rammed into the bottom of school bags.

The joint booty was hidden in a secret cache: an old but clean oil drum with a tight lid which they secreted under the school's wooden water tank stand. Led by Stella, the team set to work with cunning and precision redolent of secret agents.

Two of the young villains had observed that their hated teacher always hung her cardigan or jacket across the back of her chair. It nearly always hung there all day, unless the weather chilled off rather suddenly. But as already been said, it was an unusually warm spring that year.

Every lunch time Miss Griffiths would return to the tiny cottage across the lane from the school, rarely taking her cardigan or jacket. There she would eat her sandwiches in glorious solitude and wonder how she could possibly stay one whole year in this quite dreadful place.

It was the work of seconds for a quick pair of hands to remove the cardigan from the back of the chair and drop it through the window into another pair of waiting hands. Several minutes had to be allowed to thoroughly treat the garment with horsehair. Fistfuls of horsehair were pushed down the sleeves and into the pockets. The cardigan was then liberally treated with more horsehair: all the linings were thoroughly rubbed with it.

'I guess we'd better shake it.' Stella eyed the maltreated item with interest. 'I don't suppose we can leave the hair in the sleeves. She'd be bound to see it.'

'Yes, it does look a bit funny,' agreed one small partner in crime.

'We can leave the lining pockets full,' suggested another keen hopeful. 'She'll never notice it in there.'

'What about undoing some of the lining and stuffing more hair between the two layers of material?' was one very bright suggestion.

This clever notion was applauded by all present and the wicked band continued their work. One small girl skilled at sewing deftly unpicked a number of small stitches holding the lining in place.

'I did it just under the collar, so then the hair won't fall out,' she explained. 'It will be trapped by the hem so it can't fall out the bottom. She might not notice it either.'

'Do you think we've left enough hair on to do the job?'

'Only one way to find out,' Stella said briskly.

'Who gets to put it back?'

This honour was bestowed upon the young seamstress whom all agreed had earned it. Long before Miss Griffiths returned to commence the afternoon's school, the cardigan was in place on the back of the teacher's chair.

Stella and her band got more than they had bargained for. Miss Griffiths happened to have an extremely severe allergy to horsehair although at the time of the 'cardigan incident', as it came to be called, she was not aware of this. All she knew was that proximity to horses caused her certain stressful problems. Allergies were rarely taken seriously in the early 1980s.

One parent, arriving to collect his little daughter early from the school at the Crossroads that same afternoon, found Miss Griffiths in a state of partial collapse and surrounded by a group of extremely frightened children. He immediately sent for Doctor Mason.

It did not take Doctor Charles Mason very long to get to the bottom of the whole 'cardigan incident'. Stella Richards, bravely supported by her four stalwarts, blurted out the whole story within minutes. Miss Griffiths was treated with antihistamines and escorted back to the Doctor's Koolkuna clinic for the night, to be kept under the watchful care of Sister Braddock.

The five scamps were severely disciplined by their respective elders, all of whom Doctor Mason had enjoyed a short but excessively plainspoken talk with. Allergies were serious stuff and the young hellions must be made to realise this.

Under the kindly and sympathetic treatment meted out to her by both Sister Braddock and Doctor Mason, Miss Griffiths was gently persuaded not to make official complaints about the 'cardigan incident'. She was given two weeks leave which she spent at the seaside. The relief teacher, one Mr Geoffrey Sharpe, who took her place, was made fully cognisant of the whole situation and sworn to secrecy. He had many years of teaching under his belt and a great sense of humour: occasionally when his eye alighted on Stella Richards or one of her cronies that same eye showed the suspicion of a twinkle.

Upon Miss Griffiths' return, a truce was struck but it was always an uneasy one. She left the Crossroads at the end of the term to be replaced by Mr Sharpe, who remained at the school for the next five years. Miss Griffiths resigned from teaching and found a peaceful niche for herself in a city bank. Children were very rarely seen in city banks and horses, never.

Kirsty allowed her daughter to sob out the horrors of the past two days but stepped in before the therapeutic tears became hysterical. Slipping an arm around the girl, she whispered:

'Remember Miss Griffiths and the 'cardigan incident'?'

Gradually the frantic sobbing quietened, was replaced by several loud hiccups, a watery smile and reluctant giggle. A swollen hand feebly searched for an absent handkerchief.

'Here ...' A young flag of blue cotton was dropped down into Stella's hand. 'That's the problem with you ladies, never a handkerchief handy.'

This sally was rewarded by a second, slightly less reluctant giggle. Stella scrubbed at her face and lay quietly against her pillows.

'Drink your tea, child, before it goes cold.' Kirsty pointed to the travelling mug.

Stella obediently clutched at the mug with clumsy, trembling fingers and began slowly sipping. Each reviving mouthful of the hot, sweet liquid put new life into her.

Kirsty slipped away to the Pajero, returning with a plastic bag. From it she withdrew a small, damp hand towel. Once Stella had finished her tea, the mother gently sponged the girl's face and hands with the damp towel.

'Thanks, Mum.'

'OK, Stella, I think we'd better finish what we started. Much better to have everything out and not churning around inside you. Agreed?'

'Right, Dad.'

'I am not all surprised that you don't find it easy to trust adults anymore — can't say I blame you for that — but some of us aren't so bad, you know.'

The grey eyes looked at him levelly: 'He said that I would probably never walk again.'

'Ah, so you heard that as well? I see,' said Kirsty thoughtfully. She eyed her daughter. 'Do you like that doctor?'

Stella stared at her mother in amazed bewilderment at this unexpected question. 'Of course not. How could I?'

'Do you trust him?'

An angry shake of the head was the only reply.

'Do you think he could be a liar?'

'Of course he is!'

'Then why should we take any notice of what he said yesterday?'

'He's supposed to be the best, isn't he? Isn't that why we make these awful trips down to Sydney every month? Because he's meant to be the best?' shot back Stella.

'We won't be making these trips anymore,' was the calm response. 'Yes, Stella, we went to him because we had been told he was the best, but we were told wrong — we know that now — but we had to try. We always have to try. Now, it is time to try something else. Sometimes, when a doctor doesn't understand a patient's illness, he will give up. He appears to get frustrated and angry at the lack of results, at the absence of what he considers is his own success. The job gets too hard for him so he quits, totally forgetting that the patient still has to live every day with the pain and the illness.'

'If he thinks like that he shouldn't be a doctor!' Stella snapped.

'We know, darling, and we agree.'

'I hate wheelchairs!'

'We know, darling.'

It was startlingly clear that Stella regarded the very word as a devilish abomination, a demonic horror belonging to nightmarish dreams, an appalling apparition, a terrifying object that threatened her very existence.

'You won't put me in one?' Frightened eyes looked first at her mother then her father.

'No, Stella, we promise,' chorused Max and Kirsty.

'You honestly do promise not to put me in a wheelchair?'

'Stella, we swear to you that no wheelchair will ever cross the boundaries of Cheshunt,' Max spoke solemnly.

'Mummy?'

'I promise that we will never, ever put you in a wheelchair.'

'Do you honestly think I will walk again properly one day?'

'Yes, I truly do,' said Kirsty seriously.

'Daddy?'

'Yes, Stella, like your mother I am quite sure that you really will.'

'No wheelchairs?'

'No wheelchairs,' said Max and Kirsty.

'Morgan Luck Promise?'

'Morgan Luck Promise!' her parents spoke in perfect unison.

There was peace in the huge grey eyes that gazed trustfully back at the parents.

Chapter Twenty-four: Birds of the Bush

It had been an unusually peaceful day for Max and Kirsty. In the week since their return from Sydney Stella had made no further mention of the hated Sydney rheumatologist or the dreaded wheelchair. She had managed four full days at school and had pushed for five but Kirsty had firmly vetoed the Monday following the long drive home.

It had been Toby's suggestion that Max and Kirsty 'take a bit of a break' and ride out together to look at the waratahs.

'I'll keep an eye on the kid here.' He winked at his sister.

'Keep an eye on yourself,' retorted that young lady with spirit.

Late morning found Max mounted on his beloved Misty and Kirsty on the bay, impeccably mannered Serenade. Misty had inherited the same glorious dappled grey colouring of her famous sire, Son of Saratoga.

'Like chess pieces,' Stella called from her seat on the verandah.

'Chess pieces?' demanded her brother.

'Dark bay and silvery grey, of course!'

'Idiot!' laughed Toby.

They watched as the two riders rode away across the smaller home paddock. The riders would jump the slip rails on the far side before turning onto the track which led to the bush.

Max and Kirsty rode very close, stirrup to stirrup. Few words passed between them. This was a rare and special time: alone together and their responsibilities temporarily in abeyance.

Riding easily, his reins in his left hand, Max looked at the girl who was his wife. He still thought of her as a girl and probably always would. Beneath her broad-brimmed felt hat the black curls were tied back away from her face. Kirsty had always hated having hair around her face or in her eyes. The worried and strained look which had almost become permanent was gone and the warm brown eyes held something of their old mischievous sparkle. The strong brown hand which so capably managed Serenade's reins wore only two rings, the broad gold wedding band and the sapphire he had given her after Stella's birth. His eyes rested thoughtfully upon the gleaming sapphire.

Kirsty rode along in a dream. She had closed her mind to everything but the immediate present, revelling in the fresh, eager stride of the bay gelding beneath her. For this once she would live in the immediate now, a few stolen hours with her adored Max. It would not be for long, but just for today, for part of today, the world belonged to her and Max as it had once done so many years ago, when they were young, before her babies had died, before Stella's illness, before each hour of the day was clouded by fear for her daughter, by Stella's pain and by uncertainty. Kirsty no longer believed in a merciful God and perhaps this troubled her most of all.

The track narrowed and Misty, assuming her right as elder states-mare of Cheshunt, took the lead. The lovely mare broke into a smooth trot and Serenade, with a gay little toss of his head, followed suit. The horses seemed to sense that this was a special time.

Max suddenly turned onto an almost imperceptible track which wound away through the bush.

'Max?'

'Mystery ride.' He turned in the saddle and grinned at her.

Kirsty shrugged. 'Suits me.'

She had a secret smile on her face as the narrow track started to climb. They were on the old fire trail leading to one of the highest points of Cheshunt.

The trail threaded its way around the scented scribbly gums (*Eucalyptus haemastoma*), the creamy-trunked blue mountain gums (*Eucalyptus deanei*), the prickly-leaved paperbarks (*Melaleuca styphelioides*), the sunshine wattles (*Acacia terminalis*) and numerous hardy juniper-leaf grevilleas (*Grevillea juniperina*): all dear and familiar species.

'Listen, Kirsty, bell-birds.' Max reined Misty to a halt.

'The silver-voiced bell-birds, the darlings of daytime!

They sing in September their songs of the May-time,' Kirsty quoted softly, one hand on Serenade's warm neck.

'That's not bad for poetry,' came the grudging admission.

'It's from Henry Kendall's *Bell-birds*. Written in the 1860s, I think. I learnt it back at school.'

The horses stood quietly, shoulder to shoulder, their riders stirrups to stirrup.

'And, softer than slumber, and sweeter than singing,

The notes of the bell-birds are running and ringing,' Kirsty's voice was quiet.

Max smiled at his wife and nodded. He wasn't much for poetry — that was Kirsty and Toby's thing, not his — but those words certainly fitted in with this place and time. 'Can you remember any more?'

By channels of coolness the echoes are calling,

And down the dim gorges I hear the creek falling:

It lives in the mountain where moss and the sedges

Touch with their beauty the banks and the ledges.'

'That's pretty apt, Kirsty. Our creek starts up here somewhere. It's always a bit of an adventure to find.'

Both riders fell silent. The horses were resting, heads dropped, eyes partly closed, ears lowered to the sides. The sweet, almost spiritual, musical notes rippled through the Australian bush.

'Kirsty ...' Max touched her hand, '... we'd better get moving.'

'Welcome as waters unkissed by the summers

Are the voices of bell-birds to thirsty far-comers.'

The seldom used track began to climb steeply. The odd radiata pine tree could be seen scattered throughout the native bush at irregular intervals. As they rounded a sharp corner a dark shape hurried across the path and vanished into the bracken.

'Did you see the long tail, Max?'

'Yes, definitely a lyrebird,' he agreed, 'and an adult male by the look of his tail. It's coming to the end of their breeding season soon.'

'They're pretty shy and elusive, aren't they?'

'Very. This is probably only the fourth time I've seen one.'

'I found a tail feather once,' Kirsty told him.

'Where?'

'As a child, in the bush at home. I was out exploring one day, by myself —'

Max groaned.

His wife laughed. 'Idiot! Don't worry, I had one of the dogs with me — Shadow wouldn't have let me lose myself — he had a natural homing instinct. Dear old Shadow, he used to go everywhere with me. Well, I just saw this huge tail feather on the ground in front of me. It was a real beauty. When I got home Dad said it was definitely from the male lyrebird. My brothers were so jealous — not Peter, of course — but Charles and Phillip — Brian was just a baby. Peter made a special lock for my bedroom door — to keep Charles and Phillip from stealing my precious lyrebird feather. Phillip tried to climb through the window but fell and broke his collarbone. Mum and Dad were furious — he got scant sympathy, I can tell you.'

'What a saga,' chuckled Max. 'What happened next?'

'Peter and I fixed the feather to the highest part of one of my bedroom walls — it looked grand! It was also well out of reach of light-fingered brothers. Dad made an official family announcement that the feather belonged to me. You know, he was pretty darned smart the way he managed things. He said that any brother who entered my room without first asking my permission would get a sound hiding — with his stock whip. He also said that he was sure I would happily show the lyrebird feather to the family on special occasions, allowing everyone to enjoy the pleasure of it. I felt about two inches tall, I can tell you!'

Max roared with laughter. 'Your Dad always was a card! Good for him!'

The old wooden fire tower stood in a clearing at the top of the peak. It had been erected during the days of Max's grandparents, Robert and Eleanor Richards, when both landowners and authorities recognised the danger of bush fires and the need for early detection.

'Wow!' Kirsty tilted her head back, gazing up at the tall tower.

'You've seen it before, Kirsty.'

'Not for about twenty years,' retorted his wife.

'Slight exaggeration.' Max swung down from his saddle.

Misty and Serenade were hung up to a nearby gum tree, the bits slipped from their mouths and their saddles removed.

'Did you know it's actually called Buckridge Fire Tower on the shire maps?' asked Max as the pair walked across to the base of the tower.

Kirsty shook her head.

'Old Mr Buckridge worked for the forestry people all his life. He refused to retire — well, I think he may have had to 'officially' retire, but he was given the continued use of a forestry jeep and spent just about all his time 'looking after the bush' as he put it. He was a grand old chap — loved the Australian bush — especially this corner of it. Was adamant about keeping the fire trails clear — if he couldn't move something himself he let the boys back at base know about it and they'd be out the following day. Our fire tower never had a name and, after he died, it was officially named after him. He was pretty old and I was quite a kid when I knew him but I never forgot him. He took me up this tower for the first time when I was only six.'

They now stood at the bottom of the narrow wooden ladder.

'Ready, Kirsty?'

'Ready, Max.'

'After you then. If you fall I can catch you.'

Kirsty snorted inelegantly and grasped both sides of the ladder with her strong, brown hands. 'Better not keep too close or I might kick you by accident, buster.'

'Seriously, it's quite a climb so take it nice and steady. No super heroics please, Kirsty.'

Somewhat placated, she gave a small smile and began to climb.

Kirsty was hot and breathless when her head finally reached the hole in the centre of the viewing platform's wooden floor.

'Just a few more steps,' panted Max from beneath.

With a gasp of relief Kirsty collapsed on the rough wooden beams of the somewhat uneven floor and watched Max climb the final rungs. He shrugged off his light knapsack and tossed it down beside his wife. Then he knelt beside her.

'I'll lie with my head on the knapsack and you can rest yours on my chest. We could use a short break.'

'Let me just ditch my boots.'

'Good idea.'

Kirsty's head rested against the solid warmth of her husband's broad chest. She could both hear and feel his heart beating loud and strong. It was so peaceful and remote up here at the top of the fire tower. Contentedly she closed her eyes. She could just hear the distant silver-tongued calls of bell-birds…

'Kirsty, Kirsty, wake up!'

The voice was part of the dream she was having.

'Kirsty, Kirsty, come on, wake up!'

The voice was getting annoying, persistent. It wouldn't go away. She frowned and turned her head away.

'Kirsty!'

Now something was pulling at her shoulder. Irritably, she tried to shrug it away but it refused to budge.

'Kirsty! Wake up!'

Something was touching her face, a cold and wet something.

'Max!'

'Sorry, Kirsty but you were fathoms deep. I couldn't seem to wake you.' Max was holding a wet handkerchief in one hand, a plastic bottle of water in the other. 'To be honest, I was starting to worry.'

Kirsty struggled to her feet, groaned and stretched. 'My aching leg muscles!'

'You just climbed the equivalent of nine flights of stairs —'

'What?'

'This platform is exactly ninety feet from the ground. Mr Buckridge told me that and just to make sure I measured the ladder myself years ago.'

'Ninety feet?'

'The height of a nine-storey block of flats,' he affirmed.

'Not surprised my legs feel like chewed string.'

She leaned against the waist-high wooden rails and looked out towards the south. She could see a gleam of silver where the busy infant creek hurried away down the peak, eager to join its parent river.

'Where's the main house?'

He stood close behind her, hands on her shoulders and gently turned her to the left.

'Over there, almost due east. We can't actually see it because part of the main ridge gets in the road, but it is there, I promise you.'

She laughed and the light wind played with her tied-back curls, making them dance and flutter.

'Hungry?' he asked tenderly.

'Could you do anything about it if I was?' she teased.

'Got Stella to pack us a light snack,' he spoke nonchalantly.

'I'm impressed.' Her eyes laughed at him.

'Are you hungry?' he pressed.

She shook her head and squeezed his hand reassuringly. 'Not quite now but I know I will be soon.'

Max turned his wife to face him and the two pairs of eyes locked: brown and blue. For now, the world belonged to the two of them.

Now, as the sun dropped low in the western sky, they were riding home after a perfect day. Misty and Serenade quickened their pace as they approached the slip rails of the smaller home paddock. The rails were jumped easily and both horses were eager to race, knowing very well that they were on the home run.

'No, boy.' Kirsty grinned as she held Serenade back. 'Remember the ironclad rule: always walk the first mile out and last mile home except in emergency.'

The horses walked out eagerly, ears pricked, necks arched. They knew what was coming: a good rub down followed by a delightful roll in the dirtiest part of their paddock. Later they would be thoroughly groomed then rugged and fed. Life was good for horses on Cheshunt.

Max and Kirsty rode towards the house. It appeared unusually quiet: there was no sign of Toby or Stella. Only Jasper was in his usual place on the verandah. He rose to his feet and came to meet them.

'Hello, Jasper, you guarding the house?' Kirsty bent from her saddle to speak to him. 'He is a grand dog, Max, he really is.'

Jasper thumped his tail on the ground, trustful eyes gazing up at Kirsty. He reached up a paw and placed it on her stirrup.

'He's got such beautiful, honest eyes.' She spoke into a quietness that had turned to a strange and unreal stillness.

'Max?' Kirsty turned her head.

He obviously hadn't heard a word she'd said. He sat Misty as if turned to stone.

'Max?'

There was still no response.

Kirsty followed the direction of his fixed gaze.

It was poised arrogantly on the farmhouse verandah. It stood there: cool, insolent, alone, an almost unbelievably alien intruder to this rural fastness. The dull black upholstery was full of shadows but the silvery metal gleamed and shone in the late afternoon light.

'Toby,' roared Max, 'where the fuck did that thing come from?'

Chapter Twenty-five: Alien Intruder

I
f only Max hadn't bellowed out for the children with that stentorian roar …

If only she had reacted much quicker, shushing Max, hiding the wretched thing temporarily from sight …

If only Stella had not limped out into that perfect evening, seen the chair, stopped in her tracks as if shot …

'If only' must be the saddest and most useless words in the English language.

But, as she had later witheringly pointed out, Max's bellow could have been heard at both Bellara and Koolkuna. This upset Jasper who added his bark to his master's shouts. The cacophony brought Toby at a fast run.

After their parents had ridden off that morning, Toby and Stella had gone their separate ways.

'English essay …' Stella wrinkled her pretty nose at her brother. '… due on Tuesday.'

'I'll be in the junk shed.' Toby was referring to the large, airy, timber shed next to the workshop.

'What on earth are you doing there?'

'Just an idea I had the other day. Might not work out. Only one way to find out.'

'I'd much sooner give you a hand,' sighed Stella, eyeing with distaste her books already spread out on the kitchen table.

'Tell you what, you put in a decent stint at that essay then we'll grab a bite for lunch. Then, if you like, you can come out and help.'

Stella beamed her approval and this plan was put into action. Mid-afternoon saw Stella slowly limping her way out to the junk shed. The junk shed was one of a cluster of outbuildings behind the house, screened from it by a high brick wall.

'Your reclining chair awaits you, my lady.' Toby bowed and waved a hand at an ancient chaise lounge.

'Looks as if the mice have been eating it,' that lady observed disparagingly.

'It may appear a trifle tattered around the edges but I assure you it is sufficiently strong to support even your weight. I tried it out myself.'

Stella giggled and gingerly lowered herself onto the said piece of furniture.

'And a pillow for your back, my lady.' Toby bowed again and produced a large sofa cushion of faded ruby red satin.

'I can't imagine Mum ever allowing *that* into the house,' said Stella judiciously as she tucked the cushion behind her back, 'and that was *before* the moths got to it. But,' she added, 'it is extremely comfortable.'

'Support for your leg, my lady.' This time the bow was accompanied by a vast bolster covered in red and white striped vinyl.

'Was that out here too?' demanded Stella, poking at it.

'Of course. All accessories are courtesy of Toby's Treasure House. All needs and wishes catered for.'

'I might take it back to the house. Could be jolly useful.'

'Oh Lord, Mum'll kill me,' groaned Toby.

As Stella gradually took in her immediate surroundings, her eyes widened.

'Toby! A pony cart!'

'Well — it *was* once a pony cart,' conceded her brother.

'And you think you can fix it?'

'I *hope* I *might* be able to fix it,' he concurred. 'It must have been a very neat little vehicle once. Smart too with that dark green and cream paint job and those carriage lamps.'

Both cream-coloured shafts were splintered in two.

'They'll need replacing,' said Toby ruefully, 'but the body's in pretty good shape.'

'I like the green wicker top,' Stella approved. She eyed the two cream-coloured wooden wheels with their twelve spokes, the two green painted hubcaps on the floor beside them. 'Are they okay?'

'Need retreading and possibly realigning.'

'Are all the bits and pieces here?'

'Think so.' With his booted foot, Toby nudged a small pile of miscellaneous parts. 'The springs are here — very good springs too, and good springs are essential. I don't think any vital parts are missing.'

'Isn't it strange that both shafts are broken like that, but those two carriage lamps aren't?'

Toby shrugged. 'Shafts are nearly always the first to break in any sort of accident. Those lamps are surprisingly tough — made that way.'

'Would the pony cart fit Casper?'

'Possibly,' was the dry reply. 'But let's not jump our guns. I'm going to ask Mr Bingley if he wouldn't mind taking a look at the cart — see what he thinks. He should be able to help with the shafts at any rate.'

Hector Bingley was a retired cartwright who liked to keep his hand in, as he put it. His huge barn was home to numerous horse-drawn vehicles in various stages of repair. A few were fully restored to their original glory, others were a jumble of broken pieces piled up on the floor. The rest fitted somewhere between the two extremes. Hector Bingley delighted in supplying almost impossible to find parts to people repairing or restoring horse-drawn vehicles. He did this with little or no gain to himself because he loved to see people use these vehicles, fearing and dreading the day when they no longer graced the agricultural shows.

Toby vanished for a short while only to return, arms full. This load was dumped close by Stella's chaise lounge.

'Get busy sorting that little lot out,' he told his sister. 'No idling allowed here.'

'Pony harness?'

'Pony harness,' he confirmed, 'and sorely in need of untangling, not to mention a little basic care.'

'Where did it come from?' She eagerly pulled at the melee of straps, buckles, bands and reins which were entangled with the curved crupper and the heavier breast collar and saddle.

'Star of Bethlehem's original owner.'

'What!'

'The guy that sold Star of Bethlehem to Mum — his daughter — she had a brief enthusiasm for harness ponies. Didn't last long. This time her Dad kept a stern eye on affairs. Insisted she leased a pony, not bought one. After a spell lasting of all three months the pony has fortunately been returned to his owner, none the worse for wear. Girl did buy all the harness — her Dad said that at least harness was not a living animal and therefore could not be unduly harmed by neglect or lack of interest. Girl has now gone off to explore the wonders of Indonesia — not alone, so I hear. Left several hundred dollar's-worth of good harness in a pile on the tack-room floor at her Dad's place. Her Dad collected up said harness and offered it to Mum, at no cost. If she could make use of it and give it a good home, that was all he wanted. This is the said harness.'

Stella listened, forehead wrinkled. Her hands were already at work attempting to create some sense of order where there had been none.

'I just don't understand some people. That girl — how could she do that to Star of Bethlehem, and now the poor harness pony.'

'See what you can make of the harness — untangle it bit at a time. I'll get busy on the cart.'

Brother and sister worked companionably together, exchanging desultory remarks:

'The buckles on this breast collar are jolly stiff.'

'Need a hand?'

'No … finally got it.' Stella flexed her fingers.

'I like the original paint scheme on the cart. What do you think, sis? Shall we keep it the same?'

'Definitely. It looks very traditional.' She studied the body of the cart approvingly.

It was later deduced that the wheelchair must have arrived during the brief period when Jasper was not on the verandah. Just before four that afternoon, Toby returned to the house to collect his sister's

TENS machine and a snack for both of them. Whilst he was poking about in the pantry, the telephone rang.

'Cheshunt, Toby Richards speaking.'

There was no response.

'Hello? Anyone there?'

Still no response but he knew someone was listening at the other end of the line.

'Hello?'

Nothing. He heard a loud click followed by the disconnect tone as the caller put the telephone down.

Cursing mildly he dropped the handset back on the cradle and filled the electric jug. He and Stella could do with a good cup of tea. The kid was looking a bit knocked up.

Toby returned to the junk shed, hands laden. The TENS machine, his sister's tablets, a tin of freshly baked Anzac biscuits — good old Aussies, trust them to come up with that biscuit — and two of Stella's safety mugs filled with hot, sweet tea. Tired of his lonely vigil on the verandah, Jasper followed at Toby's heels.

Stella needed little assistance to fit the insulated wires to the flat paddles which she nearly always wore bandaged to her legs. But the girl was in pain and tired so he sat with her while she started the TENS machine and swallowed her tablets. Anzac biscuits dipped in hot tea were a welcome respite and Jasper sat between them, watching for dropped pieces of biscuit. Forty minutes passed before Toby sent Jasper back to the verandah.

'Jasper would have heard if any vehicle came up to the house, even from the junk shed,' asserted Toby. This was during a talk with Sergeant Bill Stroud two days later.

'Do you agree?' the Sergeant asked Max.

'Yes, he's a brilliant watch dog,' affirmed Kirsty. Max nodded.

'That makes it extremely interesting. Looks as if someone was watching your place, through a spotting scope maybe. They knew when the dog was out of the way and it was during that time that the wheelchair was left on your verandah; someone was dropped at your gate and walked up to the house. We can get a time on it by this phone call, which I doubt had anything to do with the wheelchair by the way. Toby here says he looked at the kitchen clock when the phone rang and it was five minutes past the hour. But why anyone would wish to go to so much trouble to do such a strange thing — well, it beats me,' the Sergeant summed up the situation. There was a short silence before he added, almost reluctantly:

'It couldn't be that someone might have thought they were helping you somehow? We get some very odd cases with so-called well-meaning people butting their noses in, often anonymously, so to speak. Honestly believing they are helping. I can vouch for that, so can my files back at the station. Don't you think that might be more likely than deliberate maliciousness?'

Toby was busy removing the handle of the small, hinged door in the rear of the cart's body, Stella attempting to neatly coil the long driving reins when the ruckus started.

'Golly! Dad's furious about something.' Toby leapt to his feet.

'Jasper's pretty upset too.' Stella dropped the reins.

'Something's very wrong. Don't you come, sis.' Toby was out the door at a run.

Slowly and painfully Stella struggled up from her chaise lounge, shedding satin cushion and striped bolster in her wake. She carefully negotiated the small hills of harness and various components of cart, reaching the wide doorway. Both the half-doors, built in the stable style, were hooked open. The evening air greeted her; the sun was just vanishing below the western horizon.

The road to shouting voices. Afterwards, she would always think of it like that because it was so unusual at Cheshunt. Her family didn't shout at each other: it was almost unknown. It was like moving along the path of a board game.

The brick paving felt hard beneath her unsteady feet as she limped past the workshop. The path sloped gradually upwards, the loud and angry voices grew closer. Breathing heavily, she approached the high brick wall. She stopped, rested on the old garden bench which stood next to the archway. For some reason she had no wish to go through that opening. For the moment she was still safe, but if she stepped beyond the sanctuary that now protected her, evil would present itself. Something was very wrong.

Stella pushed herself off the bench and took the first step. Dragged one awkward leg after the next. One slow step after another and another. It seemed to take so long yet was happening far too quickly. She had to get to her destination but feared the arrival. Disaster loomed ahead. Why did she know that? Was she going mad? Were those new drugs that the stupid medicos had started her on sending her insane? It wouldn't be the first time she had undergone a nasty reaction to their drugs. Once before she had suffered hallucinations and personality change, behaving in an irrational manner, quiet contrary to her usual self.

Irritably, she shook her head. She did not know anymore.

She was moving around the side of the house now. The loud voices and barking had stopped, replaced by a silence that was almost worse.

She saw her mother first, Serenade's reins looped over one arm. Misty's reins had been thrown to the ground: 'ground tied,' it was called. Misty stood still as a beautiful statue, for once in her life ignored by her owner. Her father, hands on hips, was glaring at Toby, who was speaking quietly. But what was Jasper doing? He appeared to be sniffing with great suspicion at a strange object on the front verandah…

Stella limped to a halt. No. It couldn't be. It just couldn't be. She let out a tiny moan.

Three heads swung in her direction. She didn't see them. She did not hear her mother's soft: 'Oh my God! Stella, no!'

She did not hear Toby's voice: 'I told her not to come.'

She did not hear her father's call: 'Stella! No, no, we didn't do it, sweetheart. We didn't do it!'

Stella slipped to the ground and into the welcome darkness.

Chapter Twenty-six: The Road to Sentinel Hill

Toby opened the door to his bedroom very quietly. The figure inside was slightly deaf and failed to hear either the turning of the handle or the man's soft footsteps. The person had their back to the opening door and appeared to be staring up at the opposite wall.

Toby stood and watched. So long as the figure didn't turn its head, he would remain free from their line of sight.

From a young age he had always insisted upon his room being plain and bare, almost stark, being excessively scornful of boys who had thick carpets, fancy curtains and other such unnecessary furnishings. It was a large, square room with big windows on the western and northern walls. The floor was well-polished wooden boards with nary a rug in sight. His mother had hung very plain curtains, the material, as she had drily remarked, being the closest thing to sacking she could find.

The walls were papered with a woodgrain pattern which made a perfect foil for his display collection. Pride of place was taken by the bayonet his grandfather had brought home from the Second World War. There were some animal skins, perfectly tanned by Old Dan, a pair of highly polished buffalo horns, a cricket bat from his boarding school days, a large photograph of Mr Kendrick Tenny, his mother and Son of Saratoga taken during that famed visit to Cheshunt more than twenty years ago and elegantly framed in rosewood, and safely restrained on its usual two highly placed wooden pegs, his prized rifle with the polished wooden stock.

It was at this display wall the figure was staring, chestnut curls tousled, barefooted and clad in pyjamas.

'You'll get cold without slippers on.' Toby moved into the room as he spoke.

The figure whirled around. 'Toby!'

'Thought you were in bed, old girl.'

'Couldn't sleep.'

'No, I suppose not.' Toby gently nudged a chair towards her and she sank into it. He pulled the folded blanket from the foot of his bed and tossed it to her. She looked very, very cold, her small face pinched.

'I like your buffalo horns,' she said at last.

'You always have,' he replied evenly.

The silence in the room lengthened.

'That's Grandad's bayonet, isn't it?' she finally spoke again.

'You know quite well it is.' He watched the white face, the restless hands and the huge grey eyes. He was bothered by those eyes.

There was another long pause. Her eyes kept returning to some object on that wall of his. Now what on earth was it? He moved his ancient wooden chair slightly, changing the angle.

'I wish I had met Mr Tenny,' she said at last.

'You did,' was the calm response.

'Yes, I know: he came back to Australia again when I was about two. I've seen all the photos and heard you all talk about it. But it's hardly meeting him when I was so small I can't remember it. Why did he come back?'

'He came after his wife died, as a sort of cheering up trip. He always loved Australia; had a real soft spot for Mum.'

Was it that framed photograph of Kendrick Tenny and company that had captured her attention so? He shifted his chair again. That was better — he now could see her direct line of sight.

This time the silence appeared to last indefinitely. He leaned back in his chair casually, watching his sister. Then his blood froze.

Her gaze was fixated, not on the framed photograph, but on the rifle which hung above it. She appeared mesmerised, almost in a trance.

'Stella!' He took hold of his sister, almost forcing her to her feet. 'Better get you back to bed. Don't want the parents on the warpath.'

She made no protest, allowing him to guide her back to her own bedroom. He gave her a brotherly hug and she looked up at him. The eyes were haunted but dry.

'Good night, sis. Things'll be better tomorrow, you know.'

She made a poor attempt at a smile, nodded and squeezed his arm.

Toby went straight to the big room where his parents always slept.

'Mum,' he called softly by the closed door.

'Toby.' His mother came out quickly, still dressed. 'What is it, son?'

'Mum, I don't want to worry you but I think you'd better sleep in Stella's room tonight.'

'I was going to,' she told him. 'I was just collecting a few things. But why, Toby?' She looked up at this tall son who was so like her.

'Look, Mum, I'm sure there's no need for panic but after today, well, after this evening, she's a bit shaky. Remember how she got that time they screwed up the medicines and she got a personality change, started doing all those strange things — the school rang up really worried one day — she's a bit that way now. I found her in my room acting a bit oddly. Took her back to bed but I think she'd be better with company.'

'Thanks, Toby.' The mother touched his cheek with one slim, work-worn finger. 'You're a good man, son.'

He bent to kiss the top of her head. 'Got to go out,' he said abruptly. 'Be gone a while. Don't worry.'

Toby returned to his room. It was cold for late September and he needed to dress appropriately for it would be a long night. Pyjamas and dressing gown were exchanged for faded blue jeans, khaki work shirt, long, hand-knitted woollen socks, a thick, warm jacket and heavy work boots. He heard his mother go across to Stella's room and breathed more easily. He felt in the jacket pockets. Yes, the leather gloves were still balled up in the left pocket. He doubted if it would be cold enough to need them, but one never knew.

The wide-brimmed felt hat was taken up from the tall hat stand which had stood by the front door for longer than he could remember. He checked his watch as he left the house: it was just past ten-thirty.

The wheelchair was snatched up from the garage where it had been removed some hours earlier, and thrust in the back of the ute. His toolbox was already there. They had been fencing on Saturday and would be fencing again on Monday — hell, that was tomorrow. He shook his head: what a day it had been.

As he drove towards Sentinel Hill, he wondered if he were over-reacting, making too much of some random movements of his sister's eyes. He hoped so. Perhaps he would never know.

Strange incidents happened on farms, especially when a gun was kept casually behind the kitchen door, fully loaded. Only a year ago young Debra Barton waited until her family had gone out for the evening, taken her father's gun from behind the kitchen door and shot herself through the roof of the mouth, killing herself instantly. She had been just sixteen years old.

The other guns on Cheshunt were kept well out of sight in their parent's bedroom. Might be best to keep that cupboard door locked, if that wasn't already taken care of. Knowing his mother, it probably was. His rifle was the only gun kept openly in view, so to speak. Well, he thought grimly, he would soon take care of that. Tomorrow it could join the cache in his parent's room.

He was bothered at times by all these drugs these wonder-doctors insisted on using on his sister. Some of them had shocking side-effects yet a solution to the illness had to be found. It angered him enormously that so much money was spent on illnesses such as AIDS where, in so many cases, the disease was self-induced. Those poor little babies and the unsuspecting wives were the only ones he had any time for. A friend of his was a nurse in a Sydney hospital and worked with the AIDS babies. The things she had told Toby made him almost despair over the human race. Money for self-induced AIDs victims appeared to flow from surprising sources; it was socially acceptable, even trendy, to support such people. Those two words shouldn't ever apply to any illness or disease. He'd never heard of anyone attempting to raise money for children with juvenile rheumatoid arthritis. Heck, most people didn't even know the disease existed!

The job had taken an hour. It was past one in the morning when he stood on Sentinel Hill, the last piece of the broken wheelchair in his hands. The backrest hit the edge of the mineshaft, throwing up the small stone which marked him, opening up his right cheek. The blood ran down his face, staining the wide collar of the thick jacket.

So the wheelchair had had the last word, had it? Well, let it think that and be damned!

Turning his back on the mineshaft he trudged down the track for the last time, leaving the old poppet-head and the stamper battery in possession. It felt good to get back in the ute. He looked over at the passenger seat where he had carefully laid the bottle: the round ender. Quite a find that had been. He got the car started, turned it around and slowly drove back past the battered old sign which once had read: Danger — Do Not Enter.

Chapter Twenty-seven: In the Feed Shed

Toby was extremely tired and worried. The cut on his right cheek throbbed. No questions had been asked but it had required three stitches. He had stopped off to pay a visit to Doctor Charles Mason on the return trip from Sentinel Hill.

Now, a few short hours later, he had removed Stella from the house, sidestepping other parties as neatly as cutting out a steer from a mob of cattle, and escorted her out to the feed shed. She was sitting on a straw bale, right leg propped up on a neatly rolled old horse rug, looking much brighter than she had the previous night.

'What were you doing in my room last night, Stella?'

'What?'

'What were you doing in my room last night?'

'Oh, that.' Her face coloured up faintly and her eyes no longer met his.

'Yes, that, Stella,' he spoke firmly.

'I was looking at your rifle,' she spoke frankly.

'I see.'

'It's ages since I handled a gun, not since this stupid illness. I was wondering if I could still use it properly. You know how ham-fisted I am these days with these pathetic hands.'

'You used to be a very good shot,' he answered quietly. 'Dad was very proud of you. But why this sudden desire for shooting?'

She flushed again and bit her lip.

'Come on, girl, come clean,' he ordered kindly.

'Well, it's going to sound kind of stupid —'

'So do lots of things. Cough it up.'

'I wanted to shoot something and I was wondering if I would be able to do it properly. Seeing I can't even use a knife and fork in the right way —' She looked at her bloated, puffy hands in disgust and went on:

'I can't hold a normal cup — my fingers can't manage the handle. So how do I know if I would be able to manage a rifle with any accuracy?'

'Is it so important?'

There was no reply.

'This all came up very suddenly, didn't it? All this shooting business, I mean. I hadn't heard any interest before this. It must be two years since you held a gun, sis.'

'It was that *thing* yesterday evening.'

'The wheelchair?'

'The *thing*,' she corrected, 'but yes, the wheelchair, if you must. I call it an evil *thing.*'

'What about it?'

'I was going to shoot it!'

'*What?*'

She looked at him, part shamefaced, part defiant. 'I told you it would sound kind of stupid.'

'You were going to *shoot* the *wheelchair!*' he exclaimed.

'Yes, but the thing seems to have disappeared, or, at any rate, it's been put where I can't find it.'

'*Shoot* a *wheelchair* … with my rifle!' Toby felt the corners of his lips twitch.

'I can't see anything funny about it,' Stella said indignantly.

'That's what you wanted my rifle for? To shoot the wheelchair?'

'Of course. What else should I need it for?' she said in obvious surprise.

After all the upset and strain of the past eighteen hours, the incredible relief was too much for Toby. He let out a vast guffaw of laughter and collapsed onto a small stack of straw bales.

'Toby! What's so funny?' She looked aggrieved.

'Sorry, sis, you'll have to forgive me.' He struggled to right himself. 'I guess yesterday was a bit much and must have got to me. I must be starting to lose it.'

'Don't be an ass.' She gave him a small punch. 'Do *you* know where the wheelchair thing seems to have vanished to? Did Dad lock it away somewhere? Did you?'

'It's no longer on Cheshunt,' he told her.

She let out a long sigh, part regret and part relief. 'I'm *really* glad it's gone,' she told him, 'but I'd still have liked to shoot it.'

'You know, Stella,' Toby strove to keep his voice serious, 'a wheelchair is not a very satisfactory target in some ways.'

She wrinkled up her nose. 'Umm, yes, I'd sort of been thinking about that.' Her young voice changed, 'But it would have made *me* feel a lot better, 'specially last night. I would have found it a very satisfactory target indeed.'

'Fair enough. Do you want to hear what happened to it?'

'*You* took it away? Oh, Toby!'

'All the way to Sentinel Hill,' he assured her and told her the tale.

'That's how you got that cut?' Impressed and awed, she stared up at her brother.

He grinned down at her. 'Satisfied?'

Still barely able to take it all in, she nodded vigorously. Toby, feeling as if all the weights of the world had been removed from his shoulders, stood up.

'Mum taking you in to school a bit late today?'

'Yep. I'll only miss the first three periods. I've still got half an hour before we have to leave.'

'Sis,' he paused for a moment, 'you know that Dad and Mum will probably tell the cops about the wheelchair appearing on our place?'

'Sure, but I can't see why.'

'Because if there is any one person who always knows what's going on in this district it's Sergeant Bill Stroud. He gets around, sees and hears things, gets told things. We have to find out where the damned chair came from.'

'Will you have to tell him about Sentinel Hill?'

'Afraid so. One missing wheelchair will have to be accounted for, especially as we're the ones reporting its magical appearance. It's better to play straight with the Sergeant — he's a good guy and a great cop.'

Stella was in the process of getting herself off the straw bale when a thought struck her.

'Toby?'

'What is it?'

'About the rifle —'

'Yes, what about it?'

'What did you think I wanted it for? You seemed so surprised when I told you about shooting the wheelchair — even seemed to think it kind of funny — so you must have had some idea of your own. Wasn't that why you dragged me out here to the feed shed?'

Damnation, thought Toby. That kid was too quick for her own good at times. Was it better to prevaricate or to tell the truth? He honestly wasn't sure.

'Why not just tell me the truth?' she spoke calmly.

'Don't get upset but I did wonder if you thought the rifle might have another use.'

'Another use? What do you mean?'

'Some people do use guns for other reasons —'

'You mean like Debra Barton?' She eyed him candidly.

'Well, yes,' he spoke awkwardly, adding hastily, 'I know it was a really dumb idea that I got into my head. Like I said before, I must be starting to lose it a bit. Old age and all that stuff starting in a bit early.'

There was quite a pause during which time Stella reseated herself upon her straw bale. She looked up at her brother, head tilted back and spoke slowly and earnestly:

'Do you know, during all the time I've had this blasted illness, I've never once thought of doing anything like that. I honestly don't know why. Sure, I get very mad and upset at times. Last night, given half a chance, I'd have shot that wretched thing to a million pieces. Wheelchairs make me so angry because people keep wanting to put me in them! You should have heard that specialist down in Sydney last week, Toby, telling Mum and Dad to get on with their lives, to make things as easy as possible for everybody by sticking me in a wheelchair. I'm not a total idiot, you know, and I have to keep using what I can. Stick me in a wheelchair and I'll be crippled in weeks. I know it's not the fault of the chair but I've got to take it out on something! I can't go round shooting medical specialists, 'though I wish I could at times.'

'Sounds jolly sensible to me, Stella.'

'Mum says that one day we'll have the right drugs to control the pain, that it is a waiting game for the present. Once we can get the pain under decent control then we can start retraining my body to work again in the right way. Mum says that's what will happen and I know she's right.'

'So do I,' said her brother soberly.

'Did you really find a round ender up at the mine last night?' the girl asked eagerly, beginning another attempt at getting herself to her feet.

'Sure did …' he grinned, '… show it to you tonight. I think that's Mum I can hear calling you, sis. Off to school with you now.'

Chapter Twenty-eight: Jindabyne

Kirsty found the school permission note lying on the kitchen table. Stella was nowhere to be seen.

Stapled beneath the permission note were a number of crumpled sheets of paper. The school was offering a five day excursion, four nights away from home. Momentarily closing her eyes, Kirsty wondered how they were going to deal with that one. There was no way in the world the school could be expected to cope with Stella on such an outing, in fact, she was surprised they had even bothered to give the child a permission note. They didn't usually. Slowly, she continued to read.

The shuffling sound which always heralded Stella's appearance nowadays caused Kirsty to look up from her reading.

'I need to talk with you, Mum. It's all right, they said I can go — if you're fine with it, of course.'

Kirsty watched as her daughter painfully lowered herself into the well-cushioned, elderly wooden rocking chair. The long school day always took its toll and Stella's face looked drawn, showing lines of fatigue and pain. She had no sooner settled herself in the chair than Sambo arrived. With his usual *here-I-am* meow, he leapt neatly onto his young mistress's lap.

'Don't let that cat sit for too long on your legs, Stella. He's far too heavy for them.'

'Just a short cuddle,' pleaded Stella. 'He feels so nice and soft and smells so lovely, you know, Mum, that gorgeous warm furry smell.'

'Do you want to tell me all about this school trip?'

'Put the jug on first please, Mum.'

Kirsty complied and Stella began, her fingers tenderly caressing her beloved Sambo:

'I was lying down in the sickbay at lunch time when Mrs Kelly came in. She told me that at the end of every year there was a special excursion for year eleven, from Monday to Friday. This year it is to the Snowy Mountains. I think we will be based in Jindabyne and take day trips from there, but I'm not quite sure. Well, Mrs Kelly said that this excursion was discussed at the weekly teacher's meeting last Monday and that my name came up. The five teachers who are going on the excursion said they really wanted me to be able to come. So Mrs Kelly and Mr Ellingham said they would be personally responsible for me, if you and Dad agree. The assistant principal has agreed.' Here she paused for breath before continuing. 'The permission notes were going to be given out during last period and Mrs Kelly wanted me to know about everything first. She said the teachers all knew that I would automatically assume I wouldn't be able to go and they knew I had missed out on different school things so they especially didn't want me to miss out on this. I've never been to the Snowy Mountains,' she ended a trifle wistfully.

Kirsty's lips twitched at this last but she felt a trifle stunned.

'Would you like to go?'

'Oh yes please, Mum!' The huge grey eyes gazed pleadingly at her mother.

'I wonder if the teachers really understand what's involved here?'

The grey eyes candidly met the warm brown eyes of the mother.

'Mum, if Mrs Kelly and Mr Ellingham weren't going I might not be so sure, but I feel perfectly happy with them in charge. Nerolee's promised to help, too.'

Later, Kirsty discussed it with Max:

'Let her go,' he spoke without hesitation. 'If the worst comes to the worst, and it won't, you know I can always drive up and bring her home; she'll only be a phone call away. After all this time at school those teachers must have a pretty good idea what they're letting themselves in for. If it was any longer I might jib but four nights is about the right length of time. My guess is that she'll enjoy it but be pleased to get home again.'

'So be it,' Kirsty sighed and signed the permission note.

Steve Ellingham set the alarm on his watch for five the following morning. As he had privately admitted to his colleague Laura Kelly a short while earlier, he was absolutely exhausted. He seemed to have forgotten to what lengths these five-days-away-from-home school excursions could stretch one.

Laura Kelly was doing night call for young Stella Richards, poor kid. He hoped she was enjoying the trip. She had looked very tired tonight, he thought. He hoped that horse trek today had not been a mistake and had not been too much for her.

The whole group had climbed to the top of Australia today, an outing especially planned by the cunning teachers in the hope that it might exhaust the lively youngsters. It had certainly exhausted *him*, he grinned ruefully.

They had started out very early, backpacks stuffed with a vast range of clothing covering every possible weather condition, sunscreen lotion, bottled drinking water, snacks, cameras and excursion notebooks. Their coach had driven them to Thredbo Village where they had taken the Kosciuszko Express Chair Lift to Eagles Nest and commenced the long hike to the 2,228 metre-high summit, a thirteen kilometre return walk.

Whilst planning this energy-consuming trip for the lively band, the teachers had put their heads together on the subject of Stella Richards. It was Erin Butler, the youngest of their quintet, who suggested a gentle horse trek for Stella and perhaps one of her friends.

At first, Steve Ellingham had been doubtful. Visions of dangerous horses bolting through the mountains, broken bones, telephone calls to Cheshunt, emergency helicopter rescues to the closest big hospital — where *was* the closest big hospital, for that matter? — and lawsuits taken out by Max and Kirsty Richards against him (he was the teacher supposed to be in overall charge of this wretched excursion) circled his mind like frenzied mosquitoes.

It was Miss Erin Butler who took the stand. In her gentle way she felt deeply for Stella Richards and was determined to do all she could to make this trip special for the poor girl. She faced her four colleagues a touch defiantly, faint colour touching her charmingly freckled cheeks.

At the very least enquiries could be made and their need explained. There appeared to be excellent advisors and guides attached to their lodge and Miss Erin Butler, for one, would be extremely surprised if facilities for a quiet trek on gentle horses were not to be found in this natural paradise for visitors. Surely this wasn't such an impossibility as some people seemed to think?

As she finished speaking, her colleagues gave her a hearty round of applause. The young teacher turned a deep scarlet.

'Nicely said,' approved Mrs Laura Kelly.

'You can get off your stump now, Erin. I think we're all with you, you know.' Mr Jonathan Penney grinned at his co-worker.

Steve Ellingham agreed. He had allowed fear of possible disaster to over-rule common-sense.

It had been Miss Erin Butler who found the riding school, a small family-run business which prided itself on providing quiet, gentle and well trained horses for small groups. She suggested that one of the teachers accompany Stella, and possibly Nerolee Turner, on a guided trail ride.

'My good woman,' exclaimed Steve Ellingham in horror, 'you can count me out! I've never sat on a horse in my entire life!'

'I've done a bit of riding,' Erin Butler told him. 'Nothing fancy but enough to manage a gentle trek, I hope.'

'You're elected, Erin,' said Jonathan Penney fervently. 'I'm with Steve. The last time I sat on one of those animals was at a fair. It was a merry-go-round horse, one of those carousel things that go up and down. That was more than enough for me!'

Gusts of laughter greeted this sally.

'How old were you, Jon?' asked Laura Kelly.

'About six, I should think.'

'What an adventurous lot,' Erin spoke in pretended disgust. 'What about you, Marcus? Have you done any riding?' she spoke to the fifth member of their group, new to the school this year.

Marcus Sanderson smiled. 'I'm in Jon's league, I'm afraid. I did ride a donkey one summer as a youngster. Nothing to speak of since then.'

'We'll leave it to you, Erin,' Laura Butler ended the discussion.

Young Stella, upon being told of the proposed plan, beamed from ear to ear. Nerolee was delighted to accompany her, having privately told Mrs Kelly that she was non too keen on the thought of climbing Mount Kosciuszko again, having done it before with her family. As she confided to the teacher, she never had been too fond of long hikes, or, for that matter, any sort of walking.

'It uses up far too much energy,' she explained to a secretly amused Laura Kelly.

Miss Butler drove Nerolee and Stella the short distance to the riding school. The car had been thoughtfully supplied by the people who ran the lodge. Stella was very quiet.

'Are you feeling up to riding, child?' The teacher looked worried.

Stella bit her lip and nodded. She was always doing this, agreeing to things before she had thought them through. Stella had been riding Casper using her Twisted Stirrups for many weeks now. She could manage an hour in the saddle with little trouble. Occasionally she rode for longer, but not often. As yet, she had not been promoted to another horse and here she was, about to face a totally unknown mount.

There was another thing. How could she have been so stupid as to forget about her special stirrups? Yes, hopefully her leg muscles had gotten much stronger, more used to riding, but how in the world was she going to cope with the remorseless and unyielding hardness of stainless steel stirrups? It might be best to try and do without stirrups altogether. Or should she tell Miss Butler she couldn't go on the ride? They had all gone to so much trouble to arrange this for her. Stella did not know what to do.

'Good morning. It's Miss Butler, isn't it? We met the other day. You'll be based at the Marple's place round the other side of the lake. Welcome, come and meet our horses.' The woman looked kind, approachable.

Before leaving the lodge, Stella had massaged both sets of calf muscles before allowing Nerolee to assist in firmly bandaging both lower legs. Now she limped slowly behind the others.

'This is Jigsaw.' The woman patted a beautifully marked pinto pony.

'He's lovely.' Stella touched his warm silken shoulder.

'We'll leave you two to get acquainted while I sort out your teacher and friend.'

Stella sat on a handy bench and looked at Jigsaw. He stood quietly tied to the fence by a piece of baling twine. Inwardly she approved. This woman seemed quite nice — should she tell her about not riding? Tentatively she stretched her right leg a little. It didn't feel too bad this morning.

Jigsaw's markings were very attractive: deep chestnut and creamy white. His hoofs were parti-coloured and his long tail a delightful combination of chestnut and cream. He was quite sturdy, rather like a Dartmoor pony; stood about thirteen hands tall and his mane had once been hogged. It was growing back now and was in the halfway stage: not very attractive to look at but still eminently practical for holding on to.

'What do you think of him? I'm Mrs Pickeral, by the way. You are Stella, right?'

'He's beautiful,' Stella spoke honestly.

'He's very quiet and trustworthy. Most of the time he's ridden by my niece. She's not very strong — got some problems with her legs and back. Jigsaw is her darling.'

Stella nodded.

'What's worrying you, child? Don't you want to ride?'

Stella found herself pouring out her concerns to this understanding woman, telling her all about not being able to ride for so long, the wonders of the Twisted Stirrup, her dear, reliable Casper and not having ridden another horse since she started riding again. Mrs Pickeral listened with interest.

'And now your teachers have very kindly arranged this ride for you but they don't really understand. How can they? They don't know about your special stirrups, do they? No, I thought not. Your uncle must be a very clever man, by the way, and your grandfather.'

Stella smiled her approval of this statement.

'I'm not surprised you're feeling a bit worried about all this but before we go any further let me show you something, Stella.' The woman vanished into the depths of the tack room.

Stella leaned back on her bench with a sigh of relief. She felt much happier. The day appeared much brighter. She touched Jigsaw's velvet nose then kissed it.

'He'll lap that up.' Mrs Pickeral had re-emerged, carrying a rather unusual burden.

Stella stared speechless, pulled herself upright on the bench.

'This is the saddle that Cherry, my niece, uses. I'm sure it's probably overkill for you but at least you should feel comfortable and safe.'

'Oh, Mrs Pickeral … why … you darling!' blurted Stella. Then her face burned with embarrassment.

'It was specially made for her by a saddler friend of ours. You can see that it's got a few extra additions.'

'It's wonderful!'

'You feel happy enough to give it a try?'

The girl nodded vigorously.

Mrs Pickeral saddled and bridled Jigsaw before leading him over to the mounting platform.

'This certainly makes it easier.' Stella walked haltingly up the sturdy ramp to the platform. With Mrs Pickeral holding Jigsaw steady, she found she could manage to get herself into the saddle.

'How does it feel, Stella?'

'A bit strange but you'd expect that.' She wriggled a little in the unusual seat.

'How about your legs?'

Stella easily fitted her left leg into the wide leather loop. 'Like a leather stirrup,' she observed, but needed help for her right leg.

The saddle had a broad sort of leather handle fitted across the pommel. The back was higher than usual, like the curved back of a chair extending up from the cantle for about six inches.

'Can I let him go?' asked Mrs Pickeral, smiling.

'Please.' Stella collected up the reins neatly. Happily she walked the pinto pony around the grassy yard, changing the rein and getting used to the feel of this different saddle.

The saddle was an extremely clever hybrid, a real character, a combination of different elements: part western saddle, part classic all-purpose saddle and with a few unique touches of its own. Stella could feel her body start to relax.

A slight clatter from the direction of the wide gate made her look up. Mrs Pickeral had returned, mounted on a pretty chestnut mare with a broad white blaze down its face and three white socks. With her were Miss Butler and Nerolee. Miss Butler rode an attractive dun gelding who featured a dark brown dorsal stripe and similarly hued wither stripes. Nerolee was astride a handsome appaloosa gelding with a straggly tail.

'You look quite at home, Stella.' Miss Butler smiled encouragingly at the girl; received a grateful look in return.

'I thought we'd ride along the edge of the lake for a while,' Mrs Pickeral told the small group, before turning to Miss Butler. 'What say you and Nerolee lead the way? Through the two gates and turn left. Just follow the trail that heads straight for the lake. Stella and I will be hard on your heels.'

The ride, originally planned for one hour, lengthened to ninety minutes and was a great success. The pace was kept slow, mainly walking with two brief runs at the canter. The visitors eagerly drank in the surroundings: the man-made Lake Jindabyne, such an important part of the famous Snowy Mountains Scheme, backed by the foothills and mountains.

'Our home lies beneath the waters out there.' Mrs Pickeral casually waved a hand towards the lake.

Horrified, Stella and Nerolee listened as the local woman told of the building of the current town of Jindabyne and the flooding of the original, much smaller town. The weatherboard house in which she had lived all her life now lay many metres below the waters of Lake Jindabyne.

'There are two sides to every story.' Mrs Pickeral reined her chestnut mare to a halt. She smiled a little at the expressions on the girls' faces. 'Not everyone was too happy about the move, especially those of us whose families had been here for generations. But,' she sighed, patting her mount, 'you cannot stand in the way of progress, or so they tell us, and the Snowy Scheme was badly needed. We are very happy here, this place has become home now. But some of the older folks, my parents among them, never really settled in the new locations.'

Miss Erin Butler later told her colleagues she warranted Stella and Nerolee learned far more during that one ride than they ever had during one of her geography classes. They certainly appeared to pay far more attention, hanging on to Mrs Pickeral's words with bated breath. Her colleagues chuckled appreciatively.

At the conclusion of the ride, the trio thanked Mrs Pickeral warmly and returned to their lodge for lunch. Stella, by now somewhat weary, retired to the room she shared with Nerolee, intending to rest, and hopefully sleep, for the afternoon. Nerolee took her current book — definitely not a piece of literature on her school set book list but a shabby old copy of *What Katy Did* which she had found in a bookcase in the front hall — and curled up for an hour in the lodge's big lounge room, where she was the sole occupant. She was far more tired than she was prepared to admit and not used to regular riding.

Chapter Twenty-nine: The Gnome Globe

Steve Ellingham awoke abruptly. He had been caught up in an absurd dream in which a pile of students' exercise books sitting on his desk awaiting his attention had suddenly each grown a pair of wings and flown round and round the room. When he'd leapt up to try and stop them, they had flown out the window, singing merrily as they went. But why on earth should they sing: *'We're off to climb a mountain, you'll never catch us, Mr Ellingham, we're off to climb a mountain, you'll never catch us, Mr Ellingham, Mr Ellingham, Mr Ellingham, Mr Ellingham.'*

He realised that at least one part of his dream was true: there was someone calling his name and that person appeared to be in this room. What in the name of the seven saints was going on?

Already confused by his rude awakening, his bewilderment was not lessened by a mysterious light that appeared to be sweeping across the walls. It was colouring his room a repellent shade of what could only be termed shamrock green. The green light flooded the room for a long moment before fading into darkness, and Mr Ellingham had just drawn a deep sigh of relief when his room lit up again, this time in vampire scarlet.

He heard the voice again:

'Mr Ellingham? Mr Ellingham, can you please help me?'

He peered in the direction of the voice just as the room went dark. When he could see again, everything had turned a nasty shade of electric blue which strongly reminded him of the blue light at his dentist. Mr Ellingham disliked his dentist so this did not help his already sorely tried mind.

Feeling as if he must have become ensconced in the middle of some very strange science fiction film, he flung back the bed covers and swung his feet to the floor. He was dimly able to perceive a rather tousled figure standing awkwardly in the doorway, one hand clinging to the half-opened door. Then the room went completely dark again.

The blackness was next replaced by sweeping beams of fluorescent fuchsia pink, a colour he could only identify thanks to the prowess of Mrs Ellingham, who had recently redecorated their newly extended living room in that repellent colour. He reached out an unsteady hand in the general direction of the bedside table upon which stood a small lamp. The resultant crash of something falling to the floor was followed by the lighter tinkle of a breaking electric light bulb.

'Mr Ellingham, Mr Ellingham, please sir, can you hear me?'

Giving his head a quick shake in an attempt to clear it, he next tried to focus on the somewhat dishevelled figure clutching at his door. It seemed strangely familiar.

'Is that you, Stella Richards?'

With the rather wavering reply, 'Yes, sir,' the room was once again blanketed in complete darkness.

His exasperated, 'For goodness sake …' was lost in a loud crunching sounding as he stood on the remains of the lamp. *Damnation.*

'Can you find the light switch, child? It should be next to the door.'

Waves of rich regal purple were now sweeping around the room.

'On second thoughts, stay where you are. I don't want you

falling. I've got a torch in my rucksack somewhere — give me a moment to find it.'

He managed to locate his rucksack under the bed just before the purple light disappeared yet again into total darkness. One remote corner of his mind wondered which colour would appear next: he didn't have long to wait, it was indisputably orange which gave him a fair amount of visibility. The torch was found at the bottom of the rucksack wrapped in a protective jumper. *Yes! They might get somewhere now.*

The torch refused to turn on and Mr Ellingham swore. The room was once more bathed in total blackness.

'Stella, stay exactly where you are and I will come across to you. I think that's best.'

Waiting till a not unpleasant shade of turquoise filled the room, the teacher picked his way carefully across the floor. He found the plate, fortunately large and old fashioned, which surrounded the light switch and clicked the switch down. The room flooded with light.

'My legs hurt so much. Please help me, sir.'

Clinging to the door in a desperate grip, Stella Richard's face was chalk white. Her eyes had enormous dark shadows beneath them. In one hand was grasped — he blinked — what on earth was that odd —?

With a swift movement he caught the child before she slipped to the ground. Cradling her in his arms, he turned into the hallway. From the only other open doorway in the vicinity it was simple enough to find her room. He lay her on the bed and was about to go in search of Laura Kelly when a small voice spoke:

'Please help me — it hurts so much.'

'Can you tell me what to do, Stella?'

'Mummy and Daddy always rub my legs down when this happens. I've taken my tablets but they take ages to work. The cream for my legs is there.' She pointed at a plastic tub on the bedside table. 'After that, can you help me put on my TENS machine?'

As Steve Ellingham later told his colleagues, he had never fully realised how much damage that wretched disease had done to that poor child. One leg was twisted inwards from the hip, about ninety degrees out of alignment, he estimated. It was a shocking sight. The other leg was also twisted inwards but not nearly so much, perhaps about fifteen degrees. The child called this her 'good leg'. He was amazed that she was able to walk at all.

He massaged both legs gently under her instructions and again, following her directions, bandaged the electrode pads in place. He made sure the leads were not tangled and put the control box in her hands. She turned the current on, confirmed everything was working and for the first time since she had woken him, smiled. Obviously the pain tablets were kicking in. Or was it that funny contraption he had just helped her attach? She certainly had a lot of faith in the thing.

'Thank you so much, sir.'

'Stella, what in the name of heaven *is* that thing?' He pointed to the object she had been clutching just before he broke her fall. It now stood at the back of the bedside table.

A small giggle broke from the girl.

The object in question appeared to be an enormous light globe. Around forty centimetres tall it had the proportions correspondent to a perfect light bulb. Obviously it was the source of all the coloured light which had appeared in his room but—

'It's my Gnome Globe.'

'*What* did you say, child?'

Another irrepressible gurgle broke from her. 'It's my Gnome Globe,' she repeated. In spite of the smile and the laugh, her face was still very white and her eyelids were beginning to droop.

'You'd better tell me all about it tomorrow,' he told her, eyeing the huge bulb in fascination.

She nodded; reached out a hand and turned the Gnome Globe on. 'It helps at night,' she told him. 'It distracts me.'

'I can imagine it might,' was the dry response.

Steve Ellingham left the room in a glow of shamrock green, his head shaking in disbelief.

Fifteen minutes later he returned to check on the patient. She lay sleeping quietly, one hand cradled under her left cheek. The room was flooded in a rich golden glow which seemed strangely appropriate.

Chapter Thirty: More Vignettes

It was much easier to remain anonymous in the city. There were no nosy coppers who knew all about you and your private storage sheds. No Sergeant Bill Bloody Stroud and his do-gooding kind to keep a 'friendly eye' on you. That's what Dean Lucas had assured his father.

There were also a lot more opportunities. 'Opportunities' was Dean's term for goods to purloin or steal. The variety of available merchandise was amazing, especially for those who were quick-eyed as well as quick-fingered.

In spite of these excellent advantages, Dieter wanted to return to the country. He had been born within the Koolkuna district, lived there all his life. It was home. If his idiot of a son hadn't arrived home with that young shaver, Sean Stevens, he, Dieter, would still be living at home, back where he belonged.

Dieter was getting excessively fed up with Dean. First there had been the business of the old kombi van, a vehicle that Dieter had always regarded with a certain affection. Within hours of fleeing the old shack he called home, Dean had insisted they dump the van. The cops would be out looking for them and the kombi stuck out like a sore thumb. It had to be swapped for something else: one of their mates would see them right.

They arrived in Sydney driving a 1983 Holden Camira, a tan-coloured vehicle which had definitely seen more than a few not-too-careful owners. When Dieter expressed his displeasure, Dean rather impatiently explained it would 'blend in with the rest of the mob in the Big Smoke' till they could get something more suited to their 'work'. This turned out to be an old panel van.

'It's a ruddy shaggin' waggon,' exclaimed Dieter in disgust.

The shaggin' wagon had stayed with them. Dieter kicked the tyres every time he walked past the hated object.

Then there was this matter of accommodation. The old shack and the accompanying three acres of native bush might have been nothing too fancy but they were home. More importantly, they were his, owned by him, one of the rare honest deals in his life. The way things were heading, he was going to make damned sure the old place never fell into his son's hands.

Here they were, living in a run-down house in one of Sydney's most dangerous suburbs, Cabramatta, and paying an arm and a leg in rent. Dieter would never admit to Dean that he was frightened, but he was; at home, they had been kings of their small domain, here, they were nobodies in dangerous and uncharted waters; in over their heads. Dieter was smart enough to know it, Dean was not.

Dean was gone most of the day and half the night. He had made strange new 'friends', always seemed to be loaded with cash. He was secretive about many of his deals, only letting the old man, as he sneeringly regarded him these days, in on some of the tamer stuff.

Dieter was lonely, homesick and frightened. He was too old to start again in the city. Not for the first time he thought about trying to make a deal with the cops. That Bill Stroud wasn't so bad, for a bluebottle. If it hadn't been for young Sean, he would have tried for a deal before now, tested the hidden waters, so to speak. But he knew they'd come down hard on him for what they'd done to the kid. He was a good kid too, better than his own son. But just the same, if only that idiot Dean hadn't brought Sean back home that night…

— TWO —

In the Phillip Street offices of Merriman and Merriman, a serious discussion was underway.

'Well, we're finally seeing a bit of action with the Bronwyn Vaughan business,' young Mr Jonathan Merriman, cheerful as ever, spoke up.

Both his elders frowned at him.

'The whole business is proving most irregular, most awkward.' This was Mr Ephraim Merriman, the senior partner, speaking in his usual thin, dry legal voice.

'Yes, but it is moving ahead.' Mr Jonathan waved an airy hand over the range of documents spread across the polished table. 'The boy is obviously very settled and happy with the Fairchilds. They wish to adopt him and he wishes to be adopted by them. Now we seem to be getting some results from Wales. Don't work at much haste over there, do they, or have we just struck one of those dilly-dallying legal firms?'

His grandfather and uncle frowned at him.

'Griffiths, Hughes, Hughes and Griffiths are a most respectable firm,' Mr Aaron Merriman spoke reprovingly.

'Quite so, quite so,' Mr Ephraim Merriman gave a short, dry cough before reaching for a blackcurrant throat pastille.

'So, to summarise the current situation: Bronwyn Vaughan's brother died three days before she left this mortal coil. Funny that. Wonder if those two will have much to say to each other when they meet again? He can, therefore, make no claim upon the Vaughan estate. He left one wife and no issue. He was quite well-to-do, left it to his wife — very right and proper. She has no claim on the Vaughan estate and intends to make no claim — not that she could — but it's nice to be sure. The boarding house place has just been put up for sale and the buyers are snapping at it like frenzied sharks. I'd say it all looks pretty promising for the young Stevens boy, poor kid. He deserves some luck.' For a brief and rare moment, Mr Jonathan looked serious.

'Substantially that is correct, my boy, although I'm not sure I approve of your colloquial language. But yes, in essence, you are correct.' Mr Aaron Merriman carefully straightened a document which had had the temerity to be slightly out of perfect alignment with the edge of the table.

Young Mr Jonathan spared a thought for the brass plate in the foyer downstairs. Highly optimistic by nature, at times even he wondered if he would ever live to see his name added to the two already engraved in copperplate script on that brass plate. There were days he seriously doubted it. Shrugging aside these melancholy thoughts, he grinned at his uncle:

'You seem to be doing a grand job of keeping those child welfare troublemakers off our backs, Uncle Aaron. How on earth did you manage it? Bribe them or threaten them?'

'Certainly not!' The junior partner eyed his nephew austerely. 'I have found them quite ah, um,' he coughed delicately, 'amenable to sensible discussion.'

Mr Jonathan, as yet no partner at all, threw back his head and roared with laughter. 'Found all their legal weak points, did you? Good for you!' Pushing back his chair from the polished table, he got to his feet. 'Well, if that's all on the Vaughan affair, I'm off to lunch. Meeting my youngster at the Pink Cockatoo.'

The two partners of Merriman and Merriman watched in disapproval as the heir presumptive to their legal kingdom vanished through the door.

'The Pink Cockatoo indeed!' spluttered Mr Ephraim Merriman.

'Really, my dear Aaron, what is the younger generation coming to?'

'He is no longer the younger generation,' replied Mr Aaron, straightening another document which had been disturbed by his nephew's departure.

Mr Ephraim shuddered delicately. Young Jonathan's son, the one he was meeting at the Pink Cockatoo, had reached the deepest depths of depravity. Instead of following the correct legal footsteps of his father, great-uncle and great-grandfather, Caleb had joined a rock and roll band, playing the drums and doing vocals.

'Jonathan is a good lawyer,' Mr Aaron conceded, with some notion of consoling the elder gentleman.

'Needs to grow up a bit, settle down properly,' was the grunted response. 'In my young days we took our responsibilities seriously. No wonder young Caleb decided to join that ah, um, band. Lack of correct parental guidance. I blame Jonathan entirely.'

Mr Aaron straightened yet another document.

— THREE —

A conversation was taking place in a house at Koolkuna:

'I do wish we could find out about the wheelchair,' the first person spoke eagerly.

Her listener shrugged. 'We made the choice to do it anonymously. This is the price we have to pay. We'll hear sooner or later.'

'It was so clever of you to work it like that. I don't know how you managed it.'

The man hid his pleasure at her words. 'It was no big deal, not really.'

'You know that's not true,' she spoke earnestly. 'It took a lot of planning. A bit like a spy story, really.'

He grinned at her. 'You casting me in a James Bond role, eh?'

'It took a lot of time, a lot of watching and waiting.'

'There's always a certain amount of luck with anything like that,' he told her. 'You can plan as much as you like but there are always the unforeseen factors. You never know what's going to spring out of the bush, so to speak.'

'It took you how long — several weeks?'

The man shook his head. 'Not really but I guess it depends how you look at it. I had to case the joint, in burglar speak, from a distance. Pick the right time, when most of the people were out of the way and that wretched dog was gone from the front verandah. I guess I might have spent about four or five days watching, spread out over several weeks, before I got the right day. Lucky I've got such a good sniper scope. Made watching the place a cinch.'

The woman looked at him proudly. In his military days he had been renowned for his marksmanship, earning the slow and grudging respect of his unit. She knew quite well he had taken on this business of the wheelchair just for her.

'How did you actually work it on the day?'

'I was in place quite early. Far too early, as it turned out, but one never knows, have to be prepared. The parents rode off late morning, had a pack on the man's back so I guessed they'd be gone most of the day. Kids waving them off like they'd be gone for a month. Girl stayed in the house for a couple of hours before going down the back to join her brother. He'd been there since the parents left. Trouble was, that dog on the verandah. I got lucky about four in the afternoon. The brother came up to the house, the dog followed him down the back again. Brother was carrying armloads of stuff so I figured they'd be staying put a while longer, even though the day was moving along a bit. Getting a bit concerned about the parents returning any moment. Gave it a few minutes to see if the dog would return to the house. Had to take a bit of a risk there but figured it was the best chance I was likely to get. Had hidden the wheelchair long before daylight this morning in the shrubbery just beyond their front gate. Was just able to get down from my tree, grab the chair, get up to the house with it and retreat. Fortunately there are a lot of trees and bushes between the house and the main gate, plenty of cover to keep behind. Not that it would have been much use if the dog had been around. As it was, I barely had enough time before the dog returned to the verandah. I'd hidden the car about a mile back down the road. Job completed.'

She flashed him a brilliant smile. 'James Bond in person!'

'What does that make you? Miss Moneypenny?' he teased.

She pouted. 'I could do worse. I've always admired her.' Then she was serious again. 'It was a very good wheelchair too. I'm sure the girl will get a lot of good use from it. It was pretty expensive, wasn't it?'

'Not too bad. Not as much as I had supposed.'

'I wonder when we'll hear?' She returned to her original theme.

He looked at her curiously. 'It means that much to you?'

She dropped her light blue eyes to her lap. 'Maybe it does.'

'I might be able to try and pick up some local gossip. Let's face it, word will soon get about once the girl's seen using a wheelchair.'

'Have you seen anyone from Cheshunt since then?' she asked.

'Saw the mother in the post office the other day, but apart from that, nary a soul.'

'Could you see if you can find something out? Please?'

'Give it a shot. Better not be too obvious about it though.'

The woman nodded in agreement, her hands dropping to the push rings of the wheelchair in which she sat. Her birth was the result of an indiscretion by Cecil Richards, Max's father, shortly after his return from the Second World War. The barmaid had fled the Koolkuna district and given birth in Sydney. More than forty years later the unwanted child returned to the place of her beginnings, wishing more than anything to be accepted into the arms of the Richards family, knowing that illegitimate by-blows were rarely welcome.

Chapter Thirty-one: 'Don't quote platitudes at me!'

Very slowly Kirsty replaced the receiver onto the cradle of the telephone. Max stood staring at her.

It had not been one of their better nights.

Stella had been hot and feverish, crying out with pain. Kirsty spent hour after hour helping the girl. First, the warm sponge bath then the careful patting dry of the pain racked body, followed by the dusting with talcum powder and clean pyjamas. Soaking wet sheets were removed to the laundry and replaced with clean, lavender-scented sheets. This routine was followed numerous times throughout the long night. The chestnut curls were damp, lank and lustreless. Kirsty tied them back with a scrunchie, keeping them away from the hot face. Finally, just before dawn, Stella had fallen into a deep sleep.

Kirsty collapsed into bed against her husband's comforting body. She sobbed from a combination of fatigue, fury and sheer helplessness.

'Why can't someone help her?' wept Kirsty. 'It's just not bloody well fair!'

Max turned over and pulled her into his arms. 'I know, sweetheart, I know.' He rocked her soothingly. 'You've had a hell of a night. I did try to help, you know.'

'You were up half the night as it is, what with that new heifer and those two horses …' Kirsty's head rested snugly against Max's shoulder. 'How are they by the way?'

'They'll all be fine, don't you worry. Stella finally asleep I take it?'

'Finally. Max, what in the blazes are we going to do? I'm honestly not sure how much longer I can take this. I feel like a zombie, whatever that may be … something that is trapped in a long tunnel with no ending in sight.' The tears began falling again.

'Shh, baby, shh, it's all right,' he comforted.

'No, it is not damned well all right! I'm coming to the end of my road with this. Why can't we find a solution?' Angrily, she pushed Max away and sat up in bed.

'Stop it, Kirsty. This isn't helping. I'll stay with Stella today and you are spending the morning in bed asleep.' Max climbed out of bed. 'I think we both need a good strong cup of tea and then I want you asleep till lunchtime.'

Returning with the large ceramic mugs of steaming liquid, Max encouraged his exhausted wife to sip slowly. He sat close to her on the bed.

'Just remember this, Kirsty, we have always found that when everything seems absolutely impossible that's when the breakthroughs come.'

'Don't quote platitudes at me.' She frowned up at him.

He bent and kissed her on the forehead. 'Finish up that tea and go to sleep. I'll keep a close eye on Stella but I'm betting she won't stir till this afternoon. Join her in dreamland, my love.'

Kirsty woke up shortly after midday, feeling much more like herself. She stretched and yawned, luxuriating in these rare moments of idleness. Her eyes moved to the neat row of books on her bedside table. She never had time for reading these days, not since Stella's illness. The range of titles amused her and she smiled a little. Pride of place was held by the Tom Roberts trilogy: *Horse Control and the Bit, Horse Control — the Rider* and *Horse Control — The Young Horse.* Closest to her reach stood her much loved Cambridge edition of the illustrated Bible, given to Kirsty at her confirmation. Then came Monica Baldwin's *I Leap Over the Wall* (recommended by her mother), Rumer Godden's *Miss Happiness and Miss Flower* (a much loved childhood favourite which she never tired of reading), *Busman's Honeymoon* by Dorothy L. Sayers (one of her favourite writers) and H. E. Bates' *The Darling Buds of May* (given to her when pregnant with Toby). In a sense, the row of books encompassed her life.

Between the Bible and *I Leap Over the Wall* were a number of thin booklets which could be said to represent the most recent part of her life. They were all about managing with juvenile rheumatoid arthritis and Kirsty knew their titles by heart. The booklets were all well-meaning but strangely unhelpful, possibly because none of them had been authored by a sufferer of the disease. She very strongly believed that, to fully understand all the ramifications of any illness, one must either have the condition or live with someone who did. Even the specialists seemed remote from the actual day-to-day struggles of their patients.

Only once had Kirsty suggested Stella read one of the booklets. It had been returned to her several hours later by a daughter with a cold little smile.

'Thanks, Mum, but I don't think I'll bother with any more of this type of thing.' The words had been accompanied by a little shudder as the green brochure left the girl's hands. It was the last time Stella had read a single word about her illness.

One or two gentle suggestions had been made: perhaps Stella would like to meet other children with the same disease? Kirsty had been hopeful but Stella had point-blank refused.

Thinking about all this, Kirsty slowly got up and dressed. It was a very hot day so she slipped into light cotton leggings and a cotton shirt with a Morgan horse printed on the front. Barefoot, she padded out to the kitchen.

'Have a good sleep?' Max looked up from where he was seated at the kitchen table, which was covered with a melee of horrifyingly official looking papers.

'I feel much better.' She smiled at him; kissed the top of his head. 'What's all this?'

'Don't even ask,' groaned Max. 'Our livestock agent's been after me again. Wally Luceno says that last lot of papers we took in are all wrong. His books don't match with ours. It's not his fault, it's the bloody government. They've got a definite down on farmers at present.'

'You've been saying that for the last thirty years,' teased Kirsty. 'Wally's a good agent though; you've always said so yourself.'

'It's perfectly true about the government having a down on farmers,' asserted her husband. 'Stella was still asleep when I last looked, by the way. Hasn't been a sound from her room.'

'Thanks. Ready for a bite of lunch?'

'Most definitely. I need it after all this brain work.' He shuffled some papers. 'All this blasted paperwork takes far more out of a man than a good day's mustering on a green horse. Australia must have been a grand place before officialdom took over.'

'It's not too dusty now …' She opened the pantry door. '… but I do know what you mean. The days when a man's word was his bond, when business was done with a handshake, must have been something to see.'

It was at that precise moment the telephone rang loudly.

'If that's Wally Luceno tell him I'm nearly finished!'

Eyebrows raised, lips twitching, Kirsty took up the handset.

'Hello, yes, this is Mrs Kirsty Richards speaking.'

As Max watched, his wife's too-slender body stiffened. (She was much too thin. Have to try and do something about that. He might have a word with young Deswyn Fairchild. Her Mrs Martin was a dab hand with doughnuts, pastries and other such delights.)

'Yes, that's right … Sorry, could you repeat that, please … Yes, about eighteen months now … She'll be eighteen in July … Where and when? … What? … Yes, I see … May I get back to you shortly? … I understand. Thank you.'

Fingers trembling slightly, she replaced the receiver and turned to her husband.

'Kirsty?'

'That was Professor Nathaniel Kotzen —'

'Who?'

'Professor Nathaniel Kotzen.'

'You mean his secretary, don't you?'

'No, I don't. It was the Professor himself. Short and sweet. He thinks he can help Stella.'

'What did he say? You didn't say much. Since when did professors make their own phone calls?'

'Shut up and listen! He did all the talking. He's been out of Australia for the past two years working and studying in the United States and in Switzerland and Austria, I think he said. Somewhere like that, anyway. He's only just been back in Australia for ten days. Doctor Mason has been talking to him about Stella — it seems he and Doctor Mason go way back — they're old friends — and he wants to see if he can help. She would have to be admitted to hospital but only for two days. We have to get back to him.'

'Kirsty! That's not telling us much!'

'He appears to have this idea of trying a different type of drug. He works on different lines from most of the other rheumatologists. New ideas from overseas.'

'Not those bloody corticosteroids that almost killed our girl!'

'It's definitely not a corticosteroid. He made that very clear.'

'In Sydney, of course?'

'I'm afraid so. A hospital we haven't been to before.'

'Stella will soon be able to write a book entitled *Guide to Every Hospital in Sydney*,' snorted Max.

'Don't be silly, Max.'

'And when is this meant to happen?'

'Next week, Monday, 2nd March.'

'I suppose we'll have to give it a go …' he frowned thoughtfully, '… but we need to find out a hell of a lot more about this chap. We don't want someone with Nazi concentration camp medicine ideas!'

Epilogue

April 1993

They were all there to watch her. The Fairchilds were out in full strength, a happy Sean Stevens now a permanent member of the family, all the legalities having finally been signed and sealed. Sean sat between Cliff and Audrey Martin, (who were visiting Sydney for the first time in twenty-five years) his smile never leaving his face. Charles, Nora and Judy Carey were also present, Charles' eyes, glued to his field glasses, seldom leaving the Twisted Stirrups. Judy's little camera was busy, her poetry notebook close to hand. It was many years since the Carey family had made the long trek to Sydney for the state's most prestigious agricultural and horticultural show.

Next to Nora Carey, Kirsty leant against Max, tears in her eyes as she recalled the night their miracle had happened. Professor Nathaniel Kotzen, who worked solely with children suffering from untreatable juvenile rheumatoid arthritis, told them that the new medications, like so many before, worked in the usual accumulative manner. It would take a minimum of twelve weeks for Stella to feel any improvement — it could take longer. It had taken exactly five weeks to the day, and it was a day, or rather, a night, that Kirsty would never forget.

Shortly after midnight Kirsty had been disturbed by the sound of her daughter's voice:

'Stella, what is it?' she had spoken half irritably, still partly asleep. It had been a long and tiring day, not helped by a kick from a visiting horse.

'Mummy, Mummy, *please, please* wake up and listen properly!'

'What's the matter, child?'

'Wake up *properly*, Mummy!'

'I am awake.' Kirsty rubbed her eyes.

'Mummy, the pain's gone!'

'*What* did you just say?'

'The pain's gone!' Her daughter's eyes were shining as they had not done since the winter of 1990, before that awful viral illness which had been the beginning.

'*Did — you — just — say — that — the — pain — has — gone?*' She had stared at Stella in bemusement, mouth gaping.

'Yes, Mummy, yes!'

Not believing what she was hearing Kirsty had suddenly shot out of bed and hugged Stella before leading her away from the sleeping Max. Max could sleep through anything.

'Tell me exactly what happened.' Mother and daughter sat very close on Stella's bed.

'I suddenly woke up — couldn't work out what woke me. I thought it was Sambo at first but he was asleep by my feet. It felt different from normal. Something had changed. It just felt different from normal, Mummy. It took me a while to work it out. There was no more pain, Mummy. The pain had gone!'

It felt different from normal. Kirsty bit her lip. Pain was normal for Stella.

It had taken Kirsty a long time to quieten and settle her daughter. Neither would sleep much, that she knew. As Kirsty left the room, the child had asked, 'Mummy, do you think it will come back again or has it gone for good?'

She had replied: 'Stella, I just can't tell you but I do know this … if it has gone once it can go again. We've finally broken through the barrier.'

Max had been ruthlessly shaken awake and told the wonderful news. He stared at his wife kneeling on the bed, her eyes burning bright, nightgown slipping from one shoulder. She looked like a small child.

'Oh Max, has our miracle finally happened? I just can't believe it! Do you think we're finally on the home straight? Do you want to talk to Stella? We must tell Toby! I feel like we should do something, call the Professor maybe!'

'Kirsty, Kirsty, Kirsty, please! Yes, it's clear that some change has been made and of course I am delighted. No, I am *not* talking to our daughter who should be trying to rest. We are *not* waking up our son. Finally we are NOT calling the Professor at almost two in the morning. Tomorrow, yes. If you don't settle down you'll be worn out tomorrow — today, rather. I am delighted, Kirsty, but please … let us both get some sleep. We need it.' Firmly Max pulled her down beside him and kissed her forehead. 'Try to settle down, love.'

In the beginning, nobody quite believed in what had happened. With bated breath almost, they waited for the pain to return and take control. It did come back but never to the same extent and the bad days grew less and less. Finally, that evil demon called pain no longer ruled their lives.

Once the pain was under management, it was time to repair all the damage done to the girl's body. Professor Kotzen, working with a small team, told Max and Kirsty it would take two years to bring Stella's body — the twisted legs being the worst difficulty — back to working order. It would be very slow, especially at first — he could not emphasise strongly enough how carefully they would have to progress, but the results would come. Special shoes would have to be made every few months; they would need to be altered as Stella's needs altered — but there, they were used to that, weren't they? The important thing was they were now no longer sliding backwards; the situation had been halted and now it was up to them to turn it around. He warned Stella that once the first euphoria had passed, that almost unbelievable delight that pain no longer ruled her life, she would most probably become impatient to progress quickly. This she would have to control. Her body had a great deal to relearn and could not be hurried. If she tried to rush things, it would only set her back.

One part of Kirsty knew that the carefree child her daughter had once been was gone forever. Parts of her body were permanently weakened and would require care and attention for as long as she lived. She would take medication for the rest of her life. There would be — had already been — reoccurrences of the illness, although hopefully not nearly so bad. Kirsty trembled with anger when she thought of certain medical specialists and clinics: the experts in the field who had not seemed to care, who had given up the task as too hard, who had almost turned her daughter into a cripple.

Kirsty turned white the day she was told Stella had been saved with only weeks to spare:

'Feet and legs so twisted and damaged, a few more weeks and all she could have done was crawl around on her hands and knees for the rest of her life. Great credit to you for keeping her active. Don't know how you did it.'

But that was then and this was now.

The commentator asked for silence while he paid tribute to that noblest of animals, the horse. The great showground grew as quiet as was possible when so many humans and livestock species were gathered together and the commentator spoke the words penned by that definitive equine writer, the one and only Elwyn Hartley Edwards:

Little Eohippus on his four-toed feet
Pondered, in his fashion, as he bent his head to eat,
Mused along the marshes at the dawning of the world,
And wondered at the swamplands where the bog sedge curled.

Little Eohippus raised his head and spoke,
"Lord, I'm slow and stupid, just as you did make,
Brute I am and brutish, the product of your hand,
I cannot know the Mystery — I could not understand."

Little Eohippus fought his misted mind,
And with one terrific effort pleaded for his kind,
Turned his eye to Heaven and asked his Maker's Grace,
"Lord, I'd find the answer by looking on Your Face."

Came God's whisper rippling through the bending reeds,
Sighing through the marrow grass and rustling through the seeds,
Shuddering the living slime in swamp and marsh concealed,
"Patience, little Brother, all shall be revealed."

Little Eohippus, as the years went on,
Found his four toes merging until they were but one,
Saw the oozing swamplands change to fertile field,
And still remained the promise, "All shall be revealed."

Little Eohippus, Equus Caballus now,
Grew in strength and beauty with pride upon his brow,
Gloriously caparisoned he journeyed wide and far,
Carrying a mighty King and following a Star.

Came they to a stable in a country wild,
Came they to the manger and gazed upon the Child,
Equus Caballus stretched out his neck to see,
Knew the Lord had granted Eohippus' plea.

Round the world the answer rang triumphantly,
Thundered through the mountains, surged about the sea,
'I now fulfil my promise to Eohippus' race,
Look, O little Brother, look upon My Face.'

The tears, unashamed and unchecked, streamed down Stella's face. She looked up at the grandstand, searched for her family, found them and gave a small salute. She was back where she belonged.

Serenade, rock-steady beneath her, arched his elegant neck. She was riding both Star of Bethlehem and Desert Star again at home now but kept to Serenade for big outings, a promise made to her parents. Her special stirrups still protected her feet and lower legs — she was one year into rehabilitation.

Serenade's neck wore a broad scarlet sash, the colour of the waratahs back home on her beloved Cheshunt. Three years ago Stella would have sniffed in disdain at riding one horse in one class, now she knew better. Every moment in the saddle had to be cherished, loved, enjoyed, gloried in.

Kirsty looked down at the sight she once thought gone forever. Across the crowd the two pairs of eyes met: brown and grey. Kirsty could read the words silently mouthed by her daughter:

'I love you, Mummy!'

That was more than enough for now. Kirsty could settle for that.

Other Titles:

Little Australian Pony Girl

(Children's Non-fiction with over 100 photographs and drawings)

About the Author

Ingrid M. Smith was born in the New South Wales country town of Moruya, famed for providing the granite for the four pylons of the Sydney Harbour Bridge.

The many and varied experiences of her own life provide the basis of her numerous non-fiction short stories and articles, although she has been known to turn her hand to light-hearted science fiction and the occasional poem.

Where the Waratahs Bloom is her first novel and was inspired by her daughter's long battle with juvenile rheumatoid arthritis. A multi-generational background in horse breeding, training and just about every form of competition from rodeo to flat racing provided the equine component for this Australian saga. Love of the native bush and of a way of life that is fast vanishing contributed additional colour.

Ingrid strongly believes that writers should be the conscience of the world.